PRAISE F

"Emotional and brilliant..."

"Tastefully erotic ... more smart than smutty..."

"Powerful and compelling..."

DEVIL'S DANCE

REBEL KINGS MC

GARRETT LEIGH

Cover Art: Garrett Leigh @ Black Jazz Design

Editing: Posy Roberts @ Boho Press

Proofing: Con Riley. Annabelle Jacobs. Mik Kuznetov

FOREWORD

This is a dark romance, featuring characters caught up in the world of motorcycle clubs (MCs) and all that comes with it. These characters are not always nice and they do things that are not nice. It *is* a romance, so the sweet moments we crave do come, but bear these words in mind before you dive in.

This is also the first book in a duet that will eventually be polyA/MMM. By the end of the duet, the main characters will have more than one love interest.

Unending thanks to Mik, my Russian sensitivity reader. So sorry you had to read this in the same room as your mum. And to Pipey, who I'm still trying to persuade to let me fall off the back of his Harley sometime. Thank you for explaining the democratic nature of MCs to me.

Trigger warnings: sex work, violence, death, recreational drug use.

PLAYLIST

Carnage - WYR GEMI
Take a Number - Stone Sour
The Witness Trees: Acoustic - Stone Sour
You Can't Fix This - Stevie Nicks, Dave Ghrol
L'Etat C'est Moi - The Blinders
Taipei Person/Allah Tea - Stone Sour
Bother - Stone Sour
Control - Puddle of Mud
For Everything - The Murder Capital
Pain and Pleasure - Judas Priest
All My Tears - Ane Brun
The Last Hangman - Hotel Lux

LISTEN ON SPOTIFY

THE REBEL KINGS MC

President: Cam O'Brian (32)
Vice President: Nash McGovern (31)
Sergeant-at-Arms: Saint Malone (29)
Enforcer: Mateo Romano (26)
Treasurer: Vacant
Secretary: John "Cracker" Delaney (58)
Chaplain: "Father" Embry Carter (25)
Road Captain: Rubi Matherson (32)

Club associates
Orla O'Brian
River O'Brian
Skylar Buchanan
Sol Bosanko

". . . I think about it all the time. That night on the beach up north, when we were just two lads on a run—me with my dad, you with that nomad crew. Damn, Saint, when I saw you letting the sand run through your fingers, the wind in your fucking hair, it was the first time in my life I'd ever felt free."

[1]
CAM

Bristol

There were many reasons why I rode my Harley fifty miles out of town for a drink, and the back view of this dude in posh clothes was one of them. At least, it was tonight. Toffs in tailored trousers and pressed shirts had never done it for me before, but I wasn't a bloke who ignored that rush of blood south.

Never had been. But whatever. My deviant habits weren't important as I watched Shirt Dude take his fancy bottled beer to a table and sit down. Nothing was. Not even the clusterfuck of a day that had sent me roaring off on my hog in the first place.

Liar. You were born for this, and you'll never be fucking free of it.

Stress squeezed my chest. I tipped beer down my throat, then leaned back in my seat, curving an inked hand around my glass. The menacing dagger tats on my fingers were smudged with oil stains, but I didn't care. I didn't become king of the road by being nice.

1

I could be nice to this dude, though. Real fucking nice.

"You're a man-whore, Cam."

Thanks, sis. Like I gave a shit.

I didn't, but my preoccupation with Shirt Dude was welcome all the same. Watching as he unfolded a copy of the *Financial Times* onto the table, frowning at whatever he saw on the pink pages, I got my first good look at his face. And, man, what a face. It was as pretty as his backside—high cheekbones, a neat hipster beard, and the kind of eyes that made a man go weak at the knees.

Weak.

Fuck.

My knees didn't waver for almost anyone, but my heart skipped a beat as I stared at him, and it wasn't often the mere sight of someone hit me anywhere other than my dick. In fact, I could only recall one time when it had ever happened before, and I'd clamped a lid on that shit so hard that it sometimes felt like it had happened to someone else—that I was watching my own pain throb and burn from another fucking planet.

On cue, my chest ached again. Meh. Maybe I'd necked too much coffee at church. Regardless, I didn't want to think about that right now—about *him* and everything I couldn't have—or the messy feelings that came with it. I wanted to think about Shirt Dude and his pretty face and what I'd do to him if we were in the right kind of establishment for me to approach him.

Trouble was, we weren't, and I really had only fled my hometown for a solitary drink and a deep breath. If I'd come out to hook up, I'd have ventured further into the city. This place—I glanced around the dark pub—was the best port in a storm I knew for a quiet, contemplative pint. An *anonymous* pint, and that was all I'd come for.

Still, I kept ogling Shirt Dude. I mean, I was only human. And subtle as a brick, apparently, because I got caught.

Shirt Dude raised his gaze from his newspaper. I expected him to look away. Most people did when they saw the leather and tats and figured out they were the real deal, not a fashion choice.

This bloke wasn't most people. He held my stare and smirked a little.

I smirked right back and the answering glint in his eyes went straight to my cock. *Down boy.* As if. Damn thing never listened to me.

Because it's not a sentient being, you fucking tool.

Who cared? Not me. The thrum in my blood was too good. And I was a reckless arsehole these days. I'd sacrificed too much to resist the simple things in life. If I wanted to fuck someone, I did.

Or at least tried.

I held my pint glass up and inclined my head at the seat beside me.

Shirt Dude rolled his eyes.

I shrugged. *You win some, you lose some.*

Or maybe, just maybe, you won the small shit that didn't mean anything, while the things that made you *burn* inside got left in the dust.

Shirt Dude moved like a ghost and slid into the spare seat at the bar. "Are you going to share why you've been staring at me for the last ten minutes?"

A cocky reply had already formed in my head, but it stuck in my throat as his smooth, low voice hit me. Refined and cultured. Like a newsreader, the kind that were on the radio when terrible things happened in the world.

There was nothing terrible about him, though. Lord, no. Up close, he was even prettier than I'd first thought. Ethereally so. His eyes were slate grey, his perfectly cut hair a cool ash brown, and those cheekbones? Yeah, they could cut fucking glass.

He smelled good too, like charcoal and the kind of expensive cologne no fucker I knew would ever waste their money on. Wood. Spice. Musk. Whatever the fuck it was, I liked it. A lot. Enough that it took me a full five seconds to remember he'd asked me a question. "I *was* staring at you," I said eventually.

Cool amusement glittered in his eyes. "I think we've established that."

"Oh, you think, do you?"

"Yes." Shirt Dude folded his newspaper on the bar. For whatever reason, he'd brought it with him. "Would you like a drink?"

I held up my Guinness. "Got one, thanks."

Shirt Dude hummed, his gaze turning speculative. "I have one too, so the question remains: why did you want my attention? I see only two options."

"That right?"

"I usually am, so tell me . . . ?" He raised a brow in question.

"Cam," I supplied.

He continued, "Tell me, *Cam*, what's your poison? Business or pleasure? And I should probably tell you that I've had my fill of business today, so choose wisely."

Colour me surprised. Either my dick was twisting

whatever he was really saying into what I wanted to hear, or Shirt Dude was up for some fun.

Despite my earlier conversation with my cock, I didn't give it that much credit. I necked my pint and set the glass on the bar while fixing Shirt with another smirk. "I choose pleasure."

He returned my leer tenfold, and it held a wickedness that sent a shiver down my spine. Those grey eyes were something else, fucking mesmerising, and as he leaned in closer, his scent got me too, reeling me in like *I* was the one who'd been hooked. "Good choice. My home is across the street. But first, a warning. If you're planning on mugging me for my Rolex, I have some advice for you."

"Oh yeah?" I licked my lips. Truth be told, though sizing people up was kind of a habit, I hadn't clocked his fancy watch. I'd been too busy drinking in the way his expensive threads curved around his knock-out body. "What's that then?"

Shirt Dude's smirk turned predatory. "Don't."

[2]
CAM

We left the pub. My hog was parked outside, but if this dude's place was as close as he said it was, I didn't need it.

We wove through the humming city crowds without talking, and I was okay with that. I wasn't trailing him for small talk. Nah. I wanted to see what was beneath those dapper clothes, and I wondered if he was as curious about me as I was about him. I mean, *damn*. We couldn't have been more different. Did he pick up dudes like me all the time?

Doubted it. There weren't many bikers out there living the life in the open. The old timers at the club tolerated my wild ways because I kept their bank accounts fat—*for now*—and I had a council around me that would light them on fire if I gave the nod. A council of brothers. A goddamn fellowship. Mostly, anyway, but I didn't want to think about politics right now. Couldn't, or I'd lie down and smash my face into the concrete pavement. Anything for some fucking peace.

Could I find inner-tranquillity in tracking a fuck-hot dude back to his place for nothing but sex and zero stress? Zero heartache and pain?

Yeah. Sometimes I could. I needed this shit in my life, and I loved it more than I loved my Harley.

As promised, Shirt Dude led me to an upmarket building a few hundred yards away and across the street from the pub. I took note of the address and tapped it into my phone, creating a location pin.

I opened my contacts and my thumb hovered, indecision warring with the need to return my attention to the pretty bloke in front of me. There were any number of brothers who had my back, but . . . I took the easy option and sent the pin to my vice president. Nash didn't give two fucks where I was or what I was doing. He didn't look at me with smothered hurt in his gaze or his jaw set so hard it might break. He accepted the message with a thumbs-up and went back to his own life. An easy exchange, and Christ, I needed something to be easy, given the week we'd just had. The only reason I wasn't scoping Shirt Dude as an assassin or a fed was the fact that he'd ignored me until he'd caught me ogling his damn fine self.

Besides, despite his warning about trying any shady shit, I had a stone on him in weight, and I'd been born with my hands curled into fists. I could handle this sweet fucker in my sleep.

He let us inside and we took the lift to the top floor, to the *penthouse*.

I whistled. "You're a rich motherfucker."

"If you say so."

"Are you going to tell me your name?"

"Is it important to you?"

Was it? Probably not. I didn't usually get around to

7

asking, but calling him Shirt Dude in my head was starting to annoy me. "Go on then. Tell me."

"That's not answering the question." The lift doors opened. Shirt Dude stepped out and to a door that had no number on it. "But I'm feeling generous, so I'll tell you anyway."

He unlocked the penthouse door, then turned to me with an outstretched hand. "Teddy Jones, nice to meet you."

Teddy. Of all the names he could've given me, perhaps I was expecting that one the least. *Because it's bullshit.*

I liked it, though, for now. It rolled around my brain like warm honey and I took his hand with a grin on my face. "Nice to meet you too."

Teddy pushed his front door open, revealing a cool, dark space that would've made me feel scruffy in my old jeans and battered leather jacket if I gave a shit.

I didn't. I stepped into his home like I rocked up in places like this all the time and let the door swing shut behind me.

"You can hang your jacket there." Teddy pointed to a row of copper hooks behind the door. "And take off your boots."

He turned on his heel and strode away into the penthouse without looking back.

Take off your boots. I wasn't used to taking orders, but man, that made my dick hard. For the first time in my life, I did as I was told, duly hung my jacket on the hook and toed off my battered motorcycle boots. My socked feet hit the polished tile floor and another shiver rushed up my spine. I was out of place here and I didn't care.

Bring it on.

I followed my instincts out of the swanky hallway and to a room that was almost a living room, though it was nothing like any house I'd ever been in. No photos, empty beer cans, or dogs snoozing on the couch. Just a couch and a drinks cabinet where Teddy stood, pouring something into a crystal glass.

He glanced at me. "You can pour your own. Open a fresh bottle if you're worried."

"Worried about what? You drugging me and having your wicked way?"

"It's a valid concern. You're a big man, but no one is invincible."

"I don't need to be if you're not a massive cunt, mate."

Teddy smiled. And wow. If I'd been into him before, I was a horny puddle at his feet the moment those lips stretched wide and split his pretty face in half. Well, kind of. It was a small smile. Reluctant. *Bewitching.* Those grey eyes had been magical from the moment I'd fallen into them, but sparkling with mirth, they were fucking enchanting.

Hypnotising.

Damn, I needed a drink before my brain overflowed with adjectives I didn't usually have call for in my life. *Only with—*

Nope.

Don't think about him.

My fucking mantra.

If you did something enough, did it ever stop hurting?

I ventured closer to Teddy and peered into the open cabinet. I wasn't worried about him slipping me roofies—he didn't seem the type—but I reached for an unopened bottle of whisky anyway. He was drinking vodka. Fuck that. I wanted to bang his brains out, not have flashbacks of my fourteen-year-old self blowing chunks behind my dad's garage.

The whisky was good, smooth and smoky. It slid down

my throat like buttered fire and added to the smouldering burn I'd carried since I'd first laid eyes on this dude.

I emptied my glass and set it back where I'd found it. "How do you want to do this? Because I'm guessing you're not one for small talk."

"Not especially." Teddy sipped his vodka, eyeing me with a narrowed gaze. "And I have some things in mind, but I'd be interested to hear your thoughts first."

"My thoughts? What is this? A fucking board meeting?"

Teddy's lips twitched, but he kept his sinful smile to himself this time. "Do you spend a lot of time in board meetings, Cam?"

More than he could imagine, but my clipped reply was swallowed up by my body's response to him saying my name. More heat flushed through me and my jeans grew uncomfortably tight. "I want to fuck you. But I'm down for other stuff if you don't want to go that far."

"That's very kind of you, but your suggestion is good with some . . . caveats."

"Caveats?"

"You are used to your partners submitting to you, yes? You throw them around, fuck them until they beg you to stop?"

For the first time, his polished accent slipped, and something else snuck in, something I couldn't quite place. "I'm used to a lot of things, but I'm adaptable, within reason."

Teddy smirked. "I'm sure you are, and don't worry. I'm not asking you to bend over for me if that's what you're worried about."

"It's not. I have zero problems saying no."

"And I have no problem listening. But that isn't what I want."

"So . . . what *do* you want?" Unable to help myself, I stepped closer to him, my entire body alight with anticipation. "You have some boundaries you want to set out?"

"The opposite, actually."

I swallowed thickly. "What?"

"Boundaries. I don't really have any, but I'm not submissive. I will tell you what I want, and I'd like you to do it."

"Where are you from?" It wasn't what I meant to say, but his slipped accent was doing strange things to me. In the pub, he'd sounded as English as the queen. Now? I couldn't tell, and my gut was churning enough to cool the blaze obliterating my common sense. "You sound Russian or some shit."

Teddy's grey eyes flickered. "Would that bother you?"

"Only if there was a reason for you to hide it from me."

"We are strangers. There is no reason for anything at all."

I tilted my head, assessing him more than I had when a simple hook-up had been on the cards. "Tell me then. Where are you from?"

"Right now? Where you found me. But I was born in St. Petersburg if placing my accent is so important to you."

"St Petersburg in Russia?"

"Yes, *Cam.*" Teddy thickened the English accent he'd started with, that dry humour lighting his eyes again. "Or is it Cameron, if we're oversharing tonight?"

"Define oversharing."

"No. You do it."

11

I couldn't figure out if he was playing with me. Or if it mattered. I didn't give two shits where he was from as long as he wasn't a shady fuck, but the sense I was missing something was hard to ignore, especially in my life. "Cameron was my dad's name, and he's long dead. You . . . Teddy *Jones*, can call me whatever you like. Is that enough for you?"

Teddy picked up his vodka with a noncommittal hum and tipped it down his elegant throat. "Follow me to the bedroom if you are happy. If you are not, you know where the door is."

He left me. Again.

And *again*, I gave little conscious thought to following him.

His bedroom was how I imagined a fancy hotel room to be—cold and impersonal, but with the bonus of a giant bed.

A blank canvas for filth.

Teddy—*not his name*—was on the far side, taking his Rolex off. He laid it on the bedside table and shot me a challenging smirk.

I scowled. "I'm not going to steal it."

"You wouldn't need to. If you wanted it, I'd give it to you."

"Why?"

"It's just a watch."

It was half a house to most people I'd grown up with, but I kept that thought to myself. I'd given away enough to him already, and I wanted what I'd come for.

I reached over my shoulder and fisted my T-shirt, yanking it over my head in one fluid movement.

Teddy watched me, unbuttoning his expensive shirt, revealing another layer beneath—a white vest as plain as my tee that I hated on sight because it denied my view of his body. "You are strong. And not from the gym, no?"

I snorted. "No."

"Real life?"

"If you say so."

Teddy nodded as if he understood a thousand times more than I'd told him. "Come here."

I raised a brow.

He raised one right back and I cracked first.

I rounded the bed to where he stood and faced him down. "Is this the part where you tell me what to do?"

"Maybe. Or you could do whatever you like and see where it takes you."

The inferno in my veins returned full force. I had no doubt that he was going to rise up at some point and give me an order I couldn't refuse, but having free rein over him, for however long, was too tempting to pass up.

I gripped his undershirt and tugged it over his head. Keeping my eyes locked on his, I backed him against the wall, then I gave in and let myself look.

A strong, lean torso greeted me, dusted with the perfect amount of dark hair and ripped with sinewy muscle. He might've been smaller than me, but it was clear his compact frame could pack a punch.

His chest called to me. I wanted to bury my face in it and breathe him in while I fucked him.

But first . . .

I undid his belt and pulled it from the loops. It dropped to the floor from my careless fingers and I went for his tailored trousers next, popping the button and unzipping the fly.

Teddy leaned against the wall, sharp gaze all over me, though his posture was languid. Was he testing me? Or simply curious to what I'd do next? Either way, I was getting him naked.

I pushed the trousers away, sending his underwear with them for good measure.

His cock sprang free. He was hard, and my mouth fucking *watered*. I didn't get on my knees for anyone, but I wanted to taste him so bad right now that a strangled sound escaped me.

Teddy trailed a cool fingertip down my bare chest. "Like what you see?"

"Yup." How could I not? His body was a work of art, and his cock? Yeah. That was pretty too, the motherfucker.

"Let me undress you," Teddy murmured.

I spread my hands, inviting him to do just that.

Teddy peeled his liquid frame off the wall and stepped close enough that my skin tingled, anticipating the moment we'd come together and the sparks flying between us would become a full-on Guy Fawkes display. He grasped the heavy skull buckle on my belt and unclipped it. Keeping his gaze on me, he undressed me in the same manner I had him, freeing my throbbing dick from the confines of its denim cage. "We're both wearing socks."

I looked down. He was right, but the issue was easily fixed. I ripped mine off and then his and tossed them somewhere.

Then I stood back, bare and proud, letting him get a good look at what he'd invited into his bed.

His hot gaze turned appraising. "So the ink really does go everywhere?"

"Not everywhere." I wrapped my hand around my cock, almost buckling at the sweet relief from the pressure. "I never found an artist I wanted near my dick with a needle."

"But you let one near your heart?" Teddy teased my chest again, tracing a circle where my heart thudded beneath my tatted skin. "You should think less with your dick."

"So they keep telling me."

"Who does?"

"No one who matters." In this situation, at least.

I let my hand drop from my cock and considered my options. We were facing each other down like alphas, prowling around until one of us made a real move. He'd invited me to do whatever the fuck I wanted, but what if it was a trick? Worse, what if I misread the situation and did something he didn't like? I liked to go hard. Rough, when the mood was right, cleansing my fucking soul, but I had no desire to hurt anyone.

"Stop thinking." Teddy tapped my temple. "You like what you see, no? Make the most of it."

All right. I didn't need telling twice. And I didn't need an excuse to get out of my head. I shut it down and let my instincts flow, grasping Teddy's hips and pulling him to my body, skin finally touching skin, his cock tangling with mine.

The spark of sensation was instant, flooding me with more heat than I could contain. A low growl rumbled from my chest, and I let my hands roam his torso and then lower, gripping his backside, palming the firm swell of muscle.

I almost kissed him.

Almost.

Instead, I bypassed his lips and went for his throat, digging my teeth in, drawing a low, delicious grunt from him.

15

He likes pain. I filed that away for reference and bit him harder, tasting blood, and the fucker didn't flinch.

Only his cock responded, surging against mine.

Yes.

I manhandled him to the bed.

He resisted enough to rile me up, grinning and showing me a set of perfect white teeth. "I will not submit. If I let you, it is because I like it."

"Works for me." I threw him down and made an educated guess that his bedside drawer was about to become my new best friend.

I reached over him and opened it. Inside, I found premium-brand lube, condoms, and . . . black metal cuffs. "Are these for me?"

"What do you think?" Teddy rolled onto his stomach. "I already told you to do what you like."

He had. And the cuffs were intriguing. I'd only played those games with women. Thinking about restraining Teddy and doing all kinds of nasty things to him made my head spin.

Did I want that right now?

Could I handle it?

Fucking A. I was unsure enough to leave the cuffs where they were and clear the drawer of everything else.

I dropped it all on the bed and knelt between Teddy's legs, taking in the expanse of his back. It was a glorious fucking sight, but I missed his dick. There was something electric about seeing a man so hard for me. I dreamt about it sometimes, on the rare nights I went to bed alone. Fantasised about it on the many nights I didn't go to bed at all. It was strange what kept you company on a long ride.

Still. This view of him was hard to give up too. And I wanted inside him. Like, now, before I burst into flames.

Fuck it. I flipped him over, shoving him onto his back and nudging his legs wider.

Teddy's lip curled in a faint snarl—*he likes that too*—and his cock taunted me, leaking fluid onto his abdomen.

I ran a finger through it, stuck it in my mouth, and tasted him. His eyes blazed—*noted*—and so did my blood. I reached for the condoms and lube, revelling in the fact that we had the same size dick, so he had some clue of what he was in for. *Because he fucks himself with that beast? Genius, mate. Absolute genius.*

Some days I was, but not today. My brains were in my balls and I was so hot for this dude I could barely see straight.

I rolled a condom onto my cock and flicked the cap on the lube bottle. "I'm gonna be a gentleman about this bit because I'm not a fucking animal."

Teddy's gaze darkened. "Shame."

"Is it?"

"Perhaps. If you liked it that way too."

"You have no idea what I like."

"Show me."

It wasn't a request, and the authority lacing the command had me scrambling forward before I caught myself. *No. Stop.* Whatever he thought he wanted, I wasn't in the business of ramming my dick into anyone before they were ready.

I nudged his legs apart again and took up the space between them. Teddy wasn't a small guy, but I loomed over him all the same, caging him with my arms as I dropped a palm either side of his head. "You said I could do whatever I wanted."

Teddy nodded, his eyes sparkling with something that would've put me on edge with anyone else. "I am interested to learn what that is."

"Want me to tell you?"

"I already said this. Show me."

His accent slipped again, and I liked the Russian flavour better than the posh drawl. I dipped down and dug my teeth into his neck again, adding to the mark I'd already left there.

Teddy growled and wrapped his legs around me, his thighs as strong as they looked, anchoring me in place.

I wasn't complaining. Trapped against his body, every part of him touched me where I wanted it to. His skin felt amazing against mine, and the thrill of fucking someone brand new took me over. I kissed a wet trail from his neck to his chest, and then down his abdomen as he arched beneath me, restless sounds escaping him.

Like his chest had, his cock called to me. I didn't suck many dudes, but this one? Yeah, I was having some of that.

I hooked my hands beneath his hips and raised him off the bed to my mouth, elbowing his legs wide enough that I could move freely.

He let me. I wasn't ignorant of that. I'd waltzed into this believing I could hold him down with one hand, but there was something about Teddy Jones.

Something dangerous.

Wily.

Wicked.

Whatever I wanted to call it, I knew I'd met my match . . . in more ways than one.

I wrapped my mouth around his cock and swallowed him

down. Teddy groaned, harsh and masculine. "Harder. Use your teeth."

That was a new one, but I was partial to the scrape of a woman's teeth against my own dick, so I happily obliged, revelling in the answering surge in his rock-hard length. I gave him the roughest blowjob I'd ever doled out and I loved it. My blood became fire, my cock digging into the mattress beneath me, desperate for friction.

When I could take no more, I pulled off and chased the wet mess down from his balls to his hole.

I slid a finger inside him.

Again, he didn't flinch. "*More.*"

One finger became two.

Three, while he watched me, apparently amused . . . and impatient.

I took the hint and replaced my fingers with my sheathed and lubed dick. His body enveloped me, drawing me in with a long, slow thrust that sent my eyes rolling around the world and back. "So fucking tight."

Teddy leered. "Is good for you?"

"You can't tell by my face?"

"I do not know your face."

"Not yet." I dropped down, bringing us closer together. We were nose to nose—closer than I'd been to anyone in a long time, despite how often I found myself with company at night. Teddy's grey eyes seemed unending. And his lips?

Fucking gorgeous. I wanted to crush them with mine and feel his neat beard against the scuff on my own jaw. I wanted to go to war with his tongue and see who goddamn won.

Me, in case you were wondering, but I reckoned he'd go down swinging.

Teddy reached up and gripped my chin. His touch was blistering, and his sinful lips twisted into that smirk again. "You are being very gentle, biker boy. Have I misjudged you?"

"Only if you think I'm a *boy*." I pulled my hips back, then punched them forward, driving into him hard enough to make anyone else's eyes water.

Not this dude, though. His smirk deepened, the only sign of impact his teeth digging into his fleshy bottom lip. I slammed into him again and again and again, until he pushed back, meeting me in the middle, and something between us snapped.

A frantic surge took over me. I fucked him like my life depended on it, hard and fast. Raw and dirty. His bed was one of those fancy divans that seemed to float like a fucking cloud. It had been a blank page when I got here, but we ruined every inch of it.

Teddy was strong and supple. Flexible. I fucked him in every position he demanded, and the need to come like a fucking train inside him became a drumbeat that echoed in my head louder than my thundering pulse.

Desire consumed me. Sweat coated my skin and my breath came in short, sharp pants.

I pulled Teddy off the bed and shoved him against the wall, kicking his legs apart. I wrapped an arm around his throat, but I didn't squeeze.

Not yet.

Not until he laughed, taunting and low. Breathless. Though like everything about him, it was subtle. "You would not dare."

"Think I'm scared of you?"

"I don't think you're scared of much."

"That's the first time you've been right since we started this." I tightened my forearm against his neck. "And if you think I wouldn't choke you, you're wrong about that too."

"Do it then."

No. The reaction came from deep inside me. Visceral and laced with an emotion I couldn't decipher. My arm stayed where it was, but the urge to force more pressure behind it evaporated.

Teddy laughed again, but it wasn't mocking. It was understanding. Fond, almost. "I don't need you to do that. Just fuck me. You are good at it."

"Good?"

"Yes. Good. I like it."

I snorted and roughly slid my other hand from his hip to his ribcage, leaving a reddened trail in my wake. "You fucking *love* it."

Teddy said nothing. Just braced his arms on the wall, his back rippling like a beautiful river.

I sucked in much-needed air and shoved inside him again, but I didn't slam. I slid in hard but slow, torturing myself as much as I wanted to torture him. I'd taken the hint that he liked it wild, but there was more than one way to skin a damn cat, or whatever. I fucked him slowly this time, drawing out every drive of my hips to the point where I groaned with each thrust. Fresh heat sluiced through me. Sweat dripped down my face. My tight balls screamed at me to finish the fucking game, but instinct kept my pace steady, digging pleasure out of us both, drowning in every sharp sound Teddy let me have.

Fuck, those sounds. If I never saw him again, I knew

they'd stay with me a long time. I let my arm fall from his throat and pressed it across his shoulder blades instead, still pumping my body in a heady rhythm.

Teddy's head dropped and a deep shudder rattled his frame. He was close. The building tension in him was unmistakable, and I wanted him to break.

I closed the minute space between us, flattening myself to his back. I tangled my fingers in his short hair and touched my lips to the hollow behind his ear. He shuddered again and my dick pulsed inside him. "I did what you said, now tell me what you want."

Teddy blew out a shaky breath. He was rigid. I snaked an arm around his waist and found his cock.

It throbbed in my hand, alive with the same ruthless energy that was eating me up, and my hips canted in response, driving me deeper inside him.

Finally, he *moaned*, and I sensed his control slipping. If there was an upper hand to be found with this dude, I had it. *For now*. And I intended to make use of it.

I started to fuck him again, even slower this time, curving my body with every thrust, moulding myself to him in a way I'd never let myself with anyone else.

But with him, it felt right. It flowed. And in a life that kept me on the edge of disaster ninety per cent of the time, I was all about the flow right now.

I needed it.

I craved it.

So I took it. I screwed him like we were goddamn lovers, one hand working his cock while I eased in and out of him, the pressure in my gut surging to boiling point, every muscle and nerve stretched so tight that when I snapped, it was going to blow my mind. *Fight it.* I tried, trembling from the effort. He had to break first or we'd failed. *I'd* failed. *He needs this as much as I do.*

How I'd come to think I had a peep-hole into his brain, I had no clue, but I knew it like I knew the sun and the moon swapped places every day.

I didn't come. I kept fucking him and fucking him until a harsh cry burst from his lungs and he came in my hand, his body tightening like a vice around my pulsing dick.

It finished me off. Like, killed me stone dead. A violence swept over me and my muscles contracted, kicking my hips forward, burying me so deep inside him, I should've come out the other side.

"Fuck." An animalistic groan tore from my chest and I came hard, seizing up, frozen with pleasure as the coil in my gut unfurled. "Fuckfuck*fuck*."

I was wrecked, vibrating with residual pleasure. I let my hand fall from Teddy's cock but kept my face buried in his neck, lungs labouring, head spinning. It took me a minute to return to earth and remember that he was the one who'd taken the worst of what had passed between us.

That the trembling wasn't just mine.

I raised my head.

Teddy's was still bowed, eyes closed, and he was breathing deep and slow, as if something had released from his goddamn soul and he was in no hurry to get it back.

I dug that. Understood it. So I did something super fucking weird and kissed his neck before I withdrew and backed off, searching his fancy-pants flat for the bathroom.

After trying a locked door, I found it attached to his bedroom and so clean it was hard to believe anyone lived

23

here. Not that I was complaining. Grimy bathrooms made me wanna hurl.

I ditched the condom, washed my hands, and grabbed a small towel from the folded stack on the shelf.

Back in the bedroom, Teddy had moved to the bed and sprawled out on it like a lion: relaxed but dangerous.

A thrill ran through me. I was sated but hungry. I could go for more if he was game.

Or maybe I was the game. I'd won the battle, but he was ready for war.

I found my cigarettes on the floor by my jeans. "Can I smoke in here?"

"No."

I dropped the box with a shrug and lay down beside him, fixing my gaze on the crackless ceiling. "Have you lived here long?"

"No."

"Not much of a talker, are you?"

"No."

I shifted my gaze to Teddy. He rewarded me with a dry smile, barely there but so intense I missed it when it was gone. "Did you get what you wanted?"

"From you?" He shifted a little, facing me on the bed.

"From whatever."

"Eloquent."

"Never said I was."

Teddy hummed and brought his hand to my chest, chasing a stray bead of sweat with his fingertip. "To answer your question, it was . . . fun, no? I like a man who does not hold back, though I think there were moments when you did."

"When?"

He glanced at my throat. Damn it. How was this dude fucking psychic on top of being satanically attractive? *Fucking A.* I had enough overly perceptive men in my life like that already.

You have one.

You have him.

Shadows threatened the filthy peace I'd found with Teddy.

I pushed them away. "Maybe I was hoping for a rematch so I didn't play all my cards too early."

"Tenacious?"

"Or optimistic. You just let me know, mate."

Teddy said nothing. I wondered if it was my cue to leave, but I didn't move. His quiet flat and complex company was everything I desperately needed, and I couldn't give it up just yet. "What do you do for a living? You look like a banker."

"Do I?"

I rolled over to face him. "I think so. Then, to me, every toff in a suit is a banker or a lawyer."

"I'm not a lawyer."

"You work with money, then?"

"Doesn't everyone?"

I couldn't argue with that. There weren't many people I knew who worked for fun. I didn't. My life was complicated enough that everything I did was so intimately entwined that I'd lost my sense of self, but work was still work. I didn't enjoy it—I just had to do it. "If you're a financial advisor or some shit, now's the time to let me know. I could do with one of those."

More dry humour danced across Teddy's pretty face, and

it still didn't feel like he was laughing at me. Slowly, he pulled his hand from my chest and reached behind him to the other bedside table, not the one with the condoms and lube.

He opened it and withdrew a notepad. He tore out a page, rolled it up, and tucked it behind my ear. "I have a proposition for you."

"Yeah?"

"Yes." He brought his hand back to my chest but didn't touch me again. Just hovered there, making me thrum with anticipation, my cock rising again as if it hadn't been all of five minutes since I'd shot my soul through it. "I don't see people I sleep with more than once, but if you fuck me again before you leave, for this—the advice you need—you may call me if you wish."

It was the strangest proposition I'd ever had, but it seemed like a win-win. I'd been half joking about needing a financial advisor, but the problem with half jokes was that they were always based on truth. I needed help from someone outside of my day-to-day life. Why not him?

And if I got to fuck him again for the privilege?

Hell to the yes.

I took the notebook page from behind my ear and stuffed it into the cigarette box I'd dropped to the floor by the bed.

Then I came upright and shoved Teddy onto his back, climbing over him, pinning him down as his flinty gaze lit up with a challenge that made my blood sing. "Shirt Dude, you've got yourself a deal."

[3]

TEDDY

I watched my biker friend leave my apartment from the coffee shop across the street. I'd left him while he took a shower. I wasn't a fan of goodbyes, even with people I liked. And I liked him. He was trouble—I felt it—but perhaps that endeared him to me. Difficult things pleased me.

His eyes pleased me too. They were obsidian dark. Everything about *Cam* was dark—his hair, his smile, the dirty sounds he made when he came—but the deep brown of his eyes held a warmth that could tear my soul apart if I let it.

I wouldn't. But I couldn't deny he'd left a lasting impression on me. If I closed my eyes, I could still smell him. While he'd drowsed between fuck sessions, I'd taken deep breaths of his scent. He'd smelled like home, which was an odd concept, as it had been years since I'd had one.

Your choice.

Hardly.

I watched Cam now, striding out of my building on his long, powerful legs, his unshaven jaw thick with inky stubble. He didn't seem to be looking for me, but I didn't expect him to. He'd enjoyed my company, of that I was certain, but he was a man with places to be. Responsibilities to honour. He'd been naked for most of our time together, but he'd worn that like a second skin. Like he wore danger, and not because of his biker leathers and the menacing tattoos that covered most of his warm skin—roses, skulls, pistols, and knives. *No*. Those things were cosmetic. What made him dangerous ran far deeper and simmered in his coal-dark gaze, something I recognised enough for a small shudder to pass through me, an adrenaline-laced shiver that should've made me sick to my stomach, but didn't.

You're the sick one.

I sighed. Maybe I was. Cam—I pondered what surname went with the subtle lilt in his accent—retrieved his Dyna Super Glide from the pub car park and gunned the engine. People tracked him as he roared away, and I didn't blame them. It was quite the spectacle, and one I knew I'd remember.

I want to see him again.

Cute. But unless my new friend called for accounting advice, there was little chance of that.

Besides, I'd spoken nothing but truth when I'd told him I didn't see people for sex twice. What was the point? If the fucking had been mediocre, then I had no desire for a repeat. On the rare occasions it was exceptional, I liked my memories to stay that way.

I watched Cam disappear into the distance, then abandoned my undrunk coffee and walked back to my penthouse flat.

It was exactly as I'd left it. Sheets rumpled, hook-up paraphernalia scattered around. Even my Rolex remained, unstolen, on the bedside table. The air was thick with the scent of sweat and sex and man. The only thing missing was the brawny biker who'd helped me put it there.

Unbidden, images of him towering over me, muscles rippling, face twisted into a half-crazed snarl, slammed into me. I'd told him we'd had fun, but the truth was, the night we'd spent together was far beyond anything I'd experienced for a long time, if ever, and his aesthetic had been only a tiny part of that. I liked rough men and rough sex, but biker boy had taken that to another dimension. He'd fought me and won—*because I'd let him*—and I wouldn't forget that.

How could I when my body was still thrumming with unspent heat? If he'd still been here—

Fuck. The things I'd have let that man do to me if we'd had more time. I eyed the bed. The freak in me was already stripping it, bundling the sheets into the bin, and erasing all trace of the stranger in my bed, but for long minutes I stood stock still and breathed deep, and when I did move, I left the sheets where they were.

I took a shower, then took my place behind my laptop screen in the spare bedroom I used as an office. The room had big windows that overlooked the city, a view I could usually ignore—if you had seen one cityscape, you had seen them all—but the grey Bristol skies seemed to call to me today. As I fielded phone calls and emails, I found myself staring into the abyss, my mind straying to pounding hips and wild sounds and a bottomless dark gaze that was as intriguing as it was unforgettable.

My body hummed with fruitless anticipation, the bruises he'd left on my skin alive with heat. I had to move, abandoning my work even as my phone lit up with a call from my biggest client. They could wait—everything could. I needed air.

The balcony in my overlarge flat was on the other side of the building. I slid the glass doors open and stepped out, breathing hard, my heart pounding that strange rhythm it fell into when emotions I couldn't comprehend overwhelmed me. It seemed ridiculous to blame Cam for it, but I did. Picking him up at the bar had been the only thing off-piste I'd done in months—the only thing outside of the *work, sleep, repeat* routine that kept me grounded. It had to be him, and I hated him for it, so why could I think of nothing else but seeing him again?

I pressed a hand to my chest and growled, low and sinister. If someone had been near me, they'd have surely stepped back the way most people did when they met my cold gaze. *Not Cam, though. You lured him in.*

No. That wasn't true. It had been the other way around, and perhaps it was this that disturbed me so.

Regardless, it was a rare day I reached for the cigarettes I kept hidden outside and lit one up, but I did today. I blew smoke into the grey drizzle, closed my eyes, and dreamt of the inked arms that had kept me safe all night long.

My phone roused me—the one I kept on vibrate in my pocket instead of the beacon of banality on my desk. I kept meaning to crush it beneath my foot and toss it from a great height, but after last night, I knew it would be a while before I had those thoughts again. *What did you give him this number for?* I did not know. Only that I had, and that I hoped it was him calling me and not the other things in this world that made my heart beat too fast.

I drew the phone from my pocket and stared at the

screen, fighting the unfamiliar sensation that rose in my chest. Was it hope?

No. It had been a few hours since Cam had left, enough time to reflect on the ice-cold robot he'd shared a bed with. It was inconceivable that he'd lived through that and decided to make contact. That man was as human as they came, warm-blooded and soulful. Sweet, even, though everything about him fought to hide it. *But* he was sharp too, and his instincts would've kicked in by now, warning him to stay away. I would not hear from him. I was certain of many things, but of that most of all.

The number lighting up the screen was Russian, not one I knew, but the voice behind it would be familiar. It always was. *"Come home, Alexei. Your father is gone now."*

Another shudder rattled through me, but it was different to the ones Cam had left behind and far less welcome. I let the call ring out—the voicemail service was disabled—and crouched low, setting the phone carefully on the floor. My leg twitched as I rose again. *Crush it.*

But I didn't. I went inside and continued my day, and it was dark the next time I passed the balcony door.

The phone was lit up again. Rage consumed me, sudden and sharp, like insects crawling beneath my skin. I slid the balcony door open, flinging it aside, and strode to where I'd left the phone. It had rained while I'd been inside, but not enough to destroy it. *Why won't you fucking die?*

I snatched it up, vision blurred with the red mist that made my nerves itch and my stomach churn. My muscles bunched, ready to hurl the device to the city streets below, but the number on the screen gave me pause. It was a landline number, and the software in my phone identified it as *Kings Building Ltd.*

Frowning, I pushed the fury in my gut aside and fished my other phone from my pocket, googling the name at lightning speed. A builder's merchant in North Devon came up, along with insignia for a motorcycle club: The Rebel Kings.

Cam.

It had to be.

I knew no other bikers, and as I sucked in a deep breath, the fire in my belly morphed to a different kind—the kind that soothed and settled me, flooding my veins with a calm I'd only found in recent years with him.

Closing my eyes, I accepted the call, and the rush of peace as the certainty that it was my biker friend settled in my black soul. "You took your time."

A low laugh answered me, as deep and throaty as when the man had come so hard inside me. "All right, mate. Fancy a drink?"

[4]
CAM

Whitness, North Devon

I wasn't really asking him for a drink, and we both knew it. He'd already told me *no* before he'd passed me his digits, but I'd been a joker once upon a time, and I hadn't got where I was in life without trying my luck.

My reward came in the form of the dry laugh that had been on my mind since I'd crawled from his bed this morning. It was close to midnight now, but it hadn't occurred to me that he might've been sleeping. I got the sense that my dude was a night owl, just like me, if he slept at all. He didn't seem like a man who needed much.

"No drink." His lush voice broke into my thoughts. "I told you what you could call this number for. Do you have a financial problem?"

I had more than one, but I wasn't about to admit that so early in our beautiful friendship. I leaned back in the crappy seat that had once belonged to my father and kicked my feet onto the ancient table. "If I did, would you be willing to help me?"

"I'd be willing to consider it. Would you care to elaborate?"

The smooth English accent he'd carried across the pub was firmly back in place, no hint of the Russian edge that had etched itself indelibly into my brain. "My books are a mess. The bloke who used to keep them died a few years ago. His old lady took over, but she was shit at it and I didn't realise until recently."

"It took you a few years to realise your company accounts were a mess? What kind of businessman are you?"

"A busy one. And too trusting, perhaps, but Magda is family, man. I didn't check up on her as much as I should've."

"That is sweet."

"Is that your way of calling me stupid?"

"Perhaps. But what I think of you isn't important. Tell me about your business."

"It's a builder's yard—a merchant, a store, whatever you want to call it. We sell construction materials and tools. Hire out machinery. Fix and service equipment. That kind of thing."

"What else?"

I sat up a little. "Um . . . clothes? Hard hats? That's about it on top of what I've already said."

The beat of silence that answered me was pregnant. Loaded. I closed my eyes and pictured Teddy on his pristine white bed, his pretty face twisted into a shrewd frown. *He doesn't believe me.* And he was right not to in most circumstances, but as far as Kings Building Ltd went, I was telling the truth. It was a legitimate business. One that would sink if I didn't get help fast.

Trouble was, my reputation preceded me round these

parts. There weren't many high street accountants who'd let me darken their doorstep. Legitimate or not, I needed help from someone who understood my world, or at least someone who didn't give a fuck.

Instinct told me Teddy was the latter. *Why would he help you, then? What's in it for him?*

I had no fucking clue, but at this point, I didn't care. If he laughed and hung up, at least I'd got the chance to hear his voice again. If not for the ache in my muscles and the scratches on my skin, I'd have been half convinced I'd dreamt him. Real life sex was never that good.

Beyond good.

Beyond *fucking* almost. And hell, if I hadn't needed that out-of-body experience.

"You intrigue me," Teddy said eventually. "And I have some time this week. Text me an address and I will come and look at your books. Thursday. In the morning. Nine o'clock. Don't be late."

He hung up. It didn't surprise me. I'd already figured out that communicating with this bloke was gonna be a fucking theme park. I lowered my phone from my ear, grinning like an idiot, just in time for the door to the chapel to bang open and my council to swagger in. Nash, Rubi, and Mateo. After them came old man Cracker John and Father Embry.

The last one made me laugh. The club's chaplain—loose term: he wasn't tied to religion any more than me—was twenty-five years old. He wore the same dark jeans, plain tee, and leather cut as the rest of us and had a face decades too young to be anyone's parent, spiritual or otherwise.

He had the heart, though. Make no fucking mistake. Sometimes I wondered if I'd still be here without him, and I channelled that in the brief eye contact we shared as the boys took their seats at the table, thankful that he always knew how to divert my attention from the simmering presence who appeared like a ghost to my right.

Saint Malone. Fuck. My head was full of Teddy Jones, but my heart *ached* for Saint. I wondered if he could tell I'd banged someone who'd made me forget about him, just for one night. If I'd taken that deep breath I'd so desperately fucking needed.

Of course he could. There was something special about Saint. He saw things no one else did. Interpreted them in ways no one else ever could.

It was why the club needed him as their sergeant-at-arms.

And why I couldn't have him in any other way.

Club secretary, Cracker, signalled for silence, then called every man's name. We swore in and I pounded my gavel on the table, every facet of me focused on my job. My family. *My brothers.* I'd die for these men, and they'd die for me, sooner rather than later if we didn't get a handle on the mess we had brewing. "We've got trouble coming," I started without preamble. "Pulling out of the bridge contracts is proving as hellacious as we thought it would be. Guys on site are already being harassed, and last night some arsehole torched our equipment stores. It's only a matter of time before things escalate. Nash, what else have we got?"

Nash McGovern, good-looking motherfucker, all gold hair and blue eyes, leaned forward, tatted elbows on the table. "We lost forty grand's worth of gear in that fire. Legitimate kit that isn't covered by insurance because it's obvious arson and the insurance provider—and the old bill—think it was an inside job. We're now blacklisted, and every policy we had for just about everything is void."

Low whistles and murmurs sounded around the table, but not from me. I knew this shit already, I just didn't want to be the one to speak it aloud when I'd warned them this would happen seven fucking years ago when I argued against bidding for the supply contracts to repair and restructure half a dozen motorway bridges. We'd won those contracts from organisations far more criminal and corrupt than us, and we'd spent every day since fighting the consequences.

And now we wanted out, guess what?

That was a shit show too. These weren't contracts that could be torn up just because we wanted them to be. We were in bed with gangs we didn't even know the fucking name of, and they were hitting us where it hurt. Money. Security. Safety. If we couldn't keep a roof over our head and our members alive, we were done.

"We have legitimate business interests." Embry spoke up, ever the voice of reason. "Just like everyone else. How can multiple insurance companies refuse our custom?"

"We're a known criminal enterprise," I said flatly. "And when you've been refused or cancelled once, it stays on your record. Like a credit score, only we now have a big fat zero."

"Can we pull money from the yard to cover the loss?"

I shook my head. "Even if we had it—and I don't know yet if we do, thanks to Magda losing her fucking marbles—we can't prop up that shit with the business we need to survive if everything else goes wrong. We can't taint it with dirty money."

Mateo lit a smoke. "Even if it's going in the opposite direction?"

I turned my attention to my fiery enforcer. "Afraid so. If we have any hope of getting out of this with anything left, we have to keep our operations totally separate."

"Still dreaming of going straight, boss?" he said with a smirk that I returned. No one sitting at our table—save old man Cracker and maybe, sometimes, Nash—was motherfucking straight. We liked it all and gave no shits how anyone else felt about it. Made for an interesting road life, let me tell you, but none of us got into this ride to be boring.

"I'm dreaming of a lot of things," I told them honestly. "But mostly finishing what my father started and getting back to a motorcycle club that runs dodgy poker games and moves a bit of green. And for what it's worth, I'm sorry you're fighting a war you didn't start. I never wanted this."

"We know you didn't." At my side, Rubi, my road captain and childhood friend, laid a fist on my arm. "Most of us were there when you spoke against getting into big-time construction rackets. We haven't forgotten."

Nash murmured his agreement. Cracker scowled. Only Saint and Embry said nothing, that part of our history before Embry's time. And Saint? Fuck, I didn't need him to speak to know he had my back.

"Okay." Mateo ashed his cigarette in the crystal dish at the centre of the table. "If we can't make the money back legitimately . . ." He shot me a look that would've chilled a civilian to the bone. Except I was no fucking civvie, and fresh out of Teddy's bed, Mateo Romano was gonna have to do better than that. "Where are we pulling it from?"

"Is that a real question, or do you have ideas of your own?"

Mateo glanced at Saint, my sergeant-at-arms, brooding, silent and beautiful beside me.

I forced myself to follow his gaze. Saint's forest-green eyes and colourful tattoos caught me in their snare and he shrugged, telling me all I needed to know. He was a man of few words by design, but he never left me wanting.

We got this.

I nodded. "Find me later when you've figured it out. And no slotting any fucker stupid enough to get in your way. I've got enough going on without worrying about shifting cadavers."

It was no fucking joke. We were working hard to move away from the kind of life that had got my dad and too many of my brothers killed or incarcerated, but however much we cleaned ourselves up, we were still an outlaw MC. People got hurt. People died. And sometimes we had to move heaven and earth to cover that shit up.

The meeting moved on. Mateo brought me up to speed on the weed shipment he was overseeing in the coming weeks. Rubi outlined details of a legitimate run to touch base with our sister chapter in the south. It was an ideal opportunity to shore up support if the shit I was expecting to fly came sooner rather than later, but more than that, I was digging the chance to get the fuck out of dodge. The wind in my face, my boys at my back, there was no better place than the open road.

Except the bed you crawled out of this morning. Damn. I could not get that bloke out of my head. My phone seemed to burn a hole in my pocket and all I could see was his lithe body writhing beneath me as I fucked him.

All I could hear was his quiet, wretched groan when he'd come.

"Cam?"

"Hmm?" I blinked and shifted my gaze to Nash. He was watching me, his blue eyes shrewder than most people gave him credit for. "What?"

"Doesn't matter. You want a drink?"

I nodded. "I want a couple."

"I'll hook you up."

He reached across me and took the gavel, pounding it on the table with a grin. "Dismissed. Get drunk and get laid while you can, boys. It's gonna be a busy week."

I rolled my eyes and wrenched the gavel from his hand, but the truth was I didn't give a shit and he knew it. I didn't run my MC like any president we'd ever heard of. My brothers rode any make of bike they fucking pleased, played shitty indie music in the clubhouse when they weren't in the mood for death metal, and banged whoever they chose. I didn't care where these bastards came from or what they were into as long as they looked me in the eye and pledged a loyalty I could believe.

Also, I wasn't a precious bastard. If I didn't want Nash's hands on my gavel, he'd have had it buried in the back of his skull years ago. Business was business, but we deserved a little fun too.

The meeting broke up, emptying out the chapel until it was just me and Embry, the closest to a confidant I had these days.

He took Nash's seat. "You look tired."

"Thanks, Ma."

"It's Pa to you, but okay. Anything you want to talk about?"

"Nope."

"Sure about that? I have time."

"Course you do. Celibate motherfucker, ain't ya? When was the last time you got laid?"

Embry gave me an angelic smile that was somehow wicked at the same time. "Is it my sexual exploits we need to talk about here? I can't remember the last time you went home after church and stayed there."

"Spying on me, father?"

"No, merely absorbing what the prospects tell me when I ask them why they're getting no sleep either."

"You think I'm fucking the prospects?"

Embry opened his mouth but changed his mind as Nash returned with a bottle of Cornish rum and two glasses. He dumped them on the table, punched Embry's arm, and left again. Clearly he had places to be.

"You sent them home last night, then rode out before they'd left," Embry said as the door shut behind Nash. "What happened to no one riding alone until this business with the bridges is done?"

I sighed. When rules were set, they applied to the whole club, even the president, and I relied on Saint and Mateo to enforce them. But as much as I didn't give a shit about prospects knowing who I was fucking at any given time, *man* ... "I needed some time to think. You know how I get if I can't get a moment of peace."

Embry smiled. He did know, all too well. As club chaplain, it was his job to take care of our mental health and he was the most diligent of us all. "There's no peace to be found taking risks. You're our most valuable asset. Without you, the club falls. And more than that, we love you. It would destroy every soul here if anything happened to you."

I knew that. Not because I was an arrogant twat, but because I'd seen it happen when my dad died. It was why I was still here and not long gone like River, my brother. I'd never been one for the easy road. Besides, I had other brothers now, and we shared more than blood and grief.

Another sigh escaped me. I nodded to let Embry know I heard what he was saying, but we both knew it wouldn't make a blind bit of difference. Nothing could shackle me, not even the club I'd give my damn life for. "I might've found us a new accountant." I changed the subject, subtle as a breeze block.

Embry reached for the rum and poured two glasses. "Who?"

"Posh dude with a fancy watch and head for numbers. It's not certain yet, but he's swinging by on Thursday to take a look."

"Where did you find him?"

"Yellow Pages." I gave Embry a dry look Teddy would've been proud of.

He rolled his eyes. "Is there a reason you didn't bring this up at church?"

"I already told you. It's not definite yet. Besides, we don't have much time to discuss legitimate business right now, so I want to make sure I know what I'm talking about when we do."

I claimed my rum glass and tipped it back in one swallow while Embry sipped his, still eyeing me as if I'd offered him a three-course dinner and only showed up with a bowl of shit soup. Whatever. I couldn't do anything about that. I wasn't gonna divulge my night with Teddy to the club. Didn't need to. He'd already made it clear it was a one-time thing.

Still. The prospect of seeing him again, business or otherwise, was consuming enough that even Embry lost his unending patience with me and wandered off.

He left the rum behind. With no one chewing my ear off for the first time in hours, I enjoyed a solitary drink, chain-smoking my way through the cigarettes I hadn't touched while I'd been with Teddy. Embry had been right: I was tired, and I thought about going home, but as much as I enjoyed the sanctuary of my house, I didn't feel like riding the coastal roads with two prospects at my back. I wanted to escape for real. Metaphorically or literally, it didn't fucking matter. On any other night, I'd grab myself a girl from the bar and take her upstairs to the residence where I had a room with a king-size bed and an en-suite bathroom. I'd lock the door and fuck her all night long.

But it didn't feel like any other night. The restlessness that plagued me was as present as ever, but the urge to silence it with a faceless bang was absent, as if I'd misplaced that part of my personality. The thought of touching someone right now made me want to puke, and I didn't have a clue what to do with it.

So I drank instead, alone and brooding. No one bothered me, they wouldn't dare, and it was three in the morning by the time I realised I'd never sent Teddy an address to meet me.

Rubbing my face, I staggered to my feet, squinting at my phone as I retrieved the number I'd punched in the evening before. I typed out a message that made no sense, hit delete,

43

and replaced it with the postcode and street address for the yard.

I sent it and stuffed my phone in my back pocket when there was no immediate reply. It was arse o'clock in the morning. Maybe I'd misjudged him and he was asleep after all.

An answering buzz caught me off guard.

I fished my phone out again and my cracked old heart flared to life. Teddy had replied, though I didn't open it until I'd passed through the bar and made it to the relative safety of my compound bedroom.

Heart thumping—*that's what you get for a skinful of rum* —I sat on the edge of my bed and swiped at the phone with clumsy fingers, opening the message on my second attempt.

Teddy: *Don't be late.*

It was hardly laced with warmth and affection, but somehow, those three words ignited something inside me I knew wouldn't quit until I saw him again. What the hell was it? Anticipation? Desire? I couldn't quite tell. It felt a lot like fear, but I wasn't afraid. Fuck my life, where was my head at these days?

I had no answer to that, and I put my phone down before I did something ridiculous and sent him a picture of my dick. Because I was hard now. Apparently even banal messages from Teddy Jones gave me a boner.

Awesome. At least I was too drunk to do much about it. I fucked my way through life with little abandon, but I drew the line at a lonely wank in my compound quarters. I took that shit home, or at least I would when I was sober enough to ride.

With Teddy on the brain, I passed out, face down in my

clothes, even my boots. I slept like a drunk man who deserved it and woke sometime later without relief to the sharp-edged fatigue scratching my brain.

I blinked. It was still dark, unless I'd done the impossible and slept through to the evening. *Unlikely.* It had been years since I'd managed more than a few hours at a time. Club life was like that. Someone always wanted a piece of me, and even if they didn't, my head was a loud place to be. The decisions I made kept people alive or got them killed, and it was a heavy cross to bear.

A cross you chose.

As if I needed the reminder. I shut my brother's sardonic voice out of my head and belatedly scanned the room for whatever had woken me. Nothing obvious came to light. On autopilot, I reached for my phone and checked the time. It was a little after five—too early to do anything meaningful and too late to go back to sleep. Were drunk power naps a thing? I hoped so. I had a long day ahead of me when the rest of the world woke.

I lit a cigarette. Changed my mind as it made my rum-soaked head spin and flicked it out of the open window. I watched it bounce to the pavement below as I tugged my boots off, shrugged out of my club cut, then flopped back on the bed.

Teddy's message taunted me. I opened it and read the words again, all three of them. *Don't be late.* Okay, first up, what made him think I'd be a tardy motherfucker? Second, how the hell did he manage to be like that in a text message? Was I losing my damn mind, or had this prick connected a live wire to my nerves when I'd been in his bed?

Cos that's how I felt right now. Fucking nervous, for no reason at all.

Nonplussed, I tapped out of the message and opened another, this one from Nash, confirming in even fewer words that he'd done the dozen things I'd asked him to do and made it home for the night. It should've been enough to settle me, but it wasn't.

I opened Teddy's message again. Stared at it. Pictured him stretched out like a fucking lion on his bed, typing it with his elegant fingers. *Don't do it. Don't do it.*

Cam: *Or what?*

Dickhead. I cringed so hard I made my jaw crack, adding to the headache I'd woken up with, but my phone buzzed before I died a complete and horrible death.

Teddy: *Or I'll leave. Why are you awake?*

Cam: *Why are you?*

Teddy: *Habit.*

Cam: *Same.*

Teddy: *Interesting.*

Cam: *Is it?*

Teddy: *I think so.*

Cam: *You need hobbies then.*

Teddy: *I have several.*

Cam: *Care to share?*

He didn't answer, and because I was a bucket of thirst, I called him.

It rang for long enough that I figured I'd fucked up. My grip on my phone tightened as I prepared to tap out. Then he answered and his smooth voice filled my senses.

"Good morning, Cam."

I smiled, glad he couldn't see me. "Is it morning for you? I didn't really go to bed yet."

"Partying hard?"

"Not exactly, though I might've sunk too much rum at some point."

Teddy hummed. "I can picture that."

What else can you picture? Cos all I can see is you splayed against that wall while I fuck you, your head lolled back on my shoulder as you come. It wasn't quite how it had happened, but it was the scene I'd seen in my dirtiest day dreams ever since. "I prefer it to whisky, but none of it does me any favours."

"I don't know. You looked all right to me with a glass in your hand."

"All right?"

"What would you like me to say?"

"The truth."

Teddy chuckled. "Is that why you called? To have your ego stroked? Surely I cannot be the only one you can think of to do that. If I am, your ego must be very neglected indeed."

His accent was Russian tonight. This *morning*. I drank it up, closing my eyes and biting my lip a moment, my cock still throbbing and yearning for him. "My ego is just fine. I called because you didn't answer my question and I'm a curious kind of bloke."

"You are *impatient*. I had left the room for coffee."

"I still want to know."

"Why?"

"Because I can't imagine you any way except what I've already seen, and I need to kill that shit before I see you."

"Again, why?"

I sat up, the bleariness I'd brought into the conversation fading away as the exhilaration of hearing his voice again took hold and brought me to life. "A few reasons, the main one being I need to make the most of the time you can spare me and focus on my accounts without wanting to throw you down and fuck you."

"You can want that as much as you like."

"Cos it doesn't change anything? You still won't let me do it?"

"Exactly, Cam."

"If you want me to stop thinking about fucking you, then *you* need to stop saying my name like that."

"Like what?"

"Like—" Fuck, I didn't know. Like a honeyed fucking prayer, but I wasn't about to admit that aloud. This dude had taken me apart enough as it was. "Never mind. Forget all that. Let's say I called to reassure you I won't be late and leave it at that."

A beat of silence bloomed between us. I wondered if I'd offended him. Then his silky voice returned. "Whatever you want, *Cam*. I will see you on Thursday."

The bastard hung up on me again, leaving me to stare at my phone and seriously question my compound wanking rules. Thursday was three days away. If I couldn't kill the fire Teddy had lit in me by then, I'd be walking into that meeting with a dick like a stone fucking column.

[5]
TEDDY

The premises of Kings Building Ltd was exactly as I expected it to be, even without the help of Google Earth. Tucked off the exit of an A road, it was a large, sprawling complex, and the builder's merchant Cam had told me about only accounted for the cluster of buildings at the front.

Behind it lay a warehouse-style structure, a breakfast café, and a gated compound that a cursory glance led me to believe was the headquarters for the Rebel Kings Motorcycle Club, the one percenter organisation Cam had failed to mention.

This amused me, though I couldn't say why. It wasn't as if Cam owed me a complete inventory of his business interests. Only the ones he needed my help with, which led me to ponder the status of his other financial affairs and what the merchant company was a front for. Not that I cared, but I was intrigued. Everything about this man intrigued me, from the hidden kindness in his deep-brown eyes to the odd feeling thinking about him gave me in my chest. The alien sensation that fascinated me enough to bring me to this place and seek him out.

I parked my car beside a row of grimy vans and got out, my boots hitting the damp, sandy tarmac the same moment as a tradesman beside me with his dirty trousers and utility belt.

He gave me a strange look.

I ignored him and strode to the main entrance, holding it open for him with a stare that made him shiver. I was good like that—it made people remember me when I wanted them to and forget me when I didn't.

The man preceded me to the front desk of the builder's merchant. I let him do whatever he'd come to do while I assessed my surroundings. It wasn't the usual category of business I frequented, but I recognised a well-oiled machine when I saw one. Staff hard at work with amiable smiles on their faces. This was a place where people liked their boss. They liked *Cam*, because there was no doubt in my mind that he was lord around here.

How could a man who fucked like that be anything else?

The shivery tradesman left with a length of something enormous that he strapped to the roof of his van. I watched him go, then approached the front desk. A woman with dark hair and eyes like Cam's greeted me, suspicion and confusion already brewing in a gaze that felt more familiar than I could bear. *She knows I don't belong here.*

I didn't even try to smile. "Good morning. I have an appointment with Cam."

The woman's eyes narrowed, swallowing up the warmth that was so like Cam. *His sister.* I couldn't say why I cared. Or why I noticed she was every bit as beautiful as him, though she did not make my stomach flutter the way her brother did.

"Can I take your name?"

"Teddy Jones. He's expecting me."

The woman nodded and signalled for a man nearby to take over her station. Then she disappeared without a word and I took it to mean Cam would find me when she'd tracked him down.

I retreated outside. An enclosed space with all eyes on me was not my favourite environment. It made me tetchy, and I wasn't a pleasant person to be around when I was irritated. Besides, I liked the outdoors and I liked to watch men work, so Cam's yard proved as entertaining as I needed it to be.

Enlightening, actually. I observed the comings and goings of the builder's merchant, men with vans and trucks, clothes grubby from manual labour. It was a brisk trade. A constant footfall. Unless someone was making gargantuan mistakes behind the scenes, it was unlikely the place didn't turn a healthy profit.

And then there was the rest of it, the steady trickle of men on loud motorcycles rumbling through the side gate and disappearing into the compound. None were Cam, but their tattooed arms and scruffy jaws were enough to let me know I was watching the Rebel Kings come and go. The activity wasn't as overt as MCs I'd seen elsewhere, but the energy was unmistakable, that quiet flurry of dangerous efficiency. *What are they up to, I wonder?*

The obvious answer was moving drugs inland and into the cities from the coastal territory they clearly controlled, but Cam didn't strike me as a man who always chose the obvious path. He'd wound up in my bed, after all. *Maybe he has a wife locked up in the compound somewhere.*

Possible, but he didn't strike me as that kind of liar either, unless she knew he liked scouting for cock in dingy Bristol pubs.

Footsteps came up behind me. Knowing it wasn't Cam, I didn't turn round. I waited for the woman from the reception desk to step around me, her scowl less prominent than it had been before. "He's on his way. You can wait in the office if you like. I'll get you the accounts."

"They're on paper?"

"Yes."

Marvellous. I really was in for an interesting morning even if Cam never showed his face.

I followed his sister to the "office"—a quiet corner of a bigger room where staff were picking and packing orders of goods that were small enough to be handed over the counter. More curious glances filtered in my direction. More suspicion. "They think I am from the local authority, perhaps?"

Cam's sister almost smiled. "I haven't asked, but people dressed like you normally means trouble around here, so it's possible."

Dressed like you. The irony. "Your brother asked me for help with the accounts, but he didn't say why. Do you know why . . . ?"

"Orla," she supplied without denying that she was, indeed, Cam's sister. "And no, I don't know the ins and outs of the accounts. I just work here. If you give me a moment, I'll fetch them for you."

I nodded and she strode away, her leather boots clumping

52

with every step. *Orla*. I liked it, and I liked her. Fiery women pleased me, just to watch them if nothing else, though I wasn't immune to their charms in other ways. If her brother hadn't already turned my head . . .

Orla returned with the books and a box of accompanying paperwork. She dumped them on the desk and left again without a word.

I started to smile, and a low chuckle from the doorway was my reward, hand delivered by the hulking frame of masculinity I'd really come to see.

"Making friends already?" Cam grinned and ventured forward, his dark hair a wonderful mess, damp from the shower and slicked back with rough fingers.

"Your sister likes me."

"Orla doesn't like anyone."

"Not even you?"

"Especially not me when I make her work the early shift."

"Early shift?"

"We're open till nine."

"From?"

"Six."

I nodded, piecing it together. "Are builders still working that late in the day?"

"Not on the sites, especially in winter, but we do a roaring DIY trade after hours for all the shit people can't get in IKEA."

Cam ventured further into the office space and I felt his gaze all over me, assessing me, dissecting me. Or at least trying to. He wouldn't get far. No one ever did. Either they gave up at the iron curtain I kept around myself or they found a way through and baulked at what lay beneath.

I didn't care either way.

You care about him or you wouldn't be here.

Inexplicable. And undeniable, but he didn't know that, and he never would.

Cam joined me at the desk. He was wearing dark jeans and a white T-shirt that clung to his muscular frame. Over the top was a leather vest—a cut—thick and battered, with the MC's insignia patched on the back. From where I stood, I couldn't see his rank, but I didn't need to. He was the king of the Kings. Any fool could see it, and I was no fool.

"So these are your books." I gestured to the pile on the desk. "You know, there is computer software for this these days, backed up in a cloud so you don't lose anything."

Cam snorted. "Mate, we only started using tills five years ago. Before that it was a biscuit tin and a change float."

"You sold building materials on a cash-only basis?"

"Yup."

"That's ridiculous. Where did it all go?"

"The bank."

I cocked my head. "Always?"

Cam gave me a look. "Why are you asking me that?"

"Many reasons, but mostly to establish how deep I need to audit your accounts if that's what you want me to do."

"I don't know what I want from you." Cam leaned against the desk. His body was a picture of casual relaxation, but his heady gaze said different. "Why did you agree to help me? I mean, I can pay whatever you want, but we never mentioned money before you got here, so . . ."

"So what? You think I'm incapable of doing a favour for a friend?"

"We're friends?"

"We are not lovers, Cam. And *you* called me. Twice."

Cam blinked and seemed to remember where he was. He glanced around, but out of respect for him, perhaps, no one was looking our way. "I called you because I like your voice. The Russian one. But you already told me where you stand on a repeat of the other night and I really could use the perspective of someone who isn't scared to speak their mind on this, preferably someone who knows their fucking shit. If that makes us friends, I'll take it."

"Well, I am not afraid of you, so I suppose we can be friends."

"Works for me."

Cam's grin widened enough to dazzle most people, I'd imagine, then sobered as he tugged the books towards us. "I already told you where we're at with these, right?"

"Only that whoever was doing them before was overwhelmed. Do you know when they are made up until?"

"Magda dumped them at my feet a few weeks ago. There are entries from this month for the timber section, but nothing else makes any fucking sense and I can't see when we last filed a tax return."

"What about corporation tax? That is due at the end of next month, no?"

"Is it?" Cam shrugged, his face adorably boyish for a moment. "You see why I need help?"

"I do. What I don't see is why you could not ask an accountant from Google to assist you. Are you going to explain that to me before I look at your records?"

"Do I need to?"

I allowed myself a smile, a compromise, when what I really wanted to do was trail my fingers along Cam's sculpted forearm, tracing the veins and corded muscle, absorbing the warmth from his tanned skin. "This is a conversation with many questions and no answers."

"Does that bother you?" Cam's gaze darkened and I felt the gravity of what he was asking me. And I appreciated it. It wasn't as though I had a lot of answers to give myself.

"It does not bother me, at least not the way you may think. But I am naturally curious. If I want to know something, I will ask."

"Do I get to ask questions too?"

"One of them should be to ask if I am a chartered accountant. I'm not, but you do not need one to file your accounts if they are up to date and correct."

"Can you tell me that by looking at them today?"

"Do you have the log-in credentials for your online account at HMRC?"

Cam blinked. "My what?"

I smiled a little wider and pulled out a chair at the desk.

It really was going to be a gloriously long morning.

His name was Cameron O'Brian Jnr and he was the registered director, along with Nash McGovern and Orla "I just work here" O'Brian, of Kings Building Ltd. He was also the proud owner of an unpaid tax bill dating back two years, news he absorbed with a resigned sigh. "That's just me, right? Not the company?"

I nodded and pointed at the screen showing the total amount he owed, including the hefty fine for persistent non-payment. "Do you have the money to pay it?"

"You tell me."

"In your personal accounts? Only you know that. Your company books will take longer to dissect before I will know if there are funds to pay you a dividend."

"Is that a hint for more coffee?"

"Not if it's the same river water you brought me an hour ago."

Cam feigned offence. "Drank it, though, didn't you?"

"Caffeine is caffeine."

"Is that your only vice?"

"What do you think?"

Heat flared in Cam's dark gaze. He held my stare a beat too long and licked his lips, an unconscious action that *almost* drew me closer to him. "I think," he said slowly, "that your vices are something you don't know yet."

"Cryptic. And vague."

"But accurate?"

I signed out of the personal tax account I'd managed to find and access for him in my search for Kings Building Ltd. "Think what you want to think. It does not make it true."

"Well, as your *friend* I'm telling you that I like your vices."

"As in?"

"As in, I liked what you offered me the other night. I know we're not doing that shit ever again, but I wanted you to know that."

"That's sweet."

Cam chuckled. "Keep your voice down. I got a rep around here."

I could believe that. While the curious stares had evaporated, demands for Cam's attention had not. In the two hours we'd spent together, we'd been interrupted six times and I'd observed the interactions with eager eyes. Absorbed the reverence and respect that the people around him bestowed on him. What he'd done to command it, I had no idea.

True to my word, I asked. "Tell me, Cam, how does a man of thirty-two become president of a motorcycle club? The only biker institutions I've ever known, their leaders were middle-aged men."

"And what *institutions* were they?"

"Angels in California. Night Wolves back home."

"In Russia?"

"The headquarters for the local chapter was across the street from my apartment when I was young. We used to watch the bikes come and go."

"We?"

"Yes." I didn't elaborate and he didn't ask me to. Despite his declaration that he had questions of his own, he'd yet to ask me any, and I appreciated that. It made his company easy enough that time was passing in the blink of an eye.

"I'm not that young," Cam said after a beat of silence.

"Is your date of birth a lie?"

"No. I've just been in this life a long time—shit." He scrubbed a hand down his face. "This isn't a conversation I can have with an outsider."

I nodded, understanding. "We do not have to talk at all if you wish."

"It's not that."

"Okay, well, let us bring the subject back to what you asked me for then." I pulled the handwritten ledger closer and opened it, tapping at the smudged and incomplete records for him to see. "As far as I can tell right now, you haven't paid corporation tax yet this year. And until you file your accounts, you won't know how much you owe."

"That'll tell me how much we've made too, though, right? How much we have in the bank as assets?"

"Correct. But to do that, you need to balance your expenses against your turnover. That will take both time and a . . . how do you say it? A fine-tooth comb? To go through this container of madness?"

I pointed at the box of receipts and invoices on the desk. I'd only taken a cursory glance inside, and that had been enough to know it would take significant time to wade through it.

Cam grimaced. "It's the right phrase. You smashed it. The rest of it makes me want to puke, though."

"It will be easier if you take your accounts online. You can do it remotely then, from your phone and a laptop at home, so you're not reliant on whoever has the right pen and paper."

"Are you taking the piss out of me?"

"A little. English people like that, yes?"

"I was born in Kilkenny, but okay."

"I knew that. You sound Irish when you—"

"Pres?"

A gruff voice cut me off, which was probably just as well. Fighting to steer clear of what had already passed between us was a battle I could not win indefinitely.

The source of the voice was a biker, a beautiful one this time, dressed much the same as Cam, though it was obvious this man was no blood relation. His chestnut hair, messy at the nape of his neck, and leaf-green eyes came from different DNA. A gene pool that had gifted him a soul-deep frown that Cam did not possess.

"What is it?" Cam spared him a glance, tension already tightening his shoulders. "You need me?"

A pause stretched out. One that seemed loaded with a curious and unexpected heat. The biker slid his gaze to me, held my stare long enough to get my attention, then flicked back to Cam. "On the road. We spilt some paint."

"You can't clean it up yourself?"

Another beat. Cam's friend seemed to measure his words at a pace that didn't match the urgency in his grim expression. "Reckon you should see it first. Before Mateo scrubs it clean."

Cam's expression marbleised. "Meet me outside."

The biker with the faintly northern accent melted away. Cam's eyes grew distant and distracted. He was no longer in the room with me, his mind working a million miles an hour on something else.

I shut the ledger with a snap, jolting his attention back to me. "Is it wise to spill paint in broad daylight?"

Cam stared at me for a long moment, then leaned forward, bringing his face so close to mine I could smell his oil and smoke scent seeping out of him. The only thing missing was the clean sweat that had sheened his skin as he'd fucked me. "Nothing about my life is wise right now, so I'm gonna take a chance and ask you this: what's your real name?"

I'd been prepared for this question since I'd let my accent slip when the prospect of him fucking me had got the better of me. Cam was a vigilant man. He'd heard it. Registered it. And he would not forget.

I had an answer ready, but for some reason it lodged in my throat and I said nothing. Just held his dark gaze until a fist pounded on the doorway beyond the desk.

"Boss, we gotta fly."

The moment was broken. Cam shifted and a second skin descended on him, obscuring the man whose eyes had been so playful and warm. It was armour and it suited him, perhaps because it *was* him, and the man flirting with me was simply after another night in my bed.

Regardless, I liked looking at him, so I watched him stand and back away from the desk. "I won't be long," he said.

"You do not know that. It might be a lot of paint."

"Might not be."

"Goodbye, Cam."

"Wait for me?"

I gave him a noncommittal shrug. Perhaps I would wait for him to come back. Then again, perhaps I wouldn't.

[6]

CAM

Saint and Mateo were efficient soldiers. It wasn't often they summoned me to clean up their mess, and never without good reason.

Today, though, I was failing to comprehend the source of their uncertainty. I eyed the unmarked and wrecked lorry from a concealed distance, its load—untold quantities of coke stashed in custard powder containers—spread out across the dual carriageway as the police picked their way through it, unaware that most of it had already gone walkabout and was now speeding towards a new supply line. "This was the plan. We disrupted the Sambini shipment with an unfortunate accident. No one saw you. You weren't even here."

Saint shot me a murky glare. "It ain't gonna take rocket science for them to figure out it was us."

"So? It's nothing we haven't done before. That's the deal if they want to move this shit through our turf. We take a slice of it whether they agree to it or not."

"They've never agreed to it."

"Exactly." I gestured to the road. "This is what happens.

An organised fender-bender. A hell of a mess, but no one gets hurt."

Saint shrugged, but I knew him well enough to read between the lines. He'd never liked any of the ties we had to the Sambini organisation, legitimate or otherwise.

Neither had I, but some things were harder to unpick than they were to carry on, even shit as destructive and risky as this.

Besides, we needed the goddamn money. I knew it. Saint knew it. But his troubled frown was hard to bear.

I slugged his arm. "What is it?"

His scowl deepened.

I sighed and tried again. "I can't fix something if I don't know it's broken."

He turned his gaze on me and I watched as he tried to find the words to articulate what was bothering him. Waited. I was used to this. Most people thought Saint Malone was just rude, but I knew better. Dude was jammed up inside, but if you gave him space to think, he had plenty to say, and all of it mattered.

Shrewd not rude.

"There's too much product here to be headed to that crew in Lambeth."

Bingo.

I pulled my smokes from my pocket and lit two, offering one to Saint as he continued to frown. "I can't see from over here. How much do you think there is?"

"Twice as much as usual. Maybe three times."

"That's a good haul for us, though, and still leaves the feds enough to let them think they've saved the world."

Saint took a deep drag on the cigarette I'd jammed into

his mouth. He blew smoke through his nose, fists clenched at his sides. To anyone else he probably looked as though he was about to lamp me one, but I knew better than that too. I saw the concealed panic—the crippling anxiety that paralysed him whenever his brain seized, trapping his words. If it had been Rubi or Nash, I might've clapped a hand on his shoulder or rubbed his arm or even taken the piss, but Saint wasn't built that way unless it was a full fucking moon. Most days, I had to wait my wild boy out and let him puzzle through his shit on his own.

"Something's changed in London," Saint ground out eventually. "This ain't the same boys buying this blow and it isn't a good time to be squaring up to a new crew. We don't have the boots on the ground."

I let that sink in, rubbing my jaw, my own deep frown creasing my face in half. He was probably right, but what choice did we have? We needed a hard hit of funds to prop up the construction business currently under siege from whoever the hell we were fighting there, and we were stone cold out of options. "Okay." I finished my smoke and crushed it beneath my boot. "Get the product moved and banked, then talk to Mateo about moving his grass early. Get all our shit done before there are too many eyes on us. That way we can hold off hitting another blow shipment until we run out of cash."

Saint grunted. It was hard to tell if he concurred or not, but he didn't argue, which was something.

I left him to observe the accident site and picked my way through the undergrowth back to my bike. It was a grey winter's day, damp with the kind of cold that sank into your bones without the beauty and wonder of frost and snow.

Most years, grey days depressed me, but I was too busy right now to pay attention to my state of mind. And . . . distracted. I'd left a Russian money man unsupervised at the compound and I was buzzing to get back to him. For business reasons, of course. Not because I found his company addictive as hell. Definitely not.

My hog was hidden in an enormous rhododendron. I dug it out and wheeled it back to the country road that had brought me here, a squirrel route only locals knew about. My mind was still mostly on Teddy—I couldn't do anything about Saint's suspicions until we had more intel—but as I hit the roadside, something stopped me in my tracks.

I froze and stared down at my bike. At first glance, nothing seemed out of place. Then my gaze fell on a splintered cable poking out where my brake lines should've been. *Jesusfuck.* I stopped rolling and crouched, pulling the cable out entirely to reveal it had been severed just enough to fail when I'd have needed it most. And worse, it had been cut with a blunt blade to make it look like wear and tear.

The cable was brand new. Nash had fitted it two weeks ago, and unless my VP—my goddamn brother—was trying to kill me, someone else was. Some cunt who'd followed me out here and sabotaged my bike while I'd been with Saint. Some *cunt* who now knew we'd been watching the coke shipment close enough to know when it had crashed.

Fuck. I pulled out my phone and dialled Nash, instructing him to come and get me without telling him why. Then I retreated from my bike and slipped into the shadows, taking the hammer from my saddle bag with me. This was bloody Devon. We didn't carry guns and blades. I couldn't have told you the last time I even *saw* a fucking piece. But we carried hammers. Screwdrivers. Heavy spanners. Tools we could explain away in a utility belt if we got pulled by the feds. Wouldn't do me much good if someone came at me with a shooter, but it was all I had.

I waited in the dark, hidden by the huge oak trees I'd used as cover in the first place, using the broad trunk of one to cover my back. In my pocket, my phone buzzed, but I ignored it, keeping every sense trained on the approach to my hiding place. Nash knew where I was. If he couldn't find his way here without chewing my ear off, I needed a new VP.

Twenty minutes later, the rumble of bikes pierced the air. Nash's Harley was as familiar to me as my own, Rubi's too, and they were flanked by three outriders. Clearly, my VP had sensed the tone.

I watched them dismount, then emerged, still scanning the horizon.

Nash was already at my bike, frowning.

We exchanged a look and he read me well enough to follow my gaze to the severed brake line.

"Fuck." He turned it over in his hand. "This was brand new."

"I know."

"Two weeks ago."

"I *know*."

"Could it have been done before you came here?"

"Unlikely. I'd have splatted on the tarmac before I arrived."

Nash stood back from my bike, circling it, a fierce frown creasing his usually amiable face. "Not necessarily. If it was a small cut, it could've frayed as you rode, getting worse along the way."

"It was fine this morning."

"Where did you park at the clubhouse?"

I gave him an idiot scowl. Where did he think I'd fucking parked? Club hierarchy dictated where we left our bikes. Had done since before we were born.

Nash shrugged. "Okay, and where did you go when you got there?"

"To the office. To meet the, uh, accountant."

He caught my slip and stared, his expression hard to read. "That was an appointment, right? He knew you were coming?"

"The fuck are you suggesting? That some random accountant lured me to a meeting, then sabotaged my bike when I was with him the whole fucking time?"

"Boss, the alternative is someone followed you here. That they knew about the coke run and our plan to raid it. Fuck, they could've done the same to every brother out on the road right now."

I swallowed hard. Unfortunately, that made more sense than Teddy trying to murder me for having fuck-hot sex with him. *Does it? You don't know shit about him. He won't even tell you his name.*

True. But I'd made contact in that pub, not him. Unless I had secret enemies who could keep up with my bouncing sexual desires better than I could, my brothers were in danger and I needed to act fast.

Raging, I booted my Harley hard enough to topple it over. "Call them off. Tell them to pull over and check their bikes, dump the load if they have to. I don't care. Make them safe." I pointed at Rubi. "Find Saint. He's up the chalk hills. Check his bike, then stay with him."

Rubi nodded. "I'll try, but you know what he's like. He's harder to keep tabs on than you are."

"Well, someone did," I snapped. "They followed me here and fucked my bike in the ten minutes I was somewhere else, so tell Saint he ain't fucking invincible, and don't let him leave without speaking to me first."

Rubi took my temper with another nod. Nash aside, he was the most level-headed brother on my crew. If anyone could deliver this news to Saint and convince him not to fly off on a murder mission, it was him. *Maybe.* It was a cold, hard fact that my sergeant-at-arms was a loose cannon when it came to protecting me.

Wild. Violent.

And I knew why. I felt the same. Only Teddy had ever made my heart pump like it pumped for Saint Malone when I acknowledged the attraction between us.

Something I did *not* have the time for right now.

Rubi tramped away, leaving his bike and keys behind, already knowing I'd be riding it home while he took the bitch seat behind Nash. When he was gone, Nash stooped and pulled my hog upright, giving me a look that reminded me why we called him the mother-fucking-hen of the group. While Embry looked after our spiritual wellbeing, Nash took care of the rest. It was how he'd come to be working on my bike in the first place.

I watched him examine the additional mess I'd made of my Dyna, knowing the guilt would kick in soon. My Harley was a part of me, of my family, my history. It was the only thing my dad had ever given me that I'd really fucking wanted. I mean, he'd given me his club, but I'd had to fight for it, and I was still fighting now. And what the hell for? So some cunt could cut my brake lines?

Man, I needed a drink.

I settled for a smoke and took a perch on a nearby dead tree, relaxing some now my brothers were with me. My hammer found its way to my belt and I took some deep, cleansing breaths, trying not to think about Teddy abandoned in the office. He was going to leave, I knew it. Would he come back? Who the fuck knew. At this point, I couldn't worry about it. I needed to make my family safe.

Rubi returned with Saint, wheeling Saint's bike. "Tyres slashed," he said when he caught my eye. "By some twat with a butter knife. Could just be kids."

Nash jerked his head up, gaze fierce again. "Why would kids cut Cam's brakes?"

"Maybe they didn't. Maybe they cut some brakes on a random bike they found hidden in a bush, then slashed some tyres for the hell of it."

"What kind of kids do you know who'd do that?"

"None. I'm just saying it doesn't have to be the worst scenario in the world here."

I sent Rubi a flat look. He was my oldest friend and I often relied on him to balance the negative side of my brain, but sometimes this prick would say black was white just for the damn hell of it. "Let's assume the worst, eh? That way we won't be disappointed."

Nash gave a grim nod and went back to his work, by now already patching the tyre on Saint's bike.

Saint said nothing. Didn't even look at me. Just scowled at the earth and trees around us as if he'd been dumped in the woods by his mother all over again.

69

Rubi sighed and came to sit beside me. He pulled a blunt from a battered cigarette box and lit up, offering it to me when he'd taken a couple of deep drags.

I waved it away. Weed was good when I couldn't fucking sleep, but I needed my wits about me today, even if they felt so sharp they were tearing me apart.

We hunkered down until we got word the boys on the road were safe. Their bikes had checked out and they'd banked the stolen product, including the payday we'd picked up in return.

They were heading home.

Nash called a prospect in with a van to pick up my bike. When it was safely loaded, I swung my leg over Rubi's bike. It was smaller than mine, a fact that irritated me for no reason at all. *Since when are you a size queen?*

Maybe since I'd seen Teddy's fat dick slapping against his gorgeous abs. I didn't bottom often. It was rare I felt chill enough to do it with a stranger, and I sure as hell wasn't doing it with one of my friends, but my night with Teddy—*not his fucking name*—had got me feeling some type of way. Like he'd dangled me out of a high-rise window and swung me around until my head was irrevocably upside down.

Stop thinking about him. You have shit to do.

I gunned Rubi's bike, noting that he had thrown a leg over the back of Nash's battle-scarred V-Rod, not giving a single toss about cuddling up to his brother for the ride home, while Saint had roared away, impatient as ever to be somewhere else, despite the fact that we were all heading to the same place. We had to. If someone was brave enough to crawl out of the woodwork and try to kill us both, we had to stick together. Safety in numbers and all that jazz.

We caught up with Saint and hit the road back to the clubhouse, me at the front, flanked by Nash and an outrider, while Saint played tail gunner at the back. There weren't many of us, but we drew attention. An unmarked police car appeared as soon as we hit the A road and trailed us all the way home.

Like a good president, I saw my boys through the gate, then doubled back to intercept the old bill before they could leave and pretend they hadn't crawled up my arse.

I waved.

They cringed and drove away. Any other day I might've laughed—the clubhouse had been here fifty years and we'd never been busted with so much as an out-of-date fire extinguisher—but I had precious little good humour left in me. Some fucker was trying to kill me. Worse than that, they'd tried to kill Saint, and that fucked with my head more.

Were they trying to kill him? It makes more sense that they disabled his bike to stop him from protecting you.

True. But still. Saint was my brother—*and the rest.* If he'd been hurt today . . .

Fuck, I felt sick. I shivered and steered Rubi's bike into the compound, noting with a sinking sensation that the Jaguar SUV Teddy had rolled up in had gone. *Of course he left. You've been gone hours. You thought he'd wait for you and take you out for dinner?*

A snort escaped me as I parked and yanked my helmet over my head, Embry already all up in my business.

He raised a brow. "Delayed reaction?"

"To what?"

"To the attempt on your life."

I snorted again. "It was a warning, not a bullet in my skull."

"This time."

I slid off Rubi's bike and let some of the pent-up frustration burning in my chest show on my face. It wasn't like Embry to be dramatic and I could've done without it. "Church in an hour. I need a piss and a fucking drink before we deal with this shit."

"Okay."

Embry stepped back, letting me go, and I blew past him with thunder in every stride, shouldering my way through the clubhouse and into the chapel, letting the doors bang shut behind me.

The building was old and filled with MC memorabilia. In days gone by, there'd been a bar at the back of the main room, keeping the table supplied with whisky and rum, but I'd taken it out five years ago, replacing it with a kitchen that kept my boys fed and watered when business consumed every hour of the day.

Mind blank, I opened the fridge and dug out enough chicken to feed an army of hungry men. Then, because perhaps I was the motherfucking hen, I loaded up the pan with every vegetable I could find.

Yeah, that's right. I cooked them dinner. Not because I was nice, but because I knew from experience that no good came from discussions fuelled by hangry men. My brothers were like wolves. I kept them well fed enough to stop them turning on me, but hungry enough that they could kill in the blink of an eye. A shite analogy, but it worked for us, and it was why the yard had a fire pit, an outdoor kitchen, and an unfinished pizza oven that had been on my list to get done since the summer.

The scent of cooking food brought my boys to the table. One by one, they trucked in, Rubi first, then Nash, Embry, Cracker, and Mateo.

Saint was last, his expression sinister enough to send a chill down my spine. I didn't need to ask to know he'd been stewing over the cut brake lines on my bike and that he was ready for revenge. Some people thought he was dead inside, but I knew different. The rage he carried came from the heart, and a fragment of that heart belonged to me.

I left Nash to dish up the meal I'd cooked and led my brother outside, unsurprised that Mateo followed. Night had fallen while I'd cooked, swallowing up the short winter day. It was cold too, but I didn't feel the frigid breeze as it hit the bare skin of my arms. I didn't feel much at all. "Hit me with it," I said to Mateo. "Who do you think is behind this?"

My enforcer ran his savage gaze over me, one eye twisted by a macabre scar that ran the entire length of his face. "We got a couple of possibilities."

"Always nice to have a choice of mortal enemy."

Mateo chuckled, but it faded fast. "The Sambinis are top of my list. They're behind the coke shipments, and us pulling out of the bridge contracts fucks them up. If we're not in line to take the fall when the fucking things come tumbling down, it's a problem for them."

I growled. Aside from the darker shadows haunting us, this bullshit was the reason I'd never wanted the club involved in corrupt construction projects. Corruption meant no one gave a fuck about anything except lining their own pockets.

Rules got broken. Corners got cut. And then motorway bridges collapsed onto traffic, killing innocent people on their way to the beach. I didn't have many morals, but I couldn't live with that shit. And Mateo and Saint couldn't live with it either. They wouldn't be here if they could. They'd be riding for another club, fighting for a president who didn't care how bloody his hands were when he went to bed at night.

Which led me to another suspect. "What about the Crows? They've been after our territory for years. You think Sambini paid them to come after us? Let the rest of the world think it's a biker war?"

Saint cleared his throat.

I waited for him to speak.

He didn't. And Mateo didn't have the answers either, only a vow that made my skin prickle. "If Frank Crow is stupid enough to start a real war with us, we'll end him and his fucking scumbag crew. Sambini money won't be any good to him then."

"We need to find out for sure." I pulled out a smoke and lit up. "I don't want to waste time Crow beating if there's a fucking eagle about to land on my back."

"Sambini isn't an eagle."

I tossed a glance at Saint.

He glared back at me, not even trying to explain himself, and I suppressed a heavy sigh, swallowing down the smoke in my lungs. One day it would kill me, but then, maybe it wouldn't. Maybe every other bullshit thing in my life would finish me first.

"Look." I scowled at them both. "We need to find out who we're fighting on this. It's one thing for Sambini to come at us on the building sites, and they expect us to hit their coke runs from time to time—it's part of the deal for letting them use our roads—but if they're trying to kill me for whatever fucked-up reason, that's personal and we're gonna need a battle plan." *And a battle chest.* Wars cost money. Weapons. Soldiers. Intelligence. We weren't fucking NATO, and none of that shit came cheap.

Mateo nodded. "I'll grab some boys and head out after dinner. I've got some people I can shake down for information. If it's the Crows, I'll know about it by morning."

"I'm staying with you," Saint said to me, his green gaze unyielding. "At least until we know who we're fighting."

I battled the urge to roll my eyes. It was standard procedure to have a brother guard me. Saint had watched my back more times over the years than I could count, but . . . I wasn't in the damn mood for the heartache that came with it. The urge to escape was deep-rooted and strong. Suffocating. I almost didn't care if a rival gang ran me down and picked a fight at the side of the road. Mood I was in, it would take a fucking army to put me down.

Maybe you're the hangry one. Mateo certainly was. I rarely saw Saint eat.

I waved him inside anyway. I needed the space.

Finally alone, another cigarette found its way to my lips, and I belatedly remembered the messages that had buzzed through to my phone while I'd waited on my boys.

I pulled out my phone and opened them up. One was from the government welcoming me back to my online tax account. A bemused laugh bubbled out of me. *What the actual fuck?* I deleted the message and opened the next. It was from my sister.

Orla: *Your friend left. He took our books. Hope he's not a fucking fed...*

I rolled my eyes. Teddy wasn't a fed. I couldn't say for sure exactly what he was, but of that, I was certain. Being a fed meant dancing to someone else's tune and the dude I'd spent a wild night in bed with wasn't a man I could picture ever doing that. *No way.* Besides, the last message on my screen was from him telling me he'd taken the accounts and he'd find me when he was done, and my only worry on that front was if I could wait as long as it took him to wade through that damn fucking box of receipts.

Newsflash: I couldn't, but as the pull in my soul became something deeper, something else took hold too. A warning I couldn't ignore. Teddy Jones—*yeah, right*—was a beautiful man, but something else lurked beneath his slate gaze and alabaster skin, a simmering danger that I hadn't absorbed the first time we'd been together.

It sank in now, belated and terrifying. Teddy wasn't a fed. He was something else entirely. Kill or cure?

I had no fucking idea.

[7]
TEDDY

There was a doorman in the building that housed my penthouse. He was six foot seven and took his job as seriously as if he were guarding the pope, so I could only assume Cam had killed him when the knock on my door came around midnight.

Because I *knew* it was Cam. Somehow, I could smell him before I'd even risen from my seat at the kitchen counter.

I didn't smell his friend, though, so the second biker lurking behind him, the beautiful one with the green eyes and tousled chestnut hair, caught me off guard. "Do you need protection from me?"

Cam smirked, though his eyes were tired. "You tell me."

I leaned against the doorframe, dressed in nothing but the black drawstring pants I'd been planning on sleeping in sometime in the near future, if I could ever tear myself away from his accounts, that was. For some reason, perhaps the one that had appeared on my doorstep, I had a primitive need to burn through them at breakneck speed. "I can tell you many things, but not all of them would be true."

"Lie to me then."

"Would you like that?"

Cam's gaze flickered over his shoulder. His wingman backed off and lounged against the wall, one booted foot kicked up on the pristine paint work. His complex gaze held a wealth of silent communication. Cam nodded and turned back to me. "Can I come in?"

"That depends."

"On?"

"On what you've done with Horacio downstairs."

"The doorman?"

I raised a brow. Cam brought both hands to the doorframe, caging me, leaning forward without seeming to know he was doing it before he noticed and licked his lips.

He didn't correct himself.

Good. I like him close. I liked drowning in his smoke and leather scent and remembering his rough hands on my skin too. He was intoxicating.

"We distracted him," Cam whispered, his breath feathering my cheek. "Slipped past when he was dealing with something and nothing. Is that okay with you?"

"You could've just asked him to buzz my intercom."

"Would you have answered?"

"No."

The lazy smirk lighting Cam's face deepened a touch, vindication flashing in his ebony gaze. "I figured."

"Did you?"

"Yeah. Answering an intercom. *Buzzing* me in. It's too . . . normal for you."

I was flattered that he seemed to have spent so much time considering my personality. He had a lot to learn, if he ever got the chance, but his assumptions so far were interesting.

Were they accurate?

I couldn't possibly say. Nor did I know why the flicker in my heart was so intense. *You have slept with this man once. Sat beside him in his open-plan office once. Why does he make you feel like this?*

No answers were forthcoming from my subconscious. Regardless, I stepped back from the doorway and waved him inside.

Cam crossed the threshold and shut the door behind him. He leaned on it, his leather jacket creaking against the wood.

"You are not wearing your cut. That is what you call those leather vests, yes? With your club colours on the back?"

He shrugged. "It's not like it is on TV. We don't wear them all the time because it attracts too much attention. I don't want every fucker I ride past to remember me."

I remember you. "What about your friend? How long are you going to leave him outside for?"

"As long as it takes."

"As what takes?"

"Whatever. He doesn't give a shit. It's his job to watch my back."

"He's your bodyguard?"

"Among other things."

I'll bet. "What's his name?"

Cam tilted his head, as if he didn't like what he saw straight on and needed a second look. "Why are you asking me that?"

He's suspicious. I almost smiled, but my gut told me he wouldn't like it. "I am a curious man. Most things I can see

79

without question, but you are a complex soul. You do not like being looked after, no?"

"He's not looking after me. He's watching my back."

"Why? I am in front of you."

"It's not you I'm worried about."

Now we were getting somewhere, though it didn't explain the heated gaze the green-eyed biker had sent Cam as he'd stepped through my front door. Or ease the painful tension gripping Cam's muscular frame.

It didn't suit him and I didn't like it. I held out my hand and beckoned him forward, then turned on my heel without waiting to see if he responded and returned to the kitchen, my bare feet making no sound on the polished tile floors.

He's behind me. I opened the fridge, ignoring my tingling skin. "Would you like a drink?"

"Just water, thanks. I gotta ride again tonight."

"What about your friend?"

"Don't worry about him." Cam's footsteps were heavy. He closed the distance between us and reached a muscular arm over my shoulder, shutting the fridge, his breath warm on the back of my neck. "Turn around."

I obeyed because I wanted to see his face.

And he knew it, but there was no victory in Cam's gaze. Only a sharpness with a faint haze of bewilderment. *He's worried I'm the enemy. That how he feels right now, with me, makes him weak.*

I drank in his subtle emotions, toying with how to respond. His vulnerability in this moment would've been easy to exploit, but pointless. All I wanted from Cam was the one thing I'd told him he couldn't have—another night in my bed. Messing with his head served nothing except to gift me with a clawing emotion I didn't entirely recognise. Guilt? Maybe. The real question was *why*? I didn't know this man. I did not care about him, not really. He had no right to be in my kitchen making me feel these things just by looking at me.

So tell him the truth.

Never. But perhaps I could scratch the surface. I raised my arm, noting that he tracked every movement I made like I was a venomous snake ready to strike, but at the same time, drowning in the heat of his gaze. He didn't want me to be his enemy. He wanted . . .

Hmm. I wasn't sure. He wanted to fuck me again, but what else? What did he need?

And why did I care?

The answers didn't come to me. My arm continued on its journey unimpeded and I cupped Cam's rough jaw in the palm of my hand. "Are you worried I am someone you cannot trust?"

"Should I be?"

"Always, in your life, no? But sometimes you will be wrong."

"I don't want to be wrong about you."

I rubbed my thumb over the shadows beneath his eyes. "Does that mean you believe I am your enemy and you like it? Or that you do trust me and it's your own judgement that concerns you?"

A low growl rumbled from Cam's broad chest, but an obnoxious buzzing from the kitchen counter cut him off. His gaze left me and flitted to where two phones lay next to his open account books. "Two phones?"

"Business and personal."

The buzzing stopped, the flurry of messages over, for

now. Messages that I would delete without reading, cursing the fact that they left a pain in my chest regardless. *I hate feeling. All of it. It hurts.*

I let my hand drop. Cam brought his bottomless stare back to me, reaching into his pocket for his own phone as he stepped back from me. He moved to the counter and regarded the phones. "Which is which?"

"Why?"

"I'm curious."

"About?"

He said nothing. Just waited for me to answer his question.

I fought the urge to rub the goosebumps from my bare skin and jerked my head at the phones. "The smaller one is personal. It's old, as you can see from the model."

"I don't know shit about iPhone models. You can't build a house with a handset."

"Is that what you'd like to do, Cam? Build houses with your bare hands?"

Yes. He didn't say it, but the fire in his gaze said it all.

Cam tapped his phone screen a few times. Moments later, my phone buzzed again, and his dark brows rose in a surprised wave. "You gave me your personal number?"

"I did."

"Why?"

Why, indeed? It was a mystery I'd yet to solve, and the only logical explanation was that I'd wanted the possibility of him contacting me again to be permanent. Business phones came and went. This one? This number? I'd had it since I'd first set foot on UK soil ten years ago. I'd come and gone since then, but despite the primal urge to destroy it, this phone had remained. "I move around," I said eventually. "And I wanted the offer I'd made to help you to stand the test of time."

"You'd have taken my call in six months' time?"

"Six years' time. I do not make offers like that and not mean them."

My phone was still buzzing. Cam killed the call and dropped his phone on the counter to join mine. The sudden silence was chilling, but I liked it. Whether he wanted to be or not, Cam was an emotive man. He didn't need to speak for me to hear him, and right now, his contemplative quiet told me he didn't quite understand what I'd said, but . . . he wanted to.

I liked that too.

It was hard to turn my back on him, but I did it anyway. I opened the fridge again and retrieved a glass bottle of water. For myself, I might've decanted it into an iced tumbler, but for Cam, I took it to him as it was and pressed it into his palm.

The cool glass against his skin startled him. For a man who'd had me in his crosshairs since I'd opened my door, he hadn't heard me coming.

Be nice.

I gestured for him to take a seat at the kitchen counter. He hesitated. I sat first and waited for him to join me.

Three, two, one. He pulled out a stool and folded his large frame onto it. He cast a distant stare over the pages of scribbled accounts spread out in front of us but took nothing in.

A soft sigh escaped him. He unscrewed the water bottle and tipped half of the contents down his tattooed throat. I watched his muscles work, aware that I should probably speak, but I said nothing for the longest time. I let him stare at me unchallenged and think whatever he wanted to think. Life was better that way. It made more sense.

"Something happened today." Cam's voice pitched low. Scratchy, as though he'd spoken too much already and he was tired of it. "I want to tell you about it because I think you'll understand, but at the same time, if you do, then everything I was worried about becomes real again."

I considered his words. Dissected them. "You assume that if I understand the world you come from that I must be an enemy."

A statement of fact, not a question.

Cam nodded, eyes tight at the corners. "It's not easy to make friends in this life."

"It isn't."

My agreement was my only answer, and he heard me, nodding slightly as a wry grin warmed his handsome face. "You said before that we could be that—friends, I mean. Was that bullshit?"

"Bullshit?" I shook my head. "You mistake me for someone who has the patience for games."

"That's what I thought. Then someone tried to kill me today and it made me wonder if it was connected to the only new thing in my life right now."

I unpicked that. Latched onto the part that didn't make me want to dig the monster from my soul and slaughter whatever poor fool had tried to hurt him. "You think I tried to kill you and I failed?"

Cam raised a brow, eyes warming with whatever it was about me he was trying to understand, the sinister clues that were starting to click into place and form a picture that he liked. "Are you telling me that if it was you who'd cut the brake lines on my bike, you'd have done it properly?"

"No. I am telling you that if I wanted to kill you, *Cam*, you would already be dead."

The truth was a funny thing. Sometimes it seemed my entire existence was dedicated to keeping it locked up. Others it slipped out of me like water running downhill and I didn't care to stop it.

I turned my attention back to the accounts for Kings Building Ltd. I was a third of the way through, still drowning in notes and receipts that made no sense. But I'd been right in my rudimentary assessment of the trading profit. There was plenty of money coming in, enough for whoever was involved to make a decent and legal living. Was that what Cam wanted? What he craved? Or was he here because he craved me?

"Can I ask you something?"

His low rumble slid over my skin like silk. I turned back to him, revelling in the fact that the warmth radiating from his large frame seeped into my exposed upper body. The only thing missing was his bare skin. "You can ask me anything you like."

"Will you answer?"

"Perhaps."

Cam's cautious smirk widened a touch. He drank the other half of his water in one long swallow, then leaned closer, his arms once again a cage of strength around my slighter frame. "Are you as dangerous as I think you are?"

I let a beat of silence stretch between us, loaded with everything I should've fought to contain but that, somehow, the acceptance in his gaze made me believe I didn't have to.

"What you think and what *is* are things you don't have to worry about as long as we are friends."

"Are we friends, Teddy?"

"Would you like to be?"

Cam didn't answer with words. He tilted his broad torso ever closer, gifting me a perfect view of the bloodied dagger tattoos on his neck. His scent overwhelmed me, and every instinct I possessed urged me to meet him halfway, but I stayed where I was, frozen as my pulse thundered in my ears. I knew what he wanted and I wanted it too, but I'd make him take it.

I was difficult like that. Unkind to myself, perhaps. But I hadn't lived a life that deserved much kindness. I hadn't led an existence that deserved the affection of a man like Cam. In his own way, he was as dark and dangerous as me, but there was a warmth in him I did not possess, and I didn't dare reach for it in case it burned me alive.

Cam chuckled and gripped my chin in his work-hardened palm. "I can't explain what you do to me."

"I would not ask you to."

"Would you tell me to stop?"

"Stop what?"

"This." Cam closed the final few inches between us and pressed his lips to mine. They were warm and dry and seemed to be connected to every nerve in my body, awakening me in ways I couldn't comprehend.

I kissed him back without stopping to make sense of what was happening to me, and the kiss deepened to a soft, sweet place that made my head spin and my blood heat.

He was still holding my face with one hand. The other slid up my flank, his long fingers traversing my bare skin until it was splayed on my chest, absorbing the impact of my thundering heartbeat. It would've been so easy to slip my tongue into his mouth, easing it past his smoky lips to tangle with his. I was already half naked. His clothes wouldn't last long if I wanted them gone, and my bedroom was four strides away.

But despite the blood-pumping wave of desire that swept over me, I did nothing but grip his neck so I felt his pulse battering my fingertips. I didn't squeeze, I just held him there, reeling from the sorcery of his beautiful kiss, until he pulled back, a shiver passing through him and into me. "I have to go."

I nodded.

Cam laid his forehead against mine and gazed at me. "I don't want to."

"I would not stop you if you wanted to stay."

"I know."

Did he? How? Those words had fallen from me unchecked. How did he know them to be true before I did?

I let my hand fall from his throat.

He stood and hovered, uncertainty creasing his chiselled face. "I came here for something else."

"For sex?"

"No."

"For business?"

"No."

I turned my back on his accounts and beckoned him closer. The T-shirt beneath his jacket had ridden up. I tugged it down and smoothed the fabric. "Perhaps it does not matter what you came here for. You will leave with more, no?"

Cam hummed. I thought he might kiss me again, and he

did, but on my cheek, a light, heady brush of his lips over the bone.

Then he stepped away and I didn't get up to see him out.

He was at the kitchen door when I called his name.

"You asked me something," I said as he shot me a quizzical stare. "In your office this morning."

The moonlight streaming through the window made his eyes glimmer. "I did."

"If we are to be friends, I suppose I should answer you."

"It's not a condition, mate. We are what we are."

I knew that, and it made what I was about to do easier. My breath flowed through my lungs as if I wasn't a man shackled in knots and chains. "My name is Alexei. You can call me that anytime you like, except when we're fucking."

"*When?*"

A small smile played on my lips and his both. I turned back to his accounts, unable to look at him much longer and stay in my seat. "Yes, Cam. *When.* Now go home and get some sleep. I do not like it when my friends are too tired to play."

[8]

CAM

Alexei. The name rolled around my mind, a whisper, an echo that haunted me every minute my attention wasn't caught up with something else. Granted, I was busy, but I still couldn't get it—get *him*—off my mind.

Alexei. It could've been another lie, but it wasn't. I knew it like I knew the kiss we'd shared would be etched on my soul until he did something else to turn my existence upside down. I mean, shit. Who kissed like that? With their whole body while barely moving a muscle? I didn't get it. I'd felt him *everywhere* from that simple touch of our lips and I didn't fucking *get it*.

This bloke was a damn warlock. There was no other plausible explanation for the spell he'd cast on me. And that was without the fact that he seemed to have done a U-turn on the possibility of us fucking—

"Pres?"

"What?" I dragged my gaze from the horizon and nailed Saint with a glare. It was dawn. We'd pulled over to smoke and put ourselves back together after a long ride that had ended in a vicious fight with the Crows we'd found trying to shift a measly haul of product through our territory. We'd won—we usually did—and I hadn't had to get my hands that dirty, but it had been a hassle I didn't need right now. Skirmishes with the Crows were part and parcel with having two MCs in the same county, but I had bigger things to worry about, like the weight of the construction cartel we'd pissed off bearing down on us. Fighting over three kilos of coke could suck a bag.

So could the ice age it took Saint to get his words out, and I hated it when he called me *Pres*, *Boss*, or any other bullshit word to avoid saying my actual name. But I swallowed my irritation. I was a grumpy motherfucker, but the man who'd fought like a beast at my side tonight deserved what was left of my patience. Fuck, Saint deserved so much more.

I lit another cigarette while I waited. Saint's stare bore down on me, his frustration rendering him more menacing than usual, but I didn't flinch. This dude would die for me. He'd proved it over and over again.

"This was a distraction," he said eventually. "They wanted us to come out and fight. They expected us."

I was inclined to agree. The Dog Crows MC had always been a pitiful operation next to ours, but even they had bigger fish to fry than a couple of kilos of blow. And who the hell needed ten men to move it? "You're right. The question is, what were they distracting us from? Mateo's shipment doesn't land until the weekend and all our premises made it through the night without any aggro. What are we missing?"

Saint shrugged, eyeing me with his penetrating green eyes. "Have you checked in with your friend?"

"What friend?"

"Your new friend."

I flicked my spent smoke into the ratty undergrowth and shot Saint a flat look as he rolled his eyes and crouched to retrieve it. "What's he got to do with this?"

"Nothing." Saint tucked my litter into a bag in his pocket. "But if we're being watched, whoever's doing it might've clocked us at his place the other night. You want to keep him safe, right?"

Bless my big-hearted sergeant-at-arms. The rebel with the sweetest soul. It should've annoyed me that I now had his curiosity to deal with on top of Embry's, but I welcomed it. Saint was my shadow, more so now than ever. Hiding shit from him was more effort than it was worth. "If anyone tailed us to Bristol the other night, all they'd have seen is us paying a visit to a swanky block of flats. No one followed us inside."

A faint smirk played on Saint's lips, a smirk I knew all too well. I'd seen it in context, more than once, when we'd shared girls in my bed at the compound. Those heady nights were how I knew Saint Malone wasn't the monster people assumed him to be. He'd kill a nun in her sleep if I asked him to, but if he had someone naked beneath him, they got nothing but respect. And me? Damn. I remembered his gentle hands on my back as I'd staggered drunkenly away from the bed, leaving him to carry the pretty girl off to his cave or whatever. How he'd steadied me as if he knew whatever I was searching for in those wild nights was just out of reach. He was a perceptive motherfucker. Perceptive and *clever*. Whatever he had to say now was annoyingly important. "Out with it, Malone. I ain't got all day."

"Just saying, boss. You walked out of there with a cock-eating glow. It'd take a fucking fool not to know whoever you went to see was important to you right now."

How can someone I've met three times leave me so fucking transparent? It should've pissed me off, but I had no scope left for new stress. I shook my head. "He's my accountant. And I'm not worried about him. If you met him, you'd understand."

"Gonna introduce us, are you?"

"You want me to?"

"What do you think?"

"I think you've noticed him more than you notice anyone else I fuck."

Silence. Quiet breaths were Saint's only answer, and the ache in my chest I carried for him ramped up a notch. *He's lonely.* So was I, but without old ladies and families to go home to, when war came, this life was like that. Brutal and cold, only brothers for company.

I gave into the urge to touch Saint and gripped his shoulder, letting my thumb rub the tense muscles beneath his T-shirt. "If you're worried he's a threat, don't. He's a friend."

Saint seemed unconvinced, but I couldn't do anything about that. Alexei was inexplicable, so I didn't try. I smoked another cigarette while I considered the fact that the next time I fucked him, Saint would likely be right outside, guarding me, hearing every sound that seeped through, feeling every jolt if I threw Alexei against the door.

I blew out a shuddery breath, the imagery fucking with my head. As if I needed something else to angst about.

Get your head in the game.

Except, this shit didn't feel like a game, especially with Saint simmering beside me like an unexploded landmine.

I headed for my bike.

He beat me to it and checked it out, then mounted his without looking at me. I followed suit, then we were on our way, speeding through the misty early morning in a race to get home before the roads were clogged with commuter traffic.

I won, pulling into the compound a heartbeat before Saint. We rumbled past the yard and to the clubhouse, the men we'd taken with us last night trailing behind.

Nash was waiting, arms folded across his chest, frown tense as he assessed us for damage. "You know, one day you really are going to have to stop doing all the dirty work yourself."

I took my helmet off and hung it on my handlebars. "It wasn't that dirty. Saint is a fucking angel. Would you rather I'd gone out with Mateo?"

"I'd rather you didn't go out at all, boss. You're the president, not a soldier."

He was so wrong and so right. Saint could've handled the Crow beatdown by himself—literally—but I'd never been a leader who could sit at the table knowing my boys were out there grafting while I got fat on the profits they brought home. Fuck that. "It was nothing. Just a dust-up to keep me sharp."

"Nothing out of the ordinary?"

I shrugged and filled him in on what Saint and I had discussed on our way home.

Nash nodded. "Makes sense. We just have to figure out what went down overnight while they kept us busy. Maybe we should lift a couple more Crows from the street. Shake them down. One of them's gotta know something."

"They didn't two days ago. And anyway, that's a short-term option. We need to be smarter."

"Shame. Mateo is gunning for fresh blood. He's pissed he got nothing out of them the first time."

"Keep him fucking tamed. For now. I don't want to waste him on petty shit."

"But you'll waste yourself?

"Enough."

I shot Nash a dark look and walked away. As my VP, it was his job to question my decisions and challenge them if he thought I was wrong—I was an MC president, not the fucking Messiah—but I wouldn't let him cage me. No fucker was ever gonna do that to me.

Not even myself.

Breakfast and a nap called my name. We'd regroup at church later, but for now, I was done with anything that didn't involve filling my belly and getting my head down to dream about a silky Russian accent and a wicked tongue. I headed into the compound and to the stairs, too tired to ride home without nodding off on the coastal roads but nowhere near tired enough to stop thinking about Alexei.

It had been three days since I'd barged into his building and kissed him, and I couldn't deny I was waiting on his call. That I checked my phone like a teenager when no one was looking.

But he hadn't called. And neither had I. No texts either, and I was running out of rope. A painful craving had settled in my soul. I *wanted* him. And I didn't know how long I could wait.

"Morning."

Fuck's sake. I slowed my pace to meet my sister as she popped up beside me. "What do you want?"

"You're talking to me like that already today?"

"It's still last night for me, girl. I need to get my head down."

Orla reached up and ruffled my hair, the only soul on this planet who possessed the damn nerve. "Bless you. I guess you don't want to know about the Jaguar-driving visitor you had this morning then?"

I stopped walking. Like, stone dead in the hallway as if the puppet master pulling my strings had yanked me backwards. "Al—Teddy Jones was here?"

It was strange how quickly my brain had adapted to *Alexei.* Teddy Jones was a stranger, but Alexei—for whatever fucked-up reason—I felt like I knew him. We were *friends,* after all.

Orla treated me to an evil leer. "Yes, your *accountant* was here. I don't know why that flusters you so much."

"I'm not flustered, I'm knackered. Did he leave already?"

"He left before you got here," Orla said, eyeing me with obvious amusement. "And he didn't give me any indication that he needed to see you. Just left the books and an envelope I'm assuming is the bill for his time, seeing as he's an accountant. You're paying him actual money, right? Not in sexual favours—"

I slammed my hand over her mouth. "Stop talking."

Orla danced out of my grip, laughing, the grin splitting her face in half too beautiful and too like our mother for me to hate her. "Okay, okay. I'm just saying, he's hot, so if you are tapping that, I don't blame you. I left the books and the envelope in your room with a bacon sandwich. You can thank me later."

She melted away, leaving me to contemplate the hell that Alexei had been here and I'd missed him, and the absolute heaven that I didn't have to go searching for my goddamn breakfast.

I climbed the stairs with heavy legs, passing the open doors of other rooms most of my brothers already occupied, blowing off steam with whoever they'd found willing and wanting. I'd usually be doing the same, but for once, getting my dick wet before I passed the fuck out held little appeal. There was only one place I wanted to slide my cock right now and he'd already left the fucking building.

As promised, I found my room blessedly empty, the accounts piled on my bed and breakfast waiting on the dresser by the window. My stomach was so empty it was going to motherfucking eat itself, but the manila envelope on my pillow called to me more than the loaded bacon sandwich Orla had left.

I rounded the bed, already tugging my clothes off, and picked up the envelope. My name was on the back, written in artful calligraphy, and I swore down, I smelt him, *Alexei*, on the paper, that expensive, musky scent. It gave me goosebumps and I shivered, glad I was alone. Saint and Orla had already snaked me, I didn't need anyone else up in my shit about this.

Stripped down to my underwear, I sat on the edge of the bed and opened the envelope. It contained a single sheet of paper—a handwritten note.

Cam,

The accounts for Kings Building Ltd are now up to date. I

96

have made allowances for undocumented expenses as personal transactions and noted the amount you will need to repay to balance these discrepancies.

Your corporation tax payment is due in three weeks. I have highlighted the amount below. After expenses, including salaries and dividends paid out, the balance you are left with is written in red. Be aware that any withdrawal from this balance is taxable . . . and traceable.

Pay your corporation tax on time.

Do not be late.

And Cam . . . I will collect payment for my services at a time convenient to you.

Do not be late with this either.

The note was unsigned, but *Alexei* whispered in my brain regardless and my phone was in my hand before I could blink. I called him, flopping onto my back as it rang and rang and rang, disappointment settling into my bones as it became clear he wasn't going to answer.

No voicemail. The call clicked out. I dropped the phone on the bed and closed my eyes. Heaviness seeped into every part of me—I honestly couldn't remember when I'd last been to bed—but agitation plagued me too, the scratchy energy that often sent me prowling for a warm, willing body to share my bed.

Not today.

I sat up and retrieved my breakfast from the dresser, eating it in three bites. It hit my empty stomach like a stone and stayed there while I retreated to the shower to wash away a night of violence and stress.

The hot water pummelled my aching body. Ink covered much of my skin, but I knew if it hadn't, I'd be black and blue. We were good fighters—the best—but we'd been outnumbered, and no fucker was untouchable, not even me. I'd taken some hits and now the adrenaline had died down, it hurt. Maybe Nash was right and it was time to step back from the road, but fuck it, I liked the pain. It kept me alive.

"I would not advise falling asleep in the shower."

I jumped a fucking mile, my bowed head jerking upright, eyes flying open, hand flailing for a weapon, cos you *know* I kept one handy in every damn room.

Alexei held up my cosh, tossing it from hand to hand, a lazy half smile twisting his full lips. "Looking for this?"

"No," I lied, reclaiming my arm and shutting off the shower. "How the hell did you get in here?"

"Far too easily, as it happens. Did you know complacency kills more people than heart attacks?"

I stepped out of the shower, water dripping down my heated skin. "I'm not a statistician, so no, I didn't, and I don't really give a fuck."

"Clearly." Alexei lowered the cosh, dropping it on the tiled floor with an obnoxious clang and an insolent sneer.

It seemed out of character for him—the noise, not the sneer—and I tilted my head to study him better. He was as put together as he'd always been, though he was dressed this time and I missed his bare chest, his sinewy muscles, and the dark hair that dusted his creamy skin. *You're out of your damn mind.*

Maybe I was, but I was starting not to care. As long as my family were looked after, the mess in my own head didn't seem to matter.

Alexei handed me a towel as though it was the most mundane thing in the world for him to have appeared in my bathroom like an apparition. "You asked me if I was the person trying to kill you."

"No, I didn't."

"I did not need the words to understand the question."

I took the towel from his outstretched hand, still dripping water on the tiled floor. This shit was fucking surreal. I'd been craving a hit of this dude's company all night long, and now he was right here in front of me, I couldn't quite believe it. "If I'd asked you in those exact words, what would you have said?"

Alexei's faint smile turned wolfish. "In my kitchen, the simple answer I should have given was no. Here, in your bathroom, I will say this one more time: if it was me who wanted to kill you, I'd have done it today—right now—and left no trace. Perhaps you should think about that next time you are discussing security with your brothers."

He was toying with me. Why, I had no idea, and despite knowing I had a viper in my bathroom, all I could think about was kissing him again. Fucking him had blown my mind, but the sensation of my lips pressed against his was permanently etched on my brain. I wanted it again and I didn't know how I was going to live the rest of my life if I didn't get it.

Hell, I didn't know how I was going to survive the rest of the day if he walked out of here without giving me a chance to claim his fucking mouth.

I dropped the towel without bothering to rub it over my wet body even once.

Alexei was slimmer than me, his slighter frame didn't fill the doorway. I slid past him and checked my bedroom door.

It was already locked. *If he didn't come to kill me . . .*

I turned back to where Alexei stood. He had shifted too, tracking me as I padded naked and wet around my room.

Fuck, I was already hard. But there was something else pulsing through me too, something more than the pent-up lust that made me feel slightly unhinged. My heart thumped like I'd banged a gram of charlie up my nose, my veins vibrating, a current thrumming between us.

Growling, I balled my hands into fists. The fuck was happening to me? This was some fated-mates bullshit I didn't have time for. I couldn't fucking *breathe*—

Alexei ghosted across the room. He backed me against the locked door, his arm at my throat, but it wasn't threatening, and because I was a sick bastard, the pressure to my windpipe was soothing, pushing the angst in my chest back where it belonged in the deep, dark pit of my gut. "You are okay, Cam."

I slow-blinked, drowning in his steely gaze and ridiculously long lashes. Honestly, they went on for days and I couldn't believe I'd only just noticed.

"*Cam.*"

"Hmm?"

Alexei ran a fingertip down my bare chest.

I shivered, and every welt and bruise on my body throbbed. "No one says my name as much as you do."

"It is a nice name. I like how it sounds when I say it."

So do I.

Alexei's trailing fingertip became his whole palm, rubbing over my chest in a soft, hypnotic circle. His gaze was piercing, flaying me open, and I couldn't stand it.

But I couldn't break it either. I *wanted* this, goddamn it. I'd fucking yearned for it in the long days that had passed since I'd last seen him. The way he looked at me was everything, and I almost didn't notice his hand descending down my body.

Then his long fingers wrapped around my hard dick and my hips bucked forward, a violent jolt that snapped me back to reality. "*Fuck.*"

"Shh." Alexei's other hand took its place, splayed over my stampeding heart. "Let it go."

How did he fucking know? Did I have every demon in my messed-up soul tattooed on my head?

Whatever it was, I was powerless to his whispered instruction. My head fell back against the door with a dull thud and I gave myself over to his magic hand.

Alexei stroked my cock, squeezing and twisting a slow rhythm that matched the final act of how I'd fucked him in his sterile penthouse. Revenge, maybe?

It was sweet enough.

I closed my eyes, lost to the push and pull of pleasure sluicing through me. I'd believed him when he'd proclaimed not to be my would-be assassin, and I believed him still, but if he killed me now, I'd die happy.

The constriction in my chest began to ease. A headache I hadn't known I had melted away. His arm returned to my throat, forcing air from my lungs, and I loved it, tipping my head back, craving more.

Alexei hissed, low and dangerous, but somehow kind too. Or maybe that was my fucked-up mind. Whatever. His attention was the cure I needed right now.

Perhaps it was everything I'd needed all along.

[9]
ALEXEI

I couldn't say what had drawn me back to the Rebel Kings' compound. Only that I had no regrets. If someone was trying to kill Cam O'Brian, it was inexplicably of great importance to me that he knew how vulnerable he was in the place he felt safest.

That he felt safe with *me* was an anomaly I hadn't prepared for.

I pleasured him with my hand, ignoring the desire burning me up inside, lost in him and every low-pitched sound he made. Cam was a grumbling beast of a man, but like this, at the mercy of my touch, he was something else. Something softer and more fragile than perhaps he knew.

His big body was tense and shaking, his inked skin covered in darkening bruises he believed I could not see. But I saw them, each and every one, and my decision to slip back onto the compound he called home was vindicated with each mark I catalogued.

He needs me. For business, pleasure, and apparently, the practicalities of staying alive.

Cam's deep groan brought me back to the present. I searched his face and found his eyes open, his ebony gaze a dark pool of wonder and heat, though he was not entirely lost to it. Curiosity was there too. Like me, he did not know what was happening between us or *why*, and he didn't like it.

Maybe it scared him.

It scared me, an emotion I ignored as Cam's pleasure peaked. He gave a full-body shudder, setting his jaw. His cock surged in my hand, and with another animalistic groan, he came.

Silence blanketed us, broken only by his laboured breath. I worked his cock until he began to soften, then brought my hand to his tight abdomen, smearing come over his clean skin.

He gave me a wicked smirk. "Trying to get me dirty again?"

"That would only serve me if I had time to shower with you."

"You don't?"

"No."

Cam's gaze flickered. Disappointment? I couldn't tell. But I did need to leave, for reasons other than a commitment to be somewhere else.

I stepped closer to him, barely keeping my shirt clean and dry, and brought my lips to his neck, kissing his pulse point, drawing another shiver from him. "Get some rest. I will hear you when you need me again."

"That makes you sound like a vampire."

My smile was deadly. "Maybe I am."

Leaving Cam was hard, but necessary for us both. He needed to sleep, and he would not do so as long as we were together in that room. And as for me, I had pressing matters to attend to, mainly the discovery of whoever was trying to kill him. I had a feeling my life would be much easier without worrying that he would be dead before I next saw him again.

I slipped out of the compound and back to my car. No sooner had I shut the door, my phone buzzed.

Cam: *tell me how you got in here*

Alexei: *No*

Cam: *the security cameras show you leaving half an hour before I got back but nothing else*

Alexei: *Get better cameras then*

It wouldn't help him with me, but I was willing to bet there weren't many souls in his corner of Devon who could move so undetected. At least, I hoped there weren't, or he was in more danger than he already knew.

I cast my phone aside and drove away from my hidden spot at the back of the Rebel Kings' compound. I had work to do at home, but there was somewhere else I wanted to check out first.

Devon was a large county—a two-hour trip from Whitness in the north to Paignton in the south. I parked my car close to the compound of the Dog Crows MC and got out, slipping seamlessly into the shadows of the rocks that surrounded their coastal club house, of course fronted by a motorcycle service and repair garage. *How quaint.*

My lip curled with distaste. I watched patched members roar through the gates, obnoxious cuts plastered to their backs, and mentally annihilated every single one of them before they reached the strip where they parked their bikes.

And that was without knowing for sure if they were the source of the failed attempt on Cam's life.

The failed part of the equation didn't work in their favour. I ran through the criminal organisations I knew to have business in South West England, and none were incompetent enough to leave cut brake lines so obvious that they would be discovered before they had served their purpose. That clue alone pointed to the Dog Crows, and I pondered the efficiency of lighting the whole place up with their entire board of officers inside. An electrical fault. Disabled fire alarms. It wouldn't be hard.

Then I spotted a woman in leather jeans entering the clubhouse with a child on her hip, and my taste for blood waned. I was a professional, not a monster.

I backed off and returned to my car, my mind spinning with possibility. There were many avenues for discovering the source of Cam's troubles, but only two were without complication: watch and wait, or ask him. Watching and waiting was a method that had kept me alive long enough to reach this point, but the second option held more appeal than I entirely understood. A test, maybe. Cam was sure enough of me to resist calling his brothers to evict the intruder in his bathroom, to stay naked and vulnerable before someone he now knew could kill him. But did he trust me enough to confide in me?

Doubt prickled my skin, and I didn't enjoy it any more than I did the compulsion to eliminate the threat to Cam's life.

Back off. You liked him fucking you because he was good at it. Saving his life is unnecessary. And complicated. You're a ghost, remember? You paid the price.

My phone buzzed. The skip in my pulse had me reaching for it on autopilot, craving a hit of Cam. But it wasn't Cam. It was something else and my eyes stung, burning with a fury I couldn't contain.

I threw the phone into the footwell of the passenger seat and started the engine, backing out of the concealed lay-by I'd parked in without checking the road in either direction. A lorry whizzed past my window. No longer capable of flinching, I didn't blink. Just pointed my car back the way I'd come and drove away.

[10]

CAM

I was *livid*. My brothers knew it, and so did I, but I was struggling to find the words to explain that our would-be accountant had broken into the compound and gifted me the handjob of my dreams while they'd been doing whatever the fuck they'd been doing at the time. Explaining myself stuck in my throat, and I found myself empathising with Saint more than I ever had.

Cracker eyed my balled fists, lips twisted in the closest to a sneer that he had the bollocks for. He was an old-timer and a friend of my dad's, but he'd voted against me taking the presidency, advocating instead for a brother that no longer rode with us. *Drummer*. A brother that now called himself a Crow. His disloyalty had vindicated my appointment, but I knew Cracker still thought me a wild card. A volatile upstart that was destroying the club from the inside out.

Some days, at least.

Others I knew he looked in his bank account and silenced the narrow-minded gobshite in his brain. I wondered what kind of day he was having today, then

107

decided he could die in a fire regardless. I pitied the fool who came at me right now. I'd kill them with my bare fucking hands.

"You are okay, Cam."

I blinked. Was I?

"Cam." I turned left. Nash stared back at me, the beginnings of a frown creasing his handsome face. "If you don't tell us what the breach was, we can't fix it."

"If you don't know, then the problem is fucking obvious."

Nash's expression flattened to the patented blankness that usually drew a laugh from around the table.

No one laughed now. They knew me well enough to shut the fuck up unless they had something useful to say, and none of them did. How could they when they had no clue what I was yelling at them for?

Come clean.

I started with the basics. "The accounts for the yard came back this morning."

More frowns greeted me, confused this time by the apparent change of subject—I was hardly known for letting shit go.

"Our accountant brought them by in person. The good news is the business is solvent enough to carry us through the next year if everything else turns to shit. There'll be no golden goose eggs, but we'll all eat. The bad news is this dude left the premises, then decided to return and walk straight into my fucking bedroom without being detected. Does someone want to explain to me how the *fuck* that happens to a clubhouse that's supposed to be protected twenty-four seven?"

The ripple spread around the table. Nash stood, already

going for the tablet that allowed him to view every security camera on the compound.

I yanked him back into his seat. "Don't bother. I already checked and there's no sign of him re-entering or leaving."

Mateo banged his fist on the table. "You let him leave?"

I snorted. "What would you have me do? Take him hostage and pull his teeth out?"

It was a stupid question to put to my friendly enforcer. I swung my gaze away from him and got caught in Embry's headlights instead. His gaze was puzzled but warm. He already understood that this was something we hadn't faced before.

"Talk to us," he said. "Make us understand."

I fought the rebellion in my heart, the one that wanted to keep Alexei all for myself. To guard him, protect him—as if he needed it—from the black hole my world became for anyone who strayed too close to the edge. "He's a hook-up from a few weeks back. Russian dude who sounds English if you're not paying attention. I figured we may as well put his financial expertise to good use and have him look at the books for the yard. At the time, I thought he was straight enough that we'd come out of it knowing if we could make a living from the yard if everything else went to shit, but I'm coming to realise that maybe I was wrong."

"He's dangerous?" A flicker of something I didn't catch passed through Embry's gaze. Disappointment? Sadness? He was an odd dude sometimes. Aside from the obvious, what did he care if Alexei turned out to be someone we could use rather than a shiny new toy for me to fuck?

Shiny new toy? Nausea rolled in my belly. Christ, even my subconscious thought I was a cunt today. "He's

109

dangerous," I confirmed to the whole table. "But not to me, that I'm aware of, at least. Hell, anyone who can walk up on me in the fucking shower is something to worry about, but he doesn't want to hurt me."

"What does he want then?"

I glanced at Rubi. "For now, just me, and I ain't complaining."

I let the influx of information sink in and rocked back in my seat. Some MCs had huge ornate chairs for their president, but my dad had never believed in wasting resources on his own ego, and I was the same. Our table was as old as the club, carved and beautiful, but my brothers and me occupied battered office chairs, dented plastic and metal, upholstered with torn fabric. With a hundred members and their families to take care of, we had better things to spend our money on.

The conversation around me went on. I kept tabs on the discussion, amusement filling me as my brothers tried to get a handle on Alexei with the vague details I'd given them, but it wasn't long before my thoughts drifted to the man himself. After he'd left me naked in my room and I'd got over the fact that he'd been there at all, I'd followed his instructions and knocked out for six solid hours. Apparently, a handjob from him was better than a Zopiclone and I couldn't wait for my next dose.

I picked up my phone, ignoring Cracker's ugly face—my secretary didn't like electronics at the table, his revenge for me banning the booze—and pulled up my message thread with Alexei. He was still saved as Teddy in my phone, a fact that amused me even more than Rubi's proposed notion that he was a mafia goon from the Sambini family, sent here as a goddamn honey trap. "Trust me, mate. If you met the bloke, you'd know how ridiculous that is."

"That's the point, though, isn't it?" Rubi countered. "That you wouldn't have a clue."

I looked up from my phone, death oozing from my glare. "You think I'm that stupid? That a good fuck would be enough for me to compromise this club?"

"That's not what I said."

"What are you saying, then? Clarify it for me."

Rubi lit a cigarette. It was all wrong for him, but I didn't allow weed in church either, so it sucked to be him. "I'm thinking out loud, boss. You're the one who brought him to our attention, and I reckon that's because you couldn't get your brain around it on your own. Let us try."

It was probably the most reasonable thing he'd ever said, but I wasn't feeling reasonable. I was restless as ever. *More.* And I was unsettled too. Every instinct I had told me Alexei meant me no harm, but what if I was wrong? What if I was so blinded by the fire he'd lit in me that I was putting my brothers and my club in more danger than we were already in?

A pack of smokes hit my drumming fingers.

Saint.

I met his gaze and he shook his head, the action minute but unmissable to anyone who cared to look.

In Saint-speak? Yeah. He had my back, and he didn't believe Alexei a threat to me either. If he did, he wouldn't be here. With Mateo at his back, he'd already be halfway back to the penthouse I'd made him stand outside while I'd locked lips with my enigmatic cat burglar.

I nodded and sparked a cigarette, waiting for the chatter

around me to die down. When it did, I addressed the whole table. "That's all I have on that right now. If anything else becomes important enough, I'll bring it back to the table, but until then, we have bigger shit to worry about. Namely, securing the compound and figuring out our next move against the Sambinis."

"We need to bring the green shipment in too," Mateo said. "I have guys on it with me, but given that everything we touch right now turns to shit, I need officers at my back while I set things up."

Saint and Rubi gave him the nod.

I took a breath, but Nash shook his head. *No. Stay off the road.*

Motherfuckers.

I held my tongue and let the business of the night play out. Then I pounded my gavel and sent my brothers away, Embry, as ever, lingering to bend my conscience in the right direction.

"I'm glad you told us about the accountant. Trust is important, Cam."

It irritated me that he tacked my name on the end of the sentence. I glowered at him. "Works both ways. You gonna tell me about every fucker you bang?"

"If it was relevant to club business, yes."

"Go on then."

"Explain the relevance first." Embry's smile warmed. He was bantering with me, and I had nothing, too wrapped up in my own shit.

I flipped him the bird. "Father, respectfully, fuck you."

"Maybe it would be easier if you did—fuck someone in the club, I mean, not literally me."

"Shame. I've been hanging out for your proposition all this time."

"Can we be serious for a moment?"

I sighed and gave my chaplain my full attention. "Is this the part where you tell me to use condoms, guard my drinks, and sleep with a kitchen knife under my pillow?"

"No, it's the part where I remind you how many balls we have in the air and how many threats we're facing on multiple fronts. If you trust our new accountant, that's enough for me, but be careful, okay? We need you. We love you."

He rose as he spoke the last few words, leaning in for an embrace I gladly accepted. For as long as we'd known him, Embry had been the family many of us so desperately needed. I held him a moment, breathing him in, then I let him go, hating that his job for the night was something he despised: frequenting the strip clubs we owned and/or protected in search of unfamiliar faces or loose tongues. He was too good at it. Without club colours, no one noticed him sipping rum in the corner, listening, watching. He was as effective as Mateo and his knife.

Embry left. For long, blissful minutes I was alone.

Then Cracker came back and pissed on my bonfire. "We need a treasurer."

"I'm aware," I drawled, reaching for the smokes Saint had kindly donated to the cause. My consumption right now was horrendous, but it kept me sane when bandits like this dickhead came at me with the fucking obvious. "Got any contenders in mind?"

"Not my job."

"It's everyone's job. That's how we ended up with Magda fucking everything up—no one else had any better ideas."

"You think letting a Russian whore look at our financial records is a solution?"

The hair at the back of my neck stood up, prickling my skin. "Whore?"

"I saw him this morning chatting up Orla. Maybe he has a thing for incest."

I sat up in my seat, staying low but ready to spring. "It would only be incest if I fucked my sister. Is that what's on your mind right now, old man?"

To his credit, Cracker didn't blink, but the old dude was pushing sixty and his beer belly was his most impressive feature. His days of holding his own in a fight without a weapon doing the work for him were well and truly over. "I'm saying you were a damn fool to show someone without ties to the club our private accounts."

"We're a limited company. You can access our records online."

"Why him, though?"

"Why not him? He found the money we needed and plugged the holes Magda left behind. Far as I can see, you got nothing to complain about."

"I still think it's fucking stupid and I ain't the only one. We don't trust outsiders."

"We were all outsiders once. You want to tell Saint and Mateo they're not welcome because they weren't born into whatever backwards universe you're stuck in?"

Cracker grimaced. It was subtle, but I saw it like the cowardly beacon it was and deepened my scowl as I leaned closer to him.

He backed off, running a hand through his mousy beard. "Fuck's sake, you'll have bitches on hogs next."

"I'll give your daughter my Bobber the next time I see her if you don't get out of my face with this bullshit right now." Hell, I'd give any woman attached to this club a bike if they wanted to ride one, and this fucker knew it. "Be somewhere else, old man, before I lose my fucking shit."

Cracker disappeared. I sank back in my seat with a heavy sigh and scrubbed my hands over my face. Embry had been right when he'd warned we were facing hostility on multiple fronts, but I doubted he'd taken Cracker and his band of discontented old timers into consideration. Mutiny was sacrilege in our world. If we didn't have loyalty, we had nothing.

Still, it wasn't like I didn't understand their concern. To them, and even to me, Alexei had come out of nowhere. I'd approached him, if an eye-fuck across a crowded bar was that tangible, but what if he'd been there all along? Watching and waiting. The spark I shared with Saint aside, it wasn't as if I didn't have a type when it came to the men I brought into my bed. What if he'd tracked me, noting my habits, and had followed me to Bristol? What if—

My phone rang.

Frowning, I answered it without looking at the screen. "Yeah?"

A warm chuckle greeted me. "You are a rude man, Cam."

The elastic band around my chest loosened. "Are your ears burning?"

"Is that a literal question or a colloquial saying that makes no sense?"

"The second one." I absorbed the smooth Russian voice like a drowning man desperate for air. "I had to tell my brothers it was you who breached our security. They think you're a honey trap."

"Ah, now this phrase I know."

"Are they right?"

"Your brothers are fools."

"Not all of them."

"Okay, maybe not the feral one who follows you around. You should keep him."

"Was planning on it. Any other advice for me?"

Alexei was silent a moment. Somehow I knew he was smiling that strange smile of his, the one that warmed me and yet sent chills down my spine. When he spoke again, his voice was lower, barely a fucking whisper. "I have some advice for you. The first thing is, keep your *bodyguard* with you as much as you can. He is . . . observant, and I would have found it more difficult to breach your compound if he'd been there. The second is to change the cameras that monitor your rear boundary. They have no motion detectors. I opened the cable and disconnected it before I unravelled your fence and entered your compound. If you watch your footage more closely, you will see the blip where the connection is lost and restarts. The rest was easy. There are no locks in your compound that cannot be picked, and you, *Cam*, need to stay alert when you are alone."

I absorbed it all with a resigned huff. "I like being alone." It wasn't much of a counter argument, but it was all I had. It wasn't like I didn't know Saint was my sharpest weapon. And talking to Alexei scrambled my brain. "What else you got for me?"

"It's more what you have for me."

"Oh yeah?"

"I still require payment for my financial services. And I will collect."

"What's your price?"

Another beat of silence passed, then Alexei treated me to another dark chuckle. "That, dear *friend*, I will leave up to you. Until then, be safe."

He hung up, of course. And yeah, I had a goddamn boner.

I also had an idea. Whether it cleared my debt or not, I wouldn't know until it was over, but I fired off a text to Alexei anyway.

Cam: *Angel Cottage, Beach Road. Thursday, 8pm.*

Alexei

Cam surprised me. And I liked surprises when it came to this man, so I didn't research the property he summoned me to. I approached it from the back and in the dark from the coastal path, keeping to the shadows, and found myself caught in the glow seeping from the kitchen window.

Beyond the old glass, Cam was at the stove, a beer in one hand, a wooden spoon in the other. He was dressed in dark unbuttoned jeans, damp hair slicked back.

He was the Cam I saw in my dreams.

Spellbound, I crept forward before I caught myself. *This man . . . he will be the death of me.*

I didn't mind. I watched him some more, enjoying his domestication, before circling his property, taking note of the green-eyed brother lounging on his bike in a shadowed corner. He didn't see me, but I had no doubt he'd see anyone else who approached. I liked him—he was good. For reasons I didn't entirely know yet, I trusted him to keep Cam safe in his home.

Cam was still in the kitchen. I knocked at the back door. He didn't look round or even blink. "It's open."

I slipped inside, leaving the crashing waves of the ocean behind, letting the scent of whatever he was cooking seep into me. "You were expecting me at the back door?"

Cam clamped a lid on a pan and turned to face me, the soft light from a nearby lamp casting perfect shadows on his chiselled face. "Actually, I half expected you to jump down from the attic, but it is what it is."

"What does that mean?"

"What?"

"It is what it is. Everything is that."

"Fucking A, mate. I don't know. You're here. That's what matters."

"Is it?"

Cam approached me, fearless and bold. God, how I loved that about him. He put his work-hardened hands on my shoulders and brought his face close enough to mine that I could've licked his unshaven jaw. "Right now? Yes. Are you hungry?"

"That depends."

"On?" More humour warmed his molten gaze.

I gave him an insolent stare of my own. "What you expect me to eat."

"Erm . . . pasta, chicken, vegetables."

"Vegetables?"

"You thought I was a slaughter the pig in the garden kind of bloke?"

"Maybe." I stretched up to peer over Cam's shoulder to his sleek range cooker. It was jet black—like his motorbike—with five burners and built into a stone alcove, and though clean, was clearly well used. "You really live here, don't you?"

Bemusement danced in Cam's dark gaze. "When I have time. After we left Ireland, I grew up here. This was my nan's house once upon a time."

I forgot sometimes that people—even MC presidents—had normal families. Ties that bound them together in mundane ways that just . . . were. "It's nice that your grandmother left it to you."

"It's not just mine. My brother owns half of it, and I'd let him have it if he wanted it, but he doesn't want to be—fuck, sorry. You don't want to hear that shit."

"How do you know what I want?"

"I'm making an educated guess, seeing as I don't give a fuck about anyone else's family drama."

"I am not you." I ducked out of Cam's hold and stepped around him, too curious about how he lived away from the club to mourn the loss of his touch just yet. "Tell me about your brother—he's your blood brother, yes? He does not ride?"

"Oh, he does. Just not with me or the club."

"What is his name?"

"River."

By chance, I stopped in front of a framed picture on a wooden shelf built from thick, dark oak. The photograph was black and white by design, not age, but I could still see the man it featured had the same obsidian eyes as Cam, the same inky hair. He had tattoos and a scruffy jaw too, but he was slimmer than Cam and his stance as he straddled a stripped-

119

back Street Bob was passive. Gentle, almost, though the resemblance to Cam was too strong for me to believe this man didn't possess the same grit and aggression. "You are not close." I made an educated guess of my own.

Cam sighed. "Not at the moment."

I spared him a glance. "But you want to be?"

"I want him to be happy. Safe. And to make his own choices. If that means he's a million miles away from me, I have to live with that."

There was a story there, I could tell, but I hadn't come here to dig into Cam's pain. I'd come for two reasons: to learn more about whatever business was putting him in danger, and because I wanted to see him—an affliction, strange as it was, that *I* was learning to live with.

I took his vague hint and wandered around the ground floor of the cottage he called home. Outside of the modern kitchen, the rest of what I found was likely as it had been when it was built. Hardwood floors, dark beams, ancient windows. Clean white walls were punctuated by the occasional family photograph or piece of MC memorabilia, and a deep leather couch sat amongst the vintage dressers and side tables.

It was . . . adorable and light years away from the style of living I'd have imagined for my biker friend if I'd pictured him outside of the bedroom.

I drifted back to the kitchen. Cam was perched on the marble countertop, two plates of food at his side, a glass of amber liquid in his hand. "I have vodka in the freezer," he said. "But it ain't the posh stuff."

"Posh stuff?"

"I got it at the supermarket."

"*You* went to the supermarket?"

"Do you see a maid around here?"

"You have prospects."

I meant the MC interpretation of the word, but Cam chose the other meaning, and his gaze darkened as he shook his head. "Nope. Never did. This was always gonna be my life whether I wanted it or not."

"Either way, I am trying to picture you in Tesco and I cannot do it."

"Where can you picture me?"

In my bed.

In yours.

On your knees.

Towering over me.

It all worked. I crossed his kitchen and stepped between his spread legs, plucking his glass from his hand and setting it on the counter. His thighs were denim-clad rocks, and they clamped around me, pinning me in place, and I don't think he even meant to do it.

But if this was his autopilot, I'd take it.

I fingered the hem of the muscle tee clinging to his body. The white was a blank canvas to the inked artistry that lay beneath, and I wanted it gone.

First, though . . .

I tilted my head in the same moment he leaned down. Our lips met in a recreation of the perfect kiss he'd floored me with in *my* kitchen, and the air shifted between us. His beautiful mouth was a vortex of sensation. It sucked me in, and any ulterior motive I'd had for coming here left my head. Evaporated. Eviscerated. I had no thoughts beyond pulling him closer and kissing him harder.

Cam's low sound of pleasure rippled through me. He cupped my face in his warm hands and pulled back, just for a moment. "You're wearing different clothes."

"Different to what?"

"To the pressed shirts you've been wearing every other fucking time I've seen you."

"I wasn't wearing a shirt at all the last time you kissed me."

"I can't believe I left you that night."

"What would you have done if you'd stayed?"

"Everything." Cam released my face and gripped the black jacket I wore over a black T-shirt and black jeans. "Don't change the subject. Why are you dressed like a ninja?"

A smirk twisted my face. "A ninja? Really?"

"I don't know the Russian word for it."

"Do you know any Russian words?"

"No."

I gave him a few. "Mne nuzhno zashchitit' tebya. Ne znayu pochemu. No ya delayu." *I need to protect you. I don't know why. But I do.*

Cam shivered, a trait I'd noticed in him when we were alone like this. "I don't know what the fuck you just said, but I liked it."

"Good."

"Good?"

"Yes." I shrugged out of my jacket and hung it over a bar stool. "But enough with the words. I want you."

The playfulness in Cam's dark gaze dissolved. Heat replaced humour and he yanked me closer, his touch no longer gentle as he took my mouth in a bruising kiss.

I let him plunder me. Let his tongue shove past my lips and dominate mine, a willing victim to his roaming hands and brutal touch.

He tore the shirt from my body, threw it away, and I didn't stop him. Untidy things bothered me, but messy sex I could live with. And I needed to see his cock, so there was that.

Cam was still sitting on the counter. I broke away from him and stepped back. "Show me your bedroom."

He speared me with his liquid stare. "I was going to fuck you on the table."

"Later, perhaps. I want you to fuck me on your bed."

Cam was a good boy. Rough and ready, but he followed orders like a dream. He slid to his feet—I noticed for the first time that they were bare, clean, and as covered in ink as the rest of him—and held out his hand. *So sweet.* "Leave your shoes by the door."

I obeyed, tucking my combat boots beside his, one pair battered and worn, the other stiff and ready for battle. Cam waited at the foot of a carpeted staircase, the cream wool pristine, as if no one ever made it that far, not even him.

"Come," he said.

I took his hand. "You will."

He chuckled darkly and led me up the stairs. At the top was a small landing covered by the same thick carpet. A leather armchair was tucked in the corner below a bookshelf, a long-stemmed reading lamp curving over it. It was too dark to see the books that weighed the shelf down, but curiosity burned a path from my gut to my chest. *He fascinates me.*

"Bedroom is this way." Cam jerked his head to the left.

I tore my gaze from his library corner and followed him through the open door.

His bedroom had the same carpet as the landing, but thicker. My feet sank into the pile as I took in the rest of the decor—the heavy wood furniture and black sheets, the monochrome art on the walls.

The single candle on his dresser.

Thick and used and wedged into a wooden skull, there was something perversely beautiful about it. I pulled a lighter from my pocket and lit it, turning to face him as the flickering flame cast the room in a soft glow. "You surprise me again. I thought your home would be more—"

"Is this the part where you tell me you thought I was a basic bitch?"

"Perhaps. I would never call you a bitch, though."

"*Good.*" His brief scowl was electric and my jeans were uncomfortably tight.

I took them off, losing my underwear along the way.

Cam swallowed and unbuckled his belt. "Come here."

"No."

He came to me and I loved that it didn't bother him to concede. Defeat only registered with a wry grin that faded as he got closer to me and shed his own clothes.

It hadn't been long since I'd last seen his body, but it seemed like a lifetime had passed since we'd been naked together. His cock tangled with mine and he laid his big palms on my chest. "What do you want? Cos I know that's what we're gonna do."

"You did what you wanted the night we met."

"Because you asked me to."

"I did."

"Alexei." It was my turn to shiver as he breathed my name. "Tell me what you want?"

There were too many things to list, but alone with him in a room that felt like a sanctuary from the real world, anything was enough. *This* was enough. Just him and his warm skin against mine, his lips claiming my lips as he pulled me close.

Cam, you do such strange things to me.

He kissed me and let his hands roam my body, sweeping down my torso until he came to my hips. One hand drifted lower, gripping my cock, and a tremor rocked me as he squeezed it tight in his fist, testing my pain threshold.

You will not find it. Physical discomfort didn't bother me. It was a distraction from the ache I'd been gifted as a teenager —the ache that in recent weeks had only been soothed by him. I wasn't about to tell him that, though. *No.* I let him search for whatever he was looking for, then brought my lips to his ear. "Will you tie me up?"

Cam wrapped his fingers around my throat. "You want me to restrain you?"

"Yes."

"Why?"

"Because I like it."

His gaze smouldered. "I could do it with my bare hands."

"I want your hands elsewhere, Cam."

He took a shuddery breath. "There isn't much I wouldn't do when you say my name like that."

He'd said something like that before, and I hadn't understood what he meant until he'd uttered my name like a prayer. Until he'd gripped my throat like he was right now and all I'd wanted was for him to squeeze so tight that there was nothing else but me and him in that moment. *It ends with us.*

I blinked, blindsided by the finality of the devil dancing through its monologue, and whether he knew it or not, Cam saw me fall and he caught me.

He threw me to the bed and advanced on me, violence seeping from every powerful movement as he covered me with his heavy bulk. He didn't kiss me again, but I didn't expect him to. I'd asked him for something else. Something sharper.

Harder.

A low growl rumbling from his chest, he ripped open a drawer by the bed. I didn't see what he retrieved, but the cool satin binding my wrists moments later was no surprise. It made sense that he was kinky as hell. He had demons to silence too.

Cam restrained my arms above my head, my bound wrists secured to the solid wood of his bed. He sat back on his haunches and regarded me with hooded eyes, his lashes so inky and dark they disappeared into the shadows of the barely lit room. "Do you need a safe word?"

"Are you going to hurt me?"

Alertness snapped into his gaze. "No."

Shame. "Then I do not need one. Tell me . . . do you trust yourself?"

"With you?"

"And without."

Cam leaned down, nudging my legs apart to make room for himself between them. "Yes and no, in any order you choose. How does that make you feel?"

"I like it."

"Do you like this?" He hinged his body forward and took my nipple in his mouth, biting down.

The effect was instant, my hips bucking from the bed, seeking friction where I craved him most. "I do."

His only response was to bite harder, and the ecstasy that rolled through me was that of a promise. This man understood me without trying, and the binds around my wrists were the last thing I would have to ask him for tonight.

[11]

CAM

There was an animal in me that only Alexei could tame, but first, we had to set it free.

We fucked all night, the meal I'd prepared long forgotten as Alexei remained bound to my headboard, his resilience blowing my rowdy mind. I took him apart in every position his restraints allowed, and still, he wanted more.

Light was beginning to creep into the darkness we'd made our own by the time I felt something shift in him. I was drenched in sweat, muscles shaking with fatigue, throat hoarse from the primal sounds he'd ripped from me all night long.

On his knees, legs spread, shoulders tense as I took him from behind, Alexei was a lake, his leaner frame rippling with every thrust inside him, but an eerie calm still gripped him.

He needs more.

I'd seen this in him the first time we'd fucked. The detachment he couldn't seem to breach. Perhaps on that night he hadn't wanted to, but behind the composed facade, I saw the desperation. He wanted this. He wanted *me*. Why else would he have come here?

There were a dozen answers to that question, but my mind was poleaxed enough to only stretch to the ones I wanted to hear.

I punched my hips forward, driving deep into Alexei, then I stayed there and reached for the binds on his wrists.

He resisted. "No."

I wrapped an arm around his throat and kept going. "Yes."

The ties fell away. Alexei snarled and gripped the headboard, knuckles white in the dim light of the early dawn. "What are you trying to do to me?"

"Whatever you need."

"You do not know what I need."

"Let me guess then. It all ends the same."

It didn't, but I took Alexei's silence as the end of his protest and pried his hands from the headboard.

I rolled him over, easing him onto his back.

His glare was biblical. "You are trying to be nice to me. That is something you need, not me."

"You don't know what I need."

He snorted. If he'd been a different man, he might've rolled his eyes around the world and back. But he was *this* man. The one who held my stare with no fear or respect that I hadn't earned.

I dropped a palm either side of his head, leaning down to kiss him, half expecting him to evade me.

He didn't. He let me claim him, a quiet sound escaping him as he fought to stay passive.

Good luck with that. I already knew how his body

responded to my lips on his. I'd seen it, felt it, and committed it to memory.

His arms were still raised over his head. With one hand, I yanked them down. With the other, I held his legs apart and slid back inside him. The new position didn't take me as deep, but it didn't need to. With his face so close to mine, his fierce gaze tearing holes in me, I was as deeply submerged in him as I dared to be.

His body clamped down on my dick. I saw fucking stars but held his gaze as I started to fuck him again, hard and slow, carving the pleasure out of us both.

Alexei's glare remained, lip curled in a snarl that made me want to sink my goddamn teeth into him.

I bent to kiss him again, pausing before our lips touched. "Put your arms around me."

"No."

"*Yes.*"

Alexei arched his back, catching me off guard. "Make me."

I didn't need to make him do anything, but fuck, if I didn't crave the sensation of his arms squeezing me tight.

The stand-off stretched out. I fucked Alexei into the mattress, holding my own release at bay while I chased his down. He'd come already tonight, we both had, but this was different. This was the pinnacle we needed to walk away from this fucked-up encounter with our heads on straight.

Yeah, that's right, we *both* needed it. Alexei could hide the whole fucking world from me, but not that. I saw it in him as plainly as I saw it in myself.

I drove hard into him and pulled out slow. Alexei bit his

lip, eyes sliding closed, concealing his intoxicating stare from me.

Nope. I gripped his chin. "Look at me."

I waited for the inevitable response. *No.*

But his lids fluttered and he held my gaze. He snatched a breath. So did I. Then his arms came around me and he held me in a vice-like embrace that anchored me to the universe.

Fuck. I needed that hold. Without it, I'd fucking soar, and I wasn't sure I'd come down.

I kissed him, plundering his mouth so roughly I tasted blood. "Tell me what you need."

He shook his head, and his dick pulsed against my belly, trapped between my abs and his.

I growled. "You want me to beg? Cos I don't do that shit, even for you."

Even for you. The fuck did that mean?

I had no damn clue, and this late in the day—or early, depending on how I looked at it—I lacked the brain power to figure it out.

"Cam."

I blinked. Alexei had moved his arms up my body, gripping my face in his hands.

"*Cam.*"

"What?"

"Stay," he whispered.

Confusion rattled me. "I didn't go anywhere."

His gaze said different. He kissed me far gentler than he had before this moment and wove one hand into the crazy mess of my hair. A slow, near-silent breath eased from his lungs, a release that tickled my jaw. "I do not need to tell you anything. Because you already know."

I was lost. The conversation, combined with the heady place fucking him seemed to take me, was too much. I had no coherent thought left.

So I stopped thinking and let instinct take me, my body doing whatever the fuck it wanted to.

A frantic climax built between us. I bent Alexei's knees to his chest and ground into him, raw sounds tearing from my chest while beneath me, he arched, taking everything from me that I willingly gave.

Dark spots began to dance in my vision. Power bunched in my nerves, ready to fly.

Alexei still held my face, gaze wild, his control finally slipping away. I bore down on him, fucking him deeper, and a crazed yell escaped him.

It was all I needed to hear. His cock surged between us, pumping wet heat onto my skin, and the threads of autonomy I'd clung to came loose.

I came with a full-body convulsion, ecstasy seizing my muscles and straining them so tight I truly fucking feared they'd snap. Pleasure burst from me and into the condom that was the only barrier left. I shuddered, and a deep groan rattled me, shaking my damn bones. "Fuck, Lexi."

The garbled mess I made of his name was distant, as if I'd left the planet. The trembling in my body was as much mine as his, and I didn't notice him laughing until I found the will to pull back.

A light I'd never seen shone in his slate-grey eyes. I laughed too, bemused as hell but willing to roll with it. "What's so funny?"

"Lexi? That is cute."

I shook my head. "You told me not to call you Alexei

132

when we were fucking. And you have too many syllables for me to handle when I'm shooting my brains out of my dick."

"That's what you can't handle about me? My syllables?"

Don't pull on that thread. I withdrew from him and ditched the condom in the bin at the side of the bed. At some point, we'd have to move and clean up, but I wasn't there yet. I was *so tired*, but his presence in my bed—in my life—right now, did something to me I couldn't give up. I couldn't sleep with him. Fuck, I couldn't miss a moment.

You're insane. Even if you knew every single thing about him, you don't have time to get this close to someone. It ain't fair.

But I got the feeling Alexei didn't care about fair. Or anything most other people did.

I turned to face him, taking in the way his elegant body poured over my bed like the silk I'd tied him up with. His skin was flushed, his hair a mess, and I dug the thicker growth on his face. There was something else, though, a peace that I plastered myself to as I stared at him. Our time together was drawing to a close, but fuck if I was anywhere near ready to let him leave. "Are you hungry yet?"

"Hmm?" Alexei seemed to come back into himself and I liked the dazed look on him. It softened him, though his sharp edges haunted my dreams.

"Hungry," I repeated, chasing a bead of sweat over his pale skin with my fingertip, a move I'd stolen from him. "I made dinner . . . I think. It seems a long time ago now."

"The vegetables?"

"It wasn't just vegetables, mate. Do I look like a fucking rabbit?"

133

Alexei raised a brow. "That sounds like a colloquialism I do not care about."

"I'm going to take that as a yes to the hunger question and move on with my life."

I kissed his temple, surprising us both, and left the bed, padding down the stairs as naked as I'd been while we'd fucked. Behind me, I heard the shower turn on and grinned. My complicated friend wasn't as filthy as he made out.

The kitchen was exactly as we'd left it. The dinner I'd dumped on plates was still there, but thankfully I'd had the foresight to stash the leftovers in the fridge.

I scraped the plates and tucked them in the dishwasher, then I found three new ones and loaded them up.

It took a while to heat. I retrieved some jeans from the dryer in the utility room and yanked them on before opening my front door to check on Saint.

He was perched on his bike, smoking, and scanning the horizon.

"You can go," I said.

He didn't turn round. Just shook his head slightly.

I rolled my eyes and schlepped back to the kitchen. The first plate I'd shoved in the microwave was done. I took it out to Saint with the herbal tea my favourite hippie maniac preferred to the coffee I needed to stay upright most days.

His fierce expression softened a touch. "Having fun?"

"Of course. You?"

"Sealwatching." He pointed at the ocean that lay beyond the coastal village in the distance. "Better than listening to you fuck."

"Liar. You live for that shit."

"Do I?"

Something bled between us. An open wound. And there was heat too—a fire untended and smouldering. "You could've gone home. No one's gonna come at me here."

Saint stabbed his fork into the food on his plate. His scowl slotted firmly back into place, but he didn't rip my head off. It wasn't his way. "You should eat too." He appraised me with his complex stare. "If you're not gonna sleep."

"You're gonna make someone a lovely wife, you know that?"

A grunt was Saint's only response. I left him to stare at the sea and retreated inside.

The food was done. I carried it upstairs. Alexei was back on the bed, still naked, but clean of sweat and come, his hair damp and pushed back from his face.

My heart skipped a beat. *Fuck, he's beautiful.* And for the first time, that scared me. It had been a *long* time since I'd last spent more than one night with someone, and I couldn't remember the last time I'd gone so long between hook-ups. I'd saved it all for him. But why?

Because you wanted to.

It should've been enough, but my head spun all the same.

Alexei sat up and took the plates from me. "Take your jeans off."

The command was gentle, but I obeyed as if he'd roared it in my ear like a drill sergeant.

I shucked the jeans and kicked them aside. Alexei tilted his head toward the space on the bed he'd left vacant for me, and I followed his direction.

He passed me a plate. "You look like you need this more than I do."

"Need what?"

"Sustenance. Did I wear you out?"

"Did you want to?"

Alexei poked at the pasta I'd cooked in a horny, anticipatory daze while I'd waited for him to appear like an apparition at my back door. "Perhaps. And myself too. I like to take things to my limits."

"Is that what happened? Did I help you with that?"

"You helped me."

I gave into the ravenous hunger rumbling inside and shovelled food into my mouth, chewing before I answered. "Is my debt cleared?"

Alexei ate a small bite of food, a slow smile teasing his lips. "The fair answer would be yes, but I'm not sure I am sated enough to walk away from you just yet."

"Maybe I'm not enough for you."

"If you think that, you should call your bodyguard—"

"He has a name."

"Which is?"

"Saint."

"Saint." Alexei nodded, his smile deepening. "Yes, you should call him in to help if you think you cannot handle me."

It was too close to the bone, and something in my face must've said so.

Alexei treated me to a penetrating stare, then set his plate aside and stood, moving to the open window. He searched the outside world below and nodded when his gaze clearly fell on Saint. "What is it between you two?"

"What do you mean?"

"I mean the current I can see that runs from him to you and back again. Are you lovers?"

"No."

"Have you ever been?"

"No."

"But you wish you could be." He nodded to himself again, like it all made perfect fucking sense.

Irritated, I gripped my plate, fighting the sudden and ridiculous urge to throw it against the wall. "What makes you say that?"

Alexei sat down beside me again and gifted a knowing smile. "He's a beautiful man and he cares about you more than he cares about himself. Why would you not want that?"

"I want you."

"That does not negate anything I just said. You could have a thousand lovers, and what is between us would be the same."

"Is this you telling me that *you* have a thousand lovers?"

"No. I have just you right now."

Relief I didn't deserve passed through me. I had no right to demand monogamy from him. But, fuck, the thought of a man who wasn't me in his bed made me want to kill someone.

"Cam." Alexei closed his hand around my forearm, squeezing tight a moment before he let go. "All I'm saying is that it's okay to feel what you feel. Don't be afraid of it, because feeling nothing is so much worse."

"Yeah." I didn't know what else to say, so I cleared my plate in silence while Alexei picked slowly at his. Sensing he needed a moment, I slipped away to the shower. When I came back, he'd eaten half what I had and set it aside.

"You don't eat much?"

He shook his head. "Not for pleasure, no. It is like sleep— neither appeals to me much."

"You don't know what you're missing, mate."

"I do."

"That makes no sense."

Alexei shrugged. "What does? Is Saint going to stay outside the whole time I am here?"

"What do you think?"

"I think it would pain him to leave you unprotected. Whatever else he is to you, he is a loyal soldier, no?"

Soldier. The pretence that my life beyond the respectable business Alexei had cleaned the accounts for was all but gone. I nodded. "It's his job to have my back and he's committed to it."

"How did someone find a way to sever your brake lines then?"

"He can't be everywhere."

Alexei hummed, his gaze more speculative than I was comfortable with. Or maybe I was comfortable with it and that was the problem. I wasn't used to pillow talk, especially about club business.

"That's the point . . . that you wouldn't have a clue."

"What are you thinking?" It came out sharper than I'd intended.

Alexei didn't flinch. I didn't suppose he would if I held a blade to his throat. "I am wondering why someone wants to kill you. What is your business? Plasterboard and concrete? Some muling on the side? Who have you offended so much?"

"I've never said anything to you about muling."

"It would be foolish to assume you were not moving something illegal this close to the coast, and you do not strike me as a man who would traffic flesh and bone."

My hackles rose.

Alexei smirked. "I am right."

He seemed to be speaking to himself as much as me. I lay down beside him, enjoying the fact that he was in my bed despite his apparent need to pick holes in me. "We don't move people. We don't allow it on our turf, and we've lost good men defending our principles. Is that good enough for you?"

Alexei rolled to face me, bringing us together in a pose that was for lovers, not pseudo friends with mind-blowing benefits. "I am not important. Instead, I am wondering if this causes you problems. Your territory is remote, with coastal access and main roads inland. I'd take it from you if I was an organisation that wanted to move sex workers from Europe to America."

"Are you?"

"Am I what?"

"An organisation. You're asking me a lot of questions for a random hook-up who likes counting money."

"I never said I liked counting money. Just that I was good at it. You understand this, I think. To excel at something that isn't part of you?"

I bought myself some time with a slow breath. He hadn't answered *my* question, and he wasn't going to, but the answers to all of his were bubbling up my throat, spilling out of me before I could stop them.

"There's another MC in our county—The Dog Crows. They'll do anything for a few quid, no fucking morals. If they had the resources to wipe us out and take our turf, they would, and then you'd see the trucks with the girls in the back, hundreds of them."

"They have the resources to move hundreds of trucks but not to take you out?"

"It wouldn't be their trucks. It'd be the cartels that run the roads—the motorways and the construction rackets." I pursed my lips, willing myself to shut the fuck up. The hell was happening to me? I didn't talk. Ever. Even to the people who mattered.

Alexei matters.

But so did the Crows and they wanted my head on a platter. They just didn't have the balls to try.

So who does?

I still didn't know, so I left Alexei's opening question unanswered and lay back, closing my eyes, just for a moment. I wondered if he would leave, but he didn't. He pressed up against me, his long leg thrown over mine, his head on my chest.

Drifting, I dropped an arm around his shoulders, and we stayed like that for a long time.

[12]

ALEXEI

The green-eyed brother put a tracker on my car. I was ninety-nine per cent certain Cam hadn't asked him to, but I left it there anyway. If Saint Malone—that's right, I knew his name now—cared enough about Cam to monitor my movements, I'd do him the courtesy of not distracting him by removing it. Besides, I liked that he had eyes on me. It amused me, along with a shade of something else that had me picturing all the things Cam hadn't admitted when I'd called him on the connection he shared with his loyal soldier.

A week after he cooked me dinner at his seaside cottage, I left my car in the space below my building and retrieved the sleek Yamaha from the lock-up I kept in the city. The sport bike was nothing like the beefy hogs the MCs rode. It was lighter. Faster.

Quieter.

They'd never see me coming.

Dressed all in black, I eased my helmet over my head and took off out of the underground car park, careful to stick to a speed that drew no attention.

The roads south from Bristol were fun to ride, and the wet weather made the long bends and fast straights thrilling enough to keep me occupied while my mind replayed my last encounter with Cam, from the cat and mouse conversation we'd shared to the axis-tilting sex. As a result of that long, heady night, I'd become certain of three things: Cam O'Brian was a dangerous, clever man, and an absolute sweetheart. *And* I didn't know what I admired about him the most. Perception or kindness, it was a tough choice.

I chose both and let my mind drift back to Saint Malone. I believed Cam when he said they weren't lovers, but something simmered between them. Something that thrilled me almost as much as Cam himself.

Stop.

With considerable effort, I reined in my wandering fantasies and picked up speed, leaving the city and built-up suburbia behind, zipping along the coastal roads, past Cam's hometown of Whitness and further south, eventually leaving Devon and entering Cornwall.

I passed Newquay and Porth Luck, the tourist hotspot where Cam part-owned a motorcycle garage he hadn't told me about, perhaps because his business partner there was his estranged brother. *River.* I liked that name too.

The Cornish chapter of the Rebel Kings MC lay just before Lizard Point, a three-hour ride from my penthouse flat.

I got there before Cam, but that had been my intention, to wait in the shadows for his chapter to roll into territory where they believed they'd be safe.

And they were ... for now. Saint Malone wasn't the only one handy with a GPS tracker, and in the days since I'd last seen Cam, I'd been busy, riding my Yamaha east to the other side of Devon, trailing the leaders of the Dog Crows. Their president was now firmly in my sights, as was an unidentified man who would ride with them today when they left their club colours behind and hit the Rebel Kings' convoy as they returned home.

You should warn Cam.

Perhaps. But it wasn't my intention to disrupt MC business, only to protect him from the threat that came from whoever the Crows had welcomed into their fold.

I still didn't know who that was, but I'd find out, if not today then another that came soon.

Watch and wait.

It was early afternoon when the Devon chapter of the Rebel Kings rolled into town. They rode in formation, Cam at the front flanked by his VP and road captain, his enforcer and chaplain at his back.

The membership fanned out behind them, around fifty strong. I searched for my green-eyed friend and found him at the rear, tail-gunning alone, alert and menacing. His demeanour set in stone what I already thought: that whatever attack the Crows were planning, it would come as far away from him as possible.

A sensible plan, but hitting the front of the convoy was madness too.

The middle then? Hmm. I wasn't convinced, unless the Crows were running a distraction for something else. Something silent and deadly that crept up on Cam when his attention was diverted by protecting his brothers.

That's it. A click sounded in my brain and the search for details expired. I observed the Whitness Rebel Kings as they swept into their sister compound and dismounted. Cam held court, his seniority over his contemporary clear to see, and I watched the Cornish president closely, searching for signs of discontent.

There were none. Cam was well liked and respected. Revered, even, by some. My gut told me the Kings were loyal and they'd fight to the death for their leader. Sound knowledge that should've eased my concern.

It didn't. The Kings could fight for Cam all they liked. Wouldn't do him much good if they didn't see the enemy coming.

I'll see it.

The Kings settled in for an afternoon of obnoxious metal music and beer. They ate charcoaled food from the outdoor barbecue and spent aeons of time examining each other's bikes, though Cam was absent for most of it, caught up in an intense conversation with his officers in a dark room at the back of the Cornish clubhouse.

Interesting.

It was late afternoon when Saint emerged into the rainy gloom, his phone in his hand. He frowned at the screen, and I wondered if he was tracking my unmoving car and contemplating why I hadn't left my flat for thirty-six hours. Then a *ping* sounded on my own phone—an alert that the Crow bikes I'd fitted trackers to were on the move—and it dawned on me that perhaps he was watching the same battle run unfold as I was.

I like him more and more.

I turned my attention to my phone screen. The Crows had left their compound and were heading south. It would take them a few hours to reach the Cornish coast, but that was on the assumption that they'd come that far. *They won't. It's safer to hit the Kings when they're on the move than mob-handed at a clubhouse.*

I glanced up as Saint found Cam in the crowd and murmured in his ear, his hand falling naturally to Cam's hip. Listening hard, Cam's expression darkened and he nodded to his sergeant-at-arms.

The club officers closed in, surrounding their leader. After a brief conversation, a flurry of activity saw younger riders instructed to remain at the clubhouse while the older men ditched their club colours and rode out.

Good. They're expecting the attack. But without their cuts, they were anonymous bikers. When the Crows hit, it would be hard for me to tell enemy from friend.

So? Stay sharp. Protect Cam. Anything else is collateral damage. As the thought completed, though, it wouldn't hold. Cam's brothers meant nothing to me, but to him they meant everything. The hurt in his heart if he lost one would be too much to bear.

Protect him. To that I was committed, but I was coming to learn that meant many things.

The Cornish chapter closed their gates. I climbed onto my Yamaha and gave Cam and his men a healthy head start, then I set off behind, tracking the Crows instead of the Kings, darting out to take a side route that allowed me to flank them all.

Losing sight of Cam made my chest hurt, and anxiety thrummed in my long dead veins, adding fuel to the fire he'd lit in me since day one. But it had to be this way. To help Cam, I had to stay in the shadows where I belonged. *You need to ghost him, not make space for yourself in his bed and his arms.* And maybe one day soon I would, but not yet.

Not yet.

I sped along the wet road, rain pelting my visor as I hugged the bends in the road, my knee to the floor. At this time of year, the roads were quiet come evening, but I still had a thousand caravans and motorhomes to weave around.

Despite my best efforts, it put me behind where I needed to be. The Crows came to a standstill, and I was three miles out.

Fuck. I gritted my teeth and pushed my bike harder, taking corners at breakneck speed, no longer concerned with being seen. The route the Crows had taken brought me to an unfinished road. I followed it, hugging the cliffs until a derelict holiday park came into view, and I realised the fight had started without me.

Skidding to a stop, I tugged off my helmet. Shouts and roars greeted me, and I scanned the scene unfolding, thirty men at full throttle with pipes and bats, kicking the shit out of each other. It wasn't a fight to the death, but it didn't need to be for blood to coat the hands of every man on the ground.

I forced myself not to search for Cam. Right now, he was as safe as he could be, surrounded by his men and moving too fast to be caught.

He's good at this, remember? Or he wouldn't be worth killing.

I wrapped the thought around me like a security blanket as I tucked my bike behind gorse bushes and retrieved a modified crossbow from a hidden compartment in my bike. I slung it over my back and took off, ducking into the undergrowth to conceal my presence, keeping a sharp eye out for any soldier doing the same.

My boots crunched fallen twigs and branches, the noise unavoidable, but covered by the sound of the fighting ahead. A deer crossed my path, wide-eyed and afraid. I stopped, letting it skitter into the nearby woodland, and the split-second hesitation took me out of the moment long enough for the brawling to die down.

I ducked behind a thick-trunked sweet chestnut tree. Took a breath, then crept around it to survey the scene before me. The Kings were bloodied and bruised, but victorious. Around them, Crows lay on the ground, already beginning to crawl back to their bikes as Cam's enforcer threw hunting knives at them, whooping his dark delight.

Fool. This one needs training.

Cam was unamused too. He barked an order and the knife throwing stopped, the enforcer turning his attention to the brother at his feet instead.

It was the road captain, his handsome face twisted in a grimace, blood dripping from a head wound.

Cam moved fast, hauling his friend upright, examining the injury, focused entirely on his brother's wellbeing.

This is it. If I was going to shoot him, I'd do it now.

My gaze drifted to the overgrown orchard behind Cam, a broken rope swing swaying eerily in the breeze as the sun disappeared behind it. With every King's attention trained on their hurt brother, it was the prime location for a shooter.

The other was the exact spot where I stood. I closed my eyes, just for a moment, using my other senses to detect another human creeping closer.

I felt nothing. I opened my eyes again. Swung my

crossbow forward and focused on the abandoned orchard. My heart thudded a torturous beat—*three, two, one*—and a lone figure emerged from the overgrown trees, gun raised and pointed at Cam's head.

No one saw him coming.

No one except me, tracking the man's every footstep as he rushed up on the gathered Kings.

Shoot him first.

I cocked the bolt on my bow and let fly as the man in my sights squeezed the trigger.

The gunshot shattered the air. Bodies collided and crumpled.

In the carnage, I didn't see who fell.

[13]
CAM

The *crack* of the gunshot battered my eardrums, shocking them so hard it felt as if the bullet had entered my brain.

I couldn't tell if I'd moved before or after whichever motherfucker had pulled the trigger. All I knew was falling, tangled limbs and blood, and the pained grunt of the brother who tumbled down with me.

Rubi. Heart in my throat, I rolled on top of him, shielding him, but there were too many arms and legs in my way. Too much weight. My body felt like lead and the coppery tang of blood filled my nose.

There was pain too, in my ribs and my back, and panic seized my soul as the unwelcome sensation of a stranger's skin against mine overwhelmed me.

Get it off. I fought like a wild animal, throwing the weight from my torso. My hands squelched in the bloodied dirt beneath me and I reared up, fist clenched, arm drawn back to strike.

Saint caught me. "Easy. It's me."

I shoved him, breathing hard.

He stood his ground, holding my gaze as if he could will me to calm the fuck down with his wild green eyes.

Apparently he could. Perspective returned to me and Saint let me go.

Nash replaced him in front of me and I latched onto my VP's levelheadedness as I took stock of the reality I found myself in.

A body lay face down on the ground at my feet, blood pooling around it. Dressed all in black, the man was wearing the wrong clothes to be one of us, and for a heart-stopping moment, my brain gifted me the memory of the last person I'd seen in black jeans and a North Face jacket.

Alexei.

It made no fucking sense, but the shaking sensation gripping my chest had only ever happened in his presence, and a fresh wave of panic sent me to my knees.

I gripped the black jacket and yanked the body over, bracing myself for the worst despite the fact that I could think of no reason, logical or otherwise, for Alexei to be dead at my feet.

A dull face stared back at me, eyes fixed and blank. Colourless, not blue or green or grey. Complete with a crossbow bolt through his skull, the dude was the deadest motherfucker I'd ever seen. "Jesus*fuck.*"

As the murmured curse left my lips, the gravity of what the hell had just happened descended. I barked orders and we fanned out, keeping low and moving fast, scanning the area for further threats. In the distance, a bike roared away. Crows crawling back to their fucking pit. I'd deal with them later.

Mateo took point, covering ground with swift feet, Nash

and Embry sweeping behind him, soldiers covering their backs.

Saint stuck close to me, and I kept Rubi between us, steadying him as he wavered from the hit he'd taken to protect Nash, keeping him on his feet as he doubled over and puked. *Fuck.* We were sitting ducks here, the pipes and hammers we'd brought to the fight no protection against an unseen enemy with a goddamn crossbow.

Or a gun.

Saint scooped the pistol from the ground—a replica that had been converted to fire live rounds. He dangled it from one finger—a *gloved* finger—as whatever happened, he'd be disposing of a body tonight, his moody face as grim as I'd ever seen. "Another distraction. Good job you got a guardian angel."

"That's what you're taking from this?"

He nodded.

I gestured for him to explain.

Saint shook his head. "Not here. Ride home in the pack. I'll speak at church."

A cold shiver passed through me, a world away from the heated shudders Alexei provoked in my nerves. But I had no leverage to argue with him. A crossbow was a silent weapon, it was dark, and we were off the beaten tracks. The chances of being detected here were slim. But the fact remained that we were out in the open with a dead body at our feet and an unknown killer in the wind.

We needed to get out of here, and fast.

"Don't be long," I told Saint. "And be safe. We need you, brother." *I need you.*

I embraced him—a gesture of affection he didn't always

want—knowing he'd feel the shakiness in my arms and not giving a shit. This life wasn't about being fearless and superhuman. It was a brotherhood, and I could've lost any one of them tonight. I could've lost *him*.

Two guys stayed with Saint to clean up. We called the prospects in with a van to pick up Rubi and his bike. "Take him to my room in the clubhouse. Or the hospital in Truro if he upchucks again."

"I'm fine, boss." Rubi grasped my shoulders, his grip strong and steady, gaze clearer now he'd left his lunch in the dirt.

I believed him, but I put the fear of God into the prospects all the same. "Don't take any chances."

They left and we set off for home, the mood sombre and tense, a far cry from the buzz we'd roared out with that morning. Despite knowing we were riding into an inevitable fight, we'd hit the tarmac for the goddamn love of it. Brothers. Bikes. The open fucking road. How it had come to a dead stranger at my feet, I had no clue, but we'd find out.

We had to.

It was late when we rolled into the compound. The van was already back. I checked on Rubi, found him dozing off his headache in my bed with Embry watching over him, and retreated to the chapel to collect my thoughts.

I was still shaking, rage replacing the fading adrenaline and fear from the fight. Fucking Crows. The Kings had been scrapping with them since before I was born, but this was some next level shit. Whoever they'd got into bed with were more dangerous than I'd ever imagined, and Saint's ominous warning returned to me, echoing in my head. *"We don't have the boots on the ground."*

But which fucking ground? The Crows had come at us like the pound-shop operation they'd always been, and somehow bullets had still flown and a man was dead. A man who belonged to someone that would no doubt come looking for him. Would that come down on us or the Crows?

Or both? There were rules in MC wars, lines none of us would cross. But there was a devil playing this game and the fucker kept dancing past me.

A knock at the door roused me from my thoughts. Nash stood in the doorway, a face I hadn't seen in a while a heartbeat behind him. "Skylar checked on Rubi. Reckons he'll be fine, but we've gotta keep an eye on him overnight, and no riding for a couple of weeks. Wanna show him your ribs while he's here? You hit Rubi's knee pretty hard when the gun went off."

"Don't say that shit in my vicinity." Skylar Buchanan stepped around Nash, a pissed-off expression keeping his face darkened by shadows. "You hurt, Cam?"

Not that I'd noticed, but I knew from experience it was quicker to let Nash have his way than to leave him to stew. Or worse, round up Embry to join the fucking chorus. "Just bruised."

"Show me."

Skylar was an A&E nurse and friend of the club, though he'd probably have called it something else. He had family ties that haunted him, so I tried not to lean on him too often. But if my brothers needed medical attention? Yeah. This kid had to suck it up as much as the rest of us.

I stripped my shirt and let Skylar prod at me with cool, practiced hands. "How's my baby brother?"

Skylar shot me a look that let me know he remembered

who we all were when the blood washed away. *As if he could forget.* "He's fine as far as I know. I haven't seen him since he serviced my bike a month ago."

"You don't keep in touch?"

"Not often. I see him in the Joker sometimes, but I'm not around much, especially when you clowns call me out after an eighteen-hour shift."

"Sorry."

"Of course you are." Skylar's tone was light. Easy, almost. But I knew this kid. Knew he *hated* the fact that he felt loyalty to an organisation that had tainted his whole fucking life. "Deep breath?"

I obeyed. Skylar listened with a stethoscope, then stood back with a frown.

"I think it's just some bad bruising, but I keep telling you, and I told them upstairs, I'm not a doctor and I don't have X-ray vision. If you're in pain, you should go to the hospital."

"I'm fine."

"Right. I'm out of here then. Unless you need to waste my time on anything else."

"Will you tell River I was asking about him?"

"Before or after I let him know you were fucked up from a fight?"

"Without all that bullshit, thanks."

Skylar rolled his eyes and left, but I knew I could rely on him. Whether he liked it or not, he owed us that.

"You know," Nash said from the corner he'd retreated to while Skylar had checked me out. "Whenever I see him, it reminds me how this all started—with your dad shutting down the trafficking rings up north."

"We fought wars before that."

"I know, but they ended. This feels like something that's been going on forever."

"You think this is about the Crows wanting to move skin through our turf?"

"Fuck the Crows. They're a tool. We've used them to do our dirty work before. Makes sense that someone else is doing that now."

"The Sambinis?"

Nash shrugged. "Maybe. That's why they wanted us working on the motorways, right?"

"Apart from the cheap labour for shoddy construction and low-grade materials?"

"Yeah. Apart from that. They wanted us to keep their routes open. Disable the cameras when they had a load coming through."

"I told you it was a distraction." Saint's voice came from the doorway. He looked as tired as I felt. "That easy raid on the coke, the scraps with the Crows. They wanted us busy while they sent snakes to take *you* out."

Saint jabbed his finger at me as he pushed off the doorframe and slunk further into the room.

He came close enough that I could sense the fury seeping from him. "That gun was pointed at your head today, and I couldn't get to you because I had three Crows on my back. If that nutter with the bow hadn't been out there, you'd have been the one dead in the dirt."

More coldness settled in my chest. "You saw all this?"

"Everything except where the bolt came from. I might've been able to guess if you hadn't swung the dead dude over your head after the fact, but you fucked that up for me."

There was no malice in Saint's grim speech, the longest he'd made in months, only plain facts.

I searched for more. "We knew they were going to come at us today. It was the obvious thing to do when they've been all over us for months. But what did they get out of it? We fucking battered them."

"They'd have got everything out of it if you'd died."

"How? We're strong without me. You'd vote in a new brother and carry on."

Nash shifted in the torn-up armchair he'd settled in. "Not necessarily. There's a lot of old guard don't like the direction you're taking us. They want the dirty cash and they don't care where it comes from."

"Okay, back up." My head was spinning, the list of enemies too long to grasp. "Are you saying—"

"Wait." Saint held up a hand and moved back to the door. He glanced out of it, then shut it behind him and leaned against it, one ear in this conversation, the other listening for approaching footsteps.

I took another breath and bore down on Nash, spearing him with my glare. "Are you saying this threat could've come from within?"

"I'm not saying anything concrete. Just that there's people among us who'd gain from you not existing anymore. People who have connections out there." Nash jerked his thumb to the window. "The Crows are nothing. We could destroy them tomorrow and they know it, so they've whored themselves out to whoever wants you dead and it's about fucking time we found out who that is."

I nodded. "Send Mateo. Tell him to do what needs doing

to make a Crow sing, and do it properly this time. I don't care what it takes."

"What are you going to do? With a target on your back, you should stay here. Lay low."

"That's what they'd expect me to do."

"You can't go home," Saint growled.

"You think I'm fucking stupid?"

He said nothing and the lack of denial enraged me, though it wasn't Saint I was angry with.

"Whatever. I'm not caging myself here. I'll kill myself before any other fucker does."

"You should still lay low," Nash said. "You got a bird you could roll with for a few days?"

"Nope."

"For real? You got no one on the hook?"

I shifted my death glare to him. "Be fucking serious."

"You could go to Bristol," Saint said. "To the accountant."

I swung my gaze to him. He didn't blink. "Even if I wanted to hide like a fucking pussyhole, you think a two-time hook-up is gonna want a houseguest?"

Saint stepped closer, sucking all the air from the room with his fiery stare. "Yes."

It was the whackest plan I'd ever heard, but in that moment, Saint did something to me I couldn't explain, and I found myself considering it and nodding like a damn fool.

Saint relaxed a touch and my bemusement deepened. I was used to not knowing what the fuck went through his head, but the sense that he knew something I didn't twisted me up.

"Saint—"

Nash cleared his throat. "We haven't got time for this. He needs to go."

The spell shattered. Saint's mask slipped into place and so did mine. He stepped back, jerked his head at Nash, and left.

I couldn't deny he took a piece of me with him, but I had other things on my mind too. So. Many. Things.

Nash stood and came to my side. He perched on the table, looking as frazzled as I felt. "None of this matters if you get killed. There isn't enough money in the world to replace you."

"Someone doesn't agree with you."

"And we'll find them. But until then, you need to stay safe."

I growled. "I'm not leaving my brothers to fight without me."

"I'm not asking you to. I'm saying, let us do some digging for a couple of days while you get some fucking rest. You're banged up, Pres. You've got bruises on bruises on those fucking ribs."

I rolled my eyes. "You're still not selling this to me."

"Okay, put it this way: if you don't put yourself somewhere safe for a couple of days, Saint is gonna run himself into the ground trying to be everywhere at once, and we can't afford that. *He* can't afford that in the situations we put him in. You want him spread so thin some fucker gets the jump on him?"

Another discontented rumble escaped me, but not for myself this time. Nash had me, and not because it was Saint, but because he was right. My brothers needed to protect themselves and protect the club, and I needed to help them do it. "Okay."

"You gonna go to the accountant?"

"I'm gonna put it to him. Can't say I'm sure of his answer."

"Saint must be if he suggested it. He doesn't usually like the blokes you bang."

"He doesn't know any blokes I've banged."

Nash snorted. "Okay, mate."

I scowled, but there was no heat behind it. What was the point? Nash had been my brother for more than a decade, and if you lived it right, club life left nowhere to hide.

Nash disappeared. I dumped ingredients into the slow cooker in the chapel kitchen, then ventured out to do the rounds of the compound, given that I wouldn't be around for a while.

The bar, the café, the yard. In the warehouse, I found Orla doing inventory. I pulled her aside. "Stay here for a few days."

"What? Why?"

"Because I said so."

"You're not God. If you want me to do something, you need to tell me why."

Irritation rattled me. Her request wasn't unreasonable, but I didn't have the energy to fight her. "There's trouble."

"I guessed that by the parade of bloody faces you brought home from the run. Can't take you anywhere, huh? Was it Crows?"

"You think I'd be this worried about Crows?"

"You never said you were worried. Just that I was

grounded." Orla put her hands on her hips. "And you can fuck all the way off with that unless you're staying here too."

"I need to be somewhere else."

"Where?"

"Somewhere that makes people waste their time looking for me."

"Like that explains anything. Fuck off, Cam. I'm going home."

"No."

"Yes. Nash can babysit me."

"Nash is busy."

"Rubi then."

"He's staying here too. He's in my bed."

Orla's brows disappeared into her hairline.

I rolled my eyes. "Not like that. He got hurt today. I know he's not the brother you'd want to play nurse to, but I'd appreciate it if you took care of him while I'm gone."

"That's a mean trick."

"What is?"

"Playing on my conscience. And fuck you with the emotional shaming. I'm not the only one hiding my feelings around here."

"For fuck's sake, I don't have time for this. Just stay, *please*. For me?"

Orla stood firm a moment longer, then her expression softened. "Okay. What about River? Does he need to be careful too?"

"He's not associated with the club."

"But he's associated with you. Anyone with half a brain would know fucking with your family was the easiest way to hurt you."

"The club is my family and they're already doing it. Just . . . stay, all right? Let me worry about the rest."

Orla let me go and I left her to take care of Rubi while I strode back to the chapel to wait on Saint and Mateo.

Cracker was already there, drinking from a bottle of nasty Bell's whisky, scowling at me, the challenge in his cloudy eyes clear.

I ignored him and checked on the food I'd dumped in the slow cooker. If he wanted to provoke me, he'd have to do better than that. Unless he wanted to talk about the fact he was becoming too much of a pisshead to ride. I didn't give a shit about most archaic club rules: if a brother wanted to ride a Triumph instead of a Harley or a biker chick wanted to roar into my compound on a fucking Honda, my gates were open. But I had no space at my table for cunts who rode drunk, and he knew it.

Didn't stop him poking the beast, though. And I had to wonder why, tonight of all nights, he wanted to fight me.

I returned to the table and took my seat. "Something on your mind, John?"

His glower deepened, hating that I sounded and looked just like my dad—a man he'd loved, once upon a time. "Nothing's on my mind, kid. Just sitting here minding my business."

"You've never minded your business your whole damn life. Why start now?"

Cracker grunted and lit a hand-rolled cigarette made from the same tobacco Cameron O'Brian Snr had smoked. He blew a lungful in my face.

I didn't blink.

Neither did he.

I sighed. "You seem annoyed. Anyone would think you were counting on that bullet blowing my brains out."

"Are you accusing me of being disloyal to this club?"

"I didn't say anything about the club. Are the two things connected?"

"Don't talk in circles with me, boy. I know that's how you get the others to do as they're told, but it won't work with me."

"I don't tell you to do anything. You've been the club secretary since the fucking nineties. If you don't know your job by now, I got nothing to say to you."

Cracker exhaled more smoke, to the side this time, thinking better of getting too far up in my face. "What about your job? You think you're doing right by the club these days? Taking boys out to ride knowing full well they're going to get jumped?"

"By the Crows?" I reached for my own smokes and lit up. "Fuck off, mate. We've been scrapping with them since before *you* joined this club. What happened today was predictable and every brother with me on the ground knew what they were riding into. Shame you couldn't make it, eh?"

"I already told you Loretta had an appointment at the hospital."

"Yeah sure, but you also told me six months ago that she didn't want you at her appointments no more because you turned up drunk to her chemo and the hospital threw you out, so . . ."

Cracker's bitter gaze flickered. *He doesn't remember.* Thought as much. Arsehole was doing a bottle of hard shit a day at this point. He had no fucking clue what was coming out of his mouth and there were pros and cons to that.

162

The pros were he was letting shit slip he used to keep to himself. The con was he was doing it with everyone so who the fuck knew what he was spilling every time he got wasted away from the clubhouse.

Watch him.

For some reason, the voice in my brain was Alexei's, and it took me out of the moment, reminding me of the stupidity I'd agreed to without his consent. I pictured myself rocking up at his place with an overnight bag, and a laugh bubbled up in my chest. It wasn't a bad way to end a day that had seen a bullet rattle my brain, but it felt like a fantasy. He wasn't gonna go for it, and yet I still wanted to ride out and put it to him, just for the sake of seeing his face for the ten seconds it took him to laugh in mine.

"Something funny, *Pres?*"

I blinked at Cracker's tone, refocussing on him, my distaste for him finally getting the better of me. I'd leaned back in my chair while I'd thought of Alexei. I let it fall forward, crashing the front legs to the floor, moving like a snake to seize Cracker by the throat.

Snarling, I ripped him from his seat and launched him against the wall, squeezing my hands around his fat neck. "Talk to me like that again, old man. Do it. I fucking dare you."

Cracker's eyes bulged, his face turning red. He said nothing, but the hatred in his glare hit me in the gut. *This is more than the shit he's been stewing over for years. Maybe he really does want me dead.*

The thought made me sick to my stomach. It was one thing for old timers to harbour resentment that the world—and the club—was moving on without them, but active

163

dissent was dangerous, and I had more than my own life to worry about.

I tightened my grip on Cracker's throat, constricting his windpipe for real, tapping into the darkest pit of my soul that would rip a man apart with my bare hands if I had to. "Don't fucking cross me. You ain't clever enough to get away with it, and I won't hesitate to end you when the time comes."

When. Not if. I never said shit by accident, and the finality of it settled in my bones. Cracker was a problem, if not right now, then soon.

"Cam." Embry grasped my forearms and tried to tug my hands from Cracker's neck. "Easy."

I ignored him, letting Cracker know it'd take a fucking army to stop me. Or at least Saint, who wasn't here and probably wouldn't stop me anyway.

"*Cam*. Stop."

Nope. Not yet. I wasn't letting this douche go until he passed the fuck out.

Which happened a split second later.

Cracker slumped forwards, body slack as his eyes rolled shut. I released him, letting him crumple to the floor and walked away without looking back.

Mateo found me sometime later, working out my frustrations in the rudimentary boxing gym we kept round the back. It was an outdoor space, sheltered only by an old tarpaulin tacked to a couple of fence posts and lit by some solar-powered fairy lights Orla had hung as a joke, thinking it would piss me off.

It didn't. They'd been there two years and I had no intention of taking them down, even if their sparkle made Mateo look scarier than he usually did.

He didn't scare me. I kept pummelling the bag that hung from the frame cemented into the ground and barely spared him a glance. "What have you got for me?"

Mateo folded his arms, dried blood flaking from his skin. "I took a couple of hangers-on from the street. Made them sing."

"And?" I'd expected nothing less. At this point, I didn't care what he'd done to get me what I needed. "Anything useful?"

"Yes and no. You were right about the Crows being in bed with a bigger crew, but they didn't know who it was, and they reckon the Crows themselves don't know who's lining their pockets either."

I caught the bag, sweat dripping from me as my chest heaved with stress-busting exhaustion. "Are you fucking kidding me?"

"Nope. Way they told it, some blokes just showed up one day and pulled Crow cuts on, and they've been calling the shots ever since."

"They've been infiltrated?"

"In plain sight. We're the ones who ain't supposed to know it."

I digested that, gathering more threads of a picture that still didn't quite come together. "What else?" I asked, sensing Mateo was holding something back.

His expression darkened, the scar on his face deepening with his mood. "They said whoever it is, they're coming for you and there's nothing you can do to stop it. And that maybe your old man should've thought twice before he shut the trafficking routes down and made everyone starve."

I tilted my head sideways. "That's pretty fucking specific

for a couple of hang-arounds. We've got officers don't know that much."

Mateo grinned a little, knowing he was one of them and not giving a flying fuck. "I promise you, boss, they were telling the truth as they knew it, but I can't vouch for the validity of it. Maybe the Crows were counting on us picking their strays up and fed them some bullshit to tell us?"

It was possible, but then, at this point, so were a million other things, and I had two options: retreat and fulfil the bridge contracts, taking the fall if something went wrong. Or carry on, pull back from construction sites and cancel the shipments of materials we'd agreed to before I'd come to my damn senses. "When's your delivery?"

"Sunday."

"That's four days away, right?"

"Five."

"Fuck, I'm losing track of time today." I unwrapped my hands and flexed my fingers, ignoring the pain in my ribs that had ratcheted up since I'd begun my ill-advised workout. "How long will it take to bank?"

Mateo shrugged. "Depends. It ain't like moving blow. Weed players are flakier. What do you need from it?"

"Fifty grand."

"What for?"

"To return the down payment on the dodgy cement order we took a few months back. We're cancelling it."

Mateo whistled. "That's gonna light a fire underneath us."

"I know, but we're already burning, man. We got no choice if we don't want to back down."

Mateo gave me a grim nod, understanding without the need for chapter and verse. "Do the others know?"

"Not yet. Fill them in for me, will ya? I got somewhere to be."

"Where?"

"Not far. I'll be back soon."

I left it at that. Nash and Saint knew where I was. No other fucker needed to.

After checking on Rubi one more time, I took a shower and wheeled a bike that wasn't mine out of the garage. I'd ditched my cut before the fight and my jacket was plain. I switched out my helmet and stole Nash's spare boots; then I left the compound without a goodbye to anyone.

I felt eyes on me as I rode away but trusted my ability to lose any fucker who tried to follow me.

No one did, and it was late enough that the roads were pretty much deserted until I reached the outskirts of Bristol. This close to Alexei, I took no chances, circling the city twice, immersing myself in traffic before I zipped into a quiet residential street and parked the bike in an unlit dead end. I ditched my jacket and shrugged on a black cotton hoodie to cover my arms.

Then I abandoned my helmet on the bike and walked away, alert for any fucker stupid enough to follow me.

Again, no one did. I reached the pub where I'd met Alexei without incident and found myself staring up at his penthouse castle in the sky, consumed by a sudden need to be as close to him as possible. A desperate need that made my stomach churn and my hands shake.

I approached the door without stopping to think how I'd get past the ageing concierge at the front desk, and as luck would have it, I found it open and the doorman distracted carrying shopping to the lift for a pregnant woman.

It was too easy to slip around them and head for the stairs. The climb was harder and my ribs throbbed with every step until I came to the penthouse landing.

I didn't knock. Alexei wasn't the only mofo who could pick a lock, even one as robust as his front door.

It took me less than a minute. I pushed the door open and stepped into his home. The hallway was dark, and so was the living room, the only low light coming from the kitchen. Anyone else might've thought he wasn't home, but I knew he was. I felt it, goddamn it, in my tingling skin, rushing blood, and clattering heart.

I shut the door behind me, closing it with a quiet *snick* that was deafening to my ears but undetectable from the kitchen.

Ditching my jacket and borrowed boots, I padded through the penthouse and reached the kitchen, following the light to the phone propped up on the counter.

A Russian voice filtered through the speakers, old and lost, while Alexei crouched on the floor staring, his unseeing gaze more haunted and broken than I'd ever felt in my life.

[14]
ALEXEI

Cam was an illusion, sent from the dark depths of my imagination to rescue me from the pit I'd fallen into the moment I'd swiped my phone screen.

He crossed the kitchen like a poltergeist and crouched in front of me, hands on my shoulders. "Alexei?"

I barely heard him, drowning in the ocean while he called my name from the moon. His grip on me tightened, strong fingers gouging bruises into my skin, but I didn't feel a thing.

He stood and moved back, taking his shadow with him. I wanted to close my eyes and summon him back, but my brain didn't work that way, not when it was paralysed like this, stuck on a loop I couldn't break.

My mother grew louder, the words indistinct, but the reedy pitch of her voice like nails on a blackboard, grating and shrill. *Make it stop.* But who was I asking? Imaginary Cam? Or myself?

A silent cry echoed in my head. I fought my frozen muscles, desperate to bury my face in my knees, cover my head, and block the universe out, but nothing happened. I couldn't fucking move.

Cam appeared again and my soul wept. *Don't leave.*

And this time he didn't. He snatched the phone from the counter and glared at the screen before sweeping his molten gaze back to me. "Fuck. This."

He ended the call and dropped the phone into the sink. The clatter made me jump, a sensation that was almost alien to me. But he was in front of me again before I could acclimate to it, taking my face in his big hands.

"Lexi." His voice was hoarse, laced with a heavy exhaustion that lined every inch of his face, but his eyes were fierce, like a wolf tending to his mate. "Whoever that was who's making you feel like this, they ain't got no place in your life."

I still had nothing. My throat was a sealed dam and I couldn't speak, not even to him.

Cam held my gaze a moment longer, then something broke in him and he hauled me to my feet, towing me out of the kitchen as if I were half his size.

He pulled me into the bedroom and shut the door. Darkness enveloped us until he flicked on a lamp, and then his arms came around me like a vice, hugging me tight against his big, warm body. "It's okay," he whispered. "Whatever it is, it's okay."

It wasn't okay and it never would be, but the cage he'd built with his arms felt like a safe room. I wanted to sink into his embrace and never resurface.

But I couldn't. Disassociation descended on me as fast as the gut-wrenching fear had before he'd reached me, and whatever words he spoke next, I couldn't hear them. I couldn't hear *him*, and that scared me more than anything.

Still holding me, Cam walked me to the bed. I wondered if he'd strip me naked and fuck me into acknowledging him, but he did neither. He lay me down, stretched out beside me, and held me until I did something I'd never done with any other man.

I fell asleep.

It was still dark when I woke up *in* my bed, not on it. I was dressed in the same drawstring trousers I'd been wearing all evening, no shirt, but Cam had shed his jeans and T-shirt and somehow manoeuvred us beneath the sheets. His arms were still around me and my head was on his chest, his heart beating steadily against my cheek.

Am I dreaming?

A quiet sigh escaped me.

Maybe I was, and the gentle hand combing through my hair was something I'd never known I wanted.

"You awake down there?"

Cam's low voice rumbled through me. I raised my head and met his gaze, diving headfirst into it before I caught myself. I still had no words, but fuck, I felt him.

I *needed* him.

Energy pooled in my veins. I squirmed in Cam's arms. He opened them, letting me go, and snatched a sharp, surprised breath as I claimed his mouth in a kiss that was too soft and sweet to be real.

I didn't kiss like that.

I didn't know how, and yet somehow, I was doing it, and Cam was kissing me back, and every part of me was powerless to stop the eclipsing epiphany that swallowed me whole. *I can't give him up.*

Worse, I didn't want to.

Cam pulled back. His hair was a tousled, dark mess and I let myself tuck it behind his ears.

He grinned a little. "Tidying me up?"

"It would take more than that."

Cam blinked. "Fuck. I was worried you wouldn't speak to me ever again."

"Why?"

His smile faded. "You were gone."

"I was right here."

His silence was his counter argument and I didn't have the mental capacity to combat it. I sighed again, pressing my forehead to his, soaking him up. "I'm sorry."

Cam rubbed my back. "Don't be. I don't need that shit."

"What do you need?"

"To know you're okay."

"Why?"

"Because it matters to me."

"It should not."

"Says who?"

"Me."

"Well, you're wrong, so fight me on it as much as you want. You won't fucking win."

I didn't want to fight him. I wanted to climb all over him and fuck the remnants of our strangest encounter yet into a distant, hazy memory. But as wrapped up in each other as we were, nothing in Cam's touch was sexual right now. He was comforting me, and I didn't know what to do with that.

"Hey." Cam nudged my chin with his knuckles, the heavy rings on his fingers cool against my skin. "You don't have to tell me shit. Just know that I'm fucking here, okay? And I'm not going anywhere."

It occurred to me that I should probably have enquired as to how he'd come to be in my flat at all, let alone why he'd come in the first place, but I didn't need those answers from him. He'd picked the lock on my front door and I hadn't heard him or seen him on my security system because I'd been . . . somewhere else, somewhere he'd pulled me back from with gentle touches and kind words.

I said nothing, shifting my weight on top of him from one side of his ribcage to the other.

He winced.

I lifted off him like I'd been burned by his radiating warmth. "What's wrong?"

"Nothing."

"You lie?"

He smirked. "Maybe."

"There is no maybe. You are hurt."

I drew back to get a better look and flicked a lamp on. Cam's skin was as obscured by ink in the light as it was in the dark, but I saw the mottled welts all the same and fury burned inside me. He'd been bruised before, but he was *battered* this time, and now I was coherent enough to assess him, the lines of pain etched on his face were unmistakable. "How did this happen?"

A pointless question—I already knew. But keeping up

appearances was important. Cam couldn't know I was shadowing his enemies. Not yet, if ever.

He gave me a slow shrug. "Some trouble with a rival club. Wasn't that bad until I beat the shit out of the punch bag before I came here."

"One fight was not enough for you?"

"I needed to think."

"It sounds like you do not think enough . . . about yourself, no?"

Cam blew out a breath. "I've had worse. Can we just leave it at that?"

Not a chance. I was a sadistic bastard and it was time he knew it.

I pressed the heel of my hand into the place I was fairly certain hurt the most, not hard enough to do more damage but with enough force to let him know I saw right through him.

Cam hissed, forcing himself to stay still as he gritted his teeth.

I leaned over him, lips a torturous inch from his. "The easiest way out of this is to tell me you're in pain and let me help you."

"This is you helping me?"

"Until you admit the truth, yes."

"You're a sick fuck."

"*Yes.*"

Humour fought a battle with the searing pain I was inflicting on him. He liked this, even if he wasn't enjoying it. "All right," he ground out. "You win."

I pulled my hand back. Cam closed his eyes and I left him to collect himself while I gathered some supplies from

174

the kitchen—ice packs and painkillers, the good ones that would help him sleep if I convinced him to take them, and some regular ibuprofen.

Back in the bedroom, he hadn't moved, save to wrap an arm around himself.

I gently pried it free and applied the ice to his bruised ribs and abdomen. "You can breathe?"

"Yeah."

"Movement?"

"I can do everything, it just fucking hurts."

"Good boy."

Cam bared his teeth at me.

I laughed and it was the most human I'd felt since we'd last been this close.

The icing took a while. I strapped the packs to him with a towel to catch any escaping moisture and held up the pills I'd brought from the kitchen. "You have options."

Cam squinted in the dim light. "Vicodin? Where'd you get that?"

"Somewhere that wasn't here."

"Is it good?"

"It will help you rest. You have not slept for a while?"

"Can't remember."

I turned that over in my mind. If he hadn't slept, he probably hadn't eaten either, and as tough as I knew Cam to be, we needed to rectify that before we put any medication in his body. "Take the ibuprofen while I get you some food. You can take the Vicodin later if you are still uncomfortable."

"I never said I was uncomfortable, Lexi. You did."

Lexi. There was not much I wouldn't do for him when he called me that. I couldn't explain it, but the affection he crammed into the fact that he was too lazy to speak my whole name did inexplicable things to me.

It made me want to open my refrigerator and *cook him* some real food. *Cam, what have you done to me?*

I fed him the ibuprofen and retreated to the kitchen. My fridge contained nothing but eggs, chicken, and spinach, but I remembered the healthy meal he'd cooked me in his cosy cottage and threw it all in a pan. The result was protein and iron heavy and seasoned with the Creole spice mix that had fallen out of a magazine I'd read on the last international flight I'd taken.

It looked passable.

I took it back to the bedroom. Cam was sitting up and poking at his phone, a deep frown marring his handsome face. "Everything okay?"

He grunted and tossed the phone aside. "I'd be better if people didn't text me shit that made no fucking sense."

"Is it your green-eyed bodyguard?"

"Saint?"

I handed Cam the plate, absorbing the light in his eyes as he studied it, cataloguing two certainties from it.

He's hungry.

No one ever cooks for him.

"Yes, Saint. Is he outside? I have more food."

"He's not here. I came alone."

"Shame."

"Is it?"

"Perhaps. It amuses me when he waits outside for you with such a fierce expression on his pretty face."

Cam laughed, then regretted it with a heavy wince. "You think Saint's pretty?"

"You do not?"

"Pretty ain't the word."

"I did not say it was the only word to describe him. Eat your food, biker boy. Then you can have the good drugs."

Cam shot me a curious stare, but hunger and fatigue won out. He ate his food, then lay down again. I took his plate away, washed it with the other dishes, then returned to the bedroom to find him pointing the remote at the flat-screen TV on the wall.

I pried it from his hand and found the menu for him. "What do you want?"

"Whatever. Except football and soap operas."

I clicked on Film4 and looked away before the screen loaded, uninterested in whatever was playing.

Cam wasn't interested either. He shifted, dumping his head in my lap at my invitation, and stared up at me. "You're the strangest dude I've ever met."

"Should this upset me?"

"Fuck no. I just don't understand you."

My fingers migrated to his hair. It was silky and messy. I brushed it away from his face. Tucked it behind his ears again, and his answering grin was as spellbinding as it had been the first time. "You do not need to understand me." *I will never hurt you.*

"I want to try." Cam spoke softly. "Who was on the phone?"

"My mother." The words slipped out of me, easing past the blocks in my heart as if they were as desperate to get close to him as I was. "She calls from the nursing home in Kolpino."

"In Russia?"

I nodded and adjusted a nearby pillow to support his back. "She has dementia, so she talks at me about things I do not remember anymore. I don't talk back, but I didn't before, so . . ."

"Before what?"

"Before she was sick. I haven't seen her since I was young."

"That sounds complicated."

"Families are, I think."

Cam hummed, eyes falling closed for a moment as I rubbed his scalp. A different man might have drifted to sleep, taking the comfort on offer and forgetting about everything else. But not him. His eyes opened a split second later. "What about your dad?"

My fingers spasmed. I forced them to keep moving, finding solace in his tousled locks. "He died a year ago. I had not seen him for many years either."

"How many years?"

"Fourteen."

"By choice?"

A humourless laugh spilled out of me, bitter and cold.

Cam flinched. He said nothing, but the questions dancing in his dark gaze bored holes in the iron curtain shielding my soul.

I pulled my hands from his hair. "You do not want me to talk about this."

Cam gritted his teeth and sat up. "I meant what I said earlier, but that doesn't mean I don't want to be there for you."

"Do you think I need that from you?

"Yes."

"You are arrogant, then."

"So?"

He was still close enough that I felt the heat radiating from his warm skin, despite the ice packs that had slipped from his battered torso.

I retrieved them for something to do. Wrapped them in the damp towel and set them aside, out of sight, to deal with later. Words I'd never spoken clawed at my insides. My whole life I'd been strong enough to subdue them, but Cam had stripped those weapons from me the moment he'd met my gaze all those weeks ago. "What was your father like, Cam?"

"Strong," he answered without hesitation. "And stubborn. It got him killed."

"My father was weak, and he lived until he was seventy-eight."

Cam shifted again, sitting up against the headboard. He gestured for me to continue.

I mirrored his pose, my gaze returning to the TV so I didn't have to look at him. "He was a gambler—he lost everything we owned and then, when he had nothing left, he lost me too."

"Lost you?"

"In an underground casino. The vor who ran it offered him the chance to clear his debt if he won the next hand. The price if he did not was me."

"He let them take you?"

"Of course he did. My father was a chemical salesman with no money or status. The organisation he'd crossed were powerful and dangerous. They took me and I never saw him again."

179

"What did they do with you?"

I rose from the bed and searched for the clothes Cam had taken off while I'd slept earlier in the night. His jacket was draped over his folded jeans, cigarettes stuffed in the inside pocket.

He always has what I need. I retrieved them and lit one, ignoring his piercing stare as I returned to the bed and offered it to him.

He plucked it from my fingers and pulled deep on it, then he returned it to my lips.

I took a lungful of my own and gave it back to him. "I do not want to talk about this for long, so I will give you the short version. My father was indebted to a crime syndicate that made their money from trafficking sex workers. They held me for two years before I was procured by someone else. I remained in their employment for ten years, and now I am here."

Cam took another drag from the cigarette and rose from the bed to flick it from the window. As he turned back to me, his broad shoulders blocked the light from the TV, shadowing his face. "You were trafficked by your own father?"

"Indirectly, yes."

"As a . . . sex worker?"

"Do you need a cruder definition?"

Cam came back to the bed, rounding it to where I sat, perching on the edge. He didn't reach for me, but I could tell he wanted to. "How old were you?"

"Fifteen."

"You were a sex worker for twelve years?"

"No. Only the first two, until the organisation was destroyed by another. Their leader saw I had other skills and gave me a different job. I did that for a long time before he set me free."

"Were you his accountant too?"

"No."

Cam reached for the Vicodin bottle on the bedside table. He uncapped it without reading the label and swallowed two pills. "Who do you work for now?"

"Myself."

"As a . . . ?"

"Financial advisor. I have never lied to you about that."

"I never asked you, to be fair."

"You did not. Would it bother you if I was still a sex worker?"

"Were you ever really that? You didn't keep what you earned, right?"

I was a slave. I shook my head. "I've never thought too hard about the words I'd need to tell this story because I've never told it."

"Why tell it to me?"

I didn't know the answer to that and Cam seemed to sense the well had run dry.

He found my hands and tugged me close enough for another of those soft kisses that drove all sensible thoughts from my head. Then he pulled back and took my face in his hands. "Does hearing your mum put you back in that place?"

I gripped his wrists, needing the contact to tether me. "Sometimes. I feel small again when I hear her voice, and it reminds me of the path I took to get to this place. It . . . drowns me, and I'm sorry you saw me like that. I am so used to being alone that I forget I cannot talk when my head is too full."

"I have a brother like that."

"River?"

"No, in the club. It's not just when he's spooked, though. It's all the time, like his thoughts come too fast for him to get them out. Then he panics and he can't speak at all."

Saint. His name whispered in my brain. "Are you patient with him?"

"Some days. Others I want to twat him with a hammer, but that's got nothing to do with how he speaks. Or doesn't speak. Fuck." Cam shook his head. "I'm so fucking tired."

And that was before the double dose of narcotics hit him. "You should sleep now."

He didn't argue.

I took his hands from my face and coaxed him back to where we'd started, me leaning against the headboard while he used my lap as a pillow. He watched the film for a while—a western with gruesome death scenes and beautiful horses. Helped along by the Vicodin, the blood and gunfire seemed to lull him to sleep, and I wondered if he was so conditioned to violence that he found comfort in the normality of it. I applied the theory to myself and decided not to think about it again.

Cam's hair, his soft breaths, and the hand he'd clamped around my thigh made the present a nicer place to be.

CAM

"What do you want?"

River's hostile growl was a dagger to my heart. I gouged my eyes with my finger and thumb, rocking forward on the edge of Alexei's bed, still groggy from the monster painkillers he'd given me. "I already told you. I'm just letting you know Rubi's gonna be late with your cheque from the yard."

Aggressive, metallic sounds made my ears bleed before my little brother spoke again. "I don't care if he's a fucking year late. Your cheques go on the fire."

I knew that. River hadn't taken a penny from a family business since he'd walked away from me five years ago. But I sent the cheques anyway; his fierce rejection was better than stone-cold silence. "Whatever, man. I just wanted you to know he's laid up, so he'll be a few days late. I didn't call to fight you."

River muttered something. Then his surroundings quieted and he expelled a pissed-off sigh. "What's up with Rubi?"

"What do you care?"

"I've known him since I was born."

"You've known me that long too."

"And you're fucking bulletproof, right? So I don't need to care."

I had bruises on bruises that said different, but his concern for Rubi was genuine, so I swallowed his malevolence and gave him the truth. "He banged his head. Got a mild concussion. No riding for a couple of weeks."

Silence.

I took a chance. "I need to talk to you about the yard."

"I don't give a fuck about the yard and your dirty money. How many times I gotta tell you?"

"It's not dirty money," I snapped. "I've told *you* that a thousand fucking times."

"Repetition doesn't make something true."

"Don't make it a lie either."

Alexei emerged from the bathroom as my epic growl rattled down the line to my brother. He gave me a steady look that I latched on to, his steely eyes warmer than I'd ever imagined when I met him. "Look," I said around a sigh that threatened to send me back to sleep. "I did what you wanted and took you off the company records, and I stopped the club using the garage to service their damn bikes. What else do you want from me?"

River made an angry sound. "You're a fucking prick, you know that? Don't guilt trip me. You still own half my garage because I can't afford to buy you out, and you took me off the yard books and replaced me with Orla so you could ruin her life instead of mine, so don't come at me like you're a fucking hero, *bro*."

He hung up. I expected it as much as I expected his rage, but it hurt more in this moment than it ever had. I lowered my phone and rubbed my chest.

Alexei ventured closer, moisture making his creamy skin shine. "A family phone call, not business, no?"

He was so Russian right now. I flailed a clumsy hand out for him and found his bare hip. "My brother. He hates me."

"Why?"

"Because he thinks I'm going to die like our dad did."

"On the road?"

"Something like that." On any other day, I'd have left it there, but I was still spinning from the horrific story Alexei had told me and I felt like I owed him something. "My dad was club president before me, and Whitness is one of the founding chapters of the Rebel Kings."

Alexei finished towelling himself dry and pulled some expensive black sweats up his long legs. "He was well respected then? He had influence?"

"Not enough in the end. A few years back, a chapter up north went off-piste and started, uh, trafficking women from Romania. He shut it down, along with every route down south, and the cartel the rogue chapter were working with killed him for it." *And then my ma died of a broken heart.*

Alexei rolled his damp towel into a complicated shape and tucked the ends in. Then seemed to realise what he'd done and unravelled it. "Did the routes open up again after your father's death?"

"No, because—"

"You became president." He sat next to me on the edge of the bed, his gaze distant a moment as his supercharged brain went into overdrive. "Do you think that is the root of your

185

troubles now? The same cartel wants you out of the way and a leader more malleable in your place?"

"Maybe. We have other business partners who don't like me, though."

"Unless they're all connected. Alliances you don't know about."

I'd already said too much. Confiding in him was a risk I couldn't take. But at the same time, a strange trust had bloomed between us, a bond I was coming to rely on. If he was playing me, I'd put a bullet in my own head to save him the trouble.

Whoa. Light-headedness ploughed into me, my heart pounding with an emotion that was as painful as it was beautiful. The fuck was happening to me? Did I love this dude? Fuck. *How* did I love him? We'd fucked a handful of times and I barely knew his name. Loving him made no sense, and goddamn, I needed things to make sense right now.

Feeling his gaze on me, I gave him a vague shrug. "Doubt it. The other beef we have is with the Italian construction rackets and they don't do business with the Romanians who killed my dad. If they're both coming at me at once, it's a shitastic coincidence. Hey, can I ask you something?"

Alexei tucked a stray lock of my hair behind my ear—he seemed to like doing that, as if it grounded him when the intensity that flared inside him got too much. "Of course. Nothing has changed about that."

I remembered those conversations, but I pushed them to the back of my mind. He'd been Teddy then, a stranger in posh clothes. He was Alexei now, and whatever relationship we had was a world away from the wild hook-up we'd shared. "Do you have any brothers or sisters?"

Alexei let his hand drop from my face, his expression shuttering before he seemed to catch that too. He closed his eyes a second and I let him have it. I'd give him anything he ever needed as long as I wasn't pushing fucking daisies.

This time, the permanence of how I felt didn't alarm me so much. I found Alexei's hands and pulled him into my lap, loving that he let me and that his legs wrapped around me on instinct. My head was foggy enough that I couldn't quite tell how long I'd been in his bed, but I dug the normality we'd somehow nurtured. The easy affection that my gut told me he didn't share with anyone else.

I kissed his neck, heat pooling in my belly, flooding south as he ground softly against me, a reflexive move that didn't match the sadness in his gaze when he opened his eyes again.

"I have no siblings," he said. "Only a distant cousin. He lives in London."

I ran my hands up his bare back. "Do you speak?"

"Not often. He is very normal. Married to a rich man and works in the city. I do like him, though. He is kind to me when I see him."

"Does he know what happened to you?"

Alexei shuddered, though it could've been from my touch. And god, I *wanted* it to be from my touch. Because I was a selfish prick and I wanted to fuck all the bad memories out of him, as if I could wipe the trauma from his soul with my magic fucking cock.

"Sacha doesn't know," Alexei whispered. "And I will not tell him."

He kissed me then, perhaps to shut me up, and I kissed him back, letting him push me into the mattress and climb all over me, tearing away the clothes we'd only just put on. He

187

was rough with me in every place except the throbbing bones in my torso, gripping my chin and savaging my mouth, pumping my dick in a merciless rhythm as I lay prone beneath him, addicted to the heat sweeping through me.

Alexei rose up on his knees, his cock so straight and hard I was almost scared to touch it, as if it would fucking shatter on impact.

I wanted it in my mouth.

I wanted it everywhere, and I wondered if he knew, if this was the moment he'd kick my legs apart and dominate me in a different way.

Alexei leaned over me, grinding his dick against mine. I flinched at the pleasure, nerves jumping, and he smiled, predatory and raw. "I want you."

"Have me." I spread my arms wide and lifted my chin. "Take anything you want."

He kissed me again while reaching for his drawer of tricks. Condoms and lube landed on my chest and I sucked in a breath. However he wanted to do this, it didn't scare me, but the renewed thrum in my pulse did. The scorching heat in my blood. The burning need to climb inside him and never come out. My heart had only ever beat this hard for Saint, and I'd swallowed it down. Drowned it under the weight of every other fucking thing in my life. As Alexei stared down at me, I forgot how to do that, and every defence in my heart melted away. "I—"

Alexei covered my mouth. "Do not think or speak. Just feel."

He tore a condom free from the wrapper and rolled it onto my cock. My hips bucked, but he held me down. "Do not move."

The command lacing the words rattled my soul. "I thought you were going to fuck me."

"Would you let me?"

"That's a complicated question."

He leered. "Too complicated for today, I think."

"If you say so."

Alexei pumped my dick with a slick hand, lubing and testing me in a filthy take on multitasking.

I held still and he smiled in a way that was as pretty as it was terrifying, if I was the kind of bloke to be scared of whatever journey he was about to take me on.

Recklessly, I wasn't.

Or maybe it wasn't reckless. Maybe I really did trust him.

Alexei widened his legs and leaned forward before tipping back and impaling himself on my cock. He took me inside him with no prep or hesitation, a tiny snarl the only sign of discomfort, and even then, I couldn't be sure.

He likes pain.

So did I, but *damn*. He was a braver man than me.

Alexei sank back, enveloping me with his tight heat. Sensation ambushed me and my muscles seized, desperate to react, but I fought it, gritting my teeth. He could push me as far as he liked. I wouldn't fucking break.

He rolled his pelvis, lightly at first, then harder, grinding pleasure from me, his thighs caging my hips. His cock jutted from his body and he leaned forward again, sliding it along my abs as he moved, the friction making it leak onto my tingling skin. "You feel so good like this."

It was probably the nicest thing he'd ever said to me, and the sentiment stoked a new flame inside me. A moan built in my throat. I kept it in as long as I could, but it burst free all the same, and I threw my head back, my hands balling into fists. "You gonna ride me, Lexi?"

"If you do not move, like I have asked you already. You are hurt enough, I think."

Nothing that felt this incredible could ever hurt. At least, that was the fantasy, but I'd been around long enough to know there was a fine line between pleasure and pain.

Between love and hate too, which made me think of River again, distracting me from the mind-bending sensation Alexei was gifting me.

He made a low sound of discontent and gripped my chin. "Stay in this moment. You deserve it."

I held my eyes open, drinking him in as he began to ride my dick in earnest, his cock still dragging forward and back on my belly.

He was so fucking hard.

I reached for him.

He slapped my hand away. "No."

"Sadist."

"Yes." He fucked me faster, dipping his head to thrust his tongue into my mouth. "But you love it, don't you?"

I groaned, fighting the instinct to arch my back and drive deeper inside him. My breath shortened to sharp pants that left me dizzy, fresh sweat coating my skin. I was a mess for him.

Fuck, I was flying.

Alexei bounced on my cock, thighs gripping me tighter and tighter as they trembled, the pale skin of his chest flushing as he began to lose his composure.

He leaned back, dropping his hands behind him, exposing his throat.

I wanted to sink my teeth into the elegant curve, claim him as mine, but I was frozen beneath him, trapped in his fucking thrall.

Orgasm rushed up on me, coursing through my veins in a blood-pumping wave. A crazed shout left me, and I punched the mattress. "Fuck, I need to touch you."

Alexei ignored me, his eyes screwed shut as he started to come apart.

I missed him. I found the unyielding muscle of his thigh and squeezed. "Look at me . . . please?"

He reared up, startled, and as he met my gaze, we both unravelled. Hot come spurted from his dick in the same moment mine erupted inside him. I came so hard my balls felt like they'd disappeared into my soul, and I fucking *roared*, lost to it—to *him*—for however long it took me to come down.

Maybe I fell asleep again, I wasn't sure. All I knew was that I had weird nightmares and I couldn't tell if they were from the after-effects of the bulldozer drugs or the horrific story Alexei had told me the night before. Either way, I saw him in my dreams, and for once it wasn't pretty.

I woke with a jump sometime later, alone in Alexei's bed. My hand flew to my chest and I bolted upright as fast as my battered ribs allowed. "Lexi?"

He appeared in the doorway. "I'm here."

I sucked in a deep, cleansing breath. "So you are."

He raised a brow, amused? Maybe? It was hard to tell. Regardless, he was too far away.

I rolled out of his bed and closed the distance between us. He was wearing work clothes—tailored trousers and a shirt that clung to his body like sin. "Are you going out?"

"I've been out," he said. "I had a meeting and you were still sleeping, so I left you in peace."

"A meeting?" My gaze snapped to the hallway window. It was light and bright outside, winter sunshine streaming through the glass. "The fuck?"

"It's the morning. You fell asleep yesterday afternoon and you did not wake up."

I blew out a breath. "That's fucking insane."

"You were tired from life, no?"

"I guess so."

Alexei nodded and presented me with a paper bag I hadn't noticed him holding. "Breakfast. I have coffee too. Then you should probably answer your phone before your brothers come looking for you."

He spun around and strode away, leaving the bag in my outstretched hand. I peered inside it. A fruit pot and a breakfast baguette greeted me, and my belly growled so loud I knew I needed to eat before I did anything else.

I retrieved my phone from where I'd dropped it on the floor after River had hung up on me and followed Alexei to the kitchen.

He was tapping on a laptop set up on the counter, frowning the same frown I'd seen when he'd scrutinised the books from the yard. Concentrated. And too clever for the likes of me.

I kept a respectable distance and demolished the breakfast he'd brought me, noting that there was nothing in front of him except a mug of coffee that looked like tar. "What are you doing?" I asked eventually. I didn't mind companionable silence, but I was curious enough that I couldn't contain myself. "Is it work?"

Alexei tore his sparkly gaze from his laptop screen. "Do you want to see?"

He beckoned me closer. I slid from my stool and stepped into his personal space, ignoring the screen in favour of burying my face in his neck. Fuck, he smelled so good. If I kept my face pressed against his skin forever, the rest of the world was a place I could barely remember.

Alexei chuckled.

Goddamn. I raised my head, more curiosity burning through me. "Are you laughing at me?"

"You are very sweet for a gangster, my friend."

"Three things wrong with that sentence, *mate.*"

He twitched a brow. "Enlighten me."

"I'm not sweet. I'm not a fucking gangster. And, Lexi?"

"Yes?"

"I'm not your friend."

Alexei stared, and something shifted between us, literally, as I tugged him closer, and a crackle of new energy wrapped around us, binding us together. I brought my hand to his throat, pressing my palm over his pulse point. It thundered, mimicking the roaring storm my own heartbeat had become. "If we are not friends anymore," he said. "Then what are we?"

"This." I kissed him, letting emotions I didn't know I was capable of seep into the rough way I held him and claimed his lips.

I didn't even know what I was trying to say to him or what it meant, but I couldn't contain it. I needed him to know he was my port in a storm right now and it meant something to me.

It meant everything.

I pulled back, already knowing Alexei wouldn't speak, but I was okay with that. If I'd learned anything about him, it was that he'd let me know if he thought I was talking shite.

That, and he was like no one else I'd ever known.

I peered at his laptop screen. "Pensions?"

He nodded. "My job most days. I help people who have lost their pensions through no fault of their own get something back."

"You mean, like, if their employer goes bust and takes everything down with them?"

"Or women whose husbands have left them with nothing."

"When they die?"

"Or they were unable to work because of ill health. My last client was the wife of a coal miner."

The information on the screen meant little to me, but the notion of Alexei being a knight in a white pressed shirt to elderly ladies in financial distress was something I'd never considered. "How did you get into this?"

"When I left my last employer, I didn't want to work for a bank or a financial institution."

"Too many wankers?"

"That is a problem with most occupations, I've found."

I couldn't argue with that. And Alexei's phone—the one that didn't give him waking nightmares—rang before I could try.

He stepped out of my suffocating embrace and picked it up, answering the call in a language that was neither English nor Russian.

It was my turn to raise a brow.

He smirked and turned his back on me, leaving me to attend to my own business.

My phone had buzzed every ten minutes since I'd left the club compound—mostly updates that didn't require chapter and verse in response, but by now, shit had started to move and I needed to check in with my brothers.

I retreated to the bedroom, easing my sore body onto the rumpled sheets. Saint didn't answer my call. Nash was next.

"Mateo swept the Crows. They're on lockdown now and we're watching them to see who comes to their rescue."

"His delivery?"

"Seems to be on schedule, no issues. Should have the early paperwork through in a couple of days."

"Don't file it in the usual place. Take it somewhere only you, me, and Saint know about."

"Got it. Anything else?"

"How's Orla?"

Pause. Nash cleared his throat. "With Rubi, last I checked. You worried about her?"

Are you? "Not as long as she has a brother with her. You got eyes on River?"

"Subtle ones. He told me to light myself on fire last time he saw me in Porth Luck."

I snorted. "Sorry, brother."

"It's all good."

We said our goodbyes. I called Rubi next. He answered with a sigh.

"I'm fine, and yes, I'm eating my fucking vegetables."

"How's my sister?"

"Almost as annoying as you."

"Prettier, though?"

"I ain't Nash, but yeah."

Out of habit, I bristled. Rubi had been ribbing me about the chemistry between my VP and my little sister since Nash had joined us ten years ago. I was a dick about it because that was the culture, but most days I had more trouble thinking up a reason to give a shit. "Are you really doing okay?"

Rubi sighed again. "I'm bored, man. Not riding makes me claustrophobic as fuck."

"Go out in the van then."

"Yeah?" Rubi's tone perked up. "You want me to take River his cheque?"

"Fuck no. I don't want the club anywhere near him right now. Go to the fucking beach, man."

Rubi muttered something I didn't quite catch. My brain ticked again, but I had too much to think about to pay it much attention. I made him promise to rest, then left him alone.

A message buzzed in as I hung up and my heart flared. *Saint.* He'd been by my side since he'd patched in and usurped my father's sergeant-at-arms. It was weird to be somewhere so long without him scowling at me from the shadows.

Saint: *all ok?*

Cam: *yup. are you?*

Saint: *taking care of business*

Cam: *nash updated me. you got more?*

Saint: *maybe. talk when I see u*

Cam: *when?*

Saint: *couple of days. got more wings to clip first*

I rolled my eyes. It made sense to reduce the Crows' capacity for launching attacks on us—we should've done it years ago—but if we were right about them working for someone far bigger, we were wasting time and resources squashing flies. And taking risks that made my stomach churn. If whoever was sending snipers to biker brawls came looking for their man and didn't find me, they'd kill a brother instead. Rubi, Nash.

Saint.

My capacity for doing nothing expired.

I rose from the bed.

Alexei appeared from nowhere and pushed me back down. "No."

"You don't even know what the fuck you're saying that for."

"I don't need to. The fire in your eyes is enough."

I was taller than him, wider, but strength was a complex characteristic, and there was logic behind his intervention. I just didn't want to hear it. "I need to go back. I have responsibilities."

"You did not come here for me, then?" Alexei spoke with a smile that was hard to decipher.

I grappled with the loose threads I needed for even the vaguest explanation of the last few days and how I felt about it. "The fight with the other club. It was premeditated by both sides. Same old shit—we can batter the Crows in our sleep—but they brought a little extra this time. Some fucker with a gun tried to end me."

Alexei didn't blink. "Another assassination attempt?"

"Yup."

"What happened?"

"That's the other messed-up thing. A motherfucking *sniper* got him from the undergrowth. An arrow to the brain."

"An arrow?"

He looked amused, which lightened my mood a touch. I loved it when he laughed, even if it was at my expense.

"Yeah, some Robin Hood shit, like I need another maniac to worry about."

"Maniac implies that person was not of their right mind, but they have killed a man undetected, by you or anyone else close enough to hear a gunshot. Unless, of course, you know the identity of this . . . crazed folklore legend."

I shook my head, grounding myself in the fact that his hands still gripped my shoulders. "I have no fucking clue. The list of people who might want me dead is much longer than the one of would-be heroes."

"Were your brothers all accounted for at the time?"

"You think it was an inside job?" I gave him a sharp look, hating that it wasn't the first time such a thing had been suggested to me recently.

Alexei shrugged. "I do not know your club. Only that beloved leaders often have the worst enemies. Love and hate, no?"

"Saint wants me to stay here a few days."

"Under my protection?" Alexei's speculative frown turned to a soft smirk that made my blood rush south. "That is very trusting of him when we have never been formally introduced."

"I'm not his fucking wife."

Alexei licked his lips, leering just enough to send another bolt of heat to my veins. "But you are his *fucking* something. I just do not know what yet, and perhaps you don't either."

"That's off-topic."

"But it is more fun to think about than some fool trying to kill you."

"Fool?"

Alexei's gaze bored into me, sucking me into a place that made my head spin and my pulse race. "Yes, Cam. They are a fool."

[16]

ALEXEI

Cam stayed with me for three days. We didn't talk much more about the reasons why, but they were never far from my mind.

Or his. He was a man in high demand. Despite laying low, his phone buzzed and beeped with little respite. I wondered how it was to have so many people so eager to talk to you. Being a lone wolf suited me as much now as it had when survival had depended on it, but I couldn't deny Cam's lifestyle fascinated me.

And irritated me. The man I'd killed hadn't acted alone, and contemplating when Cam's enemies would strike next kept me awake while he slept beside me, crashed out on his stomach, one arm flung over me as if he was scared he'd wake up alone.

He did not wake up alone. I liked being in bed with Cam. When we weren't fucking, I watched him while he watched TV, and he seemed to like tracing patterns on my bare skin. The bruises beneath his tattoos began to fade, and the fatigue he'd arrived with eased a little.

I couldn't define what we had become.

All I knew for certain was that letting him leave was more painful than I had prepared for.

"You do not like my cooking?" I stood with one shoulder propped on the hallway wall, watching him put on boots that did not belong to him.

He shot a smirk over his shoulder. "Do you?"

"Yours is better." My biker boy was domesticated beyond my wildest dreams. His mother had raised a man. "Perhaps you should stay for the entertainment instead."

"You don't want me to go? I thought you might want your space back, considering I never really asked you if I could stay in the first place."

"Saint didn't ask me either."

"You want him to?" Cam stood and came to me. His gaze was penetrating and I didn't mind. He had seen me in pieces on my kitchen floor. Emotionally, I didn't have much left to hide from him. "He'd be here in a heartbeat if I called."

"No doubt."

Cam cocked a thick, dark brow. "You bring him up a lot. Should I be worried about that?"

"Are you?" We had been dancing around his feelings for Saint a while now, but this was something different. "Remember I have never met this man."

"Do you want to?"

I didn't have an immediate answer to that question—not in the way he'd asked it. Whether either of them knew it or not yet, Saint was my ally. We shared a common cause. Anything else could wait. And if it transpired that Cam was in love with him?

Hmm. It was a pretty picture I didn't dislike.

Cam sighed. "You're so fucking complicated, you know that?"

I straightened from my slouch against the wall and stepped into my current favourite place on earth: the cage of his strong arms around me. "Things are only complicated if you allow them to be. It is easier sometimes to be honest."

The irony. And Cam felt it too. He closed his eyes, laying his forehead against mine. "I don't know when I'll be back, but I'll call you, okay?"

I said nothing. What was the point? He had to go and he'd call. It was the hand we'd been dealt.

"Lexi?"

"Hmm?"

Cam opened his eyes, fixing me with a dark stare swimming with too many emotions to count. "Be safe, okay? I don't think anyone tailed me here, but I can't be certain and it would fucking break me if anything happened to you."

"Nothing's going to happen to me."

Cam gripped my chin with rough fingers. "You don't know my world as well as you think you do."

You don't know mine. "I will be careful if it makes you happy."

He growled and I could tell he wanted to say more, but he was already running late for the brother meeting him close to his bike.

Cam kissed me, hard and claiming, and then softer, reminding me that there was far more to this man than the alpha wolf he was becoming to step out into the world again. He was good and kind. Gentle. I didn't know much of his story, but even without the claim he'd staked on my heart, he didn't deserve to die.

He *would not* die.

I pulled back. "Goodbye, Cam."

His answering smile was wistfully sweet. "Bye, Lexi."

The door closed behind him, and though he'd likely stepped straight into the lift, my brain played the soundtrack of his footsteps fading on an imaginary staircase.

Irritated, I retreated to the work I'd abandoned in the kitchen, but I couldn't digest the information on the screen. The figures swam and I felt nothing but rage.

I was scared to dissect the painful squeeze in my chest. I did not have time for it if I was going to help Cam.

Resolved, I shut my laptop and moved to the bedroom to change out of the shirt and trousers I'd only put on to tease him. I left them on the floor. Regretted it and scooped them up, folding them away in the walk-in wardrobe Cam claimed was as big as his bathroom.

Dressed all in black, I left the penthouse and retrieved my car, though the energy in my veins screamed out for my bike. The wind in my face, the freezing winter rain making the roads dangerous enough to calm me down. Was that how Cam felt when he rode his stripped-back Harley? Perhaps we had more in common than we'd ever imagined when we'd set eyes on each other that hedonistic first night.

I steered my car out of the underground car park beneath my building and took a deliberate and direct route from Bristol to Devon, circling around Whitness before heading east to the Dog Crows' compound.

Close to the clubhouse, I plucked the tracking device from my wheel arch and ditched my car, picking my way through the undergrowth on foot until I came to the perimeter fence.

The security was even easier to bypass than the Rebel Kings' HQ. I let myself into the compound and slid into the shadows, creeping into the room that housed their loft access.

I climbed into the rafters of the old building and found my way to the air vents above the room where the officers held their meetings. It was comically easy to insert a listening device and connect it to the software on my phone. So easy, I didn't stick around to eavesdrop with my own ears. I crept back to the loft hatch, dropped silently to the floor, and ghosted back to the fence.

It was as I'd left it, open and exposed. I rolled it back into place and ducked into the undergrowth, anticipation building in my veins as I neared my car, the tracking device a beacon in my pocket.

My car came into view.

Predictably, Saint Malone was crouched on the bonnet.

Cam was the most beautiful man I'd ever laid eyes on, but there was something captivating about his wingman. With his chestnut hair and piercing gaze, he was disarming, even with a fierce scowl marring his handsome face.

Saint sprang from my car as I approached, hands balled at his sides. I didn't get the sense he wanted to fight me, but he was angry about something, and I couldn't blame him. After all, a man had come a split second from putting a bullet in Cam's heart.

I was angry too.

Incandescent.

I stopped in front of him, letting my feelings show on my

face and match his so he knew we were on the same page, though for him, context was still lacking. "Have I kept you waiting long?"

Saint's eyes narrowed a touch. "Makes sense."

"What does?"

"You knew I was coming."

He paused, giving weight to my suspicion that he was the brother who struggled to get his words out, and I waited. I was in no hurry.

While a battle raged within him, I stepped closer, pondering if he was familiar enough with Cam's scent to smell him on my skin. Then I remembered we weren't wolves, and yet the proximity of Saint Malone made me feel like one. I leaned into him, noting he had the same smoke and oil smell to him that Cam carried, but there was something else too—something herbal that made me want to take a deep, cleansing lungful of him and exorcise my soul.

"You reeled me in." Saint broke into my musings. "You knew I was tracking you."

I nodded. "I have known since you placed the device at Cam's home."

"Did you tell him?"

"What do you think?"

"I think he trusts you." Saint pulled a cigarette pack from his inside pocket and offered it to me.

Tempting, but I wasn't anywhere near stressed enough to indulge. I wasn't stressed at all. I watched him light up and contemplated Cam's steely resolve to not have this man in his bed. It was a mark of his commitment to the club because Saint Malone was enchanting. "Do you think he is mistaken?" I propped my hip on the car. "To trust me, I mean."

Saint took a deep drag of his cigarette and held the smoke in before exhaling through his nose. "We know nothing about you."

We. Did he mean the club? Or just him and Cam? "What do you want to know?"

"Your name."

"Alexei."

"Not Teddy?"

I smirked. "No."

"Good."

"Good? Why is that?"

"It never suited you. I've been calling you Ghost in my head since I saw you in Cam's office."

A shudder passed through me, the subtle kind that was all on the inside, like demons dancing in my soul. "You are a perceptive man, but you cannot know everything on instinct. You haven't asked why I'm here." I inclined my head towards the Crows' compound behind me. "But you don't think I'm with them or you'd have reacted by now."

Saint took a breath but said nothing, and I let him be for a moment, giving him space to gather what he wanted to say. It was unwise to linger here for long, but for Saint Malone, I got the feeling I'd wait as long as it took.

Cam's waited years.

But for what? Did they love each other beyond their brotherhood? Logic told me I didn't know Cam enough to make that call, but my gut told me something else: that what I'd seen so far barely scratched the surface, and that the prospect of more . . . excited me.

Is one beautiful biker not enough for you?

Cam was enough. Of course he was. But he wasn't mine. And he wasn't Saint's, and everything about that felt wrong.

Saint cleared his throat. "You're not working with the Crows. It ain't your style."

"How do you know that?"

"Am I wrong?"

"You are not wrong." I threw a disdainful glance at the compound. "They are rats, no? Collateral damage for whoever wants to kill Cam."

"So you do know about that?"

"I do."

"Pillow talk?"

"Perhaps."

Saint's gaze flickered. He crushed his cigarette beneath his boot, then scooped it up and tucked it into a small plastic bag in his pocket.

I smiled. "Covering your tracks?"

"From the Crows?" He snorted. "They couldn't trail a fucking fire engine."

"What about whoever they're working for?"

Saint fiddled with the zip on his coat. He wasn't wearing club colours and his tall frame was clad in dark-wash jeans, a black T-shirt, and a battered riding jacket. "Let them find me. Then I'd have some clue who they were."

"You do not think it is the construction cartel you have upset?"

"Not directly. How much do you know about that?"

"Why do you want to know?"

"Because I need to know if I'm right before this goes much further."

I considered that he'd chosen to have this complicated conversation rather than fight me. It said a lot about his gut instinct, given that it was obvious fighting came much easier to him. *We are on the same side.* And he almost knew it. "Cam told me things are difficult with them right now. He did not elaborate on your precise business with them, and I didn't ask. It is irrelevant to me."

"Why?"

A lock of Saint's hair fell into his face.

An absurd urge to push it back made my hands twitch. "I am already aware of the Sambini operation. You are useful to them, yes?"

Saint grunted and lit another cigarette, a habit he shared with Cam. "When it suits them. They've cut us out of shit before. Now they've got beef with us because we want to walk away."

"All of you? Or just Cam?"

"We voted on it. It passed."

These sweet biker boys and their democracy. "What happens at your sacred table doesn't matter on the street or in dark corners where discontented soldiers whisper. Strip this back: construction rackets are a dying institution. Building regulations have become too rigorous for low-grade work to slip through, so these organisations must find new income."

"They already move blow. We ain't supposed to know it's them, but we do."

"And you don't care? Even if it's on your turf?"

"Cam ain't interested in hard product. He wants to move away from that too, so we're letting it go, bit by bit, unless they piss us off enough to nick it off them."

"That is the game."

208

I spoke to myself as much as Saint, but he nodded and finished his second smoke, again, ashing the butt and tucking it away.

He caught me staring. "So the birds don't eat it."

Okay. "Cam also told me about the fight and the interloper with the gun."

Saint straightened, looming over me in a way that would've annoyed me with anyone that wasn't Cam. "Did he tell you what happened next?"

"Yes."

"Did it surprise you?"

Lying came easy to me. It was a way of life when you lived in the shadows. But lying to Saint Malone was harder than I expected. The words stuck in my throat, and for a brief moment, I once again understood what it was like to be him. "It did not surprise me."

Saint nodded. "That makes sense too. What I can't work out is why you haven't told him."

"What do you think would happen if I did?"

"Honestly?"

"Or you could tell me untruths and waste our time."

Saint's stare intensified, his frown growing deeper. "I think he cares about you enough to worry you'd get hurt. He'd want to protect you as much as you want to protect him, and—"

"It would be a distraction," I finished for him. "That could get him killed as much as an unimpeded bullet."

Saint hummed his agreement and we reached that magical place where our motivations aligned. Emotions were complex beasts that did not need to be defined to wreak havoc, but in this case, our shared affection for Cam gave us a common goal: to protect him at all costs. I'd known before this day that Saint would die for Cam, but if we worked together, perhaps he wouldn't have to.

My phone buzzed in my pocket. I retrieved it and swiped the screen, opening the listening software linked to the device in the Crows' loft.

I made no effort to hide it from Saint and he took the bait, moving so he could peer over my shoulder.

"Who are you listening to?"

"Not here." I jerked my head at my car. "Follow me."

He nodded and stepped away to head back to wherever he'd hidden his bike. He was a heartbeat away from the undergrowth when I called his name.

Saint turned around. The rain had cleared while we'd talked and winter sunshine dappled his face. "Yeah?"

I opened my car door and rested my elbows on top. "You have not asked me why I am doing this."

Saint fixed his gaze on me, taking me hostage with his forest-green gaze. "I know what it's like to see him for the first time and know you'll never be the same again. That pain in your face when you talk about him? I see it every time I look in the goddamn mirror."

He melted away before I could respond.

CAM

I found Rubi asleep in the clubhouse bar, stretched out on the couch often used by brothers to get a blowjob in a quiet corner, his arm flung over his eyes.

Before he'd taken a scaffold pipe to the skull, I might've kicked him awake, but I settled for ducking behind the bar and slipping into the wash-up area to boil the kettle for tea.

He hadn't moved a muscle when I came back. I put the tea on a nearby table and shook him, careful not to jostle him too much. I already knew he wasn't going to admit to having the mother of all headaches, but he didn't have to. Orla had updated me the moment I'd got off my bike.

Rubi groaned and his arm fell away. He blinked awake and frowned when he registered it was me. "Fuck." He scrambled upright, ignoring my outstretched arm. "You're back."

"I was never gone."

"Yeah, yeah. I was starting to think Saint had offed you and buried the body in the woods."

"Nice. So you'd have left me for the worms if he had?"

"Of course. You don't wanna be cremated. I remember that shit from when we were kids."

Nostalgia flooded my heart. Me and Rubes had grown up in the club. In many ways, we were as close as blood brothers. But then, in others, we weren't. Rubi knew my history better than anyone because it was his history too, but he didn't know the things that kept me up at night and made my heart beat too fast. I'd never told him and he'd never asked.

I watched him rub his temples. "Are they getting better?"

"What?"

"The headaches." I handed him the tea. "I need you, brother, but nothing that can't wait if you need more time. You just gotta tell me."

"I'm fine."

"Fuck off."

Rubi sipped scalding tea and gave me his middle finger.

I rolled my eyes and dropped a Vicodin from the stash Alexei had given me into his free palm. "Take this and sleep it off in my bed. Then find me tonight. I got a job for you. Or at least some trouble that'll keep you out of trouble."

Faint humour flared in Rubi's gaze, but he kept it to himself, giving me a sour look instead. "If it ain't riding my bike some place to get laid, I'm not interested."

"How about if you take the van and stop by my brother's place on the way? That sway you?"

"Your brother isn't trouble."

"Not for you."

Rubi snorted. "He doesn't give you shit either. If you left him alone, he'd be sweet as a nut."

That Rubi was so certain of that added weight to the suspicion I'd carried for a couple of years now—that it wasn't familial emotions that kept Riv from walking out of my life completely. But whatever. I wasn't going to leave my brother alone. He could fight me as much as he liked. I'd still love him forever. "I need you to go to Porth Luck and take a ride out on a boat to where the Sambini shipment is coming in. See if there's anything waiting to hitch a lift for the return journey."

"You want me to go fishing?" Rubi sighed. "Isn't that a job for a prospect?"

"It's a job for someone I trust and Saint gets seasick."

"Does he balls. I've seen him move a cadaver that's been there—"

"Shut the fuck up." I held my hand up, not in the mood to contemplate all the horrible shit Saint had done for the club. "Just take the van, okay? Talk to Sol Bosanko. He'll give you grief about it, but he'd rather we brought weed through Porth Luck than anything and anyone else."

Rubi grunted and I took it as acquiescence. I left him to take his medicine and another nap and retreated to the chapel, grateful to find it empty. The slow cooker had been cleaned in my absence. I filled it up, then took up my favourite brooding spot at the table.

I set my phone in front of me, craving a hit of Alexei's sardonic voice in my ear, but I had shit to do before I could give into the reality that I missed that motherfucker already. Mateo. Embry. Saint. Even Cracker required my attention.

My stomach churned as I contemplated encountering Cracker for the first time since I'd choked him out, a putrid swirl of the worst emotions: malice, anger.

Hate.

That was the worst one. I'd been born with my hands curled into fists, boxing for fun long before I realised I was destined to fight my whole damn life. But hating a man—even one as toxic and irritating as old man Cracker—fucked with my conscience. *"Is that what you'd like to do, Cam? Build houses with your bare hands?"*

Yeah. Maybe it was.

Fuck it. I gave in and dialled Alexei, but my call went unanswered and I forced myself not to send a follow up text. Alexei had already seen right through me, but I was in the business of kidding myself that I hadn't come to need his unpredictable presence in my life as much as I needed fucking air.

Saint was next on my list. He didn't answer either—his phone didn't even ring. The only fucker I could get hold of was Embry and he appeared in the chapel ten minutes later.

"Welcome back, brother."

I glanced up from the text message I was definitely not tapping out to Alexei. "I was never gone."

Embry chuckled, sharing his warmth with me in a one-armed fraternal embrace. "Whatever. It's good to see you. How are you doing?"

"Same old."

"Around here? You'll have to do better than that."

I grunted and pushed my phone away, the message I couldn't quite articulate half-written and unsent. "I'm good. Caught up on some sleep and let my ribs rest. Happy?"

"If you are."

"I'm ecstatic," I retorted.

Grinning, Embry produced a steaming mug of coffee from behind his back. He set it on the table in front of me and dropped into the seat that Saint occupied when he was around.

"Have you seen him?" I jerked my head at the battered chair. "He's not answering his phone."

Embry kicked back with a yawn. "He hasn't been about since you left. Actually, I thought he might have gone with you."

"Nope."

"Shame."

"Is it?" I glowered, hoping Embry got the message to leave it the fuck alone, but my chaplain had other ideas, and I was starting to wonder if there was anyone who hadn't noticed the spark between me and Saint. And how the *hell* it was that my obsession with Alexei had breathed new life into feelings I'd smothered for too many goddamn years to count.

"It's a shame," Embry broke into my thoughts. "For both of you, but it's him I was thinking of. If he wasn't with you, then he's been out there this whole time chasing down enemies we don't even know we have yet. Not eating. Not sleeping. It gets to him when you're in danger, you know it does."

I did. And I felt like shit about it. One of my favourite things on this earth was Saint's rare laugh. It had been too long since I'd last heard it.

"I hear you," I said to Embry. "But I need him out there right now. I can't figure this out on my own."

Embry said nothing, but the weight of his worries for Saint, for me, for all our brothers, weighed heavily on his shoulders. He looked tired, as if he'd spent the last few days fretting up a storm. *This needs to end.* But how? If Rubi discovered the Sambinis were already trafficking girls through our turf . . . fuck. This tit-for-tat bullshit was about to go postal and there were no guarantees we'd win.

215

The unpleasant wrench in my gut expanded, sending ice to my veins. I thought about Alexei and what his father had done to him. Then I thought of my dad and the price he'd paid for the war I was still fighting. I owed it to them both to shut this shit down, but I had no fucking clue how to do it.

"Boss?"

I opened my eyes. Embry was gone and Mateo had caught me ruminating myself into a nap. "The fuck have you been?"

"Might ask you the same thing. I came by your house last night. Shack up with some bird, did ya?"

"Nope." I gave Mateo a steady look. I trusted my enforcer with my life, but he was as untamed as Saint was terminally wild. I didn't tell him much that I didn't have to. "When are you heading out for your delivery?"

"In a few hours. Do you need me for anything else first?"

"Nah, but remember what we talked about. I need that money in the bank STAT, so we can't afford any fuck-ups tonight."

"Got it."

Mateo made himself a sandwich, then left to do whatever he did with his time when he wasn't hawking cannabis or threatening Crows with his blowtorch.

The quiet enveloped me. Hours passed as my brain ticked over. It was dark when I picked up my phone for no reason at all, and it rang in my hand at the same moment Saint appeared in the doorway.

Alexei's name flashed up on the screen, and my gaze darted to Saint and back a thousand times before he crossed the room and took the phone from my clenched fingers. He answered the call and gave it back before I could react to what the ever-loving fuck he thought he was doing. "Take it. I can wait."

I shot him a *what the hell* glare.

Saint shrugged and strode to the door again.

"Wait. I mean, don't disappear, okay?"

"Yes, boss."

He fucked off anyway.

I sighed and brought the phone to my ear. "Hey."

"Hello."

"Sorry about that. I was trying to pin Saint down."

"Was it fun?"

"No."

"Hmm. I think maybe you should change your approach."

"Did you call just to wind me up about him?"

"I did not call for anything. I am returning *your* call."

Fuck. What was it about the two of them that turned my brain upside down? I wanted to bang my head on the table.

I wanted to bang *him*.

Alexei.

And Saint.

Fuck.

"Are you okay?"

Alexei spoke quietly and without the dry amusement that seemed to colour most of his vernacular when it came to me.

"Yeah."

"Are you sure?"

"Yeah—actually, no. But it's nothing you can help me with right now."

"You would be surprised how helpful I can be."

"I don't doubt that."

"Oh, but you do." The sound of a tapping keyboard filtered down the line. I pictured Alexei at his kitchen counter, bottom lip caught in his teeth as he frowned at his laptop screen and bantered in French to old ladies in Paris about their pension woes. At least, that was what he'd told me he was doing.

For all I knew, he was speaking Greek and plotting my death.

Or Italian. And there it was, the truth in his playful accusation that away from the bubble we'd found in the bedroom, I still didn't trust him and he fucking knew it.

"As fun as this is," Alexei said, "I am busy. You call me again when you have something to say, no?"

"Do you want me to?"

A pause stretched out between us. Loaded. Heavy. And devoid of the magic I felt when I'd stretched out beside him in his bed and slept.

Then Alexei sighed. "I will always want you."

And of course he hung up.

I closed my eyes. When I opened them again, Saint was in front of me, his stare more intense than I could take. "*What?*"

Nothing. It was as predictable as Alexei hanging up on me and the prickle of emotion that ran through me was the same.

I stood, getting up in his face. For weeks now, I'd been so entranced by Alexei that I'd forgotten how Saint's close proximity could make my knees weak if I didn't lock them and grit down on how crazy he made me feel.

My guard was compromised. I took a lungful of him, and the dizzying impact propelled me forward.

I backed him against the wall, pressing my chest against his. He felt different to Alexei—harder, bigger, and nothing like the dudes I'd forced myself to be attracted to since Saint had scowled his way into my orbit all those years ago—but fuck, I liked it.

I love it. "Take a breath," I growled. "If you've got something to say, get it out before my head fucking explodes."

Saint swallowed, the panic I hated so much dancing in his eyes as he fought to gather his words enough to form a sentence. His chest rose and fell too fast, like Alexei's had the night I'd found him crouching on his kitchen floor like a cornered animal. And like that night, all I wanted for Saint was to make it better. To let him know I'd take his pain a thousand times if it meant he didn't have to.

So tell him, Alexei whispered in my brain, and I glared harder. *Why?* What did it matter to him what went down between me and Saint?

It didn't make any fucking sense.

"Cam."

I blinked as Saint uttered my name. His voice was rougher than Alexei's and raked over my soul like gravel. I pressed against him harder and my gaze fell to his lips.

The chapel was suddenly airless and hot. I licked my own dry lips and took a breath that went nowhere. Alexei's voice came again in my head and I wanted to fucking scream. *No. I want you. I can't want him. I fucking can't.*

But I did. So much. And I knew Saint wanted me too. I felt it in every inch of him that touched me, from his denim-clad thighs to his ripped abs to his tattooed chest. His hair was a warmer colour than Alexei's and it had a dishevelled wave that made him look as if he'd ridden the cliff paths with no helmet, even on the rare occasions he made an effort to tame it.

He hadn't made that effort now. With his desperate gaze, he was as wild as I'd ever seen him, and for reasons I still couldn't accept, instinct drew me impossibly closer to him.

He smelled of cigarettes and the forest where he'd been left as a baby. "Saint—"

A phone rang.

Alexei.

But it wasn't my phone. It was Saint's, a man I knew to ignore ninety per cent of his calls.

He jerked to snatch this one from his pocket, breaking the mad haze that had descended over me.

I backed off, sucking in a much-needed breath, and half staggered to my chair.

Saint answered the call with a low grunt, his eyes on me, unreadable, but full of the fire I'd lit beneath us. He listened to whoever was on the line and I saw the instant that something changed—that whatever had just happened between us was obliterated by what he was hearing in his ear.

He hung up.

I stood, battle ready. "What is it?"

"Sambini shipment. It's coming in tonight and intel from the Crows says there's a truck of girls on its way to meet it."

It didn't surprise me. I'd dispatched Rubi because of the suspicion crawling in my gut. But being right hit hard. I wanted to puke. And I wanted to *kill* the motherfuckers responsible. My dad had died to stop this. I couldn't let it happen on my watch.

"We need to move." I picked up my phone, already calling Nash. "Call Mateo. Tell him he'll have to handle his business with the prospects. I need every other brother with me."

Saint nodded, still eyeing me, though the heat had morphed into something different.

He made his calls, I made mine. Then we stared at each other, my pulse thudding as his chest heaved. I had so much I needed to say to him. So many things I'd swallowed down but being with Alexei had somehow forced to the surface. I didn't understand it—it made no fucking sense—but I couldn't ignore it. Goddamn, it was burning me up inside. "Saint—"

"No, brother." He shook his head. "Not now. Keep your head. This is gonna get nasty."

He was right and I knew it. I closed my eyes. Let myself think of Alexei, just for a moment. Of his shrewd, all-seeing gaze and sardonic smirk. Of the gentle way he touched me when his guard was down.

How he kissed me like I was the air to his fucking lungs. *I miss him.*

I opened my eyes. Saint had moved. He was right in front of me, shutting down the way we all had to if we were gonna survive this night.

No.

Not yet.

I gripped his chin hard, then slid my hand along his jaw to cup the nape of his neck. "This ain't over."

He shivered. "I know."

We mobilised at lightning speed, a well-oiled machine, even without Mateo barking orders and growling bloody murder at anyone too slow to the mark.

Saint was a different battle commander. He doled out weapons in silence. Kept everyone else quiet with his smouldering glare. But he scared me just as much when he was like this and I loved him for it.

In plain clothes, we commandeered the vans we used when we needed to move en-masse and undetected and headed south to the coast of Porth Luck, a Cornish fishing town with historical links to the underworld. Club activity on the streets there had dwindled since River spat fire at me any time any brother who wasn't Rubi passed through, but the surrounding waters had different rules—rules the Kings had lost control of when we'd signed on to provide materials and labour for Sambinis' motorway contracts.

It was a cold fact that every branch of bullshit we were dealing with now could've been avoided if we'd walked away back then. *Cracker, you cunt. Is this what you wanted?* I scowled at the back of his head as the van we were both in rumbled along the road to the Cornish coast. Nash was driving—he liked to be busy—and Saint and Embry flanked me as we rattled around the back of the van. Still glaring, I nudged Saint. "Did you reach Rubi?"

"Yeah."

"You're gonna have to give me more than that," I snapped. "The fuck is he?"

"On his way."

Impatience ate me up inside. Or maybe it was something else. Despite my best efforts, I was still so hot for him. For

Alexei. For them both, and my imagination was having a fucking rave.

Get your head in the game.

I resumed my staredown with the back of Cracker's skull while Saint found his words—or didn't—and left me to stew. I had to believe he'd let me know if Rubi was anywhere other than where he was supposed to be. I had to trust him, and I did. But I still wanted to fucking shake him.

You're an arsehole.

Another cold fact. In the darkness of the cramped van, I found Saint's forearm with one hand while reaching for my phone with the other. I wrapped my fingers around leather-clad flesh and bone and sent Alexei a text.

Cam: *heading out to handle some business. Can I see u after?*

Alexei: *Yes.*

Still clutching Saint, I took a deep, cleansing breath. Alexei's one-word answer was all I needed and I let the promise of being close to him whenever this was done wash over me, finding strength in it as if he was the fucking Messiah, only he wasn't for the masses; he was all mine.

"Cam." Saint murmured my name. He took my hand from his arm and squeezed my fingers, the pressure fleeting and beautiful. "We're here."

My faculties locked into place. I put my phone away as we pulled into a lay-by close to the port where our contact kept his small fishing boat. The van doors opened and Rubi was waiting, grim-faced and pissed off. "Sol ain't playing ball. Reckons it isn't on him to police this and he doesn't want any of us on his boat."

I set my jaw. "Tell him I don't give a shit."

"I did. Then I left him to think about it, but he fucked off with your brother and I don't know if he's coming back."

"You let him leave?" I stepped up to my oldest friend, getting up in his face. "To go where?"

"They didn't say."

"What did my *brother* say?"

"Nothing."

"Sure about that?"

Anger, coloured with hurt, flickered in Rubi's gaze. But there was something else too, a defiance that let me know he was perilously close to falling off a precipice we wouldn't come back from. "I wouldn't lie to you, Pres. Not even for him."

Not even for him. I'd heard variants of that phrase too much recently. "Call River. Tell him to bring Sol back where we need him so we can get this shit done."

Rubi made the call and I watched a piece of him die as he put the club before his undisclosed feelings for my baby brother. *Tell me you love him.* But it wasn't the time, and perhaps it never would be.

Sol Bosanko agreed to meet us in the quiet cove where he kept his boat. I took Saint with me, leaving Nash with the others, and we descended the cliff path in silence, picking our way down the unlit stone steps. In the distance, the town danced with life, but this spot was dark, dangerous, and inaccessible enough that only fishermen and smugglers ever bothered to try.

By the water, our friendly fisherman waited beside his small boat. "You're a dickhead, O'Brian. I don't want anything to do with this shit."

I stepped onto Sol Bosanko's boat, ignoring both him and the fact that I'd fucked him ten years ago.

Saint followed, stone-faced, as if he wasn't going to puke his guts up the second we hit open water, and joined me at the bow. "We're just gonna stalk any random boat we come across, boss? Or you got an actual plan?"

"Now he speaks." I waited for Sol to come aboard, then faced them both. "Sambinis use trawlers for muling, then bring their shit ashore in loud-as-hell speedboats because they're fucking idiots. All we have to do is find the trawlers surrounded by dickmobile boats and we're golden, right, Sol?"

Sol rolled his eyes. "I know this coast better than any other fucker, with or without lights, but that doesn't mean I'm down for this bullshit. I already told Rubi to go fuck himself."

"You wanna fuck little girls?"

Sol blinked. "What?"

"Because that's what they're bringing to the rocks to load onto those boats and send across the Atlantic." I lit two cigarettes and passed one to Saint. "And if they get away with it this time, they'll do it again and again and again. I get that you think I'm the fucking devil, but we move a bit of weed, some blow when it falls our way. These pricks? They don't give a shit, so better the cunt you know."

Sol looked like he wanted to die, and I didn't blame him. He was a good-hearted dude who didn't deserve to be caught up in this and I liked him a lot, but I didn't have time to make him feel better.

I pointed to the black horizon. "This is your ocean. Help us clean it up."

We set off into the night with a vague idea of where to look, trusting Sol to keep our approach hidden.

"You're lucky I was a pirate in a former life," he grumbled.

I snorted, but my focus was on Saint. To anyone else he was stoic as hell, but I knew him well enough to spot the tension in his set jaw and the death grip he had on the side of the small boat. Being brave wasn't about not being afraid. It was about facing your fears head-on, and Saint was doing that right now, like he had a thousand times for the club.

For me.

I spared Sol a glance. "Your dad smuggled contraband cigs for years and I know he taught you all about it, so don't pretend you're an angel."

"Never said I was. You saw to that, back in the day."

He wasn't flirting with me. We'd had a one-night stand so long ago I could barely remember it and he'd been young enough that he'd lived a lifetime since, but Saint glowered all the same. In the pitch black, Sol didn't notice. But I did. I saw everything about Saint when I had time to look.

Focus.

Sol steered the boat west for what felt like hours, scanning the horizon until he nudged me and extended his arm. "Look."

I followed his gaze. There were lights in the distance, but to my land-person's eyes, they could've been anything. "What is it?"

"Three boats close together: one big, two small. They're by a fishing post that isn't used in winter."

"Can you get us any closer?"

"Not without them hearing the engine, but if you're right

about what they're doing, I reckon I know where they'll come ashore."

"Is there somewhere we can wait?" Saint spoke for the first time since we'd left Porth Luck behind. He flicked a glance to Sol, then turned back to the lights in the distance. "Watch them land?"

"Only from the sea," Sol said. "By land, the cove is only accessible to one vehicle at a time and that's where they'll bring the truck."

I nodded, absorbing it all. "Can you take us there?"

"Do I have a choice?"

"We haven't put a gun to your head," Saint growled.

Sol rolled his eyes. "Whatever."

He turned the boat around and headed back inland, pointing us to a rocky shoreline that would've terrified me if I'd been in the hands of anyone else. But Sol had been born to these waters and he seemed almost bored as he navigated us to a cliff and told us to scale the wet rock to a centuries-old look-out point. "Ten foot up, there's a ledge. Follow the rock ladder and you can see the whole of Cursed Cove from there. But be careful. And stay close together. I don't want you fuckers getting pneumonia."

I smirked. "That's sweet."

"Yeah, yeah." Sol manoeuvred the boat closer to the jagged shore.

I braced myself to jump out, but Saint held me back. *Me first.*

We didn't have time to argue. I let him have his way, and he leapt out of the boat, landing like a cat on the rocks.

I followed and didn't break my neck, so there was that.

Sol's directions were laser accurate. We found the stone

ladder, carved into the rocks by an ancient Cornish family I'd never heard of, and climbed to a narrow ledge that gave fuck all shelter from the bitter wind but gifted us the bird's-eye view Sol had promised.

It was so cold that I'd have snuggled Cracker eventually, and the ledge was a small enough space that we didn't have much choice but to sit on top of each other.

Saint leaned into me, by design or to hide from the gale bearing down on us, I couldn't tell, but I wasn't complaining. His body heat was everything and I pressed tighter against him, greedy for the zip in my blood I'd become powerless to ignore, a familiar warmth I craved as much as I did the thrill of the unknown with Alexei. *We need to talk.* But my brain was too fried to compute which one of them I meant or conclude that it applied to them both.

Beside me, Saint shivered, and I fought a strange urge to put my arm around him. Deep down, my baddest boy was fragile and I hated that he suffered alone.

Like Alexei. My gaze slid to the horizon and I pictured him as a teenage kid, scared and alone in a fucking cage or some shit, at the mercy of whoever his deadbeat father had lost him to. A violent shudder rattled me, laced with a bone-deep fury. I couldn't put right what had happened to him, but I—*we*—could stop it happening to the girls in that truck.

"You think he'll wait for us?"

I snapped my gaze to Saint, for a heart-stopping moment still so stuck in my thoughts that I thought he meant Alexei. "What?"

"Captain Blackbeard."

Sol. I shook my head to clear it, then corrected myself. "He'll wait. He's a mouthy fuck, but loyal."

"To you?"

"To the sea. If it was us smuggling skin, he'd let us drown."

Saint hummed, deep and low. It rumbled through him and into me, and how close we were hit home all over again, reminding me of when we'd first met all those years ago. That night had smelled of the ocean too, but the memory hurt. Only thinking about Alexei made it stop, and the fucked-up circle was complete. I wanted them both in ways that were fucking impossible and the realist haunting my heart knew that I'd end up how I'd always been: alone and yearning for someone I'd never have.

A shaky sigh slipped out of me.

Perhaps mistaking it for a shiver, Saint pressed tighter against me, and this time I couldn't fight the impulse to touch him.

I snaked an arm around his waist, slipping my fingers beneath the leather and cotton concealing his body.

My cold fingers found warm skin. I rubbed a slow circle into the flesh above his hip bone. He made a tortured sound and, for a fleeting, precious moment, dropped his head to rest on my shoulder.

[18]

ALEXEI

The Rebel Kings' compound was deserted. Dozens of bikes were parked outside, but the bar was closed, and aside from a couple of unpatched prospects and old men too past it to ride, there wasn't a brother in sight.

I disabled their cameras remotely and slipped inside, enabling them again only when I was upstairs where the bedrooms were.

The door to Cam's room was closed. Instinct led me there to wait for him, but terminal curiosity drew me past it and to the other rooms on the landing.

I found the enforcer's den first. A dart board embedded with hunting knives gave it away, though I appreciated the fact that it was clean and smelled of the abandoned mug of lemon tea on the bedside table.

A stray hooded sweatshirt was out of place on the floor. I crouched and hooked it with one finger. It was too small for the burly enforcer, but too large to belong to a woman. *A lover or a brother?*

Maybe both. I wondered if Cam had deliberately

assembled a council of sexually fluid brothers or if it had happened by chance. I wasn't an expert on motorcycle clubs, but I knew criminal gangs better than I knew myself and the diversity in Cam's was . . . unusual.

I like it.

Of course I did. I was coming to learn I liked most things about Cam.

I retreated from the enforcer's room and examined the next. It was bland and belonged to no one in particular—a fuck den for the masses, though again, it was clean.

The rest of the rooms were much the same, save one that seemed best suited for Cam's vice president, the pretty man with the wavy blond hair. A guitar graced the corner of that room and a collection of family photographs that were absent from anywhere else.

There was no room I believed belonged to Saint. He did not live here, and I couldn't say why that mattered to me.

But it did.

I retreated to Cam's room, slipping inside and locking the door behind me out of habit rather than the fear that anyone but him would venture in. This was Cam's lair, I could tell. He didn't fuck people here—not even me.

Especially not me. But then, why would he when we had nicer beds elsewhere?

Stop thinking about fucking.

I sat on the edge of Cam's bed and retrieved my phone from my pocket. I'd called Saint from the same handset only Cam and my mother's nursing home possessed the number for. It had happened with little thought, but it puzzled me now. I could've called him from one of the burners I still kept with my weapons. Or the encrypted work phone that lay dormant on my desk at home. There'd been no logical reason to open myself to Saint like that, but I'd done it as if I'd felt the same primitive trust for him that I had Cam. *Something has happened to you since you met these men. It is making you weak.*

Undeniable. But while Cam was out there facing down a sex-trafficking ring, I didn't care to do anything about it. I'd told Cam I would be there for him when he was done, and I'd told Saint I would wait here for Cam to return.

And so I would, for however long it took.

Or not, as it turned out. Patience and I were old friends, but how I felt about Cam had altered my DNA. Barely an hour passed before his cool, dark bedroom closed in on me and I abandoned lounging on his bed in favour of pacing the floorboards, scowling at my blank phone screen.

I opened the window, listening out for the sound of approaching bikes. For hours, none came. The night remained quiet and still, and as the minutes ticked by, my agitation grew to the point where I could no longer stand it.

It was another engrained habit to delete my call records, but Saint Malone's phone number had embedded in my brain the moment he'd given it to me.

I typed a message to him. Deleted it and typed it again verbatim.

Alexei: *Where are you?*

I didn't expect a reply anytime soon, if at all. The answering buzz of my phone a few moments later caught me off guard.

Saint: *the intel was right. Waiting to hit the transport vehicle.*

I swallowed, my throat constricted as if blocked by tar. It

didn't surprise me that the intel from the listening device had proved accurate—it would be stupid even for the Crows to invent the scenario they'd described at their table for no purpose but their own amusement. It was no surprise either that Cam had chosen to act so decisively and so fast.

But I didn't like it. The missing pieces in his complex war should've scared him more than they did. *You cannot win against a face you cannot see.*

A man I hated and respected in equal measure had once said those words to me and they'd never made more sense than they did now.

I resent my original message.

Alexei: *Where are you?*

Saint replied with a location pin and I was outside before my phone had dissected it.

I left the Rebel Kings' compound as unseen as I'd arrived. My bike was hidden in bushes. I retrieved it and straddled the seat, gunning the powerful engine, absorbing the shock waves through my spread thighs as I studied the map on my phone screen.

The location Saint had sent me was an hour away. *Fuck.* My fingers tightened around the screen, fury filling me, merging with the rage I'd carried my whole life. And there was fear too. Cam was something to me I couldn't describe and I'd already seen him hurt. Had pressed my hands over his black-and-blue flesh as he'd grimaced in pain. I couldn't let that happen again. If it didn't kill him, it would kill me.

I memorised the route and pocketed my phone, then I revved the engine on my bike and peeled away, zipping through the night, eating up the miles with my cracked little heart beating a panicked tattoo in my chest.

At the Cornish border, my phone buzzed again, a blank message from Saint that did nothing to ease the tension banded around my gut. A pocket dial or a cry for help? Either made sense.

I followed the map to the location Saint had sent me: another abandoned campsite. It was deserted, but as I killed the engine and lifted the visor on my helmet, it was clear that I'd missed a messy fight. Blood stained the churned-up grass, and nearby, a wrecked refrigerator truck lay on its side, crude stinger wire caught in its tyres.

They hit the transportation run and took the cargo. It was the most positive outcome I could think of, and I weighed it against the odds that the Rebel Kings had come up against an enemy they hadn't prepared for.

I did not like where my imagination took me, and I fought the images that flooded my brain. *No. Cam is smarter than this. He would not lead his brothers into a massacre.*

In my head, I knew it to be true, but my heart told me there was something else that led Cam when it came to trafficking sex workers. I'd seen it in him when he'd caught me at my weakest—the pain, the empathy. Our stories from the past were different, but the beast that had made us men was the same.

I turned my back on the refrigerator truck. It was still hissing, the crumpled bonnet cracked open and heat seeping from it. The unpleasant kind of heat that made my skin itch. Crouching on the ground, I eyed a stray hammer, congealed blood and grass stuck to the claw. There were other weapons too, carelessly left behind. Foolishly. The location was remote enough that the noise from the crash and the brawl would not been heard, but someone would come across this place eventually, and it was crawling with evidence.

Clean it up. For Cam, yes. But what if it was his blood on the hammer? *Then I will find who wielded it and burn them alive.*

If Cam had been hurt, it was not much comfort, but I let the thought settle anyway. It fed the devil I'd once been, and I would need that one day.

I left the hammer where it was and returned to my bike, already planning the tracking software I would plant on Saint when I saw him again.

If you see him again. The blood on the hammer could be his.

Another band of fear wrapped around my chest. Cam had become everything to me, but I was oddly fond of the man who already owned a piece of his heart. Saint was intriguing. Alluring. More than that, he loved Cam, and Cam needed that—to be loved. And perhaps so did Saint.

Why do you care about Saint?

Cam's voice in my head was distracting, dulling the scrape of the urgency. I liked his voice. It was rough and gravelly, with a soft Irish twang that made me go weak at the knees when I let it—when I was already naked and vulnerable with nothing to lose. Did he know how deep he'd flayed me open? Sometimes he stared at me so hard I knew he had no idea.

Others, his soulful brown gaze saw every facet of me, even the parts I'd long forgotten about—

A twig snapped, crushed by a heavy, careless tread. I whipped around, high alert activated, and scanned my surroundings, already reaching for a weapon.

My fingers wrapped around a knife Cam's enforcer would have liked as three figures loomed out of the darkness.

Bikers.

Crows.

Amused, I let the knife go—the grass was messy enough—and faced them.

They sneered, sensing a weakness that was not there, and I let them surround me, taking note of the rudimentary pipes and bats they carried, no blades or guns.

A man I recognised as their sergeant-at-arms stepped forward, twice the man of Saint Malone in nothing but the size of his gut. "What do we have here? A Rebel bitch? Or a nosy motherfucker who's just made the worst mistake of his life?"

I leaned against my bike, one ankle crossed over the other, arms at my sides. I did not speak. Not yet. I had learned many years ago that silence was often the greatest weapon of all.

The sergeant ventured closer, his clothes and skin already marked and messy from another fight. A fight, as I stared him down, I was almost certain that had been lost. *They are seeking consolation.* Amusement and relief rippled through me. There were no guarantees that Cam and Saint were safe and unhurt, but these men had not fought them and won.

These men did not traffic those women across Europe either.

Like a cursed spell, my anxiety returned. My good humour faded and I stepped up to meet the fool about to invade my space.

Still, though, I did not speak, and my would-be assailant

smirked again. "You've picked the wrong place to pull over and stick your nose in. Not a copper, are you?"

"On that bike?" One of his friends laughed. "Police can't afford hardware like that. He's probably a stockbroker having a midlife crisis."

"Too young for that." The third biker moved into view. Frank Crow: a man who had inherited his club's presidency by birthright, not merit. He had a shrewder gaze than the first biker, though I'd hardly have called it intelligent. He darted a glance to my ride and back again, taking in the Yamaha and lack of weathered leather and ink. *He knows I'm not MC.* Good for him. He knew nothing else, and if this played out how I thought it would, that wouldn't change.

Frank Crow stopped at my side and his stench of stale beer, dirty clothes, and old sweat washed over me. "Did Sambini send you to help clear up this mess?"

I cocked my head to one side, letting a smirk of my own do the talking. *Think what you want. It will not change what will happen here tonight.*

Frustration leeched into Crow's bland expression. He walked around me, checking for weapons. Then he sighed. "We don't have time for games. If he was one of ours, he'd have said so. Stick him in the truck and burn it. Torch the grass too, and pick up any tools left behind. Then we gotta end O'Brian for good before he comes for us. I'm not losing any more brothers and money to this eastern European bullshit."

My smile widened. Without me speaking a word, Crow had revealed everything I needed to know. Everything *Cam* needed to know. And now it was me who didn't have time for games.

I moved fast, striking Frank Crow hard and true enough to kill him stone dead. The sergeant didn't have time to blink. I curved my arm around him and snapped his neck, letting him slither to the ground as I eyed the last man standing.

The beleaguered Crow stared back at me, Adam's apple bobbing as he swallowed, eyes stretched wide as he realised the horror he'd walked into when he'd followed his brothers back to this scene. "Fuck. Who are—fuck. Who are you?"

I smiled, sick and deadly, and spread my hands. "Whoever your president sold his soul to is about to find out."

[19]

CAM

It was a long night. Sol took us back to dry land at a speed fast enough to make Saint hurl; then we chased the truck of girls down mob-handed and did what had earned us the reputation of the toughest chapter of the Rebel Kings. Outnumbered and outgunned—literally—we fought with our bare hands and won.

Better than that, we'd survived mostly unscathed, even Rubi who was still punch drunk from the last time. Only Saint was, uncharacteristically, bleeding, a painful fact I had to ignore as I took it upon myself to slap fake plates on the van, drive it cross country to a wooded area behind the most remote police station I could think of, and unload the cargo we'd stolen: twelve girls, not one of them over eighteen.

Motherfuckers. My blood was boiling. I needed a hit of Alexei to calm me down, but as I drove back to Whitness, daring any Crow or Sambini to get in my way, my calls to him went unanswered.

At the compound, a prospect opened the gates for me. I drove the van straight into the garage and locked it down.

Saint waited for me outside, blood still oozing from his split eyebrow.

My fingers itched to wipe it away.

I lit a cigarette instead. "Where are we at?"

A deep frown creased Saint's beautiful face. "The Sambinis sent a crew to clear the scene. I saw fire and smoke."

"You say that like it's a bad thing. Saves us the trouble."

Saint plucked my cigarette from my fingers and brought it to his mouth. He took a long drag and fixed me with a gaze that was troubled enough to make me forget how good his lips looked as he exhaled.

I gripped his elbow and pulled him aside, out of earshot of anyone else. "What is it?"

He paused, but I didn't let my impatience get the better of me this time. I gave him a moment to breathe and let my fingers splay over his forearm, embracing the butterflies it let loose in my belly. *Lexi, what have you done to me?*

"They're still using Crows to do their dirty work," Saint said.

I knew that. I'd put Frank Crow on his arse myself tonight. Only facing down some Sambini fucker with a Glock had stopped me killing him. "You think they'll do a shit job?"

"I know they will. These pricks can't do anything right."

"So watch them," I said. "Slip in behind them and finish the job."

Saint nodded but didn't move.

Neither did I, and the heated tension we'd smothered for years expanded, reaching the parts of me where Alexei already waited.

Saint stepped closer, his breath whispering my skin with a soft murmur. "Have you heard from him?"

"Who?"

"The accountant."

"Why do you want to know?"

"You miss him."

I closed my eyes, unable to deny it.

Saint wrenched his arm free and grasped my shoulders, backing me further into the shadows. "Go to him."

I let the intensity of his gaze sink into me and churn me up inside. Alexei had claimed a piece of me I'd never given to anyone else. He'd seen me hungry, tired, and in pain. He'd seen my grief when I talked about my dad and my lost relationship with River. Christ, he'd seen me come so hard I'd fucking cried. But no one had ever looked at me the way Saint did. "I don't want to leave you," I said, because it was the truth. "Come with me."

Saint's brow twitched with the words he couldn't quite say. *And what? Wait outside while you fuck him?*

No. That wasn't what I wanted. I took his hands from my shoulders and crushed his fingers in mine. "*Come.*"

"I can't. I have fires to put out."

"I'll wait. We have church anyway."

"*No.*" He shook his head. "Go to him. I'll find you later if I can."

It was a shitty compromise, but we'd run out of time to play chicken in the dark. Voices came up on us. We broke apart and the spell shattered, jolting us back to reality.

I called church. One by one, my brothers filed in, even Mateo, who was spitting feathers that he'd had an uneventful night while the rest of us had spilled blood.

Despite being a heartbeat behind me, Saint was somehow last, drifting in, transfixed by his phone screen, which was a strange enough sight that Embry did a double take.

He pulled Saint's chair out for him. "Sit, brother."

Saint didn't look up.

Frowning, I pounded the gavel and thanked my brothers for their service. "It was a fucked-up night that I gave you no warning for. So thank you. It ain't over, but we got shit done, and I'm proud of that."

A murmur of agreement went round the table.

Cracker was silent. The fucker didn't have a scratch on him and I eyed him with barely concealed malevolence and made plans to talk to Embry. I needed eyes on this mofo and Saint was already stretched thin.

We debriefed the clusterfuck the night had become. Logged injuries and weapons we'd lost.

"How did we know to hit them tonight?" Cracker spoke through a haze of cheap tobacco smoke. "Sambinis bring blow into that cove every month and you don't give a shit. Why tonight?"

"Crows have loose lips," I stated flatly. "And you can hear anything if you listen hard enough."

I left it at that, because, actually, it was all I knew. Saint hadn't disclosed where he'd got his intel and I hadn't asked. When I trusted a brother, I didn't need to know everything to make decisions.

"Just seems convenient," Cracker pressed. "That we find a lorry load of skin while you're fighting your campaign to make us fucking bankrupt—"

Cracker's chair tipped back and he hit the deck like a sack of rotten spuds. Saint loomed over him, silent and deadly, and I snorted out a laugh.

Couldn't fucking help it. "Anyway, the intel was good and we did what we needed to do. Those girls—those fucking *children*—are safe and sound with the coppers as we speak."

"What if they talk?" Embry said. "We wore no colours, but it wouldn't be hard to figure it was an MC hit if they described us enough."

"If they talk, they talk." I spread my hands. "We didn't kill anyone. But for what it's worth, I don't think they will. They don't know who we were or that our only intention was to help them. They'll be too scared to say much."

Embry nodded. "What happens next?"

"We lock down," I said bluntly. "What we did tonight is either gonna send the message that we won't tolerate that shit or we've started an all-out war, so we need to be ready."

"We were already at war," Saint growled. "If we aren't ready by now, we ain't never gonna be."

He stood, hurling his chair back with a screech, and strode from the room, leaving a pained silence in his wake. At least, it was painful for me because he was right. Every messy night and never-ending day had led us to this point, and now we were staring down the barrel of the endgame. Either we won this war and found that magical place we could just *be*, not fighting all the time just to live, or we didn't, and I'd lost my entire family for nothing.

Cracker took advantage of Saint's departure to right his chair and reclaim his place.

Mateo glowered across the table, letting him know he had no qualms repeating Saint's performance, if Mateo had any qualms at all.

More hysterical humour bubbled up my throat, but I held it in this time, giving the order to take shifts snatching rest and shoring up the compound security. To send home any fucker who didn't need to be here and tell everyone we cared about to stay alert.

I dismissed my council.

River didn't take my call. I couldn't risk sending Rubi back to Porth Luck, so I called Skylar, the friendly nurse.

He listened to my explanation with a heavy sigh, and I felt his pain. It was my pain too. "When does this fucking stop?"

I had no answer and I didn't have time to think of one. "Just tell him, okay? I need him here where I can keep him safe."

Skylar hung up.

I tossed my phone on the table in front of me and buried my face in my hands, shutting the world out, searching for the peace and quiet I needed to think clearly.

Embry put his hand on my shoulder, but I ignored him. Talking it out wasn't gonna help. I needed this shit to end.

Too bad for me Embry didn't take the hint.

He pulled out a chair and sat down so close he was practically on my lap.

I let out a world-weary sigh and faced him. "What?"

Embry handed me a mug of herbal tea.

"No beer, father?"

He smiled a little, though he looked as ragged as I felt, a shiner on his cheekbone, clothes torn and dirty. "You need to sleep."

"So do you."

"Saint rode out. He left you a message."

"Did he now?"

"He said to tell you not to wait to find Alexei."

"I can't leave the compound and fuck off to Bristol." Without Saint's body pressed to mine, I was thinking clearly enough to realise that.

Embry frowned. "Alexei wouldn't come here?"

"Because I tell him to? Fuck no." I allowed myself a tired grin, but it went nowhere because it was bathed in worry. Alexei hadn't picked up the phone since he'd sent me a one-word text the wrong side of yesterday, and it was starting to scrape at my brain. Logic told me he was fine and living his own damn life, but he'd never left a call unanswered this long. He always called me back.

Always. I wondered when I'd started thinking about him with a permanence I hadn't earned. A commitment that he'd never even hinted that he fucking wanted.

He wants me, *though. No one could fake what we've shared.*

I wrapped my hands around the mug Embry had brought me and let out another tragic sigh. He gave me a look that probed too deep and I averted my gaze. Embry was the easiest dude in the world to talk to, but I wasn't in the mood. "Did Saint ride out alone?"

Embry winced. "I offered to go with him or round up the prospects."

"Fuck." I shook my head. "He's not invincible."

"Neither are you."

"I'm here, ain't I?"

"Why don't you go upstairs for a bit? Nash can handle the lockdown and he's better at telling people things they don't want to hear when you're this exhausted."

"Critiquing my bedside manner?"

"Just advising you to delegate."

I thought about getting my head down for a few hours. Pictured myself stretching out in my bed while my calls to Alexei remained unanswered and Saint was alone on the road.

Nope. Not doing it. "Thanks for the tea, father. I appreciate it."

Embry nodded, accepting defeat. "I'll bring you some food when it's ready, if I stay awake that long."

"You cooked?"

"No. You did. Feels like a lifetime ago, eh?"

True that.

Embry left me alone. I drank the tea and counteracted the health benefits with a dozen cigarettes. I didn't call Alexei again, but he rarely left my thoughts.

I thought of Saint too and wondered where the actual fuck that was headed. But mainly I thought of my club. My family. And how the hell we were going to ride out this storm.

"Cam?"

I turned in my chair. Nash was in the doorway, the slowly rising sun behind him, making his gold hair shine like a halo. "What?"

He gave me a grim look. "We got company. Couple of Crows and some fucker I've never seen before. They want to talk."

"About what?"

"They wouldn't tell me. Said it's gotta be you."

I rose and walked to the window that allowed me to see the compound gate. A vehicle waited there, doors open, its occupants pulled out and on their knees in front of Mateo. "They packing?"

"No weapons," Nash said. "Or wires. Should we bring them in?"

"Don't suppose we've got much choice."

Nash agreed and left to action my decision. I watched it play out, then showed my face, stepping straight to the only Crow I'd ever had an ounce of respect for: Rocco St. John, their VP.

I seized him by the throat, slamming him against the wall behind him. "The fuck are you doing here?"

Rocco held my gaze, eyes bulging as I squeezed his windpipe.

"Cam." Embry's low voice counselled restraint, but for the second time in as many hours, I ignored my chaplain.

I squeezed Rocco's neck until he was a heartbeat from losing consciousness.

Then I let him fall and turned to the face I didn't know. "Who are you?"

"Lorenzo Sambini."

I froze. "You're say who, now?"

"You heard my name, O'Brian. I'm exactly who you think I am."

"I ain't got no clue who you are except that you're some mafia cunt who wants to fight me."

"We don't want to fight."

"We?"

"My uncle is the head of our organisation. He sent his son and I to represent him."

"And where's his son now?"

"I was hoping you could tell me that."

Nothing about this conversation made sense. I stepped

back, ignoring Rocco who'd collapsed to his knees. "Why would I know where your boss's son is?"

Sambini held my gaze. "After you hijacked our merchandise, we left Gianni behind with Frank Crow and a brother to clean the scene. They're missing now and I was hoping you could shed some light on that."

"Hoping?" I stared him down. "Dude, the only place any of those dickfuckers are headed next time I see them is six feet under, so unless you're about to switch sides, you've come to the wrong place."

"The Crows tell me you always send your righthand man to clean a scene. Maybe if I spoke to him, he could tell me what he saw when he got there."

"Nash is my VP and he's right here. Have at him."

I inclined my head to where Nash stood, his surfer good looks belying the beast I knew him to be when provoked.

"Not him," Sambini said. "The other one."

"My enforcer? I think you've already met."

"Fuck's sake," Rocco growled from the ground. "He means Malone. We know he'd have gone back to clean up your mess. That he'd fuck up anyone that got in his way. Get him out here so he can tell us what happened."

Real fear for Saint crept into my heart. The timings didn't add up. If the Crows were already claiming their president was missing, they'd been expecting him back before Saint had even left. But if they had Sambini soldiers lying in wait, there was every chance Saint would ride straight into their trap.

The truth was our only weapon. "He didn't ride out until an hour ago. Whatever happened before he got there has nothing to do with us."

"Bullshit," Rocco spat. "He's made Crows disappear before. You all have."

"With good fucking reason." I moved on him again, backhanding him, snapping his head back. "And we'd have good reason this time too, but I'm telling you, it wasn't us. It wasn't *him*. Maybe you have more enemies than you know about. And you—" I pointed at Sambini. "You're the fuckers who've been trying to put a bullet in my skull. You think I give a fuck that you've misplaced your prince?"

"You should." Sambini's expression darkened. "Business is what it is, but if you've hurt Gianni, my uncle will kill everyone you care about before he ends you."

"He's been trying to end me for months and now he needs a reason?"

"Hear what I'm saying, O'Brian. You don't understand who you're fighting."

"So tell me."

"Not until you give up the brother who took Gianni."

Never. Even if Saint was guilty, I'd take that fucking bullet before I betrayed him. "It's you that needs to listen. We haven't touched your prince, and if I wanted Frank Crow dead, I'd have done it myself in front of his whole damn brotherhood. Now get the fuck off my property before your uncle really does have someone to avenge."

Head spinning, I was done with the conversation. I strode away, leaving Nash to cut Sambini and the Crows loose, and stormed into the clubhouse, kicking out at a chair, booting it into the wall. "*Fuck.*"

My phone was already to my ear, calling Saint, but it didn't even ring, cutting straight to an automated message telling me his phone was either off or he was caught in the dead zone between here and the scene of the fight.

The latter explanation made most sense and gave weight to what I'd told Sambini—that he wasn't even there yet, let alone responsible for whatever the fuck had happened in their camp. But ominous dread built in my gut all the same, roiling in my belly and eating me alive. Going to war with the Sambinis over business was one thing, but if they truly believed we'd hurt the son of their top boy? Damn. We would lose brothers to this. I knew it like I knew it was going to piss it down all day long.

As the thought completed, fat raindrops began to fall from the sky, pelting the yard and rooftops.

Nash came inside, hair soaked and stuck to his face. "The Crows are missing Drummer too. Rocco reckons they should've been back from torching the truck hours ago."

"They did torch the truck. Saint saw the smoke."

"Then what happened, though? You sure he didn't run into them before he came back here?"

I snapped the cigarette I was holding. Tossed it aside and reached for another. "You think he had time to off three people and ditch the bodies before he came back here? And that he's fucked up enough not to tell us about it?"

After a beat I couldn't blame Nash for, he lit a smoke of his own and shook his head. "It wasn't him. But they don't know that and he's out there alone. Should we go after him?"

For any other brother, I wouldn't have hesitated, but Saint wasn't an ordinary brother. An ordinary man. He was an extraordinary human and his brain wasn't wired the same as the rest of us. He had a nose for trouble. An instinct. Chances were he already knew he was riding into a storm and he'd gone to ground, staying low until he could get the job done before he came home to us.

To *me*.

"If he isn't back by tonight or made contact, we'll go looking. Until then, we wait. I trust him, and I pity any fucker who hunts him down."

Nash grunted his agreement and retreated to the bar. I watched him greet my sister and then flop onto the couch I'd found Rubi on . . . yesterday? A fucking week ago? Damn, I had no idea.

I understood the look Orla sent Nash's way, though. She was worried about him. About me. About River. About the whole fucking mess our lives had always been. *I'm so fucking tired of this.*

Rubi came in from outside, rubbing his temples, still moody that he couldn't ride and whatever else was pissing him off. A couple of prospects trailed after him, grimy and sweat-covered from whatever grunt work he'd had them do. The mood was sombre but still buzzed enough from the crazy night that I walked out without a word to any fucker.

I craved peace. I needed to think. Despite knowing I wouldn't sleep, I took Embry's advice and retreated upstairs.

The room the good chaplain slept in most often was already occupied. Embry was passed out on the bed, his arm dangling from one side. The man in me that cared about my brothers more than anything went to him and tucked it back on the bed, but as the thought crossed my mind, someone beat me to it. Mateo was already there, covering Embry with a quilt before backing off to a chair by the door.

He didn't see me. And I didn't alert him to my presence. I

251

filed the scene away to think about later and kept moving to my room.

I opened the door and slipped inside, taking a moment to lean against it and close my eyes. My heart was a wreck, thudding with anxiety for Saint. Aching for Alexei. Grieving for the fact that River was never gonna let me protect him.

Without the door at my back, I might've fallen to the floor, but I found refuge in the cool wood and comfort in the aches and pains beginning to catch up with me.

"You have the best view from this window."

My eyes flew open. By now it was daylight, winter sun fighting against the incoming clouds, casting a rainbow over the compound yard.

Alexei stood by the window, eyes a live wire of energy, hair more dishevelled than I'd seen it after a solid five hours of fucking.

His smile was obscene, but I couldn't smile back.

[20]

ALEXEI

Cam needed *me*.

He stared at me for a heart-stopping moment, then he was on me like a man possessed.

And I wanted him to possess me.

Needed it more than air in my lungs.

He crossed the room in one stride and seized me by the dirt splattered jacket I was still wearing.

He hauled me close, his gaze fierce. "Are you okay?"

"Of course." I spoke with a lightness I did not feel. "Are you?"

Cam didn't answer with words. He kissed me, smashing his lips to mine and driving his tongue into my mouth. Thrown by the impact, I staggered back, enjoying the weight of him as he chased me down, forcing me against the wall. The fire in my veins burned hot enough to fight him off, but I willed it away. This was Cam. He'd never hurt me more than I wanted him to.

I let him tear at my clothes and close a rough hand

around my cock, grunting his pleasure when he found me already hard for him. He shoved his jeans down and spun me around. Then he was gone for a moment and I panicked as if I'd lost him forever.

"Cam?"

"I'm here." He covered my back again, his slick, sheathed cock probing me, sliding home, sure and sharp, gifting me the pain I needed to ground myself.

He held my hip with one hand, the back of my neck with the other. We'd been here before, but it was different this time. Now, he didn't hesitate. Or second guess what I could take. He punched into me and fucked me hard, and I pushed back against him, always, *always* seeking more.

Cam gave it to me. He slammed his hips to mine, his thick cock grinding inside me with each powerful thrust. It throbbed and it burned. It *hurt*. And for the brutal minutes I held out, I loved it.

Then I came as if a bomb had gone off inside me, sudden and violent. Pleasure surged and my cock erupted without external stimulation, swaying me on my feet as Cam groaned behind me, his climax a wild shout and a fist to the wall.

A convulsion wracked him, but he held me up.

Just.

We were a mess.

But we are messy together.

The errant thought startled me. *Together.* No. We would not be. We *could* not be. Cam had a life that did not allow for what we had. And me? I was too broken for a man like him. Cam was a rough diamond. I was a black soul. A dead one. He did not deserve my nightmares.

"Hey." Cam nuzzled my neck and I shivered. "Wanna take a shower with me?"

Weak as I was, I could not refuse.

Cam led me to the bathroom attached to his clubhouse bedroom and we shed the clothes that he'd neglected to remove before fucking me against the wall.

"What happened to your shoulder?"

"Hmm?" Dazed, Cam's sharp question caught me off guard.

"Your shoulder, Lexi. It's slashed to fuck."

"Slashed?" I turned to look at the wound in the mirror, the mark of a cheap kitchen knife the third man who'd come upon me had tucked into his boot. "You exaggerate. It is a scratch."

"From where?"

"From a stupid man."

"Who?"

I faced Cam, absorbing his set jaw and stubborn frown. He was not an easy man to lie to, so I didn't try. "I did not catch his name. Do you know the name of every man who has hurt you?"

"Don't play games with me."

"Are you scared I will win?"

"I'm scared we'll both lose." Cam reached around me and turned the shower on. "And I'm scared I won't know how to live when you're gone."

Saint will show you. I bit my tongue, letting my thoughts stray to Cam's sergeant-at-arms. He wasn't here, in any sense of the words. I'd known it the moment I'd set foot on the compound, even as the other brothers milled around, pumped from the fight they'd won—for now—but ragged and tired. I tried not to wonder too hard where he'd gone. If he was safe.

If he was coming back any time soon.

Cam sighed and nudged me toward the steaming spray. "Let's get clean so we can go to bed."

"You want me to sleep with you?"

"I want you with me, but I ain't gonna beg. You gotta do whatever makes you happy."

He stepped into the shower and closed his eyes.

I followed him, naturally, and reached for the shampoo to wash his inky hair.

Cam opened his eyes to watch me. He didn't speak, but with a gaze as open as his, he didn't need to.

I washed every inch of him, then he returned the favour, pausing at the gash on my back, switching the water to cold to rinse it.

"Of course you don't flinch," he murmured. "I wonder what it would take to break you."

"Maybe I am already broken." It was the first time I'd spoken for a while and my voice sounded far away.

Cam was closer, his warm breath on my skin. "Broken things are beautiful."

"Like Saint?"

"Yes. Like him."

"You should tell him that."

"Should I?"

"I do not think he knows he is beautiful."

Cam shut the shower off and gripped my chin. "You see it, don't you? What I see?"

"In him?" I measured my words. Cam did not know I had

spent enough time in Saint Malone's company to see the enchanting soul behind a gaze that was only flat if I looked away too soon. "I do not know this man, but I see him in your eyes, and that is enough for me."

"He told me to find you, earlier tonight. I asked him to come with me."

"Come where?"

"Wherever you were."

"But I am here."

"I know."

"And Saint is not."

Darkness coloured Cam's face. His jaw worked.

He's worried. "You do not know where he is?"

"No."

I digested that, disquiet fluttering in my belly. It was clear that Cam could not leave the compound without an army around him, but I could. With a little ingenuity, I could track Saint's phone and find him. Bring him home and ease the heartbreak from Cam's warm eyes. "I—"

A knock at the door cut me off.

Cam's gaze sharpened. He snapped to attention, no longer mine alone as if he ever had been or would be.

In a flash, he was gone, dripping water across the floor as he went.

Again, I followed, drawn to his side as if it didn't matter if whoever was at the door saw me naked in his bedroom.

By the time I reached Cam, he had pulled on a pair of grey sweatpants that hung low on his hips.

He tossed me a black pair made from the same soft cotton. "Don't even think about hiding."

"I do not hide."

"Good, cos you'll never need to here. They know who I am."

He wrenched the door open as I tugged on the sweatpants.

The weary face of Saint Malone stared back at us.

[21]

ALEXEI

Somehow, Saint was wetter than we were. Water mixed with the blood spilling from his split eyebrow, and he was soaked to the bone from the torrential rain I'd failed to notice while I'd been wrapped up in Cam.

Cam grabbed a towel and waved Saint into the room.

Saint cast a glance at me. I gave him a subtle nod and he stepped over the threshold, ignoring the towel as he closed the door behind him and leaned against it.

"What the fuck happened?" Cam demanded. "I've had Rocco St John and some Sambini cunt up my arse thinking you've lifted Frank Crow, Drummer, and the heir to the throne and dumped them in a dungeon somewhere."

The confusion in Saint's bewitching gaze was instant. He pushed off the door and moved to the window. "That's why?"

"Why what?"

"They're everywhere. I couldn't get to the truck."

You didn't need to. I handled it. I'd tell him later; it was pointless not to when it was him who'd summoned me to that place.

That means he'll know what you did.

It bothered me less than it should've done.

Cam had followed Saint halfway to the window. Then he stopped and looked back at me as if caught between us. *My sweet biker boy.* I met his earnest gaze and tapped my eyebrow before pointing to Saint's back. *He's bleeding.*

"I need to get the first aid kit," Cam said.

"For Alexei?" Saint didn't turn around. "He needs stitches."

I snorted. "That is dramatic."

"Tape, then. I can do it for you."

"It's true," Cam said. "Saint's good with blood and gore."

"You are not?"

"He's better." Cam glanced at Saint again, then retreated to the door.

He disappeared through it, leaving me alone with Saint as thunder rolled outside.

"I think he loves you," Saint murmured. Still, he did not turn around.

I moved closer to him, eyeing his wet clothes, ignoring the skip in my chest at his words. *It doesn't matter. You don't matter.* "I think he loves *you.*"

Saint made a low sound. A tortured sound. "He doesn't love me. Not like that."

"You are so sure of something you've never asked him?"

He finally tore his gaze from the window. "How do you know I've never asked?"

"I do not. I am matching your personality to his and judging you both accordingly."

Perhaps if Saint had been less fatigued, he'd have argued with me more.

Instead, he reached for me and lay cool hands on my shoulders. "Show me?"

I turned my back on him, gifting him a close-up view of the slash on my shoulder. It was far from the worst injury I'd ever suffered, but he was right that it needed closing. If not for the primal urge in my heart to reach Cam—*and him*—I'd have done it myself.

Saint examined the wound in silence. Then he put his lips close to my ear. "What happened?"

It was barely a whisper, but my gaze darted to the closed door anyway and I listened for Cam's approaching footsteps.

Nothing reached me.

"He'll be awhile," Saint said. "Kit is in the chapel and every fucker will want a piece of him."

"Do you blame them?"

"No. Tell me what happened."

"I'd imagine you already know. I was too late to help raid the trafficking run, but it seems the Kings did not need my help."

"*I* needed your help." Saint shifted his hold on me, his cold fingers grazing my neck. "Cam was moving too fast for me to watch his back."

"That's how you got hurt?"

"I'm not hurt."

"You are." I spun around, allowing his hands to remain on my bare skin and took my turn examining the injury to his face. It wasn't deep, but it needed cleaning and taping shut to protect from infection. "And I'm sorry I wasn't there."

"I tried to tell you it was over. That it was dangerous to approach."

"The blank message?"

"I dropped my phone. It's smashed to fuck."

"That is why Cam could not reach you?"

"Maybe." Saint's gaze flickered. "Stop deflecting. What happened to *you*?"

I brought my hands to Saint's face, palms to his jaw. His scruff wasn't as thick as Cam's. Wasn't as dark. "Three people came up on me. When they figured out I was not one of them, they wanted to burn me in the crashed truck."

"You didn't let them."

"No, I did not." I showed Saint my worst smile.

He didn't blink. "Are you going to tell him?"

"Cam?"

"Yeah. This is gonna come down hard on us if we can't end it before it starts blowing up."

I knew that. Had known it as I was shifting bodies and the Italian features of the third assailant had become clear. "We need to reach the organisation that is pulling the strings and persuade them that killing Cam will not solve their problem."

"It would, though, wouldn't it?" Saint glanced to the closed door. "Cracker wants the gavel, and with Cam gone, there's enough old timers who'd vote for him."

"Cracker? The old man?" Saint nodded and I let my hands slide from his face. "Interesting. I wonder if he is feeding information to the Crows."

"Course he is. But that doesn't matter if you've buried their president, does it? They'll have other shit to worry about."

"The Sambini clan is more concerning, but I can keep them at bay."

"How?"

262

I smiled again. "I have something they want."

Realisation dawned in Saint's green eyes. "You didn't kill their man?"

"Not exactly."

Saint's gaze turned thoughtful. He seemed to have forgotten he was touching me, his hands still gripping my shoulders, and I wasn't displeased about it.

I liked it.

The only thing missing was Cam.

Saint took a breath. "Do you know who the Sambinis are working for?"

"Not yet."

"Can you find out?"

"Yes, but it is not a simple phone call. It will take time and resources I did not think I would need again. Time I will need to be away from Cam."

"I have no idea who you are."

I let the malevolence fade from my face. "You don't. And perhaps you should not ever find out, but you should trust me. I love Cam and I will not let this hurt him anymore."

I love him. It seemed louder in my head than the words I'd spoken, but Saint heard me.

He believed me. "How long will you be gone?"

"I do not know."

"Will you be safe?"

"Sometimes."

"He'll come looking for you, if shit doesn't get too wild here."

"He'll try, but you will distract him. He will need that, I think. He will need you."

Saint glanced to the door again. We were running out of time. "Why can't we tell him that you're helping us?"

"You know why." I made myself duck out of Saint's hold. "Because he will want to protect me too, and he can't afford another distraction." Footsteps sounded outside the door. I pushed Saint towards the bathroom. "Go. Shower. Then I will show you how to keep him busy all night long."

Cam

Leaving Saint and Alexei alone felt like planting a bomb and misplacing the detonator. After being accosted by Nash and Rubi in the bar, I took the stairs two at a time and jogged to my closed bedroom door.

Silence greeted me, but with these two, even separate, that shit was deadly.

Together?

Fuck. I wasn't built for the rush that gave me.

The fear.

The elation.

I opened the door, every nerve stretched to breaking point. What if Saint had already left?

What if Alexei had?

But I found Alexei on the bed, stretched out on his belly as he flicked through the small stack of vinyl records I kept by the turntable my dad had left behind. I'd changed everything else about this room, but not that.

"He is in the shower," he said without looking up. "I cannot clean a wound that will get wet again as soon as he leaves."

"That sounds like you think he's gonna stay a while." I set the first aid kit on the bed. I wanted to treat Alexei's wound myself but knew I'd puke if I looked too hard at it.

He's okay. It's a scratch.

Nope. Still puking. "You two getting along okay? I forgot to introduce you."

A smirk crossed Alexei's face. "He does not need an introduction when you talk about him all the time."

"I don't do that."

"Not always with words."

"What the fuck does that mean?"

Alexei held out a vinyl record and inclined his head towards the turntable. "That we know each other already, no? You don't have to supervise us."

I glanced at the record. "Judas Priest?"

"I liked the title."

Screaming For Vengeance. I blew out a breath. "Whatever you want, sweetheart."

Alexei snorted and rolled onto his back. "Sarcasm is very strange when you do it."

I didn't want to know what he meant by that. I put the record on and set the volume low and heady. Then I shut the curtains and joined him on the bed with the bottle of aged rum I kept in my drawer for people I liked.

No glasses.

Alexei eyed the bottle and then me as I took a healthy swig. "Curative?"

"Maybe." I set the bottle aside before I tipped too much down my throat. As much as I wanted to take the edge off the night, I still needed what was left of my wits. "Want some?"

"I can think of better medicine."

The gleam in his eye was unmistakable and I wondered if he'd forgotten Saint was in the bathroom. *Course he hasn't.* I was willing to bet that Alexei wasn't a man who forgot much at all.

But was he a man who liked an audience? So much of our time together had been ours alone that I had no idea.

However he fell on it, though, I had to kiss him. Touch him. Feel his body pressed against mine before I lost my head.

I gripped the nape of his neck and hauled him closer, taking his mouth in a rough kiss that seared my senses enough that I could fucking breathe again. His low noise of satisfaction went straight to my cock, and it dawned on me that I had zero problem fucking him with Saint in the bathroom.

Or with Saint on the bed beside us.

Fuck, I want them both.

It wasn't the first time it had hit me, but with Saint so close, it punched differently now. I kissed Alexei harder, my brain swimming, heart pounding, and as the bathroom door opened, I couldn't stop.

It was the sound of the first aid kit snapping open that broke through.

I opened my eyes and pulled back, searching for Saint and finding him by the window, searching through the box that was stocked enough to be useful in an airstrike.

Dressed in yet another pair of my sweatpants, he wasn't looking at us. But he wasn't *not* looking either. With his damp hair pushed back and his tatted skin flushed from the shower, he was as relaxed as I ever saw him. Normal, almost, for him, at least.

Perhaps sensing my attention trained on him, he glanced up, meeting my gaze for what felt like the first time in days.

It wasn't, but the way his stare sank into me felt grounding, somehow, as if I'd missed him and not realised how much until he came back.

"I need to tape Alexei's cut."

"How do you know his name?"

"I asked."

As if it had been that easy, but at Saint's pointed frown, I rolled off Alexei.

Fuck. I'd forgotten they were both hurt.

Alexei gave me a droll, piercing smirk, then rose from the bed and joined Saint by the window. He took the supplies Saint was holding. "You first."

Saint didn't argue. He let Alexei lay hands on him and guide him to the bed where I was hiding my boner beneath me.

"Sit," Alexei said.

I propped myself on one elbow as I watched them encounter each other, gaze darting between them, waiting for Saint's terminal dislike of strangers touching him to surface and expecting Alexei to—actually, I had no idea what to expect from him. I'd never seen him interact with anyone else beyond a curt nod, so this shit was off the fucking charts.

Except, it wasn't. Saint's posture remained relaxed. And Alexei? His demeanour was warm. Friendly, even. As if he cared about Saint's wellbeing.

I . . . damn. I sucked in a frazzled breath, almost shaking from the impact as the two halves of my heart collided. I'd never pictured them together in any sense, but if I had, there was no doubt in my mind that it would've been sexual, not laced with kindness and compassion.

Alexei taped the wound on Saint's brow, then rose so they could switch places.

He stayed on his feet, showing Saint his back. Saint brought his hands to Alexei's skin, his touch gentle. Reverent, even, and Alexei *shivered*.

The ripple that passed through him was subtle, and perhaps a month ago I wouldn't have noticed, but I knew him —knew his body and his tells. He liked Saint's touch. It did something to him, and watching that unfold had my teeth digging into my bottom lip to contain the rumble building in my chest. The possessive alpha growl that made me want to claim them both as my own.

That works for you. What about them? What about Saint? You have no idea what's going through his head right now.

No. But I knew his tells too: his hooded eyes and his devilish tongue swiping at his bottom lip. Fuck. He liked this too, and it seemed too good to be true.

This isn't real.

It *couldn't* be. I was using all my good fortune on not getting killed, and this right here? Damn, it was a wild wet dream I'd never thought to have.

Saint dressed Alexei's slashed shoulder. I'd seen him treat brothers with far worse injuries, and every time, when it was over, he'd jerk back like he'd been burned. Or he wanted to incinerate himself to be clean. Me aside, only Orla and, bizarrely, Mateo could ever touch him without it being awkward as fuck.

But there was nothing awkward about how his hands

lingered on Alexei. Or how Alexei let them as he turned to me and beckoned me off the bed.

My cock *ached*. I stood, unashamed of how hard I was, and stepped to Alexei, kissing him fiercely, propelling him harder against Saint, an acid test for how serious either one of them was about this.

They both let it happen. Alexei leaned back against Saint's chest, and Saint stood firm, fingers digging into Alexei's pale flesh.

The sight of them lit a new fire in me. I plundered Alexei's mouth, then I pulled back, breathless, and dove headfirst into his sinful gaze.

He smirked back at me, but there was something else in his wicked leer too, something deeper that I couldn't unpick with my brain as foggy as it was. Fatigue and desire were a potent combination. I had nothing but *want* and pure fucking lust for him, a man I was pretty sure I was falling for, and for Saint, a soul I'd been enraptured with for too many years to count.

"Kiss him," Alexei whispered.

I blinked. "What?"

"Kiss. Him." Alexei grasped my chin hard, no mercy in his grip. "I know you want to."

Did I? Unbidden, my heart took a trip down memory lane, to the windy summer night on a damp northern beach and the first and only time my attraction to Saint had got the better of me. I'd wanted to kiss him then. Nearly had. But my dad had walked up on us, and a year later, he'd been dead at the side of the road.

"Cam." Alexei squeezed me harder, his gaze piercing my soul. "Don't hide from it, and don't hide it from me. I like it."

I couldn't have hidden it from him even if I'd wanted to, not with Saint a heartbeat behind him, still holding his shoulders, still silent and beautiful.

Wrenching my face from Alexei, I found Saint, and his forest-green stare terrified me, like it always had. My lips tingled, and my blood rushed. *Kiss him.* Fuck. Could I? After all these fucking years?

Slowly, I reached over Alexei and slid my fingers along Saint's jaw, my thumb finding a natural port on his cheekbone. His face was rougher than Alexei's, the scruff covering it more like mine than the velvet of Alexei's neat beard. His hair, though. Fuck, it was like silk as I tangled my fingers in it and tugged him closer.

He came willingly, his face impassive, but I knew him better than that, and the inferno in his gaze reeled me in.

I kissed him, touching my lips to his and sliding my tongue into his mouth with none of the hesitance I felt in my brain. Kissing Alexei was the adventure of a lifetime, but this?

It was like coming home.

[22]

CAM

Somehow, we made it to the bed, my lips still fused on Saint's while I kept a death grip on Alexei's hand. In the depths of my mind, I knew he was smirking, and I didn't care.

So what? He'd been right. I'd never denied it, not even to myself.

I manoeuvred Saint onto the bed, half expecting him to fight me. He didn't like being manhandled, not even by the women we'd shared in the past.

But he didn't resist. He let me lay him down, still kissing him, and cover him with my body before he drew back and looked beyond me to Alexei. He didn't speak, but I knew what he wanted.

"Lexi. Kiss him too."

Alexei lay down on the bed beside Saint. He eyed Saint and did that thing with his fingertip on Saint's chest that drove me fucking crazy when he did it to me. "Is that what you want? Both of us? Because you can just have Cam."

Saint swallowed, fighting for words. I rubbed his forearm where Alexei couldn't see. *It's okay. He'll wait for you.* And I knew Alexei would. I'd never told him my brother who couldn't speak was Saint, but there was no way he wouldn't see it now. No way he wouldn't understand.

Alexei claimed the rum bottle and brought it to Saint's lips.

Saint took a drink. A breath. And reached for Alexei. "I want you both. I don't know why, but I do."

I knew why. Because he was in love with me but unable to resist Alexei, and Christ, if I didn't know how that felt.

Or had felt. I wasn't in that place anymore. I loved Saint as much as I always had, but goddamn, I loved Alexei too. I watched him lean down, breath caught in my throat. He'd always kissed me like the viper he was, sharp and dangerous, but he was careful with Saint. Their kiss was almost sweet. Only the rising heat between them gave them away, their dicks as hard as mine.

Alexei pulled back from Saint and turned to me. By now, he was more on top of Saint than I was, and I loved how that looked, how Saint gripped Alexei's hip, while Alexei kept his hands on his chest.

I loved how impossible it was to tell who was the light and who was the dark.

"What do you want?"

It took me a second to register that Alexei was talking to me, and even longer to deduce that I had no fucking idea. I was already in heaven; I couldn't comprehend anything else.

Alexei glanced back at Saint. I wondered if he'd ask the same question of him or if he knew Saint wouldn't have an answer either, but not because he didn't know. *Because he can't say it.*

There were other ways of communicating, though. I

reached for the rum, took another healthy swig, then rolled off the bed and moved to the chair tucked under the desk I never used. "Show Alexei what you want."

Saint's gaze flickered to me. It was bottomless and tormented. If he'd been a different man, I might've felt bad for skewering him on the spot. I didn't, though. Alexei had asked me what *I* wanted, and it was this: him and Saint, however it played out. I could watch them kiss forever.

Saint sat up. He reached for Alexei again but didn't kiss him. He slid his fingers around his skull and gently pushed him down.

Alexei laughed, low and wicked. "You would like me to suck your cock?"

Of course he did. Saint loved a hot mouth around his dick, and there was no hotter mouth than Alexei's.

Alexei interpreted Saint's blazing stare and moved down his body. I liked that he didn't check with me that it was okay. Alexei had been owned before: whatever happened between us, he'd never be owned by me.

Besides, watching him strip Saint and himself bare obliterated any emotion in me but raw, dirty lust.

Yeah. Suck his fucking dick and tell me how he tastes.

Cos I really needed to know.

Naked, Saint leaned back on his elbows, tracking Alexei as he wrapped his sinful lips around his cock. He made no move to touch Alexei, to tug on his hair or push him down. It wasn't his way. Saint didn't fuck people; he screwed them gently—respectfully—and with a sensuality that I wanted him to share with Alexei. Would it hurt to see? I didn't think so. But I had to be careful . . . with both of them. I didn't want this to be complicated. More than anything, I wanted them to feel safe.

With me and each other.

Alexei began to work Saint's cock, drawing a sharp breath from Saint's parted lips. Saint's abs jumped and a subtle shudder ran through him and, *damn*, if it didn't feel good to see him react to Alexei like that. Too much of my life with Saint had revolved around anger and pain. Violence. Fear. He deserved this.

He deserved the fucking world.

They both did.

Someone moaned. I was too far into my head to know who, but the low sound reverberated in my bones. I watched Alexei's lithe body move and flex as he made Saint sweat, and it was all I could do to stay in my seat.

I was so fucking hard.

"Cam."

I blinked, again unsure of who had spoken my name. Logic reasoned it had to be Saint as Alexei's mouth was otherwise occupied, but Saint spoke even less during sex than he did any other time.

"*Cam.*"

Fuck. It *was* him.

I met his gaze over Alexei's injured shoulder. "What do you need, brother?"

His gaze darkened. He held out his hand.

I rose without stopping to think about where this was going. Moved to the bed and straddled Alexei's hips to get to him. I took Saint's hand and wrapped the other around Alexei's neck, revelling in his dirty chuckle.

Saint squeezed my fingers, like he had in the van on the

way to the end of the world. It was a fleeting gesture, but from him, it meant everything.

I leaned down, capturing his lips for a brief moment. Then Alexei did something that threw Saint's head back, his body jerking, a curse escaping him.

"*Fuck.*"

I smirked and turned my attention to Alexei, pulling him off Saint's dick and halfway upright to kiss me. Arching his neck, he thrust his tongue into my mouth. I tasted Saint on him and my eyes rolled. "Keep going," I ground out. "Make him come while I fuck you."

Alexei pressed his forehead against mine, and I felt a deeper connection with him than ever—as if he knew there was no going back from this, and he accepted it more than I did.

As if he *wanted* it.

Why? I held his face and drank him in. *Saint is everything to me, but what is he to you?*

Alexei's only answer was another crazy-hot kiss, and I felt Saint's watchful eyes boring into me, into us both, taking it all in, seeing me in a way no one else had until Alexei had found my gaze across that dingy fucking pub.

It flicked a switch inside me. I lost myself in the savagery of Alexei's mouth, the searching sweep of his tongue.

Then I kissed Saint again and the circle of flames was complete.

Alexei moved back to Saint's cock, taking him down once more, drawing a full-body shudder from Saint's muscular frame. His legs fell wider as Alexei sucked him and I kissed him, and I couldn't help contemplating how far he'd go.

I knew Alexei had no limits, but Saint?

His whole life was limited by the block in his damn head. The clusterfuck of crappy self-esteem and self-loathing his childhood had left behind.

His fucking mother—

Alexei reached back and squeezed my thigh.

I snapped to, the present reclaiming me, and focused on the men beneath me. Alexei could suck me dry in two minutes flat, but Saint had insane stamina. I'd seen it before, and his resilience gifted me the time to slip from the bed and find lube.

No condoms. I didn't know why. I'd never had unprotected sex with anyone, but I couldn't comprehend a barrier between us right now, so I held the bottle where Alexei could see it. Absorbed his nod and slicked up my aching cock.

Alexei lay between Saint's legs. I gripped his hips, bringing him closer to me, digging my fingers in hard, the way he liked. I didn't know Alexei's mind as well as I wanted to, but I knew his body. Knew he had an edge he could tumble from if I paid attention.

I slid my dick along his crease, watching the muscles in his back jump with anticipation as he worked Saint. *Easy.* I moved to rub his hip, but Saint beat me to it, squeezing Alexei's uninjured shoulder, and I knew the moment Alexei glanced up. Saw it in Saint's eyes—the fascination and wonder at the beautiful man making him feel such things.

The calm was brief, though. Alexei was an impatient lover; at least, he was with me. He pushed back, widening his stance, and I took the hint, driving inside him so harshly that Saint reared up, hands raised to shove me away.

Alexei caught him. "Is okay, wingman. Cam would never hurt me more than I want him to."

Wild eyes on me, Saint retreated, but I welcomed the fierce warning he blazed at me. His instinctive protection of Alexei made my blood sing with something deeper than the primal desire coursing through my veins. *My sweet fucking boy*.

It was my last coherent thought as Alexei's tight heat clamped down on me.

Alexei

Something changed between Cam and Saint the moment Cam slid inside me bare, and it was the first of many things I was unprepared for. I'd known they were hot for each other, loved each other, even, but the intensity as Cam began to fuck me in that brutal, sacred way of his was off the scale.

Beautiful intensity. Though I couldn't see Cam, I felt the heat of his gaze as he stared at Saint in every drive of his dick inside me. Heat that surged as I stared at Saint too.

I could still taste him on my tongue, so different to Cam, but no less potent.

No less of anything, save the fact I didn't know him as well as I knew the man behind me. The man who had such a tight grip on my heart I didn't know who I was anymore.

"Lexi." Cam growled my name, thrusting harder. "Tell him you want this."

I smiled at that. I'd seen the concern in Saint's earnest gaze when Cam had got rough. Absorbed it and filed it away to contemplate later when I left these men to their lives and continued with mine alone. I knew I'd need it then—the distraction from the gaping wound loving Cam would leave behind. "Saint." I waited for him to look at me. "I want this. I told you . . . he'd never hurt me."

Saint swallowed, his cock still rigid in my slick hand. "That's not what you said."

Beyond rasping Cam's name, they were the first words he'd spoken since he'd confessed to wanting us both. Cam. Me. As if we came as a package. And he was right, but what I'd said and what I'd meant were so deeply entwined that the semantics didn't matter.

To you. They matter to him.

I wanted to suck his cock again. More than that, I wanted to see him come as he watched Cam take me apart.

But most of all, I wanted to ease the worry in his forest gaze because he didn't deserve it.

I arched my back, anchoring myself to the heady pleasure Cam brought me, and a grunt escaped me as the force of Cam's vicious pace sent me shunting forwards into Saint.

He caught me in his strong arms, caging me like Cam did, his muscles taut and strained.

His neck was within reach of my mouth. I collected myself enough to control my unhinged jaw and nipped Saint with my bared teeth. "He gives what I ask of him."

Saint wove his fingers into my hair and tugged me off him. "Doesn't mean you want it."

"You think you know my mind better than I do?"

"Your mind isn't all you are."

It was too profound for my biker-addled brain to dissect. I gave up and returned to the one thing I could do to pull Saint out of his head.

His cock slid between my lips like an old friend. Saint's answering shiver was dynamite to the explosives Cam had already laid, and a coil unfurled in my belly. I didn't come, yet. But I heeded the warning and gave myself up to the preliminary blast.

I sucked Saint harder, no longer caring how he felt about the fact that it was my mouth on him and not Cam's. He wanted this. He wanted *me*. And I gave it to him as well as I could with Cam pummelling me from behind.

Reality began to blur. Cam reached a part of me no one else ever had, but Saint's pleasure at my touch, the bewilderment in his gaze as his composure slipped away, was a drug to my black soul. I wanted him to come, to fall apart beneath me, but I didn't want this to end. I wanted Cam to light that rocket inside me, then kill me so I didn't have to face the fact that the magic he'd gifted me was temporary.

I didn't want to lose him.

And . . . I didn't want this to be the last time I saw Saint like this either. How I felt about him was brand new and undefined, but it mattered.

Saint mattered.

As if he'd heard my thoughts, he made a sound that stuttered Cam's rhythm. We reached for Saint at the same time, me flailing wildly for Saint's arm while Cam's hand clamped down on his chest, pinning him in place.

Saint groaned again and threw his head back, arching his neck in a way that revealed a faint, jagged scar I hadn't noticed before.

A scar that had come from a knife to the throat.

My heart stopped, and as his climax peaked, pouring

from him and into my willing mouth, another section of the iron curtain around me fell.

Someone hurt him. And I hated whoever that was as much as I hated the person foolish enough to put a price on Cam's life.

Beneath me, Saint trembled, his earth-scented skin shiny with sweat and the mess I'd made of him with my mouth. I coaxed every shudder and gasp from him, then pulled back to look at him, to drink in his hooded, bloodshot eyes and the rapid rise and fall of his chest.

He was destroyed by whatever he was feeling and he didn't fight Cam's hold on him, which surprised me. He loved Cam, and he felt something beyond desire for me, but he wasn't a man that enjoyed touch when his emotions were high. I'd known this the moment I'd seen him step away from his brothers at the end of the first Crow brawl I'd witnessed, avoiding their fraternal embrace.

This seemed different. *He* seemed different. As Cam found that sweet spot inside me, I watched Saint descend to earth. Watched him register my fingers wrapped around his forearm and Cam's big hand on his chest and feel nothing but warmth, and the sense of awe and wonder returned to me.

He needs this as much as we need each other.

There was no time to ponder what that meant. Cam let Saint go and returned his hand to my hips, tightening his grip on me as his cock pulsed inside me. Without a condom between us, I felt everything—every twitch and surge, every drumbeat of frantic desperation as he chased his release while stalking mine.

He did not have to wait long for me. Sensation gathered in my muscles and nerves, and fresh heat sluiced through me.

I buried my face in Saint's abdomen, dimly aware of his gentle fingers holding my head, and I came hard, taking Cam with me as he roared behind me like a lion claiming his kill.

I floated for a while after. Cam fucking me often left me like this, subspace without the pain I'd searched out in the past. Cam didn't need to tie me down and whip me. He just needed to care—it was enough.

He was enough.

Saint was . . . oh, I did not know. I let him pull me towards him, then roll me onto my back. Fatigue oozed from every facet of him, but I sensed he would not rest until he found in me what he was looking for.

Cam left the bed. He came back with a damp cloth and cleaned up most of the mess we'd made. Then he lay down beside me and lolled his head on my bicep, halfway to sleep. I turned away from Saint to face him and tugged him against me, letting him bury his head in my chest.

Behind me, Saint's uncertainty threatened the temporary peace we'd carved out.

Do not leave. To be sure, I reached back and claimed his hand, tugging him closer until he was pressed against me and could reach Cam if he wanted to. For a moment, he lay so still I wondered if he'd died.

Then he curved his body around me, stretched to tangle his fingers in Cam's hair, and fell asleep with his head on my shoulder.

His trust in me made what I had to do next hurt more.

It was a long time before I made myself leave them.

[23]
CAM

Waking alone surprised me less than knocking out with Alexei and Saint in my bed in the first place. If not for the neatly folded towel on the bedside table, I'd have wondered if I'd imagined Alexei's appearance at all.

Saint's calling card was less subtle. His clothes from the night before were still on the bedroom floor, folded, though, cos Alexei apparently couldn't help himself.

My head was so full, I didn't know how to file what had gone down before I'd fallen asleep. I'd fucked Alexei bare. I'd kissed Saint.

Fuck, they'd kissed each other.

More.

I blew out a sigh, allowing myself a moment to digest it before responsibility called me home. But it didn't go anywhere. It stayed lodged in my chest, in my heart, and I couldn't fucking breathe.

A hot shower might've helped, but I didn't feel like washing Alexei and Saint from my skin just yet.

I found some clothes and left the bedroom, walking straight into my sister's path.

"I was just coming to get you."

"Why? What's wrong?"

Orla took my arm. "It's Rubi. I think he needs to see someone about these headaches. Cam, he's in so much pain."

My brain cleared of anything and everything that wasn't the welfare of my brother in arms. "Where is he?"

"Nash's room. He staggered in a few hours ago and passed out next to me."

In any other circumstances, I'd have asked her what the fuck she'd been doing in Nash's room, but I didn't give a shit. I jogged down the hall to Nash's room and stepped inside.

It was dark, the curtains drawn and no lights on. Nash was crouched by the bed, shirtless, obviously, because he'd been boning my sister, but my gaze didn't linger on him. I zeroed in on Rubi, who was hunched up on the edge of the bed, his arms over his head.

Nash got out of my way. I took his place and rubbed Rubi's shoulder. "Rubes, mate? You all right?"

Rubi groaned and shifted his arms just enough so I could see his face. "Headache, boss. I'm fine."

"Liar. You take anything?"

"That shit you gave me the other day."

The Vicodin. "Did it help?"

"Made me puke."

"And the pain?"

"Nah. Leave it, I'm all right."

I didn't believe him. Those pills were dynamite. They'd put me on my arse for days when I'd been with Alexei. And pain?

Man, I'd forgotten it existed when I'd been high as a fucking kite. Rubi smoked more weed than me, but it still worried me that the nuclear pills hadn't eased his discomfort at all.

Orla was right. He needed help. But how? If we left the compound, we'd ride into trouble before we got down the road, especially now it was starting to get dark again.

My fingers twitched, the urge to call Alexei so strong it almost choked me, but that made no fucking sense. He wasn't a doctor. Just a bloke who'd happened to have some American opiates lying around. *Call Skylar*.

But I didn't do that either. If there was a problem in Rubi's brain, there was nothing he could do without a hospital behind him.

"Okay." I made a decision and found Nash's gaze. "He needs a doctor. Get me a van so I can take him to A&E."

My tone left no room for argument. And Nash knew better than to try. The only fool who'd cross me was—

"You can't go out there."

I glanced over my shoulder. Saint filled the doorway, arms folded across his bare chest, a faint hickey marking his neck. Despite everything, my heart skipped a beat. *The fucker*. "I'm going. If you're that worried, do your job and protect us."

A tense silence blanketed the room, but it was fleeting. Saint blazed a glare at me, then reeled it in and nodded. "Nash, stay here with Embry and Cracker. Everyone else rides with us."

We mobilised. I helped Rubi into the van and left the compound with a ring of leather and muscle surrounding us, Mateo up front, Saint at my back.

Despite being my most aggressive soldier, Mateo was a

restrained driver. Ignoring my impatience, he eased the convoy along the roads at a pace that wouldn't attract too much attention, and we made the journey in forty minutes.

We pulled up at the main entrance. Rubi was hunched over in his seat, arms over his head again, unresponsive as Saint opened the passenger door.

He got him out before I'd shut off the engine, holding him with a compassion he usually reserved for wild animals injured on the road.

It spoke volumes of how fucked Rubi was that he didn't notice.

I scrambled out of the van and we walked him into A&E.

Saint jerked his head at the desk. *You talk.*

I signed Rubi in and kept a sharp eye out for Skylar, hoping he was working and would see the familiar name on the board. In my absence, Saint had commandeered a corner of the waiting area where we could monitor the doors and windows while keeping our backs to the wall. "You don't have to wait inside."

Saint scowled at a man punching the vending machine. "Alexei loves you."

I blinked. "What? How do you know that?"

"He told me." Saint got up and strode to the unfortunate prick having a meltdown over a Snickers bar. He inserted himself between the man and machine, daring him, without words, to hit him instead.

The man opened his mouth. Thought better of it and drifted away.

I waited for Saint to come back, but Skylar appeared first. "Cam? What's wrong? Are you hurt?"

"Hmm?"

I dragged my gaze back to where it needed to be. The irritation Skylar often felt around me was absent and he stared at me with obvious concern. "Not me." I gestured to Rubi who was slumped in the corner. "He's in pain, man. Can you help him?"

Skylar moved fast. He spirited Rubi to who the fuck knew where and told me he'd be back when he had something to tell me.

I settled in to wait.

Saint returned and sat down beside me, his knee an inch from mine, and my entire body thrummed. "Did Alexei really say that?"

He tilted his head sideways, the challenge in his gaze clear. *You think I'd lie?*

No. I just couldn't imagine those words leaving Alexei's mouth, even if something deep inside me believed them.

"You love him too, don't you?"

I turned away from Saint's penetrating stare. "I don't know him."

"So?"

"I can't love someone I don't know."

"You hate my mum and you don't know her. Love and hate ain't that far apart."

"Bullshit. I hate your mum because she abandoned you in the woods when you were a fucking baby. Her actions tell me she's a massive cunt."

Saint hummed, outwardly unaffected by the haunting trip down memory lane.

Lucky him. My hands were already curled into fists and I wanted to kill someone, anyone, but preferably the evil bastard who'd left their toddler to die. "What are you trying to say? That Lexi's actions tell me more about him than the life story I don't fucking know?"

"Lexi." Saint nodded slowly. "I like that."

"You liked his mouth on your dick too."

"That a problem for you?"

"What do you think?"

It was a strange conversation to be having in a hospital waiting room. No one was paying us much attention—save the girlfriend of the vending machine attacker who was staring at Saint like he was fucking Jesus—but I glanced around anyway as Saint stewed over his answer.

"I don't know what I think," he said eventually. "Only what's in here."

He tapped his chest, and the gesture spoke more to me than any words could've, but Skylar came back before I could answer and called me away.

The news wasn't good.

"You should've made him rest." Skylar strode beside me in the squeaky corridor. "It's gonna take longer now for him to get over this injury."

"He will, though, right? Get over it, I mean?"

"If you take care of him properly, cos Lord fucking knows you guys don't take care of yourselves."

"What do we need to do?"

"Bench him. No riding, no fighting, no stress or over-exertion." Skylar stopped walking and faced me. "I'm serious, Cam. If this gets any worse, he'll be stuck with it forever. Are you hearing me?"

"I hear you. Can I see him?"

"Where did you think we were going, to see the fucking queen?"

"Rubes ain't far off."

Skylar smirked a little, but his good humour was brief. "Look, they're gonna keep him in overnight for pain management, but there's no way I can swing you and Saint guarding his bed like angry bears on the ward. I don't have that kind of reach."

I knew that. But there was also no way we could leave a brother unprotected and vulnerable. "Can you stay with him?"

Skylar shrugged. "I can check on him, but I'm on shift down here. I can't walk out on my job."

"I'll stay with him."

I jerked around.

River stood behind me, one shoulder propped on the wall. He glowered at me, then softened his gaze for Skylar's benefit. "I fucked a nurse from the observation ward a while back. She'll let me in."

It was the perfect solution, but I couldn't get my head around it. "How the fuck are you even here?"

"Orla called me. She does that. You know, to say hello and shit."

The unspoken accusation was clear. I snorted. "You don't want that from me."

River pushed off the wall, but Skylar stepped between us before he got up in my face. "I haven't got time for family politics. If Riv can stay, that's probably the best we can do right now. Cam, you've just gotta live with it and trust us to take care of him."

I wasn't just worried about Rubi. Skylar was indelibly tied to the club, and River was my goddamn kin. There was no better way to hurt me if the Sambinis couldn't take my fucking head.

But I was out of options.

And time.

Skylar directed River to Rubi's bedside and kicked me out.

Saint waited for me at the exit. "If we leave brothers here, it lets anyone watching know we've got something inside that matters."

"You don't think they'll notice Rubi didn't come out?"

"Maybe, but they won't know River's here. He got a taxi and snuck in the back."

"*You* saw him." Of course he had. It was the only reason River had been able to walk up on me like that: Saint had let him.

Saint cleared his throat. "Rubi has to stay. There's no way around this."

Fuck, I hated that he was right. Hated that I couldn't protect my sick brother. That I hadn't protected him enough in the first place to stop him getting hurt.

I sighed. "We should go back."

Saint nodded.

And we left.

[24]
ALEXEI

I could still smell them on my skin, a reality that would've tormented me if it had been anyone other than Cam. And now Saint. It was strange how his scent was so different to Cam's, and yet so familiar it felt as if he'd put his lips to me before.

Perhaps it was in another life. Saint seemed like a man who had lived more than once. More so than Cam.

More so than me?

Maybe. It was becoming harder and harder to read myself. Before Cam, the notion of more than one man in my bed had been a hard pass. Fear was a complex emotion. It evolved and adapted, like a virus, and I'd accepted that I'd never catch up.

I miss them.

Already. After twenty-four hours. But with no idea when this purgatory would end, the longing in my heart for my biker boy and his wingman was an open wound.

The added salt came from the three missed calls lighting up my phone screen, all from Cam. I had faith in Saint to keep me in the loop if Cam needed me, but blanking him hurt.

It was only a matter of time before I cracked and picked up, but before that could happen, I had work to do—work that took me away from South West England and onto the continent, to Berlin, a city I knew well enough to despise.

At least it's not Moscow.

I drove my car to the airport, knowing Saint would be watching, and parked in an underground car park a mile away from where I needed to be. Then I got on a plane and left him and Cam behind, immersing myself in the bustle of civilisation.

It was what I did best, among other things. Crowded streets made for an easier escape than cumbersome, trackable vehicles, and I did not know if I would need that today.

Or tomorrow. However long it took to get the answers I needed.

My phone rang again as I moved through the streets. Not Cam. I did not have to look, I just knew.

Saint?

Maybe. I took a chance and glanced at the screen. It wasn't Saint, and the disappointment I felt was . . . complex. Did I want to hear his voice as much as Cam's?

No. Maybe.

But why?

Because he is a beautiful man who loves Cam too. It is logical for you to be drawn to him.

Perhaps. But I was more than drawn to Saint Malone. Watching him come had made Cam's cock inside me surge hotter. The sounds he'd made—the sounds *Cam* had made as he'd watched his friend and brother come apart at my hand.

Their dynamic was fascinating. More than hot, it was mind-altering, soul-shattering, and it should've unnerved me more than it did, but I had no nerves left. Not today. I couldn't, or I'd turn tail and run back to Cam, and then I'd have to live with the truth: that I could've saved him, but I was too scared to try.

I cancelled the Russian call and switched off the phone, just in case Saint had achieved the impossible and bugged me there too.

If I didn't like him, I'd kill him.

Or I would try. There weren't many men on earth that made me doubt my abilities, but he was definitely one of them.

Another was on the other side of the hotel room door I found myself outside sometime later, having incapacitated the goons guarding it.

I knocked. It was polite, and I was nothing if not that.

It swung open seconds later and my blood turned to ice, freezing over the parts of me that Cam and Saint had managed to thaw.

A face I knew as well as my own stared back at me, the only sign of Pavel Sidorov's surprise an infinitesimal twitch of his cold blue eyes.

Then the smile came, the one that made grown *mafiozi* weep. "My boy," he said in Russian. "You have returned."

I shook my head, fighting to keep my trembling within. "I have come for a favour. Maybe two. May I have a moment of your time?"

Sidorov peered around me, noting his guards slumped at their posts, and a wryness reached his sardonic smirk. "You do not change, eh? A phone call would have saved them whatever injuries you have left them with."

"They are not injured. Just resting. And I did not want them to see my face."

"Ah. You are still a ghost, Alexei."

I could not deny it.

Sidorov waved me into his suite. I stepped forward warily, scanning every inch of the space we occupied while Sidorov moved to the antique decanter that held the vodka he drank like water. I'd often wondered what would happen to him without it.

Then I'd stopped thinking of him at all.

I waved the vodka away.

Sidorov nodded as if he'd expected me to. "Will you sit? Forgive me, but you make me nervous when you prowl around like this."

"Liar." I stopped pacing and forced myself to stand in front of him. "You are not afraid of me."

"I should be, perhaps? Have you come to kill me?"

I snapped my gaze to him. "What?"

"It is the only reason I can think of for you to be here. It has been years since I last saw you."

"You have missed me?"

"Of course." Sidorov sipped his vodka. "You are one of a kind. It takes an army to do the job you once did."

"Perhaps you need a better army."

"That, I do not deny. Will you return to me? I would make it worth your while."

I shook my head again, resisting the urge to step back and widen the distance between us. "You would not, but that is not your fault."

Sidorov eyed me, and his scrutiny, so different from Saint's, made me feel dirty. "You are . . . not the same. Is your new life not treating you well?"

"I do not need it to. I look after myself."

"And yet, you are here. So, tell me, Alexei, what can I do for you?"

"I want to know who is trafficking women to America through Devon and Cornwall. An Italian organisation are claiming it is them, but I don't believe it to be true."

Understanding flared in Sidorov's gaze. "This upsets you."

"I need them to stop."

"Why? I mean, aside from your personal feelings on the matter."

"It is not their territory, and I am on the side of those who it belongs to." Loyalty kept me from naming the Rebel Kings, but it was pointless. If Sidorov took my request seriously, he would know who they were before the day was done.

"I am assuming," Sidorov said, "that your associates would not seek to take the trafficking trade for themselves?"

"They would not. They have fought against it for many years. It was Romanians who killed their previous leader. Do you think they could be pulling the strings behind the Italians now?"

"Which Romanians?"

"I do not know."

"And the Italians?"

"Sambini."

Sidorov snorted. "The Sambini family are not an organisation to be afraid of, Alexei. You could wipe them out by yourself."

"That would not help if they were not at the top. Besides, the group I am with doesn't have the reach of an international outfit. They are halfway to legitimacy."

Sidorov sat back in his seat, dissecting what he'd learned and what, if anything, it meant to him. A more cynical man would think nothing, but I knew him. In his own way, he had the same morals as Cam.

It was the only reason I was here.

"I can find out what you need to know," he said eventually. "And I will accept that you do not wish to compensate me in the usual way. But that does leave me with a dilemma, don't you think?"

"We are old friends. I ask for your help, you should freely give it."

"That is not how this world works."

"So, change it. You have the power."

I spoke casually, but Sidorov's eyes narrowed all the same, deciphering the faint threat for what it was. *Push me and I'll snap. I do not have time for your games.*

"May I make a phone call? Or is this a hostage situation?"

I smiled a little. "You are not my hostage."

"That is good. I have not known many you have taken to survive."

The quip reminded me of an issue I'd left behind, one that would cause Cam and Saint problems if I could not get them answers from this skin-crawling trip down memory lane. "Make the calls, Pavel. I will wait."

The answers came in the early hours of the morning. Sidorov took too many phone calls to count, then he came to where I stood at the window and offered me vodka again.

This time, I didn't turn it down. "You have bad news for me?"

"I do not know what is bad for you anymore. Just that the situation I have learned is complex."

I tipped my drink down my throat the way Cam did when he was eager to leave pleasantries behind and hypnotise me with his body.

The thought almost made me smile, but the matter at hand was too consuming to be distracted from for long. "Tell me what you know."

"You are correct in your assumption that the Italians are puppets. They are working for the Aldea cartel, and they have history with your new friends."

"You are sure?"

"The Rebel Kings MC. You are correct that Aldea killed their previous president."

I said nothing, digesting.

Sidorov went on. "It was difficult for me to explain why I was interested in a years-old disagreement."

My heart stuttered at that. I'd come here with a request for information, but Sidorov had already deciphered my true purpose and what I was asking of him. "Do you need to explain yourself?"

"Not when I had you in my stable, but times have changed, Alexei. Alliances and battle lines have moved. I need to know why this matters to you before I consider what you want."

It shouldn't have surprised me. Pavel was an intuitive

Pakhan. It was him who'd taught me to read a man before I showed him my face. "The MC are my friends. I want to help them . . . to protect them from a situation they didn't create."

"Then you should not have allowed them to hijack the merchandise. Whatever agreement I can reach with Aldea, this is something that cannot go unpunished."

"Let them punish Sambini instead. If their operation was competent, they would have known the territory the Romanians abandoned was unconquerable."

"Nothing is unconquerable. Not even you."

Frustration rushed through me. "Why do they want this route so much? There are others, no?"

Sidorov shrugged. "Pride, perhaps. These Rebel Kings, they are a small enterprise, but they cause trouble wherever they go, it seems."

"They don't go anywhere. Their territory is their home."

"Their leader is the son of the fallen president."

"So?"

"His reputation precedes him."

I took a slow, silent breath, biting down on the urge to kill any man that spoke Cam's name. "He is difficult to dissuade from his principles."

"But not impossible?"

"What are you saying?"

Sidorov propped his shoulder on the huge windowpane I stood beside. The aura of power around him made the pose seem strange, but somehow it worked. "There was an agreement in place when Cameron O'Brian Snr was deposed. Elements within the club were primed to form a council that would accommodate Aldea's business needs. His son ambushed that when he took power."

"He *took* nothing. Motorcycle clubs are democratic."

"Regardless, I warned you already that this feud ran deep. Aldea believes he has lost too much to O'Brian's boy. Even if I can persuade him to move his operation elsewhere, someone will have to pay for that."

"Are you telling me that you can make their territory safe, but the Aldea cartel will kill Cam anyway?"

The words sounded far away.

Sidorov took my arm. "The order has been issued. It is too late to recall it. Aldea has agreed to move his operation elsewhere, but his man is already paid and on the ground, a man that will not stop until it is done."

I knew this type of man. I'd been one once—the expensive gun for hire when the cheaper options had failed. "They've been trying to end him for months."

"So they tell me, and this is one thing that works in your favour. Aldea is lazy. I have persuaded him to let your friend be if his man does not find his mark this time."

"They won't come for him again?"

"Aldea? No. He has other concerns. He does not speak for the Sambinis, though. O'Brian has caused them many problems too. You will need to fix this if you wish your friend to have a quiet life."

A quiet life. I'd once asked Cam if that was what he wanted: to build houses with his bare hands and forget about the rest of it. His answer had been vague, if I took him at his word, but Cam was a man who communicated with more than his voice. How he really felt was in every molten stare. Every touch.

He wanted that quiet life.

He needed it.

So give it to him.

God, I wanted to, but as Sidorov's words sank in, panic hit me full force. *There is no time.*

Heart in my throat, I pulled my phone from my pocket. It had run flat and the power bank I'd brought with me was in an airport locker with my wallet and passport.

A string of Russian curses escaped me, ripping from my chest as Sidorov looked on. "I need to go home."

"To England?"

"Yes." I didn't know when I'd started thinking of that place as home, but it took more than geography to make such a thing. It was Cam who made me feel like that—warm, beautiful, stubborn Cam, who was going to die for his principles if I couldn't reach him in time.

My heart was already heading for the door, but there was one more thing I needed to know. "The elements you spoke of within the MC. The rats. Tell me who they are."

Sidorov nodded, understanding my intention. "It is the secretary. John Delaney. Whatever happens with the Sambinis, you will need to neutralise him and all who support him, or you may find you have too many enemies to fight."

I ignored Sidorov's superfluous words, focussing on the two that stood out. John Delaney. *Cracker.* The brother Saint had suspected all along.

Something wicked clamped around my heart. I needed to *go.* Inclement weather had closed Bristol airport to international traffic, meaning I had to fly into London. Even if I left now, it was going to take me many hours to reach Cam. Hours that could cost him everything.

Blindly, I stepped away from Sidorov and darted for the door.

He called my name and I could not understand why I stopped.

Or why I turned to face him when I'd sworn blind so many years ago that I would never lay eyes on him again. "What is it?"

"A warning and some last advice," he said. "You may find that you do not reach the home of your biker friends in time. Or that your old ways are simply not enough."

My old ways. As if I'd ever truly left them behind. I had leverage held hostage in my Bristol penthouse that laid testament to that, but was it enough?

Acid coated my tongue as I forced words from my throat. "There is an attack planned on the compound?"

Sidorov nodded. "To cover the hit and to appease Sambini for the death of his son."

He's not dead. "When?"

"It is imminent. That is all I know."

I clenched my fists. *Too imminent to stop.* "What is your advice?"

Sidorov opened his gaze to me, letting me see the man I knew him to be when mobster life didn't consume his every facet. A man with empathy and kindness—like Cam. "Tell them who you are, Alexei. I have ensured there will be a man with them who will hear you when you speak."

"I have your blessing?"

"Always, dear friend, but you should know this is the end for us—for you and I. What you make of this is yours and yours alone. I do not expect to see you again."

I nodded, knowing he'd take it as my word, and melted

away, out of the hotel suit, past the guards I'd incapacitated, and out into the street.

Fresh air hit me. Fresh panic too. The airport was too far away. I stole a car and hit the back roads, ditching under a bridge and running the rest of the way, but it still felt like a lifetime had passed before I reached the storage locker.

With shaky hands, I charged my phone while I bought a ticket for the next flight and ran for the gate, barging through families and tourists, scaring young children. *Control yourself. You do not want to be remembered.* But it was hard to care, and I pushed on until I was seated on the plane.

My phone buzzed to life as I buckled my seatbelt. With seconds to spare, I called Cam.

He didn't answer and it dawned on me that there was every possibility I was already too late.

CAM

My phone burned a hole in my pocket. Buzzing with a call I couldn't answer because I was jammed up in church for what seemed like the thousandth time in twenty-four hours.

In reality, it was the sixth, and my arse felt like it was moulded to the chair beneath me. My blood was congested and I needed fresh air. More than that, I needed my bike, the open road, and my brothers at my back without fear I'd lose one of them to a stray bullet meant for me.

Guilt ate at me as I glanced around the table and saw my mental fatigue echoed back at me tenfold. Cracker was legit asleep in his seat, not that I gave a shiny fuck about him.

Already reaching for my phone, I dismissed my brothers, watching as Saint left as if he had fire beneath his feet.

I tried not to track his retreat.

Failed, and so I had to watch the others too, like a creepy weirdo, until I finally allowed myself to focus on my phone screen.

Alexei.

My heart turned over. It had been three days since he'd

302

left me in bed. Three days of silence and mystery. My calls to him had gone unanswered and unreturned and I had no idea where he was.

If he was okay.

If he was coming back.

I returned his call. Nothing happened. A dead sound reached me instead of his voice, and more dread consumed me.

Fuck. Where are you?

Three attempts to connect the call didn't tell me. I just had to hope he'd call again.

Nash hadn't left with the others. Leaving me to fret over my phone, he got up and booted Cracker's chair. "Wake up and fuck off."

Cracker opened his eyes, sleepy malevolence in his gaze before he was fully conscious. "Show some respect, pretty boy."

Nash leaned down, his fists on the table, handsome face twisted into an uncharacteristic sneer. "Get out. Before I tell Cam what you said to Tucker about Orla last night."

Cracker paled. He rose and flitted from the room as fast as I'd ever seen the old cunt move.

I cocked a brow at Nash. "Care to share?"

"Only if you don't let it distract you from everything else we've got going on. He'll keep."

"I promise not to kill him today. How's that?"

"It'll do." Nash sank back into his seat. "I overheard him and Tucker calling her 'club snatch' and discussing what they'd do with her if you weren't such a cunt about brothers getting their dicks wet. I dealt with Tucker already, but I figured we didn't need the dissent of Cracker's minions right now by fucking him up."

"That's why you KO'd Tucker in the ring last night? I thought you were blowing off steam at being cooped up here."

"I was. And I fucking meant it."

"Club snatch." I shook my head. "When will these arseholes learn it ain't the fucking eighties anymore?"

Nash shot me a dark look. "Some of them never will."

"You think we should clean house? I promised my dad I'd wait for them to die."

It had been a humorous conversation on my part. At the time, I hadn't believed I'd ever be pres of this club. But then, I'd never imagined my dad being blown up by a car bomb either.

Life sucked. I dropped my phone on the table with a blustery sigh.

Beside me, Nash was thoughtful and quiet. I wondered if I'd made a conscious decision to surround myself with brothers who didn't shout at me. Only Rubi had stones like that, and I missed my belligerent friend.

I glanced at the antique clock on the wall. It was three in the afternoon. He'd be home by tonight, escorted by Mateo and a guard from the Lizard chapter. It boiled my blood to leave his protection to someone else, but I was the one these fuckers wanted to kill. Being close to me right now was poison.

"Cracker needs to go." Nash's husky voice reminded me we'd been having an actual conversation. "He's disloyal and disrespectful, to you and the people you care about. I know you don't want to be a tyrannical leader, but that shit can't fly."

"You think I'm weak, Nash?"

"The opposite, actually. I'm asking you to be weak and take the easy option. It's harder to keep him around and deal with the consequences over and over."

I hummed as I let Nash's thoughts percolate with mine. Saint already wanted Cracker's head. Mateo too. It *would* be easy to let them loose. But what did that make me? A bloodthirsty dictator?

No, Cam. It makes you a man who must protect his family at all costs.

Those words had never left Alexei's lips, but somehow I heard them in his voice, and a deep ache bloomed in my heart. I was as worried about Alexei as I was about my brothers, but there was something else gnawing at me too— the soppy twat buried deep inside that feared he was ghosting me. *Because this life is bullshit he doesn't need and you talked him into getting busy with your mate.*

But . . . no. It hadn't gone down like that. Even if I'd been that kind of arsehole, Alexei wasn't a man who could be talked into anything. And neither was Saint. It still blew my mind that I'd had them in my bed at the same time. Even the fact that I'd kissed Saint was too much to think about right now.

I thought about it anyway, though, tuning Nash out enough that he pulled his AirPods out of his pocket and lost himself in whatever playlist he needed to calm himself down. As the hours passed, I was glad he didn't leave. Our self-imposed confinement suffocated me, but I didn't feel like being alone, and Nash was easy company when he wasn't up my arse about club business.

Maybe that was why my sister liked him so much.

A snort escaped me.

"Something funny?"

My eyes flew open. Saint was in front of me, expression unreadable, and Nash was gone. Fuck. Had I fallen asleep? I didn't think so. The weariness in my bones was as heavy as ever, but I'd definitely left the room. "I was thinking about Nash and Orla. Should I be ragin' that he's banging my sister behind my back?"

"They ain't banging. She's lonely and he's nice to her."

"Sure about that?"

"What do you think?"

"That as observant as you are, you can't have eyes everywhere."

"It's not about seeing. If Nash was fucking her, she'd be happier than she is."

I absorbed that. "You think she's unhappy?"

"Lonely," Saint repeated. "She's trapped here with a bunch of blokes she's not allowed to have relationships with."

"I don't control her like that."

"No, but you made it clear a long time ago that your siblings were off limits to your brothers, which is fine for River—he ain't here—but Orla is, and she gets no fucking dice."

I scowled. "You're chatty tonight."

"I'm stoned." He waved a blunt at me, misting me with the herbal smoke. "Want some?"

Tempting as it was, I needed my wits. I couldn't blame

Saint for taking the edge off, though. If anyone hated being contained more than me, it was him.

Actually, I was surprised he was still here. I'd never managed to keep him in one place for so long before.

I eyed the joint. "Does it help? The weed?" I didn't specify what for. He knew.

He shrugged. "Depends how much I want it to."

"That makes no sense."

Saint finished the joint and crouched to stub it out on Cracker's seat. "So?"

One day I'd have a conversation with him that didn't give me a headache.

One day, I'd put my hands on him and it wouldn't come with a steamroller of complication and emotion.

You already did. You kissed him. Touched him. Marked him. Christ sake, the hickey was still there. I could see it peeking out from the collar of his club tee. It was fading, but the sight of it made my mouth water and my blood run hot enough to blur my vision.

I surged out of my seat and wrapped my hands around his cut, tugging him to his feet because he let me. I propelled him into the tiny kitchen and backed him into the rustic wooden counter he'd built for me. "I want to know you better."

Saint stared at me. Before that night with Alexei, that would've been it, but something had irrevocably changed between us. Something in *him* had shifted. I felt it.

His hands moved slowly to grip my hips, his long fingers sliding beneath my cut and the T-shirt I wore. He found my bare skin and hauled me closer. "You know me."

"It's not enough."

"For what?"

"For how this feels." I leaned in and took his mouth, rough and hard, the way *I* wanted it. Then I eased off, giving him what I knew he liked better, a gentle caress that made him shiver and jut his hips forward.

He was already hard. And kissing him was a lightning bolt to my dick. I thrust against him, slipping my tongue into his pliant mouth, tasting weed and mint and Saint.

Fuck, he did something to me. I could not fucking fathom how he'd been in my life so long and I hadn't claimed this from him the whole time. *Because he's not yours to claim, you goddamn Neanderthal.* But, fuck, I didn't care. I just wanted him in any and every capacity he'd give himself up.

He won't, though, will he?

My kiss-drunk brain took that literally. I cupped his face in my shaking hands and ground us together, all the while knowing he'd never spin around and let me fuck him. That he'd never let me—or anyone else—have that power over him. Saint wasn't like Alexei. He didn't know how to own that shit —how to dominate with a leer and curl of his sinful hips. He wasn't there, not yet. And perhaps he never would be.

He's not made that way. Let him be.

I eased back, taking the pressure off, letting my brain trip back to the heady night we'd spent with Alexei. I hadn't thought so hard about logistics then. For two men who could be awkward as hell, their interaction had flowed with an ease that still made no sense. They hadn't looked at each other like strangers should.

Because they're strange men, the pair of them.

True that. But still, nothing in my life had ever been that simple, so I found it as hard to believe as I did the version of

Alexei I'd seen with Saint. The softer, kinder man, as if he'd seen in Saint what I did and knew how much he needed that.

As if he'd taken the time in a moment I hadn't witnessed to truly look.

That makes no fucking sense either.

I kissed Saint one more time, then pulled back entirely, laying a palm on his chest, soaking up the frantic thump of his heart and wanting to soothe every rough edge of him. "It's going to be okay," I whispered. "Whatever happens, I've got you, I promise."

Distress flared in Saint's gaze. *He doesn't believe me.* But approaching footsteps smothered the reassurance bubbling up my throat.

Rubi was home.

Being torn between my brothers had never hurt so much, but I had to leave Saint and go to Rubi. I'd let him down by not taking his injury seriously enough and he'd suffered because of it. I needed to let him know it wouldn't happen again.

I left Saint in the kitchen in time to catch Rubi and Mateo as they entered the chapel.

Embry wasn't far behind, and then Nash.

It was telling that Cracker didn't show his face, and the mere thought of him was enough to make my jeans loose again.

"Hey, boss." Rubi and I collided at the table.

I pulled him into a hug, hating that he smelled of the hospital. "All right?"

Still in my embrace, Rubi shrugged. "They gave me good drugs that put me in a coma for two days. I feel good, man. You should try it sometime."

The only respite I'd had from this bullshit was the time I'd spent with Alexei.

Alexei and *Saint*, and like he'd heard his name whisper through my brain, Saint appeared.

He was the only brother not to hug Rubi, but he pulled out his chair for him, gestured for him to sit, and thunked a bowl of chilli leftover from the night before in front of him. "Hospital food."

Rubi grinned. "Thanks, brother."

Saint nodded and left the chapel.

After greeting Rubi, the others followed, and Rubi began eating with an enthusiasm that let me know he really was feeling better.

I relaxed a little, but the guilt remained.

"How are things?" Rubi asked.

I shook my head. "You're on sick leave."

"Sick what?"

"You heard me."

"You benching me, Cam?"

"I am. For a month. No riding, no work, no stress."

Rubi started to laugh before he digested that I wasn't joking. "The fuck do you expect me to do if I ain't working?"

"Rest."

"Here? We're on lockdown."

"Yeah, I know. There's a flaw in my plan cos I can't send you home, but I don't give a fuck. You can hole up in my room and watch porn twenty-four seven for all I care, but I'm done taking avoidable risks with my brothers."

"Did River get to you?"

"River?" My brows rose. "What's he got to do with it?"

"The avoidable risk soundbite. Sounds like him."

"He ain't always wrong." *He's never wrong.* "Just do as you're told, okay? I can't worry about anything else right now."

Rubi cleared his plate, then sat back in his seat. "I can't hide upstairs while we're at war. I'd rather shoot myself."

"You were in so much pain a few days ago you *asked* me to shoot you," I countered. "And it's fucking haunting me. I need you, brother, I told you that already, but I can't live with myself knowing that I'm not giving you what *you* need."

"I should be at your side. It's who I am."

I leaned forward and grasped Rubi's shoulder. "I know, but—"

My phone cut me off. I'd have ignored it, but madness had led me to assign a shrill ringtone to Alexei's number so I wouldn't miss his call again.

Fuck. I reached for it on autopilot before my conscience made me stop. I needed Alexei, but Rubi needed me.

The call rang out and, I swear to god, a piece of me died.

"Hey." Rubi frowned and covered my hand with his. "What's the matter?"

"Nothing. Just tired, mate."

"Sure about that? You look kinda devastated. Has something happened no one's telling me about?"

"Nah." I took a breath, trying to calm the anxiety rising in me the longer I ignored Alexei's call. "Nothing's happened since you were here. We're waiting for Sambini to move on us."

"Why, though?"

"What do you mean?"

"Why are we waiting on them? Shouldn't we move first?"

"How? We don't have a fucking clue who they really are

311

right now, let alone where to find them, and I can't risk a run out of the compound, not when I can't be sure who's at my back."

Comprehension dawned in Rubi's weary gaze. "We got a rat?"

"At least one. And no prizes for your first six guesses."

"What are you going to do about it?"

My phone rang again. That Alexei was calling me twice sent my pulse into overdrive.

Still clutching Rubi's shoulder, I fished my phone from my pocket and answered the call. "Gimme a sec."

I lowered the phone before Alexei spoke, forcing myself to focus on Rubi. "Look, none of it matters for you right now. I need you to rest."

Maybe he heard the desperation in my voice. Saw it in my eyes. Whatever it was, it gifted me a rare moment that Rubi didn't argue with me. He nodded and rose to his feet, taking the vintage map book from its place on the bookshelf. "Maybe I'll plan some runs then, get back to basics."

Despite the heaviness weighing me down, I found a smile from the pit of my soul. "We need that. It's who we are."

"'Bout time we remembered it then, eh?"

Rubi gave me a fraternal kiss on the cheek and left.

I pressed the phone to my ear. "Lexi?" Static greeted me. The line was bad. "Are you there?"

More white noise blasted my eardrums and I couldn't tell if it was in my head. I stood and drifted to the window. Saint was in the yard, turning a slow circle as he looked for something. Or someone. We had a lot of wives and kids on the compound, hunkering down with their old men while the lockdown held. I wondered if he was playing a game with the youngest sprogs. For reasons I'd never understood, toddlers loved Saint, and he didn't entirely hate them.

"Cam?" Alexei's voice returned, tinny and distant. Somehow I knew he was far away and it suddenly enraged me that I had no idea where. That he'd crept away from me—from us—without a fucking word and expected me not to give a shit.

"Where the hell are you?" I was a growly motherfucker at the best of times, but despite the fact there was no way Saint could've heard me, the viciousness lacing my tone seemed to reach him.

He turned and stared at the window where I stood.

Alexei said nothing. Or maybe he did and I couldn't hear him over the rage in my blood. "Where are you?" I repeated. "Tell me you're fucking safe."

"I'm safe, but you're not."

His voice was clear as a bell now. Wherever he'd been before, he'd moved. "I know we're not safe. That's why we're on lockdown and why you should be here with us."

"I can't—"

"No!" My shout rang out in the empty chapel and I turned away from Saint. "Stop fucking with me. You know more than you've ever admitted, and I've never questioned you because, for some fucked-up reason, I trust you. But I'm done with it. I need you to come home and tell me the truth. I need you to *tell me* who the fuck you are before I lose my damn mind."

Out of breath, I stopped shouting, half expecting Alexei to be gone—he had form for hanging up on me.

His furious growl caught me off guard. "There is no

time," he spat. "Why won't you listen to me? They are coming for you and there is no more I can do to stop them."

"Who's them? How do you know?"

"It doesn't matter how—"

"It does fucking matter. How do I know you're telling the truth? That you're not working for whoever wants me dead and getting your dick wet at the same time?"

Alexei choked out a laugh that sent a chill down my spine. A beat of terrible silence blasted between us. Then he spoke. "I am not a Trojan horse. The cartel who killed your father took a hit out on you that they cannot call back no matter what I do. The Sambinis are gathering intelligence from Cracker. They will use this to attack the compound and conceal how you are killed, leaving Cracker to take the gavel and form a new council. Even without the cartel, they have much to gain from this. Do you understand what I'm saying to you?"

I understood every damn word except the ones he hadn't said—the ones that explained how the hell he knew so many things that I didn't. My fingers tightened around my phone, cracking the screen. "How can I believe you?"

Silence answered me.

Alexei was gone.

I lowered the phone, violent energy surging through me, and hurled it at the wall, shattering it into a thousand pieces.

Idiot. No one can reach you now, not even River.

Not even Alexei if he called me back.

Fuck. I took a breath, let it rattle around my chest, and searched the yard for Saint, needing him to ground me. But he wasn't there watching me anymore. He'd vanished into thin air, and all I could see was a tiny little girl who belonged to Decoy, the brother who cut our timber. She had white-blonde hair and the biggest smile, one she bestowed on me when she saw me through the glass.

Her little hand came up in a wave.

Forcing a smile, I raised my clenched fist and uncurled it to wave back, but movement behind me spun me around before I could.

I expected Saint. He'd always been good at sneaking up on me, and I'd never asked him to stop. I lived for the flutter in my heart whenever I turned to find him standing there, his gaze on me, his strong, hard body alive with how he felt, telling me everything I needed to know without him fighting for words.

But it wasn't Saint behind me. It was a face I didn't know —a face that screamed danger and had me reaching for a weapon that wasn't there.

I lunged forward, fists raised, but I didn't get far. With a smirk Alexei would've been proud of, the bastard shot me.

[26]

ALEXEI

I drove like a man possessed out of London, praying that Saint was watching Cam instead of tracking me, his full attention where it needed to be.

My phone was plugged into the charging point, the battery flickering in and out, turning the phone off at random intervals, flashing with texts I couldn't read.

Halfway to Bristol, I ran low enough on fuel to force me to stop.

The phone was alive enough to call Cam, but his voicemail kicked in, over and over and over.

I texted Saint.

Alexei: *Plug your leak and guard the boundary. Keep him safe—I will not reach you in time.*

His answer came so fast I cursed myself for not reaching out to him in the first place. For letting my addiction to Cam sway my common sense.

Saint: *how r they going to hit us?*

Alexei: *Hard. That is all I know. Is Cam okay?*

Saint: *worried abt u. how long will u be?*

Alexei: *A few hours. Don't wait. I will find you.*

I needed to hear Saint's voice to believe he'd understood me. That he'd sensed the urgency in the few words we'd exchanged. But there was *no time*, a fact that spiked my blood pressure and made my head throb with anxiety, my brain a mess of frantic thoughts and the daydreams it defaulted to in a desperate act of self-preservation.

Stomach burning, I hit the road again, resisting the primal need to head straight for Cam in Whitness, and instead pointed the car towards Bristol. The miles disappeared as I wove the SUV through the traffic. I was rigid with tension, my jaw set as I prepared for the fight of my life, but still, my mind wandered. Unbidden, I thought of Cam the last time I'd seen him, stretched out beside me, asleep and at peace, sweat cooling on his heated skin.

I could smell him. God, I could almost feel him inside me, fucking me while Saint had filled my mouth and held me like I was made of glass. The contrast between them had bewitched me. I needed Cam's roughness like I needed to breathe, but Saint's gentle touch had felt so good. I craved that now, his sharp-edged sweetness. I craved the comfort I'd found in him.

That we'd found in each other.

He loves Cam as much as I do.

More, maybe. He'd lived it for longer.

The thought calmed me as I neared Bristol and leaving the motorway forced me to slow down, but the respite was brief. Saint was in as much danger as Cam, and it hit me like a death curse that even if Cam didn't die, there was every chance Saint would give his life to save him.

No. Nausea left me dizzy. The car lurched sideways and

317

my blood roared in my ears, deafening me as I pictured Saint, white and cold on a mortuary slab, the earthy light gone from his forest-green gaze.

No. I couldn't let it happen.

Cam wouldn't survive losing Saint.

Neither would I.

Somehow, I made it to my flat. I threw the car underground and strode inside without Horacio noticing that I was an unexploded bomb.

The leverage I'd taken from the Sambinis was exactly where I'd left it the night Cam and his brothers had rescued the trafficked girls.

I crouched in front of Gianni, the eldest son of the man pulling the strings of an organisation that had been a thorn in Cam's side for years. Thanks to the IV I'd inserted into his arm before I'd left him, he was mostly whole, and I sensed a sharpness in him that would work in my favour—an alertness to reality that was untainted by ego and status. "You have one job," I told him. "If you want to live, you will tell whoever asks you the truth about what you saw the night I took you. Do you understand?"

The Sambini prince nodded, belying the fact that I'd ungagged his mouth, giving weight to my assessment that he was not as stupid as the men he'd been caught with.

Men who had not lived.

We reached an understanding. I smuggled Sambini out of the building through the service corridors and steered him into the boot of my car.

I called Saint as I emerged above ground. It didn't connect on a conventional line or a data call, and as I sped towards Devon, I lost signal too, as if the mast had been blown from the ground, taking all means of communication with it.

Landlines severed. Wi-Fi equipment disabled. Dread cooled my simmering blood, spreading icy tendrils through my veins, stilling my pounding heart. The hired gun was close, I could feel it, and he'd already begun the process of isolating the Kings from the outside world, leaving them unable to call for help.

My right foot compressed of its own accord, pushing my powerful car faster and faster on the tight country roads.

I reached the coast and the scent of the ocean filtered through the air vents, making me yearn for the sport bike that would carry me faster to Cam and Saint. In the distance, I saw the shadows of the cliffs beneath the haunting light of the half moon. The silvery gleam spoke to me, though what it said, there was no time to dissect.

Moments later, it was shattered. An explosion rocked the earth and ethereal silver became a fiery ball of orange.

I veered off-road, cutting through a narrow lane that would take me to Whitness quicker. The rough ground shook the car from side to side, battering Sambini in the boot, but I didn't care. I was numb from the inside out, my only reason for breathing to close the distance between me and the men who'd taken my soul and turned it from black to full colour.

The mess in the sky darkened to a thick cloud of smoke. I tracked it as Whitness drew near. *It's not the compound, but it's close.* And I knew why: to distract the authorities while something more heinous occurred elsewhere.

Sirens wailed in the distance. I emerged onto the main road as fire engines swept past, and I headed in the opposite direction.

The compound was two minutes away.

I ditched my car at the rear boundary and, for the first time ever, left the cameras rolling as I picked the fence apart and slipped inside.

Quiet greeted me, an eerie silence that was as terrifying as it was necessary for me to think. *Where the hell are they?*

Not just Cam, but anyone?

They evacuated. It seemed plausible, but Cam was *here*. I couldn't say how I knew, but I did.

I circled the perimeter of the yard, torn between the chapel and the clubhouse—the bar and the residence, but I tripped before I reached either.

The compound fence saved me. I steadied myself, then glanced down and found my foot caught in the crook of a man's arm.

A man wearing jeans and a leather cut that was face down in a pool of blood.

It wasn't Cam. My heart knew it as I crouched down but pounded all the same as I revealed the man's face.

Then it sank into the pit of my stomach. The man on the ground, bleeding out from a stab wound to the gut, was the young brother with the kind and wise smile.

The chaplain.

I did not know his name, just that Cam loved him.

Help him. I didn't want to. And the ghost I'd been before I'd found Cam would've stepped over the fallen brother and walked away.

But Cam had changed me.

So had Saint.

Working fast, I stripped a layer of clothing from myself and pressed hard on the seeping belly wound.

The pain brought the brother round.

He groaned and I slapped a hand over his mouth, using the impact to force his eyes to meet mine. "Shh."

The chaplain slow-blinked. If he was alarmed by a stranger looming over his broken body, it didn't show in his glassy gaze. He was close to death and my soul ached for Cam and how much this would hurt him.

I laid a hand on the chaplain's forehead, his skin already cold, and whispered a prayer I did not believe in.

Then I rose and crept towards the yard. Up ahead, I heard boots on the ground and watched as men I didn't recognise filled the space that belonged to Cam's brothers.

They were smiling.

Like men who had won.

[27]
CAM

I woke up in a fucking fridge.

At least, it felt that way. I was the coldest I'd ever been in my life, my limbs and joints frozen as I tried to move.

A groan escaped me and somehow lit a fire inside me, searing flames that spread through my shoulder and into my arm, my fingers vibrating with every pulse of agony.

Jesus. I squeezed my eyes shut. My head hurt too, like I had the hangover from hell without the memories of the wild party that had put it there.

Fuckfuckfuck. Breathing through my nose, I tried again to move, but footsteps close by stilled me. Even my heart seemed to stop beating, though the fire in my limbs remained.

The footsteps drew nearer. A boot kicked out at me, hard enough to let me know they were enemy not friend.

"Is he dead?"

"Not yet, but the smoke will get him if he does not bleed out. Don't worry, with that much ketamine inside him, he will not get up."

The voice was eastern European, like Alexei's, but without the culture and velvet.

My skin crawled and vomit bubbled in my belly, burning its way up my throat.

By the mercy of fucking god, I kept it down. Kept still. And the man poking me with his foot moved on.

Now they knew I was alive, I let myself breathe shallow, rattly breaths that were deathly enough to leave me dizzy, and I listened hard, trying to place myself.

Last I remembered, I'd been in the chapel, but I wasn't there now. This place smelled of doughnuts and coffee, and the floor I lay on was tiled, not wood.

The café. An enterprise I'd set up for the club's old ladies to run and frequent, but rarely visited myself.

It made no sense that anyone had brought me here, except for the fact that it was the last place even Saint would think to look for me.

Saint. Concern flared in my heart. I'd last seen him in the yard. He'd been staring straight at me, but I'd turned away from him to—to what? Fuck, I couldn't remember. My brain was thick and sludgy and too distracted by being trussed up on the café floor as it dawned on me that my hands were tied.

Years ago, Saint had taught me how to unpick knots with one thumb. It was after he'd walked in on me with a woman who'd bound my hands to the bedframe with her fishnet stocking. A dirty joke that had made me laugh all night long but disturbed Saint more than he could ever explain.

So he hadn't. He'd turned boy scout on me instead, earnest and sweet, the teacher with the rough growl and savage smile. Had he imagined this moment? Any other brother, I'd know, but not Saint. As hard as I loved him, he was still a mystery to me.

I began to drift. Pain and blood loss were a wicked combination, and the jackhammer in my head was relentless enough for me to crave the blissful escape of sleep. Only fear for my brothers kept me conscious and listening.

My steady heartbeat reassured me I wasn't dying any time soon. I pondered the source of the injury to my torso. Buried deep in my mind, I knew the answer, but I couldn't reach it, and after a while, I stopped trying.

I couldn't say how much time had passed when a voice I recognised broke through the fog, slurred and angry.

Cracker. My broken body tensed. Somehow I knew he hadn't come to my aid.

"Why isn't he dead yet?"

Bastard.

The eastern European voice answered him, bored and flat. "I told your man already. He is bleeding out. The fire will finish the job. Are you ready to set it? I want my money."

"You get your money when that cunt doesn't have a pulse."

Nice. I didn't even have it in me to be angry. I'd known for months that Cracker was against me enough to want me dead and I'd done nothing about it, too caught up in the club business that had led us to this point. If I died today, it was as much my fault as his.

"Also, I'm docking your payment for the fuck up with the chaplain. I wanted Malone dead, not Embry. He'd have been useful to me."

Fuck. Embry. No. Grief was a blade that only grew sharper. My heart broke, and it was all I could do to stay prone on the ground, biding my time as my thumb worked to untie the knots at my wrists, my only comfort in the implication that Saint was alive.

The man Cracker had bought my death from moved fast, doing something to Cracker that made him gurgle and gasp. "You do not get to make that decision. The biker got in my way. I killed him. It is how it works and is why so many pay me to kill this one, no? He is in the way?"

"Who else paid you?"

"It does not matter. The job will be done."

"What about the rest of them?"

"They are quiet for now, like we agreed. You have time to do what you need to do before you make your escape."

"Malone is still breathing. He'll know this was me and he won't stop until I'm dead."

"That is your problem. Perhaps you should've been more specific when you ordered the hit on your president."

"I should've killed him myself."

"You should. Now you have a bullet in a man who is not yet dead and I have run out of patience to assist you with that. I will take my payment now."

"No," Cracker spat. "You fucked up, and not just for me, for whoever else you took money from. He's still alive—"

He cut off with a strangled splutter I'd heard from him before, the one that had oozed from him when his face turned purple beneath the force of my forearm against his throat.

I chanced a flicker of my heavy lids and my hazy gaze fell on Cracker against the shiny countertop in the café's kitchen. A man bore down on him, body tense with aggression. His stance wasn't one I recognised, but his face was familiar. Of course it was—he was the arsehole who'd put a bullet in me.

He killed Embry.

And he'd hurt my brothers. It was the only explanation for their absence. The only reason they hadn't come stampeding through that door to kill these motherfuckers.

Orla. Fuck. Where is she?

The fresh wave of fear was enough to clear my mind of drowsiness and pain. I darted a glance around the kitchen and found the magnetic strip that held the knives. It was three feet away. If I could force my body upright and lunge for it, I had a chance.

Cracker was losing his fight. I took advantage of his misfortune and lurched to my feet, eyes only for knives.

My fingers closed around the cool metal handles. The sensation reminded me of Alexei in every circumstance except when I was inside him, fucking him until he felt human enough to let it all go. *Don't think about him. He's not here.* I felt him, though. And it was his voice, again, that urged me on.

I grabbed the knives and spun around, clumsily knocking over a nearby chair, but despite the clattering, I still held the advantage.

They didn't see me coming.

I ripped the stranger from Cracker and buried the knife in his neck, twisting hard until I was sure I'd inflicted an unsurvivable injury, dodging his flailing hands as he went for my throat with a switchblade I'd failed to notice.

The blade caught my face, a sharp scratch that went nowhere I had time to worry about.

I punched it from his hand and kicked it away, then I shoved him to the floor and stamped on his head. "That's for Embry."

The bloke was gone, life seeping from him in a slow gurgle. Later, it would hit me that I'd killed a man, but as his eyes rolled and fixed in the back of his head, I felt nothing but rage. Embry was dead, my brother, my friend. If I didn't fight, I'd break.

Cracker. I turned on him, growling as pain rocketed through me, and intercepted him as he fled for the door.

I dragged him back, manhandling him to the tiles, one knife at his throat, the other pressed beneath his overhanging belly. "You fucking rat. I should gut you right here."

Cracker gulped, but the fear in his bloodshot eyes wasn't as deep as it needed to be. *He doesn't believe I'll kill him.*

And he was right. He was a rat, but he was still a brother, and there were better, more humiliating ways to end life as he knew it. My dad had taught me that.

I cold-cocked Cracker with the knife handle, knocking him out with one well-aimed blow.

He fell slack beneath me. I shoved my arms under his shoulders and dragged him out of the café, dumping him where I could keep eyes on him while I figured out what the fuck was going on.

The café was tucked away in the corner, a hole in the wall that turned out toasties and tea to locals affiliated to the club. There wasn't much around it—just a couple of parking bays and the play park me and Saint had built one summer when I'd been so obsessed with him that I'd needed a plausible excuse to keep him shirtless and sweaty without acting on the fierce desire coursing through me.

It was why we had four double swing sets when, at the time, the sum total of MC kids the right age to play on them had come to a round three.

I couldn't say why my head went there as I crept around them, every sense on high alert, but my brain was unmanageable right now.

Slow.

Dreamy.

And still throbbing like a motherfucker.

Clutching the kitchen knives, I reached the storage bins that stood between me and the yard. I leaned against one, taking the weight off, just for a moment.

My head swam, the buzzing in my ears so loud I doubled over and puked.

I wiped my mouth with the back of my hand. It was bloody, but I couldn't remember if it was mine or the intruder I'd killed. I didn't *want* to remember. *Stay sharp. It's all you've got.*

Nice pep talk, but I was spinning too hard to absorb it.

I came upright and took a slow breath, focussing on the knives in my hands, tightening my grip, gritting my teeth against the pain in my shoulder.

Don't fight it. You need the pain to survive.

I heard Saint's voice this time and something inside me snapped, triggering a surge of energy I desperately needed.

Voices reached me.

Unfamiliar voices.

Fuck, I didn't even recognise the language.

Crouching, I crept around the storage bin and squinted in the darkness at the yard. At first, I saw only men in cuts that weren't ours. *Crows.* Then I noticed the others—the men in smarter clothes with slick hair and clean shoes.

Sambinis.

Or were they cartel? At this point, I couldn't recall who wanted me dead the most.

Somewhere I couldn't see, a door opened. A dragging sound reached me, and I watched the expression of the nearest Crow change.

It was Rocco St John and he looked as sick as I felt. "You killed them all?"

A Sambini goon—*Lorenzo*—laughed. "Not quite. Just gassed them a bit to keep them quiet while Aldea's man takes out O'Brian. The boss wants that one, though. We'll load him up when the fat man comes back."

That one. I didn't have to look to know he meant Saint. That the Sambinis still believed he'd killed Frank Crow, Drummer, and their goddamn prince.

Dread filled me. Saint was innocent, but with no evidence to prove it, they'd kill him without question, and that was the kind option. *They'll torture him first.* I'd heard shit about the Sambinis.

They'll burn him alive.

The gruesome image propelled me to my feet faster than my broken body was prepared to take. More nausea rattled me, but I pushed it down and stepped away from the shelter I'd found behind the bins, revealing the expanse of the yard and the sight of my brothers laid out, face down and unconscious with their hands bound behind their backs.

Nash. Mateo. Saint.

Only Rubi was missing.

And Embry, but I already knew his fate and the pain in my heart nearly sent me crashing back to my knees.

One thing kept me standing.

"*Not quite.*"

They were still alive and as I drove forward, forcing my heavy legs to keep moving, Saint was already twitching, the true rebel in him refusing to stay down.

No.

Not yet.

But it was no good. He groaned and rolled over, attracting the attention of a nearby Crow.

The scrote stepped up, drawing his foot back to put the boot in, to kick my brother when he was down.

Rocco St John stopped him, stepping between them with a subtle shake of his head, and it was the window I needed.

I burst into the yard, covered in blood, a maniacal energy surging through me. "Someone want to tell me what the *fuck* you think you're doing with my brothers?"

Every man present and awake jumped out of their skin. Despite the fact that they were waiting on Cracker and his departed murder pal, they hadn't heard me coming.

On instinct, the Crows backed up, grouping together.

Rocco's eyes were conflicted.

Worried.

I absorbed that and turned my back on him. Whatever plan he'd arrived with, he didn't like it. He didn't like *this*, and it was all I could bank on as I faced the Sambinis alone.

Hardening my glare, I found the gaze of the one who'd marked Saint for certain death. Lorenzo Sambini—the same cunt who'd come here searching for his cousin. "Speak," I growled. "You're on Rebel property."

Lorenzo laughed. Again. "Not for long. Look around you, O'Brian. You're barely standing and your brothers are dead."

"They ain't dead." *Not all of them.* "And neither am I, so

330

I'm warning you now, tell me what the fuck you want before I rip your head from your shoulders."

"How are you going to do that with a bullet in you?"

"I'll manage. I already killed your hitman."

"He wasn't ours. Your secretary hired him."

"Either way, he's dead and I ain't. What makes you think I can't end you?"

"Logic. I have five men with guns, plus the hired help." Lorenzo gestured behind me to the wavering Crows. "You are alone with a carving knife, so let me tell *you* what is going to happen here. I am going to shoot you, properly this time. Then I am going to collect the man that took Gianni and take him to my uncle. Your other brothers can live, but your business here is done. Razed. What becomes of them is not my concern. Is there any part of that you don't understand?"

"I understand it all, but you're wrong."

"About which part?"

"The part where you kill me here and Sambini is happy about it. My brother didn't touch your prince. It was me. I put a bullet in his head when I buried Frank Crow and Drummer."

Lorenzo blinked. Then he smiled, as if I'd played into a trap even he hadn't been aware of. "Even better." He darted a glance to the man standing next to him. A man who looked more like Alexei than a man of Mediterranean descent. "But all it means is that your brother dies now instead of you. We don't have time for the inconvenience he would wreak on us if he survived your death."

He nodded to someone I couldn't see and the Sambinis separated, half advancing on me while the others darted to where Saint lay prone on the ground behind me, still vibrating with the effort to wake up.

I spun around as they raised their weapons, a silenced gun in the hands of each man. Rocco St John charged forward, but whatever his motives, he wasn't going to get there in time, and neither was I.

They were going to kill Saint. They were going to shoot him in the dirt like a rabid dog and there was nothing I could do to stop them.

Cold hands closed around me, wrestling me to the ground. I fought them like a wild animal, thrashing and stabbing air with the knives in my hands.

Booted feet kicked them away, dislocating one of my thumbs. I growled at the fresh pain and used all my strength to throw my assailants off me, but the respite was brief. The muzzle of a gun touched my temple at the same moment the rest of Sambini's crew reached Saint.

It was over. I'd failed, and the first man I'd ever loved was going to die.

"I would not do that if I were you."

The new voice was close, and my skin broke out in goosebumps before the familiarity of the answering rush registered. That hypnotic wave. The addicting heat. Even broken and defeated on the concrete, my body felt it.

Alexei.

My eyes fluttered, struggling for focus. To stay conscious. Fuck, maybe I wasn't conscious. Maybe I was already gone and dreaming of him, like I did every day he wasn't with me.

The gun disappeared.

"Cam."

No. Don't say my name like that.

"*Cam*." Smooth hands grasped my wrists and slid up my forearms. "Get up. There is work to do before I can treat your wounds. Stay with me. It'll be okay, I promise."

He let go and only the desperate need to touch him again kept me from falling back to the ground.

I lurched upright. Alexei was already ten feet from me, striding towards where Mateo and Nash lay on the ground.

Nash was still out cold.

Mateo was awake.

Alexei unbound him, all the while speaking rapidly in a language I didn't know to the man I'd already pegged as closer to his ethnicity than the Sambinis.

The man paled. Even in the darkness, I saw it—the twist of a man's face when he saw a ghost. He said something to the men still looming over Saint.

They backed up like they'd been burned, rejoining the men who had already retreated from me. Then he faced Alexei and said something else.

"You will wait," Alexei snapped in English. He took a car key from his pocket and pressed it into Mateo's hand. "My car is in the undergrowth behind the rear fence. Your chaplain is in the back seat. Take him to the nearest hospital and hurry. There is not much time if you want him to live."

Mateo's bleary eyes widened. He scrambled to his feet, then seemed to remember himself and turned to me.

"Go," I ground out. "Don't stop for anything."

Mateo sprinted away, staggering a little as whatever fucked-up thing these cunts had done to my brothers lingered in his system.

Rage filled me, but before I could take a step, Alexei was back.

He stood next to me, one arm held out, guarding me, as his gaze fixed on Saint, watching as he started to come round again. "No one touches a Rebel King."

His voice was pitched low, but it sent a shiver down my spine, as if my body knew I was witnessing something I'd never been meant to see.

Saint opened his eyes and sat up. He glanced around, blinking, taking in Nash unconscious beside him, the Crows slowly slinking back, and the huddle of worried Sambinis.

Then his gaze fell on me and Alexei, guarding me like a goddamn lion. I waited for the confusion to hit, but it never came.

The motherfucker smiled. At *Alexei*. And sank back on his elbows. "You're late."

ALEXEI

Cam's confusion was painful. It hurt almost as much as seeing him so badly injured and not being able to help him yet, but I jammed a lid on the rising distress in my soul and kept my gaze on Saint, anchoring myself to his steady calm.

His wisdom.

Somehow this man knew me better than I'd known myself before I'd met him.

Before I'd met Cam.

"You're late."

I smiled without humour. "No, friend. I am right on time."

Barely. But this wasn't the time for details. I was here. We all were. And only some of us would make it out.

Satisfied that Saint was contained, and that Cam was too injured to do anything drastic, I forced myself to leave him and bore down on the Sambinis.

Sidorov's man had extracted himself from them. He met me halfway and spoke in rapid Russian. "I was warned something was coming. I never imagined it would be you."

"Imagination is dangerous. I speak passable Italian, but I think this would be better coming from you. What is your name?"

"Viktor."

"Good. Now tell them who I am and what will happen to their entire organisation if they don't do exactly as I say."

Viktor obeyed, giving the Italians the good news. It should've pleased me to watch the disbelief colour their faces, and then horror-laced realisation dawn as they pulled out a satellite phone to validate Viktor's claim. But I was distracted by the final Rebel King—the VP—waking up and Cam lurching towards him.

Saint got there first. He unpicked the tight knots binding the VP's wrists in the time it took Cam to stagger twenty feet and collapse beside him.

I noted the skill, then left them to care for their brother.

A man I believed to be Lorenzo Sambini, nephew of their *Pakhan*, was on the phone. I approached him, enjoying the way he baulked as I got closer, and whoever he was conversing with gave him an answer that made him believe I was going to kill him.

I liked his fear. It fuelled me.

You hurt Cam.

You hurt Saint.

Now I will hurt you.

The Sambinis bunched up, turning their backs inward as I circled them. It amused me that they had not noticed I carried no obvious weapons.

Lorenzo spread his hands. "We didn't know."

"Know what?" I tilted my head sideways, toying with him.

"That the Kings were in bed with the Sidorovs."

"They are not." I walked around them again, stalking my prey. "They are in bed with me."

"You're Sidorov's attack dog."

"Am I?"

"They call you The Ghost."

A lazy laugh escaped me. "I am not a ghost. I am very much alive, wouldn't you say?"

Lorenzo swallowed. "We didn't know."

The repetition gave away his fear and I wasn't sure of the emotion that swept over me. I wasn't used to it—to feeling so much. *It is Cam's fault.* I glanced at him. He was on his knees, helping his VP sit up, but he was listening, watching, and he turned his molten gaze on me.

I had never known something so alive.

I'd never *felt* it.

I circled back to Lorenzo. "Your uncle is already being instructed on how the rest of his life will play out, but let me tell you how it will be for you. Are you paying attention?"

"I'm listening."

"Good. I will switch to English now so the Kings can understand us. Show them the respect they deserve or this conversation will end without the resolution you need to walk out of here alive."

Viktor edged closer. He held a satellite phone of his own, letting me know that Sidorov had known exactly how this would go down. That it would be my name and not his that ended this, leaving him free to whatever he pleased if the scraps left behind intrigued him.

I could not even hate him for it. Sidorov was a ruthless crime boss, but despite how he'd acquired me, he shared

Cam's distaste for trafficking flesh and bone. The war that had cost Cam his parents was won.

Lorenzo shifted, reminding me that I'd yet to speak.

I glanced at Cam again. He wasn't looking at me anymore, but Saint was, and his gaze hooked into me, finding purchase somewhere I did not know he could reach.

Lorenzo.

Focus.

I took a breath and turned back to Sambini. "The trafficking operation is over. Your partnership with the Aldea cartel has severed. You will not do business with them again in this country."

"We have an arrangement with them," Lorenzo protested. "We can't just walk away."

"You do not need to. They already have, and they will not come back. That avenue of income is closed to you now. They will not take your call and I will not take kindly to you seeking a new partner."

"What about the coke shipments? We owe them a percentage."

"That goes to the Kings to repay the damage you have caused here."

Lorenzo's brows rose and I realised how young he was— too young, perhaps, to know how a conversation like this worked. "How do we know Aldea won't come after us for payment?"

"You do not. But your uncle will by now."

"It's a lot of money."

"I know."

Lorenzo glanced around. "How will they launder it?"

"That ain't your business."

The growl came from behind me. I didn't have to look to know Cam was on his feet, and I suppressed a smile, an easy enough feat given how badly I knew he was hurt.

"They will figure it out," I said. "I have it on good authority that they have an excellent financial advisor."

Lorenzo didn't get the joke. His frown deepened as he scrambled to gather loose ends. "What about construction? The Kings still owe us an order of cement."

"We cancelled it," Cam said. "Sent your money back. If you ain't got it, that's on you."

"And your labour force?"

"Give them honest jobs. We don't want no part of dodgy work that gets people killed."

My noble biker boy. This time I did smile, but it wasn't pleasant, and Lorenzo Sambini shivered. "We'll need to meet again to iron out the details."

"You will," I agreed.

"Wait for our call." Cam appeared at my side, tension and heat radiating from him like an incoming firestorm. "And be patient. We've got a shitshow here to clear up."

His rage made my cock twitch.

Oblivious, Lorenzo nodded and turned back to me. "Will you be there too?"

I leered at him, then spoke in Italian. "Maybe. Or perhaps you will never see me again. But nothing will change. Do you understand, Lorenzo?"

"I don't understand how the Kings crossed your radar. There's nothing they can do that we can't do better."

"You are mistaken," I told him truthfully, then switched back to English. "The Kings do not work for me. I work for them. That should be enough for you."

It was. But I had one more thing up my sleeve. I looked over my shoulder, past where Saint had hauled his VP to his feet and to the boundary that I had breached, again, to enter the Kings' compound undetected.

I whistled. "Come out."

Gianni Sambini stumbled out of the shadows. He was hungry, tired, and terrified, but otherwise unharmed.

He came to my side, fear making him tremble, and Lorenzo's mouth fell open.

I smiled again. "What? You thought he was dead?"

Lorenzo shook his head, stunned. "The Crows told us Malone killed him and incinerated his body."

"What a colourful lie."

Beside me, Cam grunted, but I couldn't tell if it was through the dismantling pain he had to be in or amusement.

I resisted the urge to check, just, and pushed Gianni forward, making him trip on his shaky legs. "The Crows were seeking vengeance they are too weak to inflict themselves. I killed their president and his friend. I kept this one alive as a consolation prize."

"It's true," Gianni said. "He snapped their necks with his bare hands."

I smiled again. "Good boy."

The Sambinis tugged their prince into their fold, backing up, inch by inch. Only Lorenzo remained, and I began to admire him a little. I would not have enjoyed killing him.

You haven't killed anyone yet.

Yet. A tiny word with so much power.

I stepped closer to Lorenzo, ignoring the wrench in my heart as the movement put distance between me and Cam. Russian words surged up my throat and I let them, knowing

Viktor would translate. I was bored with this. I needed it to be over. *Cam* needed it to be over. "Gianni knows what will happen to you and everyone you've ever cared about if you do not follow my instructions. Believe him when he tells you what I am capable of."

Lorenzo nodded, but it was autopilot more than acquiesce. I'd frightened him and I liked it enough that the devil I was fighting to contain battered the walls I'd built around it. I wanted to frighten Lorenzo more. Only Cam's suffering presence at my back restrained me.

"Go," I whispered. "Remember what you have seen and heard today. I do not like repeating myself."

Lorenzo Sambini held my gaze for a fleeting moment; then he stepped back, escaping the web I'd snared him in when I'd invaded his personal space.

He rejoined his men and they melted away.

Viktor went with them, leaving me alone in the darkness, but barely a heartbeat passed before I felt him.

Before I felt *them*.

Cam was too wrecked to speak. As Saint held him up, he pressed his lips to the hollow behind my ear.

"You're not as cold as you think you are."

341

I had no idea who he was.

How he'd bewitched and terrified two international crime families into bowing to his word.

I just knew I wasn't scared of him.

That I loved him in a strange and beautiful way that was as inexplicable as it was consuming.

I buried my face in Alexei's neck, absorbing the impact of what he'd done for us had inflicted on him. I felt his pain and trauma in the tiny, subtle shiver he let pass through him, and I knew Saint did too.

Saint and Alexei. I was missing something there, but I was too destroyed to figure it out.

I swayed on my feet.

Only Saint's arms kept me upright as I raised my head.

"Where's everyone else?" I choked out. "Orla—"

"We evacuated." Nash limped to my side, casting Alexei an unreadable glance. "Saint knew something was coming so I gave the order."

"Rubi?"

"He led them out. Did six runs to get everyone to safe houses and sent the rest to Lizard. I ain't heard from him in a while, though. My phone's bust."

"They took out the mast," Saint said. "That's how I knew it was starting, but most of the members were out by then."

I didn't understand how I'd missed that happening.

"You weren't in the chapel when I came to tell you." Nash read my thoughts and guilt passed through his features. "The lights were off. I didn't see the blood on the floor until we came back to do a sweep and they locked us in and gassed us."

"Jesus." I scrubbed a filthy, bloody hand down my face. "I killed the dude Cracker hired to kill me."

"Aldea hired him too. He was a double agent." Alexei's voice was distant.

I was still clutching him like a starving man.

He peeled my hand from his wrist and stepped back, looking beyond me to where Cracker lay unconscious on the ground.

I saw where his brain went, but he moved before I could stop him. "Lexi."

He ignored me and I staggered after him until strong hands pulled me back.

Saint.

"Get the fuck off me." Whole, I might've fought him off, but Saint's hold on me was absolute.

Alexei reached Cracker. He crouched.

Moments later, I knew Cracker was dead.

I felt sick. "*Lexi.*"

It was a whisper this time, but it reached him and he turned his glittering gaze on me, shaking his head. "This man

343

conspired to have your father killed long before he came for you. As long as he lived, you would never have the life you want."

Saint's tightening grip told me he agreed.

I turned to Nash, my level-headed VP.

He met *Alexei's* gaze and nodded. "Sits right with me."

Fucking hell. The realist in me accepted the logic—Cracker had been happy to burn me alive in the café, after all—but I wasn't sure if Alexei knew that. If any of them did, and I wasn't about to tell them. This crazy night was fucked up enough as it was.

Spinning, I leaned heavily on Saint. His hand slipped under my grimy T-shirt and he swiped his thumb over the base of my spine. The touch was hypnotic, and I almost passed the fuck out, but the roar of approaching bikes jarred me to life.

Lots of bikes.

Tension rocketed through me. I lurched away from Saint and spun around as the lights of too many bikes to count illuminated the yard.

Rubi swept in, every brother in arms at his back, and then dozens more from every chapter from Cornwall to Reading.

Jesusfuck, it was a sight to behold, one that nearly sent me to my knees again.

The bikes began to park up. A beat-up hog with faded red paint was closest to me. The rider dismounted and ripped off his helmet.

Only it wasn't a he. It was a woman with chocolate locks down to her waist and furious obsidian eyes.

"Orla? What the fuck?"

She threw her helmet at my feet. "Don't fucking start. You look like you died already."

Nash caught her as she flew at me, seizing her by the waist. "Easy. I didn't give you a bike so you could run your brother over with it. This shit ain't his fault."

I had nothing. I believed Saint when he said they weren't banging, but giving her a goddamn bike?

In the MC world, he might as well have wifed her.

So let him. You want her to be happy, don't you?

It was Embry in my head this time, and my scrambled, wandering thoughts screeched to a halt.

I whirled around again. Saint wasn't there to catch me, but Alexei was. "The bullet went straight through, but if you don't let me treat you for blood loss and shock, soon it won't matter."

"What?"

"Cam, you got shot and you are not made of Kevlar."

"Embry—"

"Mateo's with him." Saint was somewhere behind me. "Fix the landline so he can get through when he calls."

I had no clue who he was talking to. Only that Alexei's iron grip was holding me upright, his soft breath and lips at my ear keeping me conscious.

"Give your orders," he whispered. "Then let me help you."

I passed out, drifting. I came round to a floating sensation and a hand that wasn't Alexei or Saint wrapped around mine. "Riv? That you?"

"It's me." My brother loomed over me, his face coming together as the present returned to me, along with the throb in my skull. "You alive down there?"

"Think so." I took a moment, then tried to sit up. Agony ripped through me and River cringed.

"Easy. You got shot, bro."

That much, I remembered. I gritted my teeth and forced myself up with the arm that wasn't tied into a sling. The room —the clubhouse bar—swam for a few seconds, but I didn't knock out or puke, so I took the win.

River steadied me. "Don't do anything wild, you've got an IV in your arm."

"Hmm?"

He jerked his head at a trailing plastic tube. "You have an IV," he repeated. "Your Russian friend said you needed it and Skylar agreed."

"Skylar?"

"He's not here. I called him, but Vladimir didn't seem to need any help, so I didn't ask him to come."

"Vladimir?"

River rolled his eyes. "He didn't tell me his name."

"It's Alexei."

"I know."

"Why are you—fuck, never mind." I swallowed a wave of nausea and tried to put my fragmented brain back together. "Embry?"

"Saint left a while ago to find out. He's with Mateo at the hospital. Skylar said he'll check in when he goes on shift in the morning."

"It's not morning yet?"

"Depends what time and what day you think it is. You've been out cold since yesterday."

No wonder my bladder felt like it was gonna explode. "Where's Alexei?"

"Around. He said he wouldn't leave until you were okay."

"I don't want him to go."

"Why?"

"Hmm?"

"What is he to you?" River peered at my face as if it was doing strange things. "I thought you were in deep with Saint?"

"What?"

"Come on, bro. I called that shit years ago."

"To who?"

"Orla. No one else."

I blew out a breath. "I love Saint. And Alexei. It's complicated." But fuck, it felt good to say it out loud, and I needed all the good I could get. "Why are you here?"

River helped me stand. He was smaller than me—an inch shorter, a stone lighter, but his gaze was darker, in every sense, and the last time we'd been this close, he'd told me it would be easier if I'd died. "Orla called me. She told me the worst had happened so it was time to decide if I really didn't give a shit."

"And?"

"It was never that, and you know it. It was the opposite. I love you and I've been terrified my whole fucking life that you're gonna get killed and it'll just be me and Orla."

"I'm still here, Riv."

He cut me a vicious glare. If I hadn't been used to it, I'd have flinched. "You got shot because one of Dad's brothers

347

wanted you gone. Because the shit Dad got involved with never went away. Where does it stop?"

Skylar had asked me that once. I couldn't remember what I'd told him, and no sensible answer came to me now. "I don't know. I can't even tell you what happened to get to this point, cos I'm not fucking sure."

"Where did Alexei come from?"

"I met him in a bar."

"Then what?"

I shrugged the shoulder that wasn't strapped, swollen, and humming with bone-deep pain. "I guess we were more alike than I realised, except I still don't know the truth of it."

"Orla thinks he's a mafia don."

"Maybe he is."

"You really don't know?"

"Nope."

"But you love him anyway?"

"Yep. Fuck, I need to piss."

River steered me in the direction of the shower room attached to the bar. It was for non-resident brothers to clean up after a long ride and smelt of sweaty leather and old socks. I staggered to a urinal and took a piss that felt so good I swayed on my feet.

Then I puked in the sink with a violence that shook my fucking bones.

When I was done, I ran the tap and stared at my reflection in the cracked mirror. I looked like hell—black eyes, sallow skin, dried blood everywhere I could think of. Worse than that, though, was the darkness weighing me down. Man, I was so confused.

"Cam?" River appeared at my side. He pressed a

toothbrush into my hand and rubbed my back. "Come on. You'll feel better if you get cleaned up."

I didn't believe him, but I scrubbed the crappy taste from my mouth anyway and drank the sports drink he forced on me. "Cracker's dead," I blurted for no reason in particular.

River nodded. "Rubi told me. The masses don't know yet, though, so you need to talk to them when you feel up to it."

"We need church first."

"No. Your brother is right."

I jerked upright from where I'd slumped over the sink. Alexei was in the doorway, impeccable as always, the tightness in his slate-grey gaze the only sign of stress I could see.

Fuck, he was beautiful. "Where's Saint?"

Somehow, it made sense to ask him before anyone else.

"He just called." Alexei glanced over his shoulder before looking at me again. "Your chaplain is going to be okay, so he is coming home. The enforcer will stay at the hospital until someone can relieve him. But, like I said, your brother is right about your church. It can wait until your members are reassured. Your council is loyal. Lean on them."

"You're so wise."

"Sarcasm, Cam?"

"I don't know."

Alexei smiled. Had we been alone, I believed he'd have come to me, but he stayed where he was, and so did I.

Eventually, he disappeared again.

I shivered.

River whistled. "He's intense."

"I know."

"Orla said he saved you. And the club."

"He—"

River shook his head. "I don't want the details. I just need you to be okay."

"I am."

"You're not. You're fucking lucky, that's what you are. That bullet went straight through the muscle. If it hadn't, you'd have bled out while whatever shit they stabbed you with kept you down."

"What?"

River rubbed a tender spot on my neck. "Nash said you were missing for ages. Alexei found the needle mark in your neck. Some cunt must've drugged you to keep you down."

Disquiet flooded me, a grimy sensation that threatened the peace I'd forced on my stomach.

River drew back enough to find my gaze and hold it. "Hey, it's okay. They didn't do anything else to you. Saint checked the security footage before he wiped it."

How my kid brother knew the depths my mind had sunk to, I had no idea. I pried his hands from me and held them in mine. "I'm glad you're here. Will you come back when it ain't world war three? Spend some time with us?"

"I don't know, man. I mean, what's changed? You're still pres and the club is still toxic as hell."

"I'm working on that. Have been this whole fucking time. What do you think this mess was all about?"

"I can't think, Cam. I just. Fuck, I told you. I just need you to be okay."

"I—" I rubbed my lips, willing my brain to work. "Okay. I mean. I'm all right, Riv. Honest. Just got some shit to clean up, then we're good, I promise. As legit as we're ever gonna be."

"Don't make promises you can't keep."

"Why don't you trust me?"

"I do. It's every other cunt."

"What about Rubi?"

River's distant gaze snapped to me. "What's that supposed to mean?"

"He ain't a cunt."

"I didn't mean brothers."

Brother. The word was starting to blur in my head. "Where did Alexei go?"

River sighed. "He didn't leave. I told you, he said he wouldn't."

"When?"

"When you were sleeping off a shit ton of blood loss and fucking horse tranquillisers or whatever. Man, you were so sick from that crap, I thought you were gonna die."

I felt like I had. "I need to speak. Fuck." I turned back to the sink and stuck my good hand beneath the tap, scooping up water to run it through my hair.

It made no difference whatsoever, but River laughed, and that made all the difference in the fucking world.

30

ALEXEI

River O'Brian watched Cam speak to the crowd of assembled brothers, keeping to the shadows like I did but on the other side of the yard.

I kept eyes on him for no other reason than it distracted me from the urge to run away. Not from Cam, but perhaps from myself.

Not that I would've got far. Cam was distracted, but I felt Saint's penetrating gaze on every inch of my skin, and I did not mind it much.

Cam spoke like a leader. He made no promises and told no lies, but it was enough. The brothers that dropped their cuts and left were not his brothers at all.

After a lingering, yearning glance at the Rebel Kings' road captain, River O'Brian left too. Cam watched him go, then sank onto the stone steps in front of the clubhouse again, flexing the fingers of the hand trapped in the sling, testing the dislocated thumb I'd reset while he'd been unconscious.

His expression was distant, his skin pale in the dim light of the early evening.

I sat beside him and claimed his other hand, sheltering the gesture in the shadow his bigger body cast over mine.

He chuckled. "You don't have to hide that for my benefit. No cunt here would fucking dare."

"Dare what?"

"Come at me for who I love."

"You love me, Cam?"

"As much as I can when I got no clue who you are."

That was fair. But I wasn't his priority right now. I could not be when there were so many other things claiming his attention. "You will have your church soon?"

"When Mateo gets back. He's on his way."

"Then what?"

He turned to me. "In life or in business?"

"It is all the same to you, no? That is why it is so . . . messy." I spoke with humour, but it was strained. For some reason, English was difficult to find. The words slipped away when I needed them most.

"I want you to be with me . . . in church, I mean. I don't want to tell your story for you."

"It is that important?"

"In my world? Yeah, Lexi, it is. I know you ripped yourself open to do what you did for us. And I know why, even if you can't say it to my goddamn face yet, but I don't know who you are or where you came from, and my brothers need that, man. They need to know it was real and the shit that went down here ain't gonna happen again."

"It won't." The growl in my voice made me sound like him. "Sambini knows what will happen if he breaks the agreement."

"I get that, but why? Who the fuck are you?"

"I thought I would never have to tell you. Even after I knew my heart would belong to you forever, I thought I would help you give yours to Saint, and then I would leave."

Cam swallowed. He was in a lot of pain, but it was nothing compared to the hurt in his dark gaze. "I felt that— that you wanted me and him to be something, but I never figured out why. There was so much going on, it was enough for me that you'd seen him . . . like, really seen him, you know? Not many people do."

"I see him."

"You're gonna have to explain that to me sometime."

"Explain what?"

"The bit I'm missing in this fucking shitshow."

I squeezed his fingers, a reflex that warmed my soul. "You think what you have shared with us is a shitshow?"

"No. I'm just confused as hell at how easy two awkward-as-fuck people can be around each other when they've only met twice."

"We were naked for one of those. That helps with inhibitions, no?"

"Didn't know you had any, mate."

I laughed, a quiet sound that seemed to belong to a man I did not know yet. "I will come to your church if it makes you happy. Then maybe you will let me take you home?"

"I want Saint to come."

"So do I."

Cam took a breath, but he was interrupted by approaching boots. The bustle in the yard had thinned out since he'd spoken, leaving his closest brothers behind. They stood before him now, all of them, save the injured chaplain.

It was time.

I did not help Cam to his feet.

No one did—he didn't give them the chance. He rose as if he hadn't been shot through the shoulder less than twenty-four hours ago and waved his soldiers inside.

Then he looked to me. "Are you coming?"

I hesitated only a moment before I shrugged. "Whatever you want."

"I want *you*."

Cam turned and stomped inside.

I followed him through the bar where he'd slept all day and into the space he called the chapel—a room with an ornate table and a collection of decrepit office chairs.

His brothers were already in place, exhaustion heavy in their faces, especially the enforcer who'd come from the hospital.

Only Saint seemed unaffected by fatigue, a facade, I assumed, as I knew he'd been awake as long as I had.

Cam took his seat. He gestured to one of three empty chairs.

I shook my head and propped a shoulder against the wall. Sitting with them would send a message they had not voted for. I was not one of them, and I didn't want to be.

Cam gave me a hard stare, then pounded his gavel on the table. "We're three men down on the council alone. Cracker's dead, Embry's laid up, and we ain't had a treasurer for so long I can't remember what it was like when Whistler was counting our money. When the dust from all this settles, I'm gonna need names of the brothers you think could step up."

"I have some ideas," Nash said.

The road captain raised a hand. "Me too."

Cam nodded. "We'll talk again in a couple of weeks."

A murmur of agreement went around the table, then Cam pointed his gavel at the enforcer. "Embry?"

"Lost a ton of blood like you, and the shank damaged his guts. Surgeons repaired the damage overnight and he spent the day in ICU."

"He's out now, though, right?" Cam frowned deeply, trying to remember.

The enforcer nodded. "Woke up this afternoon. Took himself for a walk already. He's doing good, Pres."

Cam blew out a breath. "Motherfucker scared the hell out of me. Did he tell you what happened?"

The enforcer's gaze flitted to me. "Said he heard someone coming over the fence. There was no one around and he didn't have his phone, so he challenged them on his own, thinking we'd see it on the cameras."

I snorted. "Your system at the boundary fence has always been weak. I have disabled it many times."

"Why?"

"To show you."

My answer made no sense to the enforcer, not yet. He thought I was playing a game. He did not know I loved Cam. "Anyway, none of us showed up and a couple of dudes jumped him from behind. Got him on the ground and shanked him. He doesn't remember much else except . . ."

"Alexei," Saint supplied.

The enforcer blinked. "Alexei. Yeah, he remembers you pulling him up and carrying him to your car. If you hadn't done that and tossed me your keys, the doctors said he'd have bled out."

"Thank you," Cam said. "From all of us. I don't know if we could survive losing Embry."

I believed that. The enforcer was rough around the edges. Untrained and raw. But the bond he had to the chaplain showed in every inch of his haunted and scarred face. "You did not lose him. It seems that you've only cut your obvious dead weight."

Cam nodded. "Saint, where are we at with that?"

"Loaded and ready to deliver later tonight. Nash helped me."

Cam's VP cringed. "Freaky motherfucker didn't even puke."

"You get used to it," Saint replied flatly. A pause stretched out before he spoke again. "And puking just leaves me more work to do."

"You're an efficient grim reaper," Nash concurred.

A ghost of a smile warmed Cam's face, but it was brief. "We haven't heard from the Sambinis yet. I think we can trust their word from last night, but we still need to stay sharp. Wouldn't put it past them to retaliate if their boss man decides we've taken the royal piss shutting them down like that."

"They won't retaliate."

Cam flicked his gaze to me. "How do you know that?"

"They have been warned."

"By who?"

"My former employer. I went to him when I realised the Romanian cartel was coming for you. The Sambinis you could've handled alone, for a while at least. Aldea is a different operation."

I spoke to Cam, but every eye in the room was now on me, and I knew the time had come. I had revealed myself to Sambini, and to Aldea through Sidorov.

It was Cam's turn now, and that of his brothers who put so much trust in him that they'd waited for this moment as long as he had.

I pushed off the wall and walked around the table, coming to a stop behind the three empty chairs. "In eastern Europe, the industries you are involved in are controlled by three organisations. One each in Romania and Hungary, the other in Russia."

"The Sidorov family?"

I smiled faintly at Saint. It pleased me that it was him who knew. "Yes. They are stronger than all others. The top of the tree."

He tilted his head sideways. "Is that where you're from?"

"I worked for them awhile."

"Ten years," Cam said softly.

"Yes. Pavel bought me from the Pakhan my father lost me to. I was the blade of his knife for a long time."

"His hitman?"

"If you like."

Cam shifted in his seat. The pain he was in was making him sweat a little, but relief coloured his drawn features too. What he knew of me was starting to make sense. "You have a reputation, don't you? One that the Romanians knew?"

"The older Sambinis too. The younger one, Gianni, he was there when I dispatched Frank Crow and his friend. That is probably enough for him, I think."

"What did you do to him?"

I was almost glad he didn't seem to remember what Gianni Sambini had told the masses. "What he said he would do to me, but I gave him the privilege of killing him first."

"Good." The enforcer dipped his chin at me. "I hated those cunts."

I could only agree. "I did not wipe them out, though. And you have men that may want to avenge your . . ."

"Secretary," Nash filled in. "And they probably think Cam or Saint killed him. We might have more trouble with that. No offence, but they ain't worldly enough to understand the politics you've brought to the table. Without the Sambinis, they might band together and start shit of their own."

It made sense. Restless, I continued around the table. *I need to smoke.*

Saint read my mind and held up a box of cigarettes.

I took one and leaned down to the lighter he held in his hand.

When I straightened, Cam's gaze was on us, sharper than before, as if puzzle pieces were slotting together in his head. He did not know yet that Saint and I had worked together behind his back, but it wouldn't be long.

I took a deep drag on my cigarette, then passed it back to Saint. "You can handle an MC insurgency. It is what you are good at, yes? Why your rivals sought outside help in the first place?"

Cam nodded. "As long as they don't come too hard and too soon, we can handle them. Been putting that shit down for years."

"You enjoy it," I stated. "It is part of the life."

"Until the next johnny big bollocks comes along."

I tore my gaze from Cam and gave his road captain my attention. "What is your name?"

"Rubi, mate."

I glanced at the enforcer. "And you?"

"Mateo."

Cam chuckled. "Sorry. You seem to know everything else without me telling you, it didn't occur to me to make formal introductions."

"It's okay. I did not need to know their names before today." I kept my gaze on Rubi. "There will be no other incursions from Europe. At my request, Pavel Sidorov has made it known that your territory is unavailable for the purposes the Aldeas wished to use it for."

"How long for, though?" Rubi looked to Cam, to Saint, and then back to me. "He's protecting us because you asked him to. What happens when you leave?"

"What makes you think I would leave?"

Silence. I could only hear my own heart thumping.

Rubi cleared his throat. "Okay. But say you did, what happens then?"

I shrugged because I did not know, and I did not feel like explaining that it wasn't Sidorov's reputation that would keep wolves from their door. "Maybe you will not have to find out, but whatever the Sambinis make of what occurred here yesterday, your business with them is multifaceted. You should prepare to encounter them again."

It was a good enough answer for now.

Rubi nodded, his curious gaze not unfriendly, and rubbed his temples. "This shit is getting complicated. I feel like I've had my head in a gas oven for weeks."

"Ain't you that got gassed," Nash grumbled.

I liked him. He was the easiest man to read at the table, and straightforward people kept the world turning.

"Are you doing okay with that?" Cam addressed the brothers who'd been incapacitated in this very room.

Nash shrugged. "I'm not spinning anymore."

"I forgot about it," Mateo said.

Because of Embry.

Saint said nothing.

Cam sighed. "We should wrap this up. At some point we gotta talk about the fact that half of you wanna bang my siblings or each other, but I haven't got the head for that right now."

Rubi tensed.

Nash too.

Cam held up his hands. "I said talk, not fight. We'll figure it out. Lord knows, I've spent too many years telling myself no. I can't live with myself if I put you through that fucking pain too."

"You can't leave it at that. What about the rest of it?" Mateo leaned forward, dropping his elbows on the table. He still looked as if the bottom of his world had fallen out, but as he glanced at me and then Saint, it was clear where his mind had tracked the deeper hurt in Cam's gaze and found the battered jackpot.

Cam saw it too, and I gave him an out. I did not need to be here for this.

I stole Saint's cigarette pack and gifted him a smile I hoped wasn't too sardonic.

Then I strode from the room and made it all the way to the stone steps before my heart decided it was as far as I could be from him right now.

It was late. There were a few brothers dotted around, but none paid me much attention.

361

I smoked Saint's cigarettes and considered where I would find my next cup of coffee. I did not think about when I would eat or sleep. Such things didn't bother me. *Cam needs those things, though.*

He did, and as the thought took root in my gut, the door behind me opened and Saint folded his long body into a crouch at my side.

For a long moment, he did not speak. I sensed his struggle and gave him time, lighting a cigarette for him and placing it between his lips.

He took a deep drag. "I have to leave. Take the rubbish to landfill."

I read between the lines: he was taking the dead bodies to be disposed of. "You will come back?"

"In a few hours, but he needs to go home before then."

"Okay."

"You'll take him?"

"I'll try. He is stubborn."

"You're worse."

"Am I?"

Saint relaxed a little and sat down, extending his legs in front of him. "I think so. It suits you."

"Why have you thought about that?"

"I don't know."

I nodded and stubbed out my cigarette. There was a bin nearby but I wanted to know if he still carried the bag in his pocket for the sake of the songbirds.

He did. I let him pluck the butt from my fingers and tuck it away.

"I love him too," he said.

"I know this."

"It doesn't bother you?"

"Only in the sense that you do not believe he should love you back."

"Cam loves everyone."

"Not like he loves you."

"Not like he loves *you*."

I hummed and tilted my head back, gazing at the stars above us on this clear and frosty night. "I will take him home," I said. "To the cottage on Beach Road. We will wait for you there."

"Why?"

"Because he needs both of us."

Saint turned to face me. In the darkness, his face was a chiselled mess of angles and insecurity. "I'll come, and whatever happens, it needs to be about him, but . . ." He stopped to fight with himself.

I waited, but he did not speak again. Instead, he took my hand and placed it on his bare forearm.

The contact burned as bright as the explosion the Sambinis had set off on a nearby industrial estate to distract the police. My fingers squeezed the warm, unyielding flesh of their own accord, and I rubbed my palm over Saint's skin.

He shivered, pleasure sparking in his complex gaze, and I felt it in the pit of my stomach. It unnerved me, but I smiled.

Saint deserved to feel good, perhaps as much as he deserved Cam's heart.

31

CAM

Saint's departure was abrupt, but it didn't surprise me. He had limited bandwidth for convoluted conversations. And this one? When our brothers were burning with curiosity over something that so involved him so intimately?

I saw the discomfort creep through him. Saw it manifest in his restless hands and darting gaze. He was tired anyway, but this hurt him, and I couldn't fucking bear it.

"You gotta leave him alone." I addressed the table when Saint was gone. "Don't get in his face about whatever this is."

Silence greeted me, bemused and brutal. They wanted to understand, but nothing I'd said made any sense to them.

"It's complicated," I said around a deep sigh. "And I don't know where any of it is going."

Opposite me, Mateo leaned forward. Of them all, he seemed the most interested in the unconventional place my personal life had become. "Are you with them both?"

"I want to be."

"Are they with each other?"

"I don't know."

Mateo reached for his coffee cup. Found it empty and dropped it again. "The Russian—"

"He has a name."

"I know, boss, but I'm trying to separate your boyfriend from business for a minute and I'm fucking tired."

My brow ticked up at the edge in Mateo's rough voice, but I let it go. Embry getting hurt had done something to him perhaps even he didn't understand yet. "He's not my boyfriend, but whatever."

"Is he gonna be your old man?"

"Fuck, I don't know." Was he? The thought made me choke on a laugh. Old ladies were an indelible part of MC culture, but the world—our slice of it, at least—had moved on. I didn't need or want a partner tied down by club rules and traditions. Besides, the notion that Alexei would ever agree to it was fucking ridiculous. "*No*," I said when I'd contained the strange emotions bubbling inside. "I don't know what's gonna happen, but he ain't gonna be that."

"What about Saint? He want the job?"

"Are you fucking crazy?"

Mateo shrugged. "Sometimes."

Then he paused, and it was a hesitation that seemed to go around the entire table.

I glanced at each of my brothers in turn—three of them, as Embry and Saint were missing—and each man had the same look on his face. The same odd mix of emotions that made my heart warm and my skin crawl at the same time. "What is it?"

Nash averted his gaze.

Rubi opened his mouth. Shut it again.

Once more, Mateo leaned forward, eyes flashing. "I'm

just gonna say it cos I'm out of fucks to give if you take my head off my shoulders today—

"Excuse me?"

"Let me finish."

I waved a hand my only working hand for him to continue.

Mateo held my gaze, unaffected by whatever rage I had left in me. "Cam, there ain't a man at this table doesn't know you love Saint. That you have for fucking years. Why is this happening now? Why ain't you been together all along?"

Air left my lungs. Blood left my body. I felt dead inside, like I had since I'd made a fateful and misguided decision so long ago. Nausea clawed at my insides. There was so much shit I needed to say, to my brothers, and to my family, but all I had right now was the truth. "Because I'm a selfish cunt."

It wasn't good enough. Mateo stared, forcing me to elaborate. I closed my eyes, hiding from him, but he didn't go anywhere. None of them did.

I opened my eyes. "We've been at war since my dad died. I met Saint two months before that, and I was in deep the moment I saw him, but the club needed him more—needed *all* of you, on a council they could trust was led by my head and not my fucking dick and my heart."

"*We* trusted you," Rubi said. "We still do. That wouldn't have changed if you'd been with Saint. It ain't changed now."

"Yeah, well. Time and hindsight are wonderful things. But there's something else too—something I only realised when I met Alexei. I was scared, man. I watched my mum die because she couldn't live without my dad, and I knew I'd love Saint that much if I let myself and..." I choked, but forced the words out the way he so often couldn't. "I couldn't lose him like that. I'd have thrown myself off a fucking cliff and I had too many people depending on me."

Nash leaned back in his chair, eyes heavy with fatigue. "He's always loved *you* that much. You never asked him what he wanted?"

"What do you think?"

Nash blew out a sigh that seemed to age his pretty face ten years. "I think it's not always about what people want, bro. It's about giving them what they need."

"Wise words."

"Call me the oracle from now on."

"Yeah, okay." I turned back to Mateo. He nodded, letting me know I'd pacified him for now, and I wondered if his questions had been for his benefit or Saint's. They were as close as Saint ever got to anyone who wasn't me.

Or Alexei.

"All right." I scrubbed a hand down my face. "I know we've got a lot more shit to work through, and I *know* I've fucked up, as president, and as whatever I am to him, but I'm gonna fix it, okay? I just need time. And, like I said, I need you to not get in his face about this. Dude needs to breathe, and we gotta let him."

"What about Alexei?"

My gaze snapped back to Mateo. "What about him?"

"He's protecting us," Mateo said. "Protecting *you*. What if things get shitty and you don't want to bang each other's brains out anymore? What happens to the truce he's brokered for us then?"

"I don't know." Fuck, I was sick of those words, but the truth was all I had. I didn't lie to my brothers. I couldn't. "This is so fucking messy," I said to no one in particular.

Rubi shoved his chair back. For a moment, I thought he would walk out like Saint had, but he came to me and gave me a careful, fraternal hug instead.

"It'll be okay, Cam. He looked at you the same way Saint does."

Another twisted laugh escaped me. "And how's that?"

"Like he'd burn the world down for you." Rubi let me go. "Are we done here? I gotta sleep before my head explodes."

I reared back to look at him. "You doing okay? You shouldn't have been riding yesterday."

"You'd prefer it if I'd left your sister here?"

"You brought her right back."

"I'm not taking responsibility for that. Nash is the daft cunt who gave her a hog and a fucking machete. She was going to cut my nuts off."

I could believe that. Orla was as fierce as our mother, and I was as sentimental as my dad. I let it go. Orla on a bike was something I'd have to get used to, but I would. This was a new dawn, and she deserved her piece of it.

Rubi left.

Mateo rose too. "I'm going back."

Embry. I nodded. "I'll be there as soon as I don't look like I've been in a shoot-out."

It was the only reason I wasn't haunting Embry's bedside. A single instance of knife crime could be written off as random. A hoard of bloody bikers milling around in its wake?

That was attention we didn't need.

I stood to embrace Mateo.

He was gentle with me, which I appreciated. Then he left, striding away with a single purpose that made my heart ache and warm in a contradiction I was more familiar with when I thought about Saint.

I looked to Nash. "Make sure he eats and doesn't kill anyone?"

Nash nodded.

"Orla—"

"I got her, Cam. She's safe with me."

I grunted, more because I'd run out of words than anything else.

Nash rolled his eyes and reached over me for the gavel. He pounded it on the table, then made his escape too, leaving me alone, but not for long. I stood and leaned heavily on the table for support.

Alexei appeared like a ghost. "I am taking you home."

"That an order?"

"Perhaps. But not mine."

"Saint?"

Alexei's lips twitched. On anyone else, it might've been a smile, but not him. *He's a hitman. Russian mob. You've probably never met anyone more fucking dangerous in your life.* But I wasn't scared of him. I loved him. "I don't want you to leave."

"Leave?"

"When you're done babysitting me. I don't want you to go back to Bristol and live in your ivory tower."

Alexei took my hand from the table and draped my good arm around his shoulders, taking my weight before I could stop him. "You want me to live here? In your clubhouse?"

"I want you in my bed. That ain't always here."

"Wanting to fuck me more often doesn't mean much."

That stung. I twisted in his grasp to face him. "That's not what I meant."

"I know. I just do not want to have this conversation here."

"Why?"

"Because it is not what you need."

It was. So fucking much. But no argument came to me.

I kissed his cheek and reclaimed my arm. Then I walked myself out of the chapel and into the night air.

It was freezing. I shivered, colder than I'd ever been. My heart cried out for Saint. Before Alexei, being around him was the only time I'd felt warmth since my parents had died. *I need him home.*

"He won't be long," Alexei whispered.

I shook my head. "He's never been in my house."

"Nothing stays the same unless you want it to."

He moved past me and down the steps.

His car was in the yard, parked between my Harley and Saint's as if it had always been there. Unlocked, like my fucking soul. But what about his?

Alexei slid behind the wheel of the Jaguar SUV. I took a last glance around the compound, catching Rubi's eye, then I opened the passenger door.

Sleek white leather swallowed me up, alien to anything I was used to.

Alexei laughed as he put the automatic car in drive and eased out of the space where Mateo had parked his car. *Next to my bike.* "Would it help if I found a death metal radio station?"

"Help what?"

He didn't answer. Just laughed again and drove us out of the compound.

My house was six miles away, fifteen minutes that I was prepared to spend in silence, but my loose tongue had other ideas. "This doesn't work without you," I blurted.

"What doesn't?"

"Me and him. He needs more than I am."

Again, Alexei said nothing, and it felt like I was in the car with Saint. Was that it? Were they so similar and yet so different that I couldn't handle one without the other?

I hadn't been thinking about Saint when I'd first met Alexei. Years of practice had left me proficient in pushing him out of my mind, a skill that filled me with fucking shame. Saint didn't just need more than me, he deserved it. "You understand him," I realised. "Don't you?"

Alexei sighed. "Sometimes. He is a unique man, though. I do not think he understands himself."

"He's not used to anyone giving a fuck. Did you know he was born in prison?"

Alexei muttered something in Russian, then he sighed again. "No. I know nothing about him except that he loves you, and . . ."

"And?"

"There is something about him I cannot look away from."

I chuckled. "Trust me, I get it."

"I do trust you."

"Yeah?"

Alexei cut me a dry scowl. "Yes. And you do not have to look so delighted about it."

I was delighted. So much of him was still a goddamn

mystery, but I felt this victory. Claimed it, as much as I claimed him.

His phone pierced the heated air. His *Russian* phone.

Alexei's expression shut down.

Fuck that. I snatched the phone from the console and tossed it out of the window. "No more."

Alexei chuckled, shaking his head. "You are unmanageable."

"I'm a choir boy compared to Saint. Good luck managing him."

"Maybe I will not try. It is not like he can manage me. And neither can you. You should know that before you ask things of me. I am not like you—an open book with new secrets on every page. I burned those pages a long time ago and I do not want them back."

There were too many metaphors for my tired, uneducated brain to contemplate. "I don't care about any of that. I just want you. And him. And you and him. Fuck, that sounds like a lot, eh?"

I was losing it, and he knew it, of course. I might've been unmanageable, but he was too fucking clever to care.

We pulled up outside Angel Cottage.

Alexei helped me out of the car and to the front door, taking the keys from me to unlock it.

Inside, he leaned me against the wall and took my face in his cool hands. "I am not going anywhere. We do not have to understand it to let it be."

"Do you love me?"

"Yes."

Alexei smiled, but panic surged in my chest. I gripped his wrist. "You don't owe me anything. I want you with me, but not if it makes you unhappy. I know what it's like to be caged by something you love."

"Being caged by something you hate is much worse. But I do not hate this place, so I will stay awhile, if you want me to."

"Here? At the house?"

He shrugged. "Wherever you are. I should warn you of something, though."

"What?"

"I heard your conversation about *old men*. This is not a role for me. You know this, don't you?"

A wry smile split my face. "I'd rather you sat at my table."

"As a brother?"

"And a lover."

"That could get complicated for you. And I would not help. I don't enjoy authority unless I asked for it."

"I'm not talking about sex, Lexi."

"Who mentioned sex?" He pressed against me, his lean, hard body moulding to mine in all the right places. "Unless you have fantasies about all your brothers?"

"No. God, no. Just Saint."

Alexei laughed again, and I swear, it was the warmest sound he'd ever made. I wanted to bottle it so I could keep it forever.

"You're tired," he said when he'd composed himself. "Shower. I will find you some food."

"You're not gonna leave?"

"I am not."

Alexei pressed his forehead to mine. It was something I did with my brothers when I wanted them to hear me. It was familiar and comforting and settled me enough to release the death grip I'd apparently claimed on his arm.

He stepped back and waved me towards the stairs. "I will follow you."

I believed him.

Showering with a hole in my shoulder that couldn't get wet—Dr Lexi's orders—was a pain in the arse. It took longer than I anticipated. By the time I was done, Alexei had followed me upstairs.

He'd made me a sandwich. How fucking cute. But though I was so famished I couldn't see straight, the sight of him lounging on my bed sparked a different hunger in me. One I had no business feeding while I was such a goddamn mess.

I swallowed it down, making a meal out of towelling off until he came to help me.

It didn't help. Despite the pain radiating throughout my body, my dick hadn't got the memo and I was hard as a rock.

Alexei smirked. "I was worried about you, but perhaps I didn't need to be."

"You thought it was broken?"

"Not specifically." Alexei grazed his fingertips along my length.

I shuddered. "Fuck. Let me lie down before you do that again."

"You are lying down regardless."

Alexei set the towel aside and steered me to the bed. He lay me down, then stretched out beside me, still fully clothed.

I glowered.

He touched my face with a gentleness I didn't need from him. "What's wrong?"

"I need you."

"I'm here."

"I know, I just—" I clenched my eyes shut, searching for words to explain the anxious, horny inferno coiling in my stomach. "I'm so fucking tired, but I feel like I'm gonna explode. Like I need to kick the shit out of something or—"

"Come." Alexei smirked. "I know this feeling. It is violent, but it does not have to be."

I snatched a lungful of air that went nowhere. "I can't fucking breathe."

"You can."

"Can you take your clothes off?"

"Of course." Alexei rose and stripped, revealing his elegant body to me.

I drank it in as if I'd never seen him before—his long limbs, lean muscles, and the pale skin that smelled so damn good.

Still hyperventilating, I reached for him. "Come back?"

"I never went anywhere. It is you that is not present."

"I'm present."

Alexei returned to the bed and lay down beside me. His skin against mine calmed me, but it wasn't enough. I needed something from him that I hadn't wanted from anyone in more than a decade.

I needed oblivion.

I needed dominance.

I needed him to hold me down and take it from me until my brain shut the fuck up and I could breathe again.

"Cam." Alexei laid a hand on my chest, pressing down, as if he could force some calm back into me. "Look at me."

"I am."

"*Look* at me." He still cupped my face with his other hand. His grip turned brutal and I tethered myself to it, clinging to it like a free-falling bird with a broken wing.

His voice, always quiet, dropped to a low murmur that rattled my bones. "I will give you what you need, but you must do something for me."

"Anything."

He smirked and reached over my injured arm to the drawer he knew held everything we needed. "You will tell Saint I was gentle."

It was the only lie I'd ever tell him.

Alexei kissed me and brought his lubed hand to my dick, wrapping slick fingers around me, drawing a gasp from my tight chest. He jacked me hard but slow, dragging pleasure out of me as he plundered my mouth, his tongue dancing the same devil's dance as his wicked hand.

The other held my torso still, and he chuckled as my hips rocked of their own accord. "I did not think you would ever want this so much."

"I want *you*."

"You realise my cock won't heal you?"

"Never asked it to."

Alexei nudged my legs apart, draping them over his hips. He poured more lube on his hand. "Do you want me to—"

"No. Just do it."

His smirk softened. "You did not let me get away with that the first time we were together."

"I'm a hypocrite."

"You are." Alexei dropped forward, catching himself with one arm while the other went to his dick. "But you want it enough that I will allow it."

His cock pressed against me, easing inside me enough to make my body tense up.

I fought it, forcing myself to relax, and Alexei slid home with a rough thrust that made me groan.

"Fuck." The pain was as dizzying as anything else I'd experienced recently. Breath left my body and I gripped Alexei's arms hard enough to bruise. "*Fuck.*"

Alexei held still, giving me a moment to collect myself, but it was brief—a fleeting heartbeat in time that was over before I could blink.

He held one of my legs to his chest and began to fuck me, taking care not to jar my injured body in the wrong places, while still ruining me where I needed him most.

I'd been cold for days. Suddenly I was blazing hot, sweat coating my skin. I still couldn't breathe, but the burn in my lungs felt good.

It felt right and I gave myself up to it.

Alexei groaned and snapped his hips harder. The pace and rhythm were nothing compared to the brutality I'd inflicted on him when he'd asked for it, but it was raw and dirty and rough.

It was everything I needed.

The coil inside me began to unravel. Sex as therapy was bullshit, but the release I felt as he drove into me was everything. "Don't stop, Lexi."

Another tortured sound wrapped around us—his, mine, I had no damn clue. My head burst open, every gnarled knotty thought escaping. They'd come back, I knew, but in this moment, right here with him, a different intensity smashed into me.

Nerves I didn't know existed sparked to life . . . and then exploded, leaving seared flesh in their wake. Alexei's movements grew deeper, scavenging every ounce of energy I had left. He held my face with slippery fingers, thrusting in and out of me, over and over. I wanted his lips on mine, but he was too far away.

He heard me, though, the freaky, psychic motherfucker. Goddamn, he was more like Saint than I'd ever realised.

They felt like one soul.

"Cam." My name fell from his lips, his mouth slack with pleasure, eyes glazed. "Cam . . ."

Fuck it. "Kiss me. Please?"

It was a boneheaded move. Buried inside me, he had to lean on me, adding pressure to an injury that already felt like death itself, but I didn't care. His mouth crashed to mine and I was overcome.

Undone.

Dead.

And so fucking full of him our pulses felt synched, his heart hammering with mine as urgency pumped my blood. I fucking *yelled,* the force of it scraping my throat raw. My dick erupted, and then white-hot pleasure surged through me, arching my back, twisting every muscle and tendon tight.

I came as if it was the first time a man had ever laid hands on me.

In some ways, it was.

Alexei held me as I shattered to pieces. Then he came too, violent and sudden. His breath staggered, eyes rolled back.

God, he was beautiful. Sex with him had always been mind-bending, but this was something else. *He* was something else, even to the man I'd met all those months ago. "I love you."

Alexei trembled, still reeling from his climax. "I know, Cam. I love you too."

He lifted his weight from me, releasing the pressure from my shoulder.

I blew out a shaky breath. He pushed my sweaty hair back from my face and something passed between us. I couldn't say what, but I felt it, and so did he.

"You are all dirty again," he whispered.

"What are you gonna do about that?"

"Wait here."

As if I was capable of anything else.

Alexei rolled off the bed. He disappeared, then came back with a warm cloth. He cleaned us up, then bullied me into bed.

I closed my eyes, drifting, then something I couldn't fathom pulled me back.

Saint.

I opened my eyes, and there he was, lounging in the doorway, eyes wild, his hair a feral mess. Another seismic shift rocked me. I sat up, reaching for him, but he moved for me, at my side before I could blink, sinking onto the bed, long fingers wrapped around mine.

He swallowed hard. "There's something you should know."

"What?"

Saint jerked his head at Alexei, a slow grin warming his face. "This ruthless motherfucker rides a Yamaha."

THE END.

I know, I know, I'm evil ending Devil's Dance there, but rest assured, Saint's Song is OUT NOW.

And read on for a sneak peek into Saint Malone's world. I cannot wait for you to get to know him better.

Love pretty paperbacks? I'm DELIGHTED to tell you that I'm in the process of releasing entire Rebel Kings MC series in special limited edition paperbacks, with BONUS CONTENT. Keep flipping those pages for a glimpse at that gorgeous new cover.

Not ready to let go of this instalment? No, me neither. **Sign up to my newsletter for an exclusive bonus scene of CAM and SAINT in their younger days** *swoon*

My bonus scenes are also often extended on my Patreon platform.

Cam. Saint. Alexei

DEVIL'S DANCE

THE BESTSELLING REBEL KINGS MC BIKER SERIES

GARRETT LEIGH

REBEL KINGS

SAINT'S SONG

GARRETT LEIGH

Saint

The window in Cam's clubhouse bedroom looked out over the whole compound. Some nights when he was somewhere else, I let myself in and stood by the glass, watching and waiting. For what, I'd never figured out, but I couldn't count the hours I'd lost to watching *him*.

Cam.

My brother.

My president.

His cottage by the sea was different. I'd never been inside, and my observations had been limited to coastal traffic and wildlife. Never him.

Never Alexei.

I sensed their presence before I opened my eyes, but a guttural sensation woke me with a jump all the same, a gasp that ripped from my scratchy throat.

Habitual panic squeezed my chest. It was rare that I didn't wake up and think I was somewhere else—another time, another place. My senses came to life too fast, and I fought the bedsheets, shoving them away before a *cold* hand hit my chest.

"It's okay, wingman. You are with Cam."

That voice. *Alexei.* My eyes flew open. He was beside me, crouching on the floor next to the bed, and I couldn't decide what surprised me more: that he was still there or, that I was there at all.

In Cam's bed.

He's hurt.

Heart slowing, I sat up. Alexei's hand fell from my chest and he rose, stepping back. His retreat felt wrong, but I couldn't rectify it until I knew Cam was okay.

Cam.

My gaze found him. He was next to me, asleep, like he had been the first and last time I'd woken up in bed with him. Only difference was I wasn't naked, and Alexei had stayed.

Cam was naked, though, a fact I got no joy from as I leaned over to look at him properly. Nothing had happened when we'd crawled into bed together. He'd passed out the second we'd all laid down together, and eventually, so had I.

Had Alexei slept?

Cam would want to know. I'd find out for him, just as soon as I knew he was still fucking breathing.

I inched closer, taking in the dressed bullet wound on his shoulder and the sling supporting his arm. The slash mark on his cheek, and the raised contusion on his neck where he'd been stabbed with a needle. *He won't like that.* A stupid fucking thought, but it was true. Cam could handle a bullet. In our world, it made sense. The rest of it was a violation that would haunt him forever. The lost hours, the confusion. He probably didn't remember how sick he'd been after, but I did, and it haunted me too. I watched his chest rise and fall with steady breaths, but all I saw was it heaving as I'd held him up over the bar sink. His pained groan as the drugs had torn him up inside.

His peaceful face now didn't seem real.

I touched his uninjured shoulder. His skin was cool and it was so unlike him that *my* chest fucking burned.

A blanket was bunched around my waist. It hadn't been there when I'd gone to sleep. I kicked it off, snagged it, and lay it over Cam. I wanted to cup his jaw, and run my fingers through his messy hair, but despite everything we'd lived through, I still didn't know how to touch him for no other reason than I *wanted* to.

Alexei returned to the bed. He came up behind me, his quiet footsteps louder than usual, so I heard him coming.

He reached around me and grasped my wrist, pushing my hand back to Cam's skin. "It is good that he is cold. If he was warm, we would worry about infection."

I knew that. It was me who'd broken into a clinic to steal the precautionary antibiotics we'd dosed Cam with while he'd been unconscious in the bar. But I felt Cam's warmth in my dreams, and its absence scared me.

"Come."

Alexei backed off and beckoned me from the bed. He was dressed in Cam's sweatpants and a T-shirt that must've been River's as it was too small to be Cam's. Me? I was rocking the same grimy jeans I'd rolled in with. Only my shirt was missing.

I need a shower.

Perhaps that was where Alexei was taking me. He liked things clean and tidy.

Except blowjobs.

And sex.

Don't think about sex.

Alexei led me downstairs and to the kitchen I'd never been in.

It was very Cam.

It was *warm*.

Alexei opened the fridge and pointed at the contents. "He will need to eat and I'm a terrible cook."

I couldn't imagine Alexei being terrible at anything, except maybe being nice to people he didn't like. I wasn't good at that either.

Cam is. It was why Cracker had survived so long.

Why *Alexei* had killed him instead.

"Saint. Come on now. You do not have to talk, but at least look in this food dungeon and tell me you know what to do."

Food dungeon? I joined Alexei at the fridge and peered not inside, but at him. "You're not hungry?"

"I could eat."

"That's not the same."

"Clearly."

He sounded annoyed, but it was hard to tell if it was with me and my fat tongue, or with himself for not knowing what to do with the farmer's market Cam kept in his fridge.

It was hard to tell anything about Alexei, and as twisted as it was, I liked that about him. He made me think. Made me look deeper at just about everything.

Whether he knew it or not, he made me stronger.

Was it wrong that I thought he was cute?

Maybe. This dude was a stone-cold killer. A hitman for the Russian mob. Wanting to pinch his cheeks and make him smile was fucking weird.

"I can make omelettes." I pointed at the eggs. "With green shit. He always wants the green shit."

"For himself or for you?"

"You really do know him, don't you?"

Alexei fished spinach and mushrooms from the fridge, leaving me to grab the eggs. "I am trying, but it is not so hard. He is open to those he wants to be. It is you that puzzles me."

I opened my mouth to ask him why, but nothing came out. An imaginary brick blocked my throat and the words scrambled in my head.

"Do you have your phone?"

The question seemed off topic. I frowned and patted my pockets. Somehow, it was still stuffed in my jeans.

I held it up.

Alexei jabbed a finger at the blank screen. "If you want to talk and you can't."

I wasn't used to anyone being so direct. Most people got bored and wandered off. Or assumed I had nothing to say.

Cam was patient when he had the time.

Ragey as hell when he didn't.

Alexei's easy acceptance unnerved me. I waited for cold-hot embarrassment to flood me, but nothing happened. Alexei waited as if it was the most normal thing in the world to text him when he was right in front of me.

I opened my phone and tapped the screen.

Saint: *why?*

"Why do you puzzle me?"

I nodded.

Alexei pointed at the stove. I followed his direction and joined him there. "You are hard to read. Not about Cam, but with everything else."

Saint: *the club?*

"No."

Everything else. He meant him. And Cam. And me.

The three of us.

Saint: *I can't read me either, but you can't talk about being cryptic AF*

Alexei smiled and opened a cabinet. He found a frying pan and held it up to me.

I nodded and he placed it on the stove with undue care.

Then he hoisted himself onto the counter.

Apparently, I was cooking alone.

I didn't mind. Keeping my hands busy made my speech work better, and I was pretty good at breakfast foods. Which was lucky, cos I sure as shit couldn't cook anything else.

Alexei watched me slice mushrooms and hack up spinach. Actually, he watched the knife and I wondered if he was nervous of me. Most people were, but he wasn't most people. Rumour had it that he'd snapped Frank Crow's neck, that cunt Drummer too, and neither man was fucking small.

I found a bowl and a fork and pointed at the eggs.

Alexei cracked and whisked them, then passed them to me with a strange expression on his face. "I've never done this before."

"Cook?"

"With someone. I am alone a lot."

"Do you like it?"

"I've never thought about it."

"Why not?"

He slid from the countertop and washed his hands. Twice. "Why would I think about it? It would not change anything."

I wanted to know if being alone was something he chose, but the words didn't come, and my hands were occupied. I made myself focus on making Cam something edible to wake up to, and then Alexei too, though I had the weirdest feeling that he wouldn't eat it.

"For yourself too, wingman."

I glanced between him and the two omelettes I'd already cooked. "How did you know I wasn't going to?"

"You are selfless. In your head, you do not want to eat Cam's food in case he needs it more."

"That sounds more misguided than selfless."

"The result is the same." Alexei slid the board with the leftover mushrooms closer to me. "Cook."

I liked the way he ordered me around and it didn't occur to him for one second that I might tell him to go fuck himself. I was used to people—my brothers, even—dancing around me. Only Orla regularly called me on my shit, and she didn't do it like this.

She was nicer about it.

Nicer than I deserved.

I made the omelette. Then I stared at it, and Alexei did too, until Cam cleared his throat from the doorway.

"The fuck are you two doing?"

Alexei turned slowly to face him, but said nothing.

I stayed where I was and found some words. "You need to eat."

Cam came closer—I felt him. My skin tingled and the hair on the back of my neck stood on end. How the hell did he still do this shit to me, when being around Alexei seemed so fucking normal?

Because you're not normal. And neither is Alexei. Freaks and geeks love company.

Cam slid an arm around my waist. His hands were still too cold and I tried not to flinch. *He should be warm by now.* "You never told me you could cook."

"How do you know it wasn't Alexei?"

"He doesn't look murderous enough."

Alexei raised an eyebrow. "My cooking is better than your jokes."

"I wasn't joking. I've seen you cook before, remember? Though, I suppose if you ain't doing it now, I'm not dying."

"Do you feel like you are dying, Cam?"

Cam grunted while I absorbed their back and forth. It wasn't exactly banter, but it flowed like they'd been lovers for a lifetime. And despite the tension Cam had been carrying for months—*years*—still seeping out of him, I felt the strange peace Alexei brought him. Understood it, because Alexei gifted me that too.

"No one's dying." I slipped out of Cam's hold and passed him a plate. "Except you if you don't eat. Or whoever gets in your way."

Cam turned his grumpy scowl on me. "Was it laughing gas they knocked you out with?"

"You think I'm funny, boss?"

His frown deepened. "Don't call me that."

Okay.

I let him glare at me, because I liked it. Angry Cam was beautiful—his coal-dark eyes lit by honest fire. Cos that's what he was: honest. I rarely looked at him and didn't know what he was feeling.

What he was *thinking* was a different story, but specifics didn't always matter.

Alexei stepped closer and placed a fork on Cam's plate. "Sit down."

Cam held my stare a moment longer, then followed Alexei to the kitchen table.

I trailed after them, then remembered my breakfast and went back for it.

Alexei had left his behind too. I grabbed it and took it to the table, sensing Cam's gaze on me.

On us. It was only a matter of time before he got in my face about how much I'd known about Alexei before him.

I set Alexei's plate in front of him.

He ignored it.

Cam sighed. "Fucking hell, did you two fall out of the same womb?"

Alexei glanced at me.

I shrugged. "Sit down. He's obsessed with the dinner table."

"It is not dinner time." He sat down anyway, though.

So did I. Regardless of whatever Mother Hubbard shit Cam was about to pull, it was the quickest way to get him off his feet.

Cam eased himself into his chair at the head of the table while me and Alexei flanked him. It felt kinda royal, but it worked.

Alexei pushed Cam's plate at him. "I have good drugs if you eat that."

"I don't need drugs. I'm fine."

"You are scared," Alexei said. "The needle in your throat has made you crawl out of your skin."

Cam glared at him. Nearly. It should've been funny that he changed his mind at the last minute, but I couldn't laugh at Cam being in pain. Also, I was fascinated by the spy hole Alexei seemed to have into his brain. I knew Cam well, but Alexei was picking shit up faster than me and I wanted to know how.

They hadn't been fucking that long.

It's not just fucking, though, is it? They love each other.

A two-way street. Lucky them.

Cam loves you.

Fuck, I knew that. I just didn't know if it was the same. He'd never looked at me the way he was Alexei right now. Never holed up in this house with me and fucked me all night long.

You even want that, bro?

Cam leaned across the table and beckoned Alexei close.

Alexei didn't move.

Then he did and their kiss was inevitable.

Beautiful. I couldn't look away, and the pinch in my heart I'd felt that night in Bristol when I'd first seen them together... it was a distant memory. Now all I felt was a rush of heat I struggled to contain without lunging across the table and trying to figure out who I wanted first.

"Saint."

I blinked. Cam was as up in my face as even he would dare to be. I frowned. *What?*

393

He beckoned me close too. I leaned forward, the heat in my blood squeezing my heart so tight I couldn't breathe. Was I scared of him kissing me?

If I was, it was only because I wasn't sure how I'd survive the resulting inferno.

I wasn't used to this shit feeling so fucking good. I hadn't fucked many men. I'd fantasised about it more than I'd done it, and every time it had happened, I'd thought of Cam. Pictured him doing the things to me that I was doing to someone else.

Imagined an impossible world where our positions were reversed.

As if he'd let you fuck him.

I'd never dared dream he would, but his dynamic with Alexei twisted reality. Something simmered between them that blew apart the status quo I'd imagined and nothing felt impossible.

Cam kissed me as if it was the first time all over again. He was gentle with me, testing me, then he claimed my mouth and I knew if he'd had two working hands he'd have pinned me to the chair.

I'd have let him. That night I'd learned how good it felt to have his body pressing down on me. In the few hours of sleep I'd snatched since, I'd dreamed about it. Of him. Of me.

Of Alexei.

I kissed Cam back and let my hand skate up his uninjured arm, his skin warmer now, as if Alexei had heated his blood as much as they both had mine. My lips parted, letting his tongue slip through, and if he'd been anyone else, I'd have pulled him into my lap.

But he wasn't anyone else.

He was my president.

My brother.

He was *Cam*.

I faltered. Cam grinned against my lips and drew back, his gaze as loopy as I felt. He said nothing, but only because he knew I'd say nothing back.

Alexei was no longer at the table.

My head whipped around, but he was already on his way back with the coffee that would put a real smile on his face.

Cam rolled his eyes. "You'll be awake for another week if you drink that."

Alexei made a noise that sounded more like it had come from me. "Eat your breakfast, biker boy."

Cam ate, and watching the colour come back into his pale face made my dick hard, distracting me from my own food.

Alexei didn't even look at his, and I reckoned I knew why. As he sipped his coffee and tapped his fingers on the table, it was obvious that he ran on his nerves. That he was used to being tired and hungry, and he clung to it when he was stressed.

Cam couldn't handle shit like that. He liked to take care of people. It was only a matter of time before—

"The fuck is wrong with you two?"

You two. It was the second time he'd called us that, and I liked it as much as Cam's irritation amused me. If we were all he was worrying about right now, I'd take it.

Alexei's gaze sharpened. He'd drifted while Cam had been eating, not as fascinated by it as I was. "What are you talking about?"

"You don't eat. Either of you. It's like you're fucking scared of it."

Cam shoved his empty plate away, grimacing as the aggressive movement jostled him.

A frown flickered across Alexei's face and he tilted his head a little, darting a glance at me. "I cannot speak for Saint, but for me, it is complicated. When you have been without something, it's hard to accept that you won't be again."

Cam absorbed that, perhaps matching it to all the horrible things he knew about me. "Are you worried that once it's gone you won't get any more?"

"Maybe."

"What about you?" Cam turned his consuming stare on me. Honestly, he had eyes like melted chocolate and I could never look at him without thinking about the biscuit factory I'd once worked for three days before I'd punched my boss and realised I wasn't built for that life.

Cam waited. I didn't have an answer for him, but Alexei kicked me under the table.

"Use your phone."

I sighed. Really? I didn't want to text Cam. I wanted him to glare at me until he figured it out on his own. Or moved on. He had a fifty-fifty score sheet.

"Saint." Cam reached for me with his good hand and put his damn fucking palm on my bare skin. "Tell me? Please?"

Bastard. I fished my phone from my pocket and tapped out everything he wanted to know and probably a shite-load that he didn't.

Saint: *I used to hoard food when I was a kid. Knowing I had it felt better than eating it.*

I dropped the phone on the table, pushed my chair back, and left the room. It wasn't my house, so I had nowhere to fucking go, but I needed a shower. So I did that.

When I got out, Alexei was waiting for me on the landing, peering at a bookshelf next to a tatty leather chair. "I need to go home for a while," he said.

"Why?"

"Work."

"You have a job?"

"Does that surprise you?"

"No." *Yes.*

Alexei gave me a knowing smirk. "I will come back tonight. You will stay with Cam, yes?"

"If he lets me." He didn't always. He got claustrophobic as fuck and ran away.

"He will let you."

"How do you know?"

"Because he wants to be with you. He missed you when you left the kitchen."

Alexei had the kind of voice that was hard to read. I couldn't tell if he was speaking the truth or taking the piss.

But...I didn't suppose it mattered. Outside of this house, I wasn't letting Cam out of my sight.

I nodded.

Alexei stepped closer and straightened the grimy T-shirt I'd tugged back on.

He smelled good, as if he hadn't been up for days and days and days. I wanted to touch the neat stubble on his face, but Cam wasn't there, so I didn't know if I should.

Or, if he even wanted me to.

The moment passed. Alexei turned away and ghosted to the stairs.

I followed and Cam was by the front door, scowling

because Alexei was leaving. "You can take my bike if you want."

Cam's gaze snapped to me. "What?"

"Not you." He couldn't ride, or even drive a car.

"I knew that."

"So?"

"So..." Cam shook his head. "Whatever."

Alexei rolled his eyes. "Is okay, wingman. My car is outside and it's fast enough that I can reach you if you need me."

That wasn't what I'd meant, was it? Fuck. I had no idea. It was a rare thing that words fell out of me by accident, but it happened with Cam. Always with Cam. And now Alexei too.

You are so fucked.

Cam pulled Alexei close and whispered something in his ear. Alexei smiled, and then he opened the door.

He glanced at me.

I didn't move or speak, and he slipped outside, shutting the door behind him.

The air he left in his wake was heavy.

Suffocating.

I clenched my fists, choking on the rock that settled in my throat, unable to decipher why him leaving hurt so much.

Go after him.

But why? What was I going to do? Drag him back to my fucking cave?

No. But I couldn't let him go. Not like this.

I ripped the door open and darted out of the house.

Alexei was at his car, door open, about to slide behind the wheel.

I caught his shoulder.

He let me.

Then I gripped his chin and kissed him. The chaos inside me settled, and it dawned on me that maybe, just maybe, this strange new world was fucking real.

OUT NOW

ABOUT THE AUTHOR

Right now, **Instagram** is the best way to keep up with Garrett. Search @garrett_leigh

Bonus Material available for all books on **Garrett's Patreon account**. Includes short stories from The Rebel Kings MC, Misfits, Slide, Strays, What Remains, Dream, and much more.

Facebook Fan Group: Garrett's Den

Garrett is also an award winning cover artist, taking the silver medal at the Benjamin Franklin Book Awards in 2016. She designs for various publishing houses and independent authors at **www.blackjazzdesign.com**

Connect with Garrett
www.garrettleigh.com

Made in the USA
Middletown, DE
09 May 2023

30317828R00246